ONCE AND FOR ALL

ONCE
AND FOR ALL

a novel

SARAH DESSEN

Viking

VIKING
An imprint of Penguin Random House LLC
375 Hudson Street
New York, New York 10014

First published in the United States of America by Viking,
an imprint of Penguin Random House LLC, 2017

LIBRARY OF CONGRESS CATALOGING-IN-PUBLICATION DATA IS AVAILABLE
ISBN 9780425290330

Printed in U.S.A.

3 5 7 9 10 8 6 4 2

Book design by Nancy Brennan   Set in Berling LT

To Regina Hayes
for making me think, making me laugh, and,
always, making me better.

ONCE AND FOR ALL

1

WELL, THIS was a first.

"Deborah?" I said as I knocked softly, yet still with enough intensity to convey the proper urgency, on the door. "It's Louna. Can I help you with anything?"

According to my mother, this was Rule One in dealing with this kind of situation: don't project a problem. As in, don't ask if anything is wrong unless you are certain something is, and as of right now, I was not. Although a bride locking herself in the anteroom of the church five minutes *after* the wedding was supposed to begin did not exactly bode well.

From the other side of the door, I heard movement. Then a sniffle. Again, I wished William, my mother's partner and the company's appointed bride whisperer, was here instead of me. But he'd gotten hooked into another crisis involving the groom's mother taking issue with preceding the bride's mom down the aisle, even though everyone knew that was how the etiquette went. Work in the wedding business long enough, however, and you learn that everything has the potential to be a problem, from the happy couple all the way down to the napkins. You just never know.

I cleared my throat. "Deborah? Can I bring you a water?"

It wasn't ever the true solution, but a water never hurt: that was another one of my mother's beliefs. Instead of a response, the lock clicked, the door rattling open. I looked down the stairs behind me, praying I'd see William approaching, but no, I was still alone. I took a breath, then picked up the bottle I'd grabbed earlier and stepped inside. Hydration for the win.

Our client Deborah Bell (soon to be Washington, ideally), a beautiful black girl with her hair in a bun, was sitting on the floor of the small room, her fluffy white dress bunched up around her. It had cost five thousand dollars, a fact I knew because she had told us, repeatedly, during the last ten months of planning this day. I tried not to think about this as I moved quickly, but not too quickly, over to her. ("Never *run* at a wedding unless someone's life is literally in danger!" I heard my mother say in my head.) I'd just opened up the water when I realized she was crying.

"Oh, don't do that." I eased down into what I hoped was a professional knees-to-the-side squat, drawing a slim pack of tissues from my pocket. "Your makeup looks great. Let's keep it that way, okay?"

Deborah, one false eyelash already loose—some lies are necessary—just blinked at me, sending another round of tears down her already streaked face. "Can I ask you something?"

No, I thought. Now we were at nine minutes. Out loud I said, "Sure."

She took in a shuddering breath, the kind that only comes after you've been crying awhile, and hard. "Do you . . ." A pause, as another set of tears gathered and spilled, this time taking the loose eyelash with them. "Do you believe that true love can really last forever?"

Now someone was coming up the stairs. From the sound of it, though—large steps, lumbering, with a fair amount of huffing and puffing already audible—it wasn't William. "True love?"

"Yes." She reached up—God, no! I thought, too late to stop her—rubbing a hand over her eyes and smearing eyeliner sideways up to her temple. The steps behind us were getting louder; whoever they belonged to would be here soon. Meanwhile, Deborah was just looking at me, her eyes wide and pleading, as if whatever happened next hinged entirely on my answer. "Do you?"

I knew she wanted a yes or no, something concise and specific and if this were any other question, I probably could have given it to her. But instead, I just sat there, silent, as I tried to put the image in my head—a boy in a white tuxedo shirt on a dark beach, laughing, one hand reached out to me—into any kind of words.

"Deborah Rachelle Bell!" I heard a voice boom from behind us. A moment later her father, the Reverend Elijah Bell, appeared, fully filling the space of the open doorway. His suit was tight, the shirt collar loosened, and he had a handkerchief in one hand, which he immediately pressed to his sweaty brow. "What in the world are you doing? People are waiting down there!"

"I'm sorry, Daddy," Deborah wailed, and then I saw William, finally, climbing the stairs. Just as quickly he disappeared from view, though, blocked by the reverend's girth. "I just got scared."

"Well, get it together," he told her, stepping inside. Clearly winded, he paused to take a breath or two before continuing. "I spent thirty thousand nonrefundable dollars of my hard-earned money on this wedding. If you don't walk down that aisle right now, I'll marry Lucas myself."

At this, Deborah burst into fresh tears. As I put my hand out to her, helplessly patting a shoulder, William managed to squeeze past the reverend and approach us. Calm as always, he didn't look at me, his eyes on only the bride as he bent close to speak in her ear. She whispered a response as he began to move his hand in slow circles on her back, like you do for a fussy baby.

I couldn't hear anything that was said, only the reverend still breathing. Other footsteps were audible on the stairs now, most likely bridesmaids, groomsmen, and others coming to rubberneck. Everyone liked to be part of the story, it seemed. I'd understood this once, but not so much anymore.

Whatever William said had made Deborah smile, albeit shakily. But it was enough; she let him take her elbow and help her to her feet. While she looked down at her wrinkled dress, trying to shake out the folds, he leaned back into the hallway, beckoning down the stairs. A moment later the makeup artist appeared, her tackle box of products in hand.

"Okay, everyone, let's give Deborah a second to freshen up," William announced to the room, just as, sure enough, one bridesmaid and then another poked their heads in. "Reverend, can you go tell everyone to take their places? We'll be down in two minutes."

"You'd better be," the reverend said, pushing past him to the door, sending bridesmaids scattering in a flash of lavender. "Because I am *not* coming up those stairs again."

"We'll be right outside," William told Deborah, gesturing for me to follow him. I did, pulling the door shut behind us.

"I'm sorry," I said immediately. "That was beyond my skill set."

"You did fine," he told me, pulling out his phone. Without even looking closely, I knew he was firing off a text to my mom in the code they used to ensure both speed and privacy. A second later, I heard a buzz as she wrote back. He scanned the screen, then said, "People are curious but there is a minimum of speculation noise, at least so far. It's going to be fine. We've got the eyelash as an explanation."

I looked at my watch. "An eyelash can take fifteen minutes?"

"It can take an hour, as far as anyone down there knows." He smoothed a wrinkle I couldn't even see out of his pants, then adjusted his red bow tie. "I wouldn't have pegged Deb as a cold-feeter. Shows what I know."

"What did she say to you back there?" I asked him.

He was listening to the noises beyond the door, alert, I knew, to the aural distinction between crying and getting makeup done. After a moment, he said, "Oh, she asked about true love. If I believed in it, does it last. Typical stuff pre-ceremony."

"What did you say?"

Now he looked at me, with that cool, confident countenance that made him, along with my mom, the best team in the Lakeview wedding business. "I said of course. I couldn't do this job if I didn't. Love is what it's all about."

Wow, I thought. "You really believe that?"

He shuddered. "Oh, God, no."

Just then the door opened, revealing Deborah, makeup fixed, eyelash in place, dress seemingly perfect. She gave us a nervous smile, and even as I reciprocated I was more aware of William, beaming, than my own expression.

"You look beautiful," he said. "Let's do this."

He held out his hand to her and she took it, letting him guide her down the stairs. The makeup lady followed, sighing only loud enough for me to hear, and then I was alone.

Down in the church lobby, my mother would be getting the wedding party into position, adjusting straps and lapels, fluffing bouquets, and straightening boutonnières. I looked back into the anteroom, where only a pile of crumpled tissues now remained. As I hurriedly collected them, I wondered how many other brides had felt the same way in this space, standing on the edge between their present and future, not quite ready to jump. I could sympathize, but only to a point. At least they got to make that choice for themselves. When, instead, it was done for you—well, that was something to really cry about. At any rate, now the organ music was rising, things beginning. I shut the door and headed downstairs.

My mother picked up her wine. "I'm going to say seven years. Long enough for a couple of kids and an affair."

"Interesting," William replied, holding his own glass aloft and studying it for a moment. Then he said, "I'll give it three. No children. But an amicable parting."

"You think?"

"I just get that feeling. Those feet were awfully cold, and asking about true love?"

My mom considered this. "Point taken. I think you'll win this one. Cheers."

They clinked glasses, then sat back in their chairs, each taking a solemn sip. After every wedding, when the bride and groom were gone and all the guests dispersed to their homes and hotels, my mom and William had one last ritual. They'd have a nightcap, recap the event, and lay bets on the marriage it produced. Their accuracy in predicting both outcome and duration was uncanny. And, to be honest, a little unsettling.

To me, though, the real test was in the departure. There was just something so telling about that moment when everyone gathered to see the bride and groom off. It wasn't like the ceremony, where people were nervous and could hide things, or the reception, which was usually chaotic enough to blur details. With the leaving, months of planning were behind them, years of a life together ahead. Which was why I'd always made a point of watching their faces so carefully, taking note of fatigue, tears, or flickers of irritation. I didn't make a wager as much as a wish for them. I always wanted a happy ending for everyone else.

Not that the clients would ever know this. It was the secret finish to what was known in our town of Lakeview as "A Natalie Barrett Wedding," an experience so valued by the newly engaged that both a spot on a waitlist and a huge fee were required to even be considered for one. My mom and William's price might be high, but they delivered, the results of their work bound in the four thick, embossed leather albums in their office sitting room. Each was packed with images of glowing brides and grooms getting married in every way possible: beachside, while barefoot. Lakeside, in black tie. At a winery. On top of a mountain. In their own (gorgeous, styled for the occasion) backyard. There were huge wedding parties and small intimate ones. Many billowing white dresses with trains, and some in other colors and cuts (signs, I'd found, of second or third marriages). The difference between a regular wedding and a Natalie Barrett one was akin to the difference between a pet store and a circus. A wedding was just two people getting married. A Natalie Barrett Wedding was an experience.

The Deborah Bell Wedding—it was company policy that we referred to all planned events by the bride's name, as it was Her Day—was pretty much par for the course for us. The ceremony was at a church, the reception at a nearby hotel ballroom. There were five bridesmaids and five groomsmen, a ring bearer and a flower girl. Their choice of a live band was increasingly rare these days (my mother preferred a DJ: the fewer people to wrangle, the better) as was the dinner brought out by waiters (carving stations, buffets, and dessert bars had been more popular for years now). The night had wrapped up with fireworks, an increasingly popular request that added a permitting wrinkle but literally a final bang for the client's buck. Despite the earlier dramatics, Deborah had run to the limo clutching her new husband's hand, flushed and happy, smile wide. They'd been kissing as the door was shut behind them, to the obvious disapproval of the reverend, who had then dabbed his own eyes, his wife patting his arm, as the car pulled away. *Good luck*, I'd thought, as the tail lights turned out of sight. *May you always have the answers to each other's most important questions.*

And then the wedding was over, for them, anyway. Not for us. First, there was this recap and wager, as well as a final check of the venue for lost items, misplaced wedding gifts, and passed out or, um, otherwise engaged guests (you'd be surprised—I know I always was). Then we would pack our cars with our clipboards and file folders, mending kits, double-stick tape, boxes of Kleenex, spare power strips, phone chargers, and Xanax (yep), and head home. We usually had exactly one day to recover, after which we were right back at the office in front of my mother's huge whiteboard, where she'd circle the next wedding up and it all began again.

Despite how my mom and William joked otherwise—often—they loved this business. For them, it was a passion, and they were good at it. This had been the case long before I'd been old enough to work with them during the summers. As a kid, I'd colored behind my mother's huge desk while she took meetings with anxious brides about guest lists and seating arrangements. Now I sat alongside them, my own legal pad (in a Natalie Barrett Wedding leather folio, of course) in my lap, taking notes. This transition had always been expected, was basically inevitable. Weddings were the family business, and I was my mother's only family. Unless you counted William, which really, we did.

They had met sixteen years earlier, when I was two years old and my dad had just walked out on us. At the time, my parents had been living in a cabin in the woods about ten miles outside Lakeview. There they raised chickens, had an organic garden, and made their own beeswax candles, which they sold at the local farmers' market on weekends. My dad, only twenty-two, had a full beard, rarely wore shoes, and was working on a chapbook of environmentally themed poems that had been in progress since before I'd even been conceived. My mom, a year younger, was full vegan, waited tables in the evenings at a nearby organic co-op café, and made rope bracelets blessed with "earth energy" on the side. They had met in college, at a campus protest against the public education system, which was, apparently, "oppressive, misogynist, cruel to animals, and evil." This was verbatim from the flyer I'd found in a box deep in my mother's closet that held the only things she'd kept from this time in her life other than me. Inside, besides the flyer, was a rather ugly beeswax candle, a rope bracelet that that been her "ring" at her own "wedding" (which had taken place in the mud at an outdoor music festival, officiated by a friend who signed the marriage certificate, also included, only as "King Wheee!"), and a single picture of my parents, both barefoot and tan, standing in a garden holding rakes. I sat on the ground beside my mother's feet, examining a cabbage leaf, completely naked. My name, an original, was a mix of their own, Natalie and Louis. I was Louna.

The box in the closet holding these things was small for someone who had once had such big beliefs, and this always made me kind of sad. My mother, however, only reflected on this time of her life when clients wondered aloud if it really *was* worth spending an obscene amount of money for the wedding of their dreams. "Well, I was married in a mud pit by someone on magic mushrooms," she'd say, "and I think it doomed us from the start. But that's just me." Then she'd pause for a beat or two, giving the client in front of her enough time to try to imagine Natalie Barrett—with her expensive, tailored clothes, perfect hair and makeup, and ever-present diamond earrings, ring, and necklace—as some dirty hippie in a bad marriage. They couldn't, but that didn't stop them from signing on the contract's dotted line to make sure they wouldn't meet the same fate. Better safe than sorry.

In truth, the reason for the demise of my parents' marriage was not the mud pit or the officiant, but my father. After three years in the woods making candles and "writing his poems" (my mother claimed she never once saw him put pen to paper) he'd grown tired of struggling. This wasn't surprising. Raised in San Francisco by a father who owned over a dozen luxury car dealerships, he'd not exactly been made for living off the land long term. Ever since he and my mom had exchanged vows, his own father told him that if he left the marriage—and, subsequently, the baby—he'd get a Porsche dealership of his own. My mom already believed that commerce was responsible for all of life's evils. When her true love took this offer, it got personal. Three years later, long estranged from us, he was killed in a car accident. I don't remember my mother crying or even really reacting, although she must have, in some way. Not me. You don't miss what you never knew.

And I knew my mom, and only my mom. Not only did I look just like her—same features, dark hair, and olive skin—but I sometimes felt like we were the same person. Mostly because she'd been disowned by her own wealthy, elderly parents around the time of the mud pit marriage, so it was always just us. After my dad bailed, she sold the cabin and moved us into Lakeview, where, after bouncing around a few restaurant jobs, she got a position working at the registry department of Linens, Etc., the housewares chain. On the surface, it seemed like a weird fit, as it was hard to find a convention more commerce-driven than weddings. But she had a kid to feed, and in her previous life my mom had been a debutante and taken etiquette classes at the country club. This world might have disgusted her, but she knew it well. Before long, brides were requesting her when they came in to pick out china patterns or silverware.

By the time William was hired a year later, my mom had a huge following. As she trained him, teaching him all she knew, they became best friends. There in the back of the store, they spent many hours with brides, listening to them talk—and often complain—about their wedding planning. As they learned which vendors were good and which weren't, they began keeping lists of numbers for local florists, caterers, and DJs to recommend. This expanded to advising more and more on specific events, and then planning a few weddings entirely. Meanwhile, over lunch hours and after-work drinks or dinner, they started to talk about going out on their own. A partnership on paper and a loan from William's mother later, they were in business.

My mom had a fifty-one share, William forty-nine, and she got her name on the door. But the legalese basically ended there. Whatever foxhole a particular wedding was, they were in it together. They made dreams come true, they liked to tell each other and anyone else who would listen, and they weren't wrong. This ability never did cross over to their *own* love lives, however. My mom had barely dated since splitting with my dad, and when she did, she made a point of picking people she knew wouldn't stick around—"to take the guesswork out of it," in her words. Meanwhile William, who had been out since about age eight, had yet to meet any man who could come close to meeting his exacting standards. He dealt with this by also leaning toward less than ideal choices with no chance of long-term relationship potential. Real love didn't exist, they maintained, despite building an entire livelihood based on that very illusion. So why waste time looking for it? And besides, they had each other.

Even as a kid, I knew this was dysfunctional. But unfortunately, I'd been indoctrinated from a young age with my mom and William's strong, oft-repeated cynical views on *romance, forever, love,* and other keywords. It was confusing, to say the least. On the one hand, I lived and breathed the wedding dream, dragged along to ceremonies and venues, privy to meetings on every excruciating detail from Save the

Date cards to cake toppers. But away from the clients and the work, there was a constant, repetitive commentary about how it was a sham, no good men really existed, and we were all better off alone. It was no wonder that a few years earlier, when my best friend Jilly had suddenly gone completely boy-crazy, I'd been reluctant to join her. I was a fourteen-year-old girl with the world-weariness of a bitter midlife divorcée, repeating all the things I'd heard over and over, like a mantra. "Well, he'll only disappoint you, so you should just expect it," I'd say, shaking my head as she texted with some thick-necked soccer player. Or I'd warn: "Don't give what you're not ready to lose," when she considered, with great drama, whether to confess to a boy that she "liked" him. My peers might have been flirting either in pairs or big groups, but I stood apart, figuratively and literally, the buzz-kill at the end of every rom-com movie or final chorus of a love song. After all, I'd learned from the best. It wasn't my fault, which did not make it any less annoying.

But then, the previous summer, on a hot August night, all of that had changed. Suddenly, I *did* believe, at least for a little while. The result was the most broken of hearts, made even worse by the knowledge that I had no one to blame for it but myself. If I'd only walked away, said no twice instead of only once, gone home to my bed and left that wide stretch of stars behind when I had the chance. Oh, well.

Now my mother downed the rest of her drink and put her glass aside. "Past midnight," she observed, taking a glance at her watch. "Are we ready to go?"

"One last sweep and we will be," William replied, standing up and brushing off his suit. As a rule, we all dressed for events as if we were guests, but modest ones. The goal was to blend in, but not *too* much. Like everything in this business, a delicate balance. "Louna, you take the lobby and outside. I'll check here and the bathrooms."

I nodded, then headed across the ballroom, now empty except for a few servers stacking chairs and clearing glasses. The lights were bright overhead, and as I walked I could see flower petals and crumpled napkins here and there on the floor, along with a few stray glasses and beer cans. Outside, the lobby was deserted, except for some guy leaning out a half-open door with a cigar, under a NO SMOKING sign.

I continued out the front doors, where the night felt cool. The parking lot was quiet as well, no one around. Or so I thought, until I started back in and glimpsed one of Deborah's bridesmaids, a tall black girl with braids and a nose ring—Malika? Malina?—standing by a nearby planter. She had a tissue in her hand and was dabbing at her eyes, and I wondered, not for the first time, what it was about weddings that made everything so emotional. It was like tears were contagious.

She looked up suddenly, seeing me. I raised my eyebrows, and she gave me a sad smile, shaking her head: she didn't need my help. There are times when you intervene and times when you don't, and I'd long ago learned the difference. Some people like their sadness out in the open, but the vast majority prefer to cry alone. Unless it was my job to do otherwise, I'd let them.

CHAPTER

2

"YOU KNOW," Jilly said, from inside my closet, "this job of yours is really putting a damper on my love life."

"You always say that," I told her.

"And I always mean it." There was a thump, followed by the sound of something falling. "Wow. Is this pink one really strapless? How unlike you. I'm trying it on. Crawford, about face."

I looked over at her ten-year-old little brother, who was standing by my desk, studying my math textbook. He pushed up his glasses, sighed, then turned around. Meanwhile, I shifted her baby sister, Bean, to my other hip, trying to extract my hair from her tight grip. As I did, she gummed my shoulder, leaving a streak of spittle across my shirtsleeve. Since she had two working parents juggling their empire of food trucks, a visit from Jilly was always a family affair.

"Okay," she announced after a moment, emerging in a watermelon-colored sundress that was too small for her. Also, not strapless last I checked. But Jilly liked things tight and short, all the better to accentuate her ample curves. As much as it was not my personal style—by a long shot—I had to admire her body confidence. Most girls at our school were constantly talking diets and thigh gaps, but my best friend had always been one to zig where others zagged. It was but one of about a million things I loved about her. "What do you think?"

"That there are straps," I pointed out, coming over and wriggling one loose. "See?"

She glanced over a freckled shoulder. "Oh. Well, they're slim at least. Pop that other one up for me?"

I did as I was told as Bean tried to reach for her, chubby fingers grabbing. Jilly always came to my house in one outfit and left in another. I had an entire rack in the closet of her clothes, as organized as my own, which she ignored every time she went in there.

"So, about tonight," she said, wriggling an arm under the strap and adjusting her ample chest into the bodice. I was a hopeful C cup at best, and she was a legit D, so she always added to my clothes a va-va-voom factor I couldn't even hope for. "The guys are meeting us late night at Bendo, after the last band plays. It's that Catastrophe one."

"Brilliant or Catastrophic," I corrected her.

"Right." She turned around, presenting her back to me to do the zipper. "You can come after the event. You said you'd be done early, right?"

"No. I said it was a six o'clock wedding. It'll be ten or after."

"That dress is too tight," Crawford said in his signature flat monotone. It was the way he'd talked since he was a baby and the family had moved in behind us, just over the slim creek that separated our two houses. At the time, Jilly and I were ten, he was two, and the twins and Bean not even around yet. Jilly's parents were busy when it came to everything, including procreating.

"Don't worry about me. Just read your book," she told him in reply, pushing up her boobs a bit.

"It's Louna's book," he grumbled, and flipped a page. "Also Bean needs changing."

So that was what I smelled. Crawford, wicked smart and socially awkward, was always a step ahead of the rest of us. Without comment, Jilly took Bean from me, plopped her on the floor, handed her one of her bracelets to gum on, and continued.

"Enough with the excuses, okay?" she said to me. "It's been almost a year. Time to get back out there. You can't hide behind work forever."

"And 'out there' is a dirty, sticky club?"

"In this particular case, yes."

"Germs cause viruses," Crawford opined. "And viruses make you sick."

"Just come, listen to some music, we'll hit a party or two," Jilly said to me, as Bean began crawling under my bed. "It'll be fun. I promise."

"Wait a second. You didn't say anything about a party. Or parties, plural."

She exhaled loudly, this time without the benefit of a breath beforehand. "Louna," she said, reaching out and taking me by my arms, "I'm your best friend. I know what you've been through, and I know you're scared. But we are still young. Life is ahead of us. What a privilege, right? Don't squander it."

This was the thing about Jilly. In so many ways, she was over the top, a big, loud, spirited girl who cared not one bit what anyone thought about her. She always had at least two of her siblings in tow, co-opted my clothes, and was hell-bent on finding me another boyfriend, even if—and especially when—I didn't want one. And yet for all these frustrations, and our absolute polar opposite personalities, every once in a while she could say something like this, heartfelt and direct and, damn it, true. Her heart, as misguided as it could be on other levels, always managed to zero out everything else. What a privilege, indeed.

"I'll try to get there," I told her.

"That's all I ask." She leaned forward, giving me a sloppy kiss on my cheek just as her phone beeped. Pulling it from her bodice—her preferred storage space—she glanced at the screen. "Twinnies need to go to gymnastics. I totally forgot."

"I hate gymnastics," Crawford said. "The whole place smells like mats and feet."

"He's not wrong," Jilly told me, checking herself in the mirror again. Then she looked into my closet, raising her eyebrows. "Wait, are those new sandals I see back there? Hold the phone! I just got a pedicure."

With this, she ducked around me, past the rows of my everyday shoes and into a back corner of the closet, reaching out to grab a pair of thin black sandals with a gold ring closure I'd worn only once. Just seeing them dangling from her hand, straps hooked over her thumb, made my heart sink. "No," I said, my voice sounding harsher, more abrupt than I meant. "Not those."

She looked down at them, then at the place they'd been, away from the others. A beat, and she got it. Quietly, she set them back down on the floor. "Oh, right," she said. "Sorry."

I didn't say anything, just tried to collect myself—why was this still so hard?—as she bent down to retrieve Bean. When she lifted her up, I felt Crawford watching me, his face somber as usual, and even though I knew he was just a kid and knew nothing, I had to turn away.

They left a few minutes later with the usual noise involved in any scene change, Bean shrieking while Jilly and Crawford bickered down the stairs. Once out in the backyard, she looked up at my window, waggling her fingers, and I waved back, then watched as they made their way across the grass. Jilly jumped the creek, light on her feet even with the baby in tow, but Crawford stopped, bending down to closely examine something by the water's edge. A moment later, she yelled at him to hurry up, and he moved on.

In my room, things were quiet in that special way they only were when the Bakers left the building. As a family they were a lot to handle, for sure, but I couldn't imagine what my life would have been like had they never moved in. My own house was so clean and still, just my mom and me, everything in order. Knowing their brand of dependable chaos was always nearby was a comfort from day one. We all need to lose ourselves in a crowd once in a while.

But I was alone now as I went back into the closet. There

in that small, dark space, I picked up one black sandal, then another, and placed them back where they'd been, in the corner under a black dress, also worn only one time. They no longer felt like mine, as much as another girl's from another time. And yet, I still couldn't get rid of them. Not yet.

⁂

"I love a third wedding," William said happily, as we stood by the country club pool, watching guests take their seats. "Everyone is so relaxed. I feel like we should just specialize in them, corner that niche market."

"Not enough business in it," my mother, always the realist, told him. "Plus you'd miss the neuroses of young brides. It would be a waste of your gift."

"True," he agreed, as his eyes followed an older man in a tight-fitting suit who was about to sit in one of the front rows of chairs reserved for family. William was the most hyper-aware person I knew, like a cat always ready to pounce. I realized I was holding my own breath until the man's wife took his elbow, pulling him back to a farther row. "Speaking of young brides, I spoke to Bee and she's confirmed for first thing Monday morning for her preliminary."

My mother sighed. "You know I hate a rush job, William."

"The wedding is in August. It's April."

"*Late* April," my mother countered. "Which would be fine, if it *was* a third wedding. But it's not. It's high society, and high maintenance, which means we should have started planning a year ago."

"You're leaving out high budget," William pointed out.

"Money isn't everything." I waited a beat for what I knew was coming next. Sure enough: "You can't put on a price on your sanity."

"But if you could, they'd pay it."

They both fell silent as another guest started for the front row. It would be only a matter of minutes before William pulled out the pre-printed RESERVED cards (in his almost calligraphy-like handwriting, aka the official font of a Natalie Barrett Wedding) and put them on the seats. He usually tried to resist, eschewing any extra clutter in a venue, even nicely printed cards. But you could never underestimate the Moron Factor. That was another one of my mother's mantras.

"Twenty minutes," she said now, flicking her wrist to check her watch. "Put down a few cards, just so we don't have to police. Louna, can you take BRR?"

I nodded, pulling out my phone to double-check it was on silent. Back Row Right was often my spot at events like this one, when there was a walking factor involved. It was a variation of our three-pronged approach: she launched the wedding party, I kept tabs as they were moving, and William was positioned up front. There, he'd be ready to spring into action in case of someone fainting, rings being dropped or forgotten altogether, or flower girls and ring bearers going rogue mid-ceremony. (Which often happened, although only one time all at once, at an event we now referred to simply as The Disaster.)

Now we broke, each taking our positions. This event, the Eve Little Wedding, had been in the works for the last nine months, and William was right: it had pretty much been a breeze. The bride was in her fifties, the groom his seventies. They had plenty of money and few specific requests, other than wanting the nuptials to be at the Lakeview Country Club, where they'd met on the tennis court. The club was handling the food, they'd hired our preferred DJ, and the whole thing was expected to wrap up by ten p.m. sharp.

The only wrinkle had come from the bride's daughter, Beatrice. When she'd gotten engaged a couple of weeks ago, she decided she, too, had to have a Natalie Barrett Wedding. Complicating things was the fact that she and her fiancé were getting married in mid-August before moving across the country at the end of the summer for a medical residency, so everything had to happen ASAP. Normally, with the waitlist and my mother's obsession with organization, we didn't take on anything that came close to last minute. But Eve Little had been so easy, and they were spending so much money, that William, at least, had capitulated. Which was, well, forty percent of the battle.

I walked to the back of the rows of chairs I'd helped set out a couple of hours earlier, taking my place on the aisle. As usual, there were a few people clumped in the back row, which was sure to annoy William, who liked his audiences uniform. "What are they even thinking? It's not like they're going to get called on to participate," he'd huff. In extreme cases I'd even witnessed him pulling his rank and reseating people, although that only happened when he was feeling especially pissy.

I didn't have such strong feelings, so I just nodded at the couple a few seats away from me as I pulled out my phone, checking the time. There were fifteen minutes to go when the first group text from my mom arrived.

SWIMMERS HEADED TO POOL.

A beat, and William appeared, magically, from behind a light-draped topiary. Smoothly, he intercepted a woman and her kid, both in bathing suits, then redirected them back past the AREA CLOSED FOR EVENT sign.

There was then a burst of organ music, so sudden I was not the only one who jumped in my seat upon hearing it. Before my mom could type the inevitable WTF??? I slid out of my chair, hustling to the back of the pool patio, where the DJ, Monty, was already holding up his hands apologetically. Under control.

Twelve minutes. I turned, looking back to the entrance to the patio, where my mom was now bent over a tow-headed ring bearer. With everything that could go wrong in a ceremony, she particularly disliked the chaos factor associated with kids and dogs, and took what she considered to be appropriate offensive action with both. For canines, this was an ample supply of cut-up hot dogs, stuffed up her sleeve in a Ziploc bag. For children, candy bribes and a stern voice usually did the trick, although balance was important when it came to the latter. There were enough emotions at stake without a crying kid kicking off the whole thing.

By seven minutes, I was back in my seat, watching William survey the crowd as the final guests found seats. Whenever he saw the lack of bodies between the fourth row and last one, he winced, although I was pretty sure only I noticed.

At six on the dot, the music was supposed to begin. Instead, my phone vibrated again. I read the text twice and still didn't understand it.

SOB AWOL 4 AISLE WALK.

Up front, William was also getting this message. He looked at me, raising his eyebrows.

WHAT? I typed, as the man two seats down from me checked his watch.

GET HERE NOW, was the reply, and I didn't even finish it before I was on my feet and moving.

Don't run, don't run, I reminded myself, trying to hustle in an efficient but not panicked-looking way across the patio. When I got to the club lobby, the wedding party was lined up, the now teary-looking ring bearer in the front. Past him, and the pairs of bridesmaids and groomsmen, was a confab of Eve Little—looking radiant in a light yellow gown with petal sleeves; I loved third weddings!—her daughter Bee, and my mother. Everyone was talking at once.

". . . have to be confident of the precise order to do our job properly," my mom was saying as I came up. "Last-minute additions make that difficult if not impossible."

"I understand that," Eve said, as Bee, her own phone to her ear, scanned the room. "But he was just here!"

"He's stealthy that way," Bee told me, as if I knew what this was all about. "Maybe check outside?"

I looked at my mom, who said, "You heard her. Go check outside!"

"For who?" I asked. "Everyone's here."

I knew this, because the Cheat Sheet was one of my assigned jobs. The night before every event, I put together a single piece of paper containing a list of the wedding party and pertinent family, contact info for the vendors we'd hired (caterer, DJ, florist) as well the final, approved wedding schedule from arrival of guests to our departure. Now, only moments in, that was out the window.

"Ambrose," Eve said. Hearing this, my mother tried (or actually, didn't) to mask her frustration.

"Who?"

"My brother," Bee told me, shifting her bouquet of white roses and lilies to her other hand. She was a gorgeous girl, blonde with creamy skin and blue eyes, the kind of good-looking that would be annoying if she wasn't so nice. "He wasn't going to be here, but now he is. Tall, blond like me, most likely talking to a girl. Smack him if you have to."

SOB was Son of Bride, then. And the more colloquial meaning, if he really was singlehandedly holding all this up. "On it," I said to my mom, starting to the lobby exit. Before pushing the door open, I took one last look behind me, just in time to see William moving quickly down the aisle, his phone clamped to his ear. If he and my mom had moved to actual talking on the phone, this was even worse than I thought.

Outside, I took a quick scan of the parking lot. Two golfers were standing by an Audi with clubs poking out of the trunk, talking, while a guy in chef whites stacked vegetable crates by the kitchen entrance. Otherwise, nothing to see. Or so I thought until I heard the melodic tinkle of what could only be, in any world, a pretty girl's laugh.

It was coming from behind a florist's van a few spaces down from me, and was followed by another chuckle, this one distinctly male. I started toward the van, wondering again why I hadn't just chosen to work in a coffee shop, bookstore, or some other place that didn't involve corralling strangers against their will. I rounded the van's back bumper, clearing my throat.

When I first saw Ambrose Little, I had two distinct thoughts, cementing how I would feel about him from that point on. I didn't know this at the time, though. All I registered was this: First, he was incredibly good-looking. Second, just the sight of him—a mere glimpse, in profile, from a distance—annoyed me in a way I couldn't quite explain.

First, his looks. Bee was right: they did share the same coloring and features. But Ambrose, who was in a tux and white shirt, was tall, almost gangly, with long arms and legs, distinct cheekbones, and a swoop of blond hair just tousled enough that you knew he had to spend time on it. He was like that upside-down exclamation point at the beginning of a sentence in Spanish, the mere appearance of which warned of something complicated ahead.

As far as the annoyance factor, it was harder to quantify. Maybe it was that he *was* so good-looking, like the chiseled, flat-chested surfer boy doll of my childhood morphed into human form. Never before, though, had I viscerally disliked someone purely on sight. It made me feel shallow in a way I didn't like.

At that moment, however, he hadn't even noticed me, too busy leaning into a curvy Indian girl wearing khaki shorts and a golf shirt with the country club insignia. She, in turn, was resting against a Toyota, a set of car keys dangling from one hand. They were about as close to entwined as you could be without touching, and despite my vocal warning, neither of them noticed me.

"Ambrose," I said, in my stern voice. This time, he looked over, that curly swoop moving to the other side of his forehead. Straight on, I saw it was a perfect curl, so intact you couldn't help but want to reach out and pull on it. Just thinking this annoyed me again. "The wedding is starting. We need you in place."

He smiled at me then, a lazy, rich boy smile, all teeth and confidence. "Well, hey there. Who are you?"

The girl made a face, clearly unhappy with this development. I said, "I work for Natalie Barrett, the wedding planner. I need you to come with me. Now."

He laughed, then saluted me, his hand brushing the curl. "Yes, ma'am! Just give me two shakes." And with that, he turned back to his friend, who tilted her head up once she had his attention again.

Some people asked themselves in difficult situations What Would Jesus Do? For me, when it came to work at least, there was only one true example to follow, and I knew that in my shoes she'd take whatever measures were necessary to get things back on schedule. Next summer, a bookstore or coffee shop, I promised myself. Then I marched over, clamped a hand around Ambrose Little's wrist, and started dragging him toward the club entrance.

"What the hell?" the girl said, her eyes narrowing. "You can't just—"

But I could, and I was. I'd expected resistance, which was why I'd grabbed him with such gusto. Instead, he immediately lost his balance, stumbling forward into me while flailing for something to grab on to, which turned out to be my left breast. Now I was dragging someone while being groped, while the golfers looked on. Nice.

"Normally I like an assertive girl," Ambrose said, regaining his footing as I shoved his hand off me. "But you're coming on a *bit* strong."

I ignored this, afraid of what I'd say if I did respond. We were almost to the club entrance; once over the threshold, he'd be my mother's problem and I could get back to BRR duty, where I belonged.

"I feel like we haven't been properly introduced," he continued, as I yanked open the glass door with my free hand. "I'm Ambrose. And you are?"

"Finally," my mother hissed, intercepting us the moment we stepped inside. I looked at a nearby clock: it was six fifteen. As she was someone who deeply prided herself on the timeliness of her events, every minute of a postponement caused an uptick in annoyance. Ambrose might not have known it, but if he'd dawdled any longer, more than his wrist would have been twisted. As it was, he gave her the same charm-confident smile, which she countered with a stare so icy I almost felt sorry for him. Almost.

"This way," she barked, as I dropped his hand, relieved to step out of the way and the fray. He followed her without any comment, protest, or dragging involved. Even he knew right off who was the boss.

My phone buzzed. William. UPDATE?

ALL IN PLACE, I replied. HEADING TO BRR.

I walked past Ambrose and his mom, then the rest of the wedding party, which had been lined up for so long their restlessness was obvious. As I passed the bridesmaids, I felt a hand on my arm. When I turned, Bee gave me a grateful smile. "Thanks for retrieving my stupid brother."

I nodded, markedly *not* assuring her he was nothing of the sort. "Of course."

Back in the last row of chairs, there was an obvious buzz of speculation as to the delay. To the untrained ear, all waiting sounded the same, but I knew the difference and so did William, who claimed the energy of a bad start had the potential to curse any event that followed it. When I spotted him behind a pillar, I was not surprised his mouth was a thin line, the closest he'd allow to a frown while working.

Finally, at 6:23, the processional music began. I pivoted in my seat, looking over my shoulder as the ring bearer and flower girl plodded adorably down the aisle, tossing rose petals in front of them. As William ushered them into their spots, the bridal party followed, two by two, like animals to the ark. When Bee passed me, she smiled at me again, and I got the distinct feeling she was used to apologizing for her brother. In contrast, when he and Eve came along next, the crowd oohing at her yellow dress and him so handsome in his tux, he didn't even see me.

A wedding is a series of special moments, strung together like beads on a chain. Sure, by themselves, they are lovely, but put them all together and you get art. If we did our job right, the fact that the initial moments were off wouldn't even be remembered after the first dance, toasts, and cake cutting were done. But really, in a perfect wedding—or world—you wanted the best possible beginning. Start on a high note and, no matter what song follows, chances are just better that it will be music to your ears.

⚜

At 9:47, despite the strict ten p.m. sharp ending on the schedule, the dance floor remained crowded. Still, I took no comfort in the fact I'd been right talking to Jilly earlier. The day had been unexpectedly hot for the end of April, and the combination of stress, sunshine, and multiple hours on my feet had taken a toll. I didn't want to go to Bendo, much less make the effort required to be "out there," with two boys I didn't even know. And I definitely didn't want to dance. Which was why, when Ambrose Little emerged from the back of a rather sloppy-looking Electric Slide line, spotted me, and beckoned, I only shook my head.

This was a no-brainer, but not because of anything to

do with him. The Golden Rule of working a Natalie Barrett Wedding: remember your place. It wasn't unusual for clients, over the course of many months of planning, to develop a certain dependency on us. Huge life events that were fraught with emotion often led to displaced feelings. However, "Nobody wants to look at their pictures later and see their wedding planner acting like a guest," my mom always reminded extra employees we took on from time to time for bigger events. "If we don't stay out of frame, we haven't done our job right."

So I wasn't surprised to be asked to dance. It happened, especially at open bar events. I was, however, not expecting him to respond to my *no* by shaking his own head, then walking right over and sticking his hand out to take mine.

"Dancing is healing," he said, opening his palm wide to me as the music faded out and another song began. "Let's heal."

"No, thank you," I said.

He wiggled his fingers wildly, as if imitating a sea anemone might suddenly sway my opinion.

"Thanks, but no," I told him, switching up my three allowed words in this situation.

"Ambrose!" a girl in a short pink dress, her now bare feet crisscrossed with the evidence of previously worn sandals, hollered from the floor. "Get over here! We need you for the conga line!"

"Hear that?" he said to me. "Conga! You gotta get in on this." When again I shook my head, he sighed loudly, then bent over with his hands on his knees, as if my response was now so tragic it had knocked the wind out of him. After a second, he lifted his head, then one hand, busting out the sea anemone move again. "Conga. Healing. Let's go."

"No, thanks," I told him.

People were starting to form the line now, stumbling as they grabbed on to each other, laughing and flushed. If there was a benchmark of the Beginning of the End of a reception, this was it. Ambrose looked over, grinned, then turned back to me. "Don't worry," he said. "I don't have to squeeze tight."

"You won't have to squeeze at all," I said. "Because the answer is still no."

"Aren't you supposed to be working this event?"

"I am."

"So you should dance, then."

"That's not how it works."

"Why?"

The last thing I felt like doing was getting into the parameters of my job with a clumsy, wavering conga line approaching. "I'm not a guest, I'm an employee. We don't dance. We work."

He considered this briefly. "Okay, then I'm asking you to be my date. You're off duty."

"That's not how it works either," I told him.

"Man! You are *tough*!" He shook his head, that curl I couldn't seem to *not* focus on bobbing. The conga line was now winding around a nearby chair, a red-faced man with a cigar clamped in his mouth leading it. "So what you're saying is that you are never going to dance with me right now, no matter how I plead or beg you, even if conga is involved."

"Correct," I said.

"Really?" He made a face. "Shoot. I hate not having what I want."

This was such a weird thing for him to say—arrogant, honest—that I found myself, for the first time, without a set response at hand. But as the conga line came up behind him, the girl in pink letting out a whoop as she reached for his belt buckle, I almost wished for a final beat to address this thought, one I still had myself, more often than I could admit.

I hate not having what I want.

"Don't we all," I said quietly, as the line blurred past me, weaving through the tables. And just like that, I reached the point where the whole thing was too much color and life and laughter, and all I could do was turn and walk away.

CHAPTER

3

ETHAN ASKED me to dance at a wedding, too, and I said no. The first time.

But that was later in the story, this one I'd once told others so eagerly, and now could only repeat to myself, in my own head. You'd think in retrospect time would become linear, as if distance from events forced them to take their proper places. But something like this, I'd learned, was more fluid, as if the story was always being retold, in progress, whether you could bear to listen or not.

I was doing it again, jumping around. But it was so hard to start at the beginning when you knew how it would end.

It all happened at the Margy Love Wedding, the previous summer. My mother did not like doing out of town weddings and rarely took them on, maintaining that she was only as good as her vendors, which were all local. Margy Love's grandpa, however, was dear friends with William's mother. As the original benefactor of the business, Miss May—as she was known—had a certain clout even my mother couldn't deny. Aged eighty and in assisted living, she rarely asked for favors. But when she did, the answer was always yes.

So that August, after ten months of long-distance planning with Margy (in D.C.) and her mother (in California) we
packed up for a weekend in the beach town of Colby (where
they'd vacationed as a family every summer of Margy's life).
The venue was only about three hours from our house door
to door, and, actually, *not* a bleak, unpopulated place where
weddings had never happened before. Not that you could tell
this by how stressed my mom was or the amount of stuff she
insisted we bring (three vans' worth, one of us driving each)
to ensure she'd have everything she required. My mom was
wound pretty tight as a rule, at least when it came to work.
But even I had rarely seen her so tense and snappy, which
was why, when we finally pulled out caravan-style from the
front of the house, I was happy to have the ride all to myself
with just the radio for company.

Still, I missed Jilly, who had been planning to come along
with me and hang out on the beach or in my room while I
worked. This would have been a first for her, an entire weekend away from her family, and we'd both been looking forward to it. It wasn't easy for the Bakers to do without her and
juggle their two Cheese Therapy food trucks (they sold gourmet grilled cheese and the richest, creamiest tomato soup I'd
ever tasted), which was why she usually ended up being the
substitute hands-on parent to one or all of her siblings. This
weekend, though, they'd promised her a pass in return for
a busy summer of ferrying the twins and Crawford around,
as well as changing endless diapers of Bean's. Two days earlier, however, Cheese Therapy had been one of only twenty
trucks selected for a food truck rodeo at the state capital

celebrating small local businesses. It was a big deal, and they needed all hands on deck, so our getaway was out.

So Jilly would spend the weekend corralling her siblings and working the Cheese Therapy register while scoping out cute boys in a bigger city. Meanwhile, I'd go to Colby, where I'd spend Friday night assisting my mom and William with the rehearsal dinner—a clambake on the beach with a Tiki Hut theme—and Saturday working the main event (formal, at a hotel overlooking the ocean, surf and turf stations to follow).

If I'd actually been a guest, this probably would have sounded great. As it was, all I could think about was the combination of food and sand (never good in practice) and a very important wedding taking place in a venue I'd not yet seen. At home, we had extensive notes on every place we'd staged ceremonies, detailing pertinent issues like hard-to-find exits, squeaky floors, or rattling pews. Out of town, though, we were everywhere for the first time.

At least it was a nice weekend, warm with sunny and clear skies forecast, and I would be at the beach. With this in mind, I'd splurged earlier in the week on a new black sundress and gold-accented sandals for the occasion. As we drove east, the subdivisions and interstates giving way to farmland and two-lane roads, I could feel the work-related kink in my neck slowly relaxing. I could only hope the drive was having the same effect on my mother in the van ahead of me.

Once over the bridge to Colby, we turned onto the main road, which was bottlenecked with tourists. FRESH SHRIMP! read one sign I studied as I crawled along, followed by WHO

NEEDS TRAFFIC? RENT A BIKE FROM ABE'S! with an arrow pointing to the nearby boardwalk. After what felt like an hour of exhaust, brake lights, and the occasional glimpse of ocean, blue and wide, we finally turned into the lot of a high-rise hotel called the Piers. The main building was so white in the bright sun that just looking at it made my head hurt. As I parked, pushing open the door, I could already hear my mother complaining. So much for a relaxing drive.

"This *sun!*" she said to William, instead of hello, as he walked over. As usual, he was perfect and unruffled in his khakis, short-sleeved checked shirt, and very clean white Adidas sneakers. In contrast, my outfit, after three hours in the car, looked like I'd balled it up in my hand multiple times. There were a lot of things I envied about William (just about everything, actually) but top on the list was how he always looked serene and flawless, even under the most dire of circumstances. "Old New England suppression and deni-al," he called it, which made it sound less like something to covet. I still did, though.

Now he just looked at my mom, reflected in his aviator sunglasses, flapping her arms around and trying to kick up a breeze as she continued, "At almost exactly this time tomor-row, we'll have a sixteen-member wedding party in full dress out in this. If everyone doesn't faint it will be a miracle."

"You're forgetting the pergolas," he said mildly. "We didn't insist on them, and the fluttering tulle, purely for the looks of it."

"We'll need a lot more than fluttering tulle to deal with

this," my mom grumbled, dabbing at her (not sweaty, from my view) brow. "But that's tomorrow. Let's find the caterer and see how this dinner is shaping up. Louna, can you start the unloading? The ballroom door is supposed to be just over there, behind the Dumpsters, and unlocked. They're expecting us."

Great, I thought, even as I nodded. They'd go into the A/C to talk tiki torches while I schlepped boxes of center-pieces, my mother's preferred table linens, and glassware across a hot parking lot. I could still hear her complaining as they walked away.

That night, the rehearsal went well, with only a few basic wrinkles. (Meltdown from flower girl, bossy wedding plan-ner wannabe aunt of bride, impatient officiant. This last was a pet peeve of us all. Nobody liked a snappy minister.) By the time Margy and her groom, Josef, play-walked down the aisle together, with her carrying the bouquet of ribbons from her bridal shower, everyone was ready for a drink. As they adjourned to the beach, my mother had the caterers wait-ing with trays of champagne, the tiki torches lit and flaming around them. Let the party begin.

"Well, that's done," she said to William, giving a cordial-but-not-exactly-warm nod to the bossy aunt as she passed us. "Here's hoping the actual event goes so smoothly."

"That was smooth?" he asked, his eyes following a brides-maid in wobbly platform sandals who was trying to navigate the steps to the beach. "Just once I'd like to get an officiant who was happy to do their job."

"Like you're always happy to do yours?"

"*Exactly,*" William replied. A pause. Then they both laughed, as if this was hysterical. I rolled my eyes, turning back to the party as two of the groomsmen walked by us. One of them was about my age and built like a football player, with dark hair cut short and blue eyes. The kind of boy that you can easily picture as a little kid, that cute. As he passed by, he smiled at me, and I felt my face flush, even as I tried to imitate my mother's efficient, businesslike nod in return. Once he went down the stairs to the beach, I realized William was watching me, amused, and felt embarrassed all over again.

After the dinner, the guests moved the party to the hotel bar and, thankfully, out of our jurisdiction. I helped my mom, William, and the caterers break down the tables and chairs, then brought a purse, a phone, and a monogrammed flask to the hotel lost and found. (Someday, I'd write an entire book about the things people left behind at weddings. I just had this feeling it all meant something.) By ten thirty, I was back in my room eating a pack of crackers from the vending machine and texting with Jilly, who was in a hotel room with Crawford watching a marathon of swamp fishing shows while the "youngers" (her term) all slept.

SO BORED, she reported. IF I SEE ANOTHER CATFISH I MIGHT SCREAM. TELL ME YOU ARE GOING TO GO OUT AND DO SOMETHING EPIC TONIGHT.

OF COURSE I AM, I wrote back.

SURE. I BET YOU ARE IN BED ALREADY.

I balled up the cracker wrapper, threw it in the general direction of the nearby trashcan, and missed.

I'LL DO EPIC TOMORROW. PROMISE.

YOU BETTER. IF I CAN'T, YOU HAVE TO!

I made a face. This was a familiar rant from Jilly, who had been long convinced that I squandered the relative freedom I enjoyed as an only child of a single, non-food-truck-owning parent. In my shoes, she was fond of telling me, she'd be the kind of person who was always out Doing Stuff and Making Things Happen. (The specifics of what, exactly, these terms meant were never explained; as with any fantasy, vagueness was part of the appeal.) Moreover, it wasn't just a waste of my life but of hers as well, that I willingly spent time away at the beach sitting in bed watching a news special about a murder mystery while covered in cracker crumbs. I wasn't Jilly, and never would be, but I would have given her some of my open hours if I could have. She definitely deserved them.

The next morning, I went for an early run and jumped into the hotel pool before showering and meeting my mom and William for our scheduled nine a.m. strategy breakfast. Over a table of pastries, coffee, and fruit, we synchronized schedules, divided up our to-do list for that morning, and went over the cheat sheets I'd printed out in the hotel business center. By ten thirty, I was back in one of the vans, navigating the streets of Colby in what was basically a glorified scavenger hunt. According to my (bullet-pointed) list, we needed a hardback, attractive but not *too* embossed bible (the family one had been forgotten back in California), four black bow ties, and "two rolls of pennies, preferably polished."

These items could have been challenging to procure even back in Lakeview, which had several malls and a thriving retail district downtown. Colby, however, offered up much less in terms of options, which was why an hour later I'd only gotten the bow ties. Lillie's Occasions, the only formal wear place, did not look kindly on renting out accessories last minute. I had to promise they'd be returned by noon sharp on Sunday, pay twice the normal price, and slip the owner forty bucks cash before she'd let me take them, and even then I could feel the stink eye on me all the way out to the parking lot. So I was already visibly beaten down by the time I found a bible at the local bookstore and basically pleaded with them for some rolls of pennies from their safe, which they gave me purely out of pity.

"There you are," my mom said to me when I finally returned to the private dining area off the ballroom we were using as ground zero for our planning. All the flower arrangements were lined up on a nearby table, programs already folded and stacked beside them. "Did you get the pennies?"

"I got *some* pennies," I said, pulling the rolls from my pocket and putting them next to where she was sitting at the head of a table, her folders organized in a clock face pattern around her. Each one held a task that needed to be completed before the ceremony began, and she'd move through them accordingly, checking each off as she went. "But they aren't polished."

"That's not as important as getting them on the cards."

"Cards?"

Instead of answering, she reached for a yellow folder not in the clock face, pulling it toward her. Everything at Natalie Barrett Weddings was color coded, so I didn't even have to see the (neatly printed in William's writing) label on it to know it held Last-Minute Items. She flipped it open, taking out a sheet of paper and handing it to me. "Josef's mom was named Penny. She died of cancer when he was ten. They've decided to honor her by handing out cards with her name, dates, and a bright, preferably shiny penny to each guest."

"And this happened in the last two hours?" I asked, having no recollection of hearing anything like it during the previous months of planning.

"It was decided last night, at the gathering after the dinner."

This was such a dreaded practice we actually had an acronym for it: a last-minute DAB, i.e., Decided at Bar. "Please tell me you are kidding."

"I wish I was." She sighed, her face tired. "Now, I know you are going to hate me, but I need you to go back out and pick up the cards from the printer. They were a rush job and are already paid for and ready."

"Seriously?"

"I said you'd hate me," she replied, as if this actually made anything better. And plus, I couldn't hate her, anyway; she'd never made a DAB. She was way too organized. "Just remember; next summer, you'll be almost out of here to college. No more tasks like this. You can get a nice, normal job, like selling produce."

This was what she'd started saying to me at times like

this, as if a promise of weighing cucumbers in the future softened any current blow. It was also as close as she'd come to addressing me leaving for school, something so fraught with emotion she wasn't even able to joke about it. Yet. I said, "I know you're trying, but the idea of working at a farmers' market is hardly a comfort right now."

"No?" She gave me a sympathetic look. "How about this: get the cards and I promise, barring any unforeseen disasters, you can knock off early tonight."

"Define disasters."

"No. I refuse. It's like tempting fate." She shut the folder. "Just say yes to the offer, will you? A free night at the beach! You can study up on the produce business."

"You're not funny," I grumbled.

"Maybe not. But I *am* desperate." She took a quick, apologetic glance at the van keys, which I'd deposited next to the pennies. "In all seriousness, I wouldn't push on this. But . . ."

". . . the client gets what the client wants," I said, before she could complete yet another one of her mantras. I picked up the keys. "But I am not polishing pennies. I draw the line there."

"That's fine. William will do it."

"Wait, what?" William said, entering the room at precisely that moment. "What am I doing?"

My mom pretended she didn't hear him. "Just think about weighing those cucumbers next summer!" she called out as I started to the hallway. "So easy! So relaxing!"

I didn't reply, just waved a hand behind me as William said, confused, "Cucumbers?"

At six p.m. sharp, Margy walked down the aisle on the arm of her father, looking gorgeous in her cap-sleeved gown with a bejeweled bodice, and crying happy tears. We'd hit the jackpot on the weather: warm but not *too* hot, a good breeze but not enough to send veils and dresses billowing up. The only wrinkle was a loud Coast Guard Helicopter flying by low over the beach and drowning out the beginning of the vows. Even my mother couldn't control the military, although I would not have put it past her to try.

After the ceremony, I sat in the BRR as the wedding party and then guests exited to the ballroom, where the bars were open and the DJ already playing beach music, the bride and groom's favorite. Once the chairs were empty, I helped some guys from the Piers fold and stack them to clear space for what would later be the dance floor. Left behind were crumpled programs, a few stray tissues, and, to me, entirely too many of the penny cards William and I had hastily assembled in record time before the ceremony. Oh, well.

Once the ceremony was complete, there was always an easing in my mother's tension. So I wasn't entirely surprised when she joined me during dinner as I stood guarding the display of M & J cupcakes on the cake table. While guests rarely messed with a wedding cake, something about cupcakes brought out serious grabby hands, and not just in children. Until the pictures were taken, though, they were off limits, which meant body blocking them while saying "Not yet!" in a cheerful, yet firm, voice to anyone who tried to approach. It was one of my least favorite jobs, and one William loved. But he was tied up taking over for a queasy bartender until backup arrived, so it fell to me.

"Did you see how many people ditched those penny cards?" my mother said, her eyes moving over the crowd in front of us. "Talk about dishonoring the dead."

"DABs are *always* a mistake," I told her, as a flower girl, carrying a full plate of steak and pasta, started for the cupcakes. When I stepped forward, she veered off, her dress hem dragging on the carpet behind her. "If any idea is good, we've already thought of it."

She looked at me, smiling, proud. "Listen to you. Spoken like a real wedding planner."

"Or a future cucumber seller," I replied. "And I'm still knocking off early tonight. You promised."

"I know, I know." She reached behind us, picking up a stray crumpled napkin and tucking it in her pocket. "I also know I've been lucky to have you working with us these last few years. Although it's not like I really gave you a choice."

"I am getting another job once I start college," I told her.

"God, I hope so." She shuddered theatrically. "I cannot be responsible for sucking someone else into a lifetime of this business. I already feel bad enough about William."

I looked over at the bar across the room, where at that moment the man in question was chatting away while salting the rim of a margarita, two older women in jewel tone dresses hanging on his every word. "I don't think he minds it so much."

She smiled, seeing this too. "Oh, he does. He just can't do anything else, like me."

This was big talk, and I was used to it. My mom and William always discussed the business as if it, too, was a bad relationship they couldn't wait to break off. And yet, they kept coming back, bickering over choices of clients and laughing at inside jokes I'd never understand. The longest, most successful relationship either of them had ever had was with this business and each other, and they knew it. Maybe it wasn't true love, but it worked. Somehow.

Finally, Margy and Josef cut the cake, each feeding the other a bite (skipping the smashing of it in each other's faces, which we as a company lobbied against, always). With the dessert table fair game, I went to the bathroom, where I checked all the toilets for problems and paper and wiped down the sink counter. Then it was back through the ball-room and outside to the patio, where a few kids were running around on the dance floor as the DJ got ready to start playing the real music. I swung by the nearby bar, picking up two waters, then delivered one to him, asking if he needed anything. When he said no, I walked over to the steps that led to the beach, where someone had left a couple of little plates and a wine glass with a napkin stuffed into it. I was just putting them on a tray table when I heard the early first notes of a Motown song. By the time I turned around, people were already coming through the doors, following the music.

There are always phases to dancing at receptions. Usually kids and older people are first to take the floor, due to a lack of self-consciousness. By the second song, you could count on a few of the more tipsy people to join them, often in the form of a clump of girls, all out shaking it together. Younger couples were next, followed by single guys, who tended to need some coaxing to join in. Eventually, though, if the drinks were flowing and the DJ decent, you had a packed floor of all types. William always said the best part of weddings was the dancing, and I had to agree with him. People just stopped caring. One night away from the norm, with the people you know best or barely at all. If you couldn't cut loose then, when could you?

I edged past a circle of bridesmaids bumping hips, then an older couple doing some complicated spin-out-and-back footwork, my eye on a nearby ledge cluttered with empty champagne glasses. I was so focused I didn't even notice the young groomsman from earlier approaching until he was right beside me.

"Want to dance?"

I turned, taking him in: the short hair, those blue eyes, the black bow tie I'd picked up earlier loose, but not undone, around his neck. "No, thanks."

He looked surprised and—I realized, horrified—embarrassed. "Oh. Okay."

"I'm working," I said quickly, stepping over his last syllables. Now we were both blushing. "For the wedding planner. So I can't—"

"Oh, right." His face relaxed. "I didn't realize—"

"I know, it's fine." I looked at the floor, tucking a piece of hair behind my ear. "Thank you anyway."

He smiled then, and there was something about the way

it changed his face, taking it from cute to outright charming, that suddenly made me wish I could say yes. To a boy,
and a dance, and also to having that chance, one night, to be
away from everything. We stood there a minute, until the
bridesmaids nearby opened up their circle, whooping, and
pulled him in. I walked over to the ledge I'd seen earlier,
collecting the glasses and putting them on a nearby tray.
Underneath one of the chairs was another penny card, face
down, and I picked it up, rubbing my finger over the coin.
When I looked back at the dance floor, the boy and the
bridesmaids were gone.

That could have been it. And sometimes, on my worse
nights when I couldn't sleep for all the tears, I wished that
it was. Because then, Ethan wouldn't even have been Ethan
to me, but just a guy I said no to at one wedding among so
many in a long summer. Nothing more, nothing less. Nothing to lose.

As it was, a few minutes later I stopped by to check in
with William and my mother, who were standing off to the
side of the dance floor, watching one of Margy's aunts dance
suggestively against a heavyset man in a sport coat.

"The power of champagne," he said as the woman turned,
bumping her ample rear against the man's hip. "She's told me
twice tonight she never drinks it, each time with a mostly
empty glass in her hand."

"Weddings are a different world," I replied, using one of
his favorite phrases.

"Indeed they are." The couple were now outright grinding

each other. "And right now, I want to go home."

"My *eyes*," my mother said in a low voice, fake-horrified at the spectacle. "I'm too old for this."

"They're senior citizens!" William said, and they both cackled.

"And I was promised an early night off," I said, looking at my mom. "Can I go?"

"Wait, Louna gets to leave? How is that fair?"

"Because she's seventeen and paid poorly," my mom told William. "Her bosses are awful people."

"I have heard that," he agreed. He smiled at me. "What are you going to do?"

"I don't know," I said. "Whatever I want?"

"Look at our girl, single and ready to mingle at the beach. She's acting like a real teenager!" He beamed at me, then looked at my mom. "I so hoped this day would come."

"Stop," my mom said, pretending to fan her eyes. "I'll get emotional."

"Shut up, both of you," I said, and they laughed again. "I'll see you tomorrow."

"You are young and so is the night! Carpe diem!" William called out after me as I walked across the patio.

"That means day, William," my mom said.

"Carpe night, then!" They dissolved into more laughter.

Fine, I thought, as I started across the patio, to the lobby. So what if I did go back to my room and be non-epic, by Jilly's definition? It had been a long day and weekend, and I was tired. I had all of senior year and college to throw down, if I so chose, and maybe I would. If I didn't though, it wasn't my mom and William's business by any stretch. And really, I was only what they had made me.

As I thought this, the DJ began another song, slower this time. As some couples began to leave the dance floor and others headed in that direction, I stepped out of the way. On the other side of the crowd, my mom and William were still talking, occasionally breaking into bouts of laughter. Finally a path cleared inside to the ballroom, but instead of taking it, I went down the steps to the dark beach below. Later, I'd think of this as the true, real start of that night, where everything began. Maybe that was why halfway down I kicked off my sandals, stepping into the sand with my feet bare.

CHAPTER

4

"I CAN'T believe you waited until now to buy an outfit for graduation," Jilly said from outside the dressing room. "You don't leave anything until the last minute. That's my thing."

"True," I told her, pulling my shirt over my head. "But I've been busy. And I told you, I didn't think I needed something new, anyway. My gown will be over whatever I wear."

"At the *ceremony*." Her voice grew closer, along with her feet, toes dark red, in platform espadrilles, now just under the door. "But what about all the parties afterward?"

There was that word again. I made a face in the mirror, hearing it.

"And don't think you're getting out of being social this time," she said, as if she had actually seen this reaction through the door. "We're Making Memories, remember?"

Now I groaned aloud, and she laughed. A couple of days earlier, we'd stood in line to pick up our yearbooks during lunch period, one of what felt like endless senior year milestones in the days leading up to graduation. The books themselves were heavy and smelled of leather, with this year's theme embossed in big yellow letters across the cover: MAKING MEMORIES. It was cheesy and ridiculous, which was why Jilly had claimed it as our summer rallying cry, starting, well, now. No longer was it enough to Do Things and Make Stuff Happen. It all had to be memorable, as well.

It was also imperative, apparently, that I have a new dress for graduation, even though because of work I had more than enough options in my closet. So here I was, at one of Jilly's favorite boutiques, only hours before the ceremony, with her twin eight-year-old sisters, Kaitlyn and Katherine—collectively known at KitKat—hunched over her phone nearby bickering as they played Igloo Melt.

"It's my turn," I heard Kitty say. Although they were identical and often dressed alike by choice, their voices were the dead giveaways. Kitty was loud, boisterous, while Kat often didn't speak above a whisper unless implored to do so. She must have responded, because Kitty said, "Okay, but then I get an extra-long one. *And* your bonus cubes."

"Pipe down, loudmouth, we're in public," Jilly told her. There was a clank, and another dress appeared over the top of my dressing room door, this one cobalt blue. I pulled the first she'd picked, a bright pink dress with a short skirt, off the hanger and stepped into it, reaching behind me for the zipper. One glance and I knew it wasn't me, but still, I opened the door.

"Nope," she announced from the seat she'd taken on a polka-dotted chaise directly across from the dressing rooms. "Too much. I was going for pert and perky, but it's more like startling."

"This from a person who is basically the brightest thing in the room right now."

She looked down at her yellow romper, which out in the actual sun had almost blinded me. "Yes, but I *like* color and can therefore pull it off. Try the next one."

"I like color," I grumbled. As I turned back to the room, a salesgirl studying a laptop by the register gave me a sympathetic smile.

"My turn!" Kitty bellowed. "Now!"

"Work it out or nobody plays," Jilly told them in a tired voice, then said to me, "Try the A-line next. That's the blue one."

"I know what an A-line is."

"Do you, though?"

I rolled my eyes at my own reflection, reminded again why I always hated being on this side of the dressing room door. I was used to tagging along shopping with Jilly, who believed strongly in the power of retail therapy. But things always worked better when I was flipping through magazines waiting for her to model the looks. Our friendship worked because we each knew our strengths, and now I felt like we were both miscast.

The blue dress *was* better color-wise, but it made my boobs seem sort of pointy. This seemed strange to opine aloud, however, so I went back outside without comment.

"Nope. Your boobs look weird." She squinted at them. "Although it *is* kind of interesting; torpedo-like. You'd definitely get attention."

"That's not the kind of attention I want." I went back to

the dressing room, shedding the dress, then eyed my last selection, a deep plum sheath with a V-neck. "Are you serious with this purple? Really?"

"It's eggplant, and very much in fashion right now," she replied. "Put it on."

I did, glancing at my watch as I pulled my arm through. It was just after three thirty, which meant I didn't have long to stop by my mom's office to check in, then get home and change before meeting her and William at school for the ceremony. They were coming straight from a meeting for Bee Little's wedding, about which everything, it seemed, was happening last minute.

Bee was lovely, which was good, because her event, despite William's initial confidence, had become your basic wedding planner nightmare. First, the venue—a gorgeous old house with expansive gardens and a pond—had caught on fire just after she put down a hefty (last-minute) deposit on it. Then the caterer she insisted was her only deal breaker in terms of vendors had a nervous breakdown, although not over this wedding. (My mother was not yet convinced of this.) All this would have been bad enough even if her own mother's event—which had gone so well, her son's vanishing act aside; oh how we loved a third wedding!—had not resulted soon after the honeymoon in a separation due to "incompatibility issues." (Even my mother and William had been blindsided: they didn't bet on third weddings, feeling that by then you should know what you're doing.) The upshot: with nine weeks to go, they now found themselves in the busiest part of the wedding season with no venue, no

caterer, and a mother of the bride who was even more cynical about the process than they were.

I pulled on the last option Jilly had chosen for me, slipping it over my head. When I glanced in the dressing room
mirror, it *did* seem awfully purple, although I liked the plain
yet classic neckline and the way the skirt's hem flared up
and out at the bottom. I had just stepped out to see what
Jilly thought when the salesgirl gasped, putting a hand to her
mouth.

We both looked over at her. "What is it?" Jilly asked.

She looked up at us, startled, like she'd forgotten we
were there. "Sorry. I was just . . . it's the news. There's been
a shooting."

I felt a prickle at the back of my neck, hairs raising up.
Immediately, Jilly glanced at the twins, who were still ab-
sorbed in their game, then put a hand on my arm. "This one
looks good. Who knew eggplant was your color?"

"What kind of shooting?" I asked the salesgirl, although I
could swear I already knew. There was something in her face
I recognized.

"I'm sorry," she said again. She dropped her hand, shaking her head. "It's a school. In California. Just breaking news,
right now. They don't have any—"

"Come on," Jilly said, her voice firm as she steered me
back into the room, shutting the door behind me. From outside she said, "You don't really need a dress. Like you said,
you have tons. Let's just go."

I stood there a second, looking at my reflection. I could

see myself blinking, quickly, before I turned away, fingers fumbling to pull the dress up over my head. Ignoring the hanger, I left it in a heap on the bench in my haste to put my shorts, T-shirt, and flip-flops back on and grab my purse. Outside, Jilly was waiting, reaching down wordlessly to take my hand. As we walked behind the counter, with the twins in tow, the salesgirl was still focused on her computer, and I averted my eyes so I wouldn't see the screen. But I knew what was most likely there, as well as to come. A long shot of a flat, nondescript building, maybe with a mascot on the side. People streaming out doors, hands over their heads. The embraces of the survivors, mouths open, caught in wails we were lucky not to hear. And, in the worst case, pictures of kids just like the ones in my own yearbook, lined up neatly, already ghosts.

⚮

By the time I got to my mom's office, I'd somewhat calmed down. Jilly had helped, turning up the radio loud as she drove us through town, now and then taking glances at me she thought I didn't notice. It was gorgeous out, with a bright blue sky, and people were out on the sidewalks and in their cars, windows down—while elsewhere, someone's worst nightmare had only just become real. It seemed wrong, like there should have been a stain on the day or something.

"Are you sure you don't want us to hang out for a few minutes?" Jilly asked me as she pulled into the lot of my mom's office, where I'd left my car parked earlier. "All I have left to do is to pick up Crawford's new glasses and then grab him from Tae Kwon Do."

"Another pair of glasses?" I asked.

She glanced at the twins in the rearview, each looking out a separate window, sitting close to each other. "The kid got suspended this time. We'll see if it makes a difference."

Although I found Crawford's monotone and awkwardness appealing, it made him a huge target for the bullies at his school. Martial arts had made him strong, but not made much of a difference in the lunch line, at least not yet. In the meantime, the Bakers spent a lot on replacement eyewear.

"I'm fine, you should go," I told her. "I'll see you at the amphitheater."

"Here's hoping Steve passes out and doesn't make it."

"Fingers crossed."

She laughed, and I did too, if only to convince her I was, in fact, okay. With her Baker and me Barrett, we'd spent our lives in this small town with Steve Baroff wedged between us for every alphabetical occasion, except when he was too stoned to show up for school. We'd long hoped this would happen for graduation, if only for the continuity of us being on the stage at the same time. Making memories, indeed.

As she drove off, already cranking the radio, I started toward my mom's office. Natalie Barrett Weddings was located in the center of a modern office building with a dentist's office on one side, a high-end stationery store called RSVP on the other. Entirely too much of my paycheck had gone to the latter due to my weakness for cards, writing paper, and, especially, blank books. Life seemed so much more manageable when you could write it down neatly on paper, which was probably exactly why I could only do it for a day or two, and hadn't even tried in the last year. When I looked through those old barely begun journals now, the events on the pages seemed too small to even fill the lines, that inconsequential. Thinking this, I had a flash of the salesgirl and her computer, and felt a chill come over me. I pulled open the door to my mom's office, where the A/C was always blasting and I wouldn't notice my own drop in temperature.

William saw me, though, immediately getting up from his seat at the conference table across from Bee and coming over. "I had a news alert on my phone," he said in a low voice. Distantly, I heard my mom, also at the table, saying something about head counts. "You okay?"

"Fine," I said automatically. "Go back to your meeting. I just came to drop off the tickets."

He nodded, but still waited a beat, as if I might change my mind, before returning to the group. Meanwhile, I slipped into the back office, where I reached into my pocket, pulling out the two passes I'd picked up for the ceremony. You were allowed up to six, but it wasn't like I needed any more. I slid them into my mom's purse, which was sitting on her side of the big desk they shared, then went back out into the main room.

". . . were supposed to meet me a half hour ago," Bee was saying to her brother Ambrose, who had joined the group in my brief absence. Dressed in jeans, a short-sleeved blue button-down shirt, and tennis shoes, he looked freshly showered, as if just beginning his day at this late hour. Maybe this was why his sister, usually so pleasant, seemed annoyed. "It's no wonder you can't get a job if you're incapable of getting places on time."

"My watch is broken," he said. "And then I had to get here, so . . ."

Bee's cheeks were flushed. "You have a *phone*, Ambrose. And there are clocks!"

An awkward silence settled over the room, during which he spotted me and smiled, waving energetically, as if we were longtime friends finally reunited. His complete lack of caring for the trouble he'd caused would have been impressive if it didn't seem so demented. I was still deciding how to react when my mom said, "So, Louna. How does it feel to be almost free from the compulsory education system?"

Now everyone looked at me. Even when I wasn't working, I was working. "I won't believe it until I flip my tassel," I replied.

"Louna's graduating tonight," William explained to Bee. "High school."

"Really?" She smiled at me. Beside her, Ambrose noticed William's fancy stainless-steel tape dispenser—we were both suckers for office supplies—and pulled it toward him. "Congratulations!" Bee said. "What a milestone. I remember every minute of my commencement."

"Me, too," Ambrose said. I noticed that his hair, although damp, was in full effect, that one curl pushed away from his face but about to tumble down again.

"You didn't graduate," his sister pointed out. To us she added, "It was one of those leave-quietly-and-we-won'texpel-you kind of situations. Classic Ambrose."

"I was talking about *yours*," he said, pushing the button on the dispenser. It whirred, spitting out a single piece of tape. "And it was never proven that I brought the cow in, if you'll recall."

My mother raised that one eyebrow. "Cow?"

"So what are you doing next year, Louna?" Bee said quickly, turning her attention back to me. Whatever had happened with farm animals, she didn't want to dwell on it.

"I'm going to Rice-Johnson," I replied.

"It's a private liberal arts college, her first choice, *and* she got a partial scholarship," William added proudly.

"That's great," Bee told me, as Ambrose hit the switch again. Then again. Two pieces of tape popped out and he grabbed them, sticking them to his thumbs. "I went to Defriese. Majored in public policy. I *loved* college."

"It's just so hard to believe," William told her. "I feel like she just started kindergarten. Time just *flies*."

Oh, dear, I thought, hearing his voice grow tight as he finished this sentence.

"William, pace yourself," my mom, also noticing, advised. "We've still got the whole night ahead of us."

He nodded, even as he took out a folded tissue, dabbing at his eyes. If my mom and William were one person—and it often felt like they were, to me—she'd always been the head and he the heart. Sure, they were equally cynical when it came to their business and the main concept that underscored it. But if she could joke or reason away anything that made her feel, it was often because William took it to heart twice as hard. This was especially true when it came to me. First day of kindergarten, first sleepover, first time my heart was broken; it was William who sympathy cried or clung to my hand just a beat too long before I walked out the door. And thank God for it. I loved my mom, but with just her I might have never known what compassion looked like.

"Speaking of later plans, we need to move this along," he said now, looking at the notebook open in front of him. "To recap, we've touched on the latest with the venue and catering, and I'll reach out to these top three of the five ideals for the rehearsal dinner to check on availability. Are the guest numbers still pretty firm for that?"

Bee, in pearl earrings with her hair pulled back in a daisy-patterned headband, flipped open the cover of her tablet and swiped through a few screens. Beside her, Ambrose picked up the dispenser and turned it upside down, examining its base. "Seventy-eight with wedding party and all out-of-town family."

"And you have sent invitations?" my mom asked.

"Four weeks ago," Bee replied, sitting up straighter. It was obvious she sensed my mom's apprehension about this event and was eager to please her. "So far we're at two hundred RSVPs, with a final estimate of two hundred fifty."

My mom glanced at William, who gave her a smug look. Big weddings meant big money and, with Bee's fiancé, Kevin Yu, from a family that owned a big pharmaceutical company, big attention. Personally, I wanted to know if she planned to change her name, switching from Bee Little to Bee Yu, but had not found a way to work this into a meeting. Yet.

"You really think any place that you'd want to use can handle a party of seventy-eight on a Friday night only nine weeks out?" my mom asked, as Ambrose, apparently still fascinated by the dispenser, put it back on the table and pushed its button several times in a row: *click, click, click.*

"If there's a possibility of a magazine spread, yes," William replied, over the sound of the machine whirring, discharging tape pieces.

"You can't make room where there isn't any."

"There's always a way."

In the midst of all of this, the machine started making a grinding noise. Then, a long squeak. We all looked at Ambrose, who reached out and hit the button again.

"I just feel that you—" my mom said, but that was as far as she got before Ambrose picked up the dispenser again, trying to turn it off. When he couldn't, he stuck it in his lap, under the table, where it continued to grind louder and louder until I heard a pop. Suddenly there was a lot of tape on the floor at my feet, as well as a faint smell of smoke.

"Ambrose!" Bee screeched, losing her cool entirely. She whirled in her seat, snatching the dispenser from his lap. "*God!* Stop it!"

"I was just—" Ambrose said. Delicately, my mother reached down, pulling a piece of tape off her foot and putting it on her folder.

"I don't care!" Bee said. "You're always doing something and it's never what you should be doing and now Mom's had enough and I'm stuck with you so fucking shut up and sit there and don't touch anything!"

Silence. Out of habit, I glanced at William, who looked both horrified and thrilled by this development. I had to admit I was, too. Bee cursing was wholly unexpected. My mom, however, was hardly fazed as she said, "All I'm saying is that I think you need to keep your expectations in check."

At this, Bee burst into tears. As she put her hands to her pretty face, shoulders shaking, Ambrose patted her arm, then said to us, "It's a stressful thing, a wedding."

"*Oh my god!*" she screeched, wrenching away from him. She pushed back her chair, getting to her feet. "I'm sorry. I just . . . I need. . . ."

"Of course," William said smoothly. "Restroom is around the corner. I'll get you a water."

I wasn't sure that was going to help, especially after I heard how hard the bathroom door slammed a moment later. Nevertheless, he disappeared down the hallway with a bottle in hand, leaving me, my mom, and Ambrose alone. I looked down at the floor. Tape was everywhere.

"You know, Ambrose," my mother said after a moment, "it would be a *huge* help to us if you didn't drive your sister insane before August."

Despite Bee's breakdown and the tape explosion, there was only one thing I noticed as my mother said this: for the first time, she was talking in We when it came to this wedding. Bee was surely embarrassed. But thanks to said outburst, it looked like my mom was finally in.

"People never believe me when I tell them this," Ambrose replied, folding his arms on the table. "But I'm not *trying* to annoy her. She's just very sensitive."

"You really think that's the issue?" my mother asked.

He nodded, somber. "Always has been."

"I heard your mother sent you here because she was so frustrated with dealing with you."

"True," he agreed. "And I wrecked her car. But in my defense, she is *also* very sensitive. I think it's a genetic thing."

Oh, for God's sake, I thought, fighting the urge to roll my eyes. Of course it was everyone else's fault. Next he'd blame the tape dispenser. My mother, however, smiled at him, clearly amused. "Did I hear Bee say you need a job?"

"That's what I'm told," he replied.

"You're told?"

"It's actually more of an ultimatum," he admitted. "Apparently I am both annoying *and* expensive."

Instead of replying, my mom just studied him, one hand twisting the diamond necklace she wore every day. I didn't like the look on her face even before she said, "How about this: you work for me this summer, and I'll take your wages off my fee, which your mother is paying."

"Really?"

"Mom?" I said, stunned.

Ambrose grinned at me. "Did you hear that? We'll be co-workers!"

"But you have to actually *work*," she told him, firm now. "I don't do annoying or expensive. And you show up on time. Is that clear?"

"Absolutely," he replied. "When do I start?"

"Now." My mom pushed out her chair, then pointed under the table. "Pick up all this tape. Then come find me for a coffee order. I need caffeine."

"On it," Ambrose said, giving her a mock salute as she started into her office. I followed her, glancing behind us just before shutting the door to see him crouched down on the carpet, picking up the tape one piece at a time. He saw me looking at him and gave me a cheerful thumbs-up. Jesus.

"Are you crazy?" I said to her, closing the door. "Why in the world would you hire him?"

"It's our job to keep brides calm and focused," she replied, pulling her wallet out of her purse. "This wedding is a mess so far, and yet the only time I've seen Bee upset has been because of Ambrose. This way, he's out of her hair and helping us at the same time."

"No way," I said, shaking my head. "You've never hired anyone on the spot like that. You background check the rare person you do take on. There's no way you'd risk your name and your event just to keep someone busy."

"I can't do a good deed?" she asked, amused.

"You *don't* do good deeds," I said flatly.

"Hey!" she protested. I just looked at her. Finally, she sighed and said, "Okay, fine. I *may* have gotten a phone call earlier from Eve about how Bee was at her wits' end with her brother and asking if, for an additional fee, we could divert him somehow."

"She's paying you to babysit him?"

"Not babysit. He's working, or no deal. I told her that."

She slipped a twenty out of her wallet, handing it to me. "And I'm not going to trust him with anything crucial, God knows. Errands, physical labor, last-minute details, and coffee runs."

I thought for a second. "But that's *my* job."

"Exactly." She smiled. "And you are about to graduate and have your last summer before college. I'd like to see you actually try to enjoy it."

"Do *not* do this for me," I said, in a warning voice. "I've already dealt with him enough to know I'd rather work alone than with that kind of help."

"You're welcome," she said, as if I hadn't spoken at all. Then, before I could protest further, she leaned forward, pressing her lips to my forehead. "Give him this and the standard coffee order and point him toward Jump Java. Then you're officially off duty. Okay?"

I wanted to keep at this, stop what would surely be a runaway train before it even had a chance to gain speed. But over her shoulder, the clock said four fifteen and I had a date to meet Jilly in line, Steve Baroff between us or not, in two hours. Plus, based on all I'd already seen of Ambrose Little, he wouldn't need me to sabotage him: he'd do it himself. Probably before I even flipped my tassel.

"Okay," I said, taking the bill from her. "It's your funeral."

"What a charming way to put it," she replied. "Spoken just like a high school graduate."

I rolled my eyes, reaching down to open the door. When I pushed it open, it banged hard against something on the other side. Which, I saw as I peeked around it, was Ambrose, who was still on the floor and, most likely, close enough to have heard everything. Whoops.

"I think I got it all," he said now, not sounding offended at least. "Man, that is some sticky tape."

"That's why we keep it in the dispenser," I told him as he got to his feet, picking pieces off his hands and dropping them in a nearby trash can. "My mom wants coffee. I'm supposed to give you her order and point you there on my way out."

"Great," he replied, so easygoing, like a person who'd never had a reason not to be. Of course he hadn't heard what I'd said. Even if he had, I was sure he'd figure I was talking about someone else. Or that I was just sensitive. "Lead the way."

≈

"It may seem like just coffee," I said, as we stood in an unexpectedly long line at Jump Java. "But nothing is just *anything* when it comes to my mother. That's the first thing you need to know."

He nodded. "She's a tough nut, is what you're saying."

I looked at him. "Never call her that. Like, ever."

"Noted." He shook his head, that one curl bouncing off to the side. "You know, I'm getting the sense you don't have a lot of confidence in my ability to do this job."

"You're correct," I replied, as the line finally moved a bit.

He had the nerve to look offended. "Why? You don't even know me."

"Maybe, but let's recap my experience with you so far. You delayed your mother's wedding—"

"Which, in retrospect, might have been a good thing.

Imagine if I'd been talking to Demi even longer? She might have come to her senses and saved herself a lot of anguish."

"—and just today," I went on, "you broke company property and made a client cry."

"I made my sister cry," he corrected me. "At the time, I was not yet an employee. Let's be clear here."

The line inched forward, slightly. "Do you always deflect anything that might make you accountable for a problem?"

"For some reason, blame is often directed toward me. I have to be vigilant."

"For some reason?"

"Weren't you going to give me the coffee order?"

My jaw clenched, hard, and I told myself to relax. When I couldn't, I distracted myself by looking over the woman William and I had christened Phone Lady. Every weekday, no matter what time I came in for coffee, she was at that same single table, her laptop open, phone to her ear. There, she would talk, loudly, as if compelled to make everyone hear her end of whatever conversation she was having. Sometimes, it was about her work; she did some kind of medical record transcribing. More often, though, the talk was personal. Earlier in the week, for example, I'd learned both that one of her friends had recently gotten a breast cancer diagnosis and that she herself was allergic to wheat germ. And that had been a short line.

Sure enough, during a pause of the espresso machine, I could now make out her high, slightly twangy voice saying something about airline fares. I said to Ambrose, "William will always want a tall chai latte with skim milk. He's the constant.

It's my mom that's the wild card. Most days, she's going to want an espresso with whole milk. If she's really stressed, she'll ask for a double. But if she snaps at you, just get a single. She won't know the difference and it's better for everyone."

Ambrose didn't respond, and I realized he was studying the pastries. Great. "Hello?" I said. "Are you even—"

"Tall chai latte, skim. Mom asked for a single espresso, so don't have to make judgment call. Plus two chocolate croissants, warmed up so they're nice and melty."

I blinked, surprised he'd at least gotten some of it right. "I didn't say anything about croissants."

"Those are for us," he said.

"I don't want a croissant."

"You seem a little crabby. It might help," he advised. "Don't worry, it's on me. Although I might have to borrow a couple of bucks until payday."

Later, I'd realize that this response pretty much summed up everything that made me nuts about Ambrose in one simple sentence. At the time though, I just stood there, unable to respond. Then my phone beeped. Jilly.

ARE YOU GETTING EXCITED? WORD IS PARTY AT THE A-FRAME WILL BE AMAZING. MAKING MEMORIES!

"Party at the A-frame, huh?" Ambrose asked, reading over my shoulder. "Where's that?"

I jerked my phone to the side. "Seriously? Do you have any manners at all?"

"You're the one who pulled out a phone during our conversation," he noted. When I glared at him, he said, "You know, you *really* might want to rethink that croissant."

"Next," called the bearded guy behind the counter, a little older than me, whose preference for plaid shirts had made William christen him the Lumberjack. "Hey. How's the wedding business?"

"Crazy as ever," I said. I gestured at Ambrose. "He's got the order. But you probably know it better than even I do."

"Probably," Lumberjack said. "But tell me anyway."

"I'm out of here," I told Ambrose. "Don't forget extra napkins."

"Okeydoke," he said, as I turned away, toward the door. "Have fun at graduation!"

This last comment was said in such a cheerful and easygoing tone, the absolute opposite of how I was feeling, that I felt my jaw clench again. How on earth could someone be so immune to basic social cues, so entirely oblivious to how annoying he was? I was still wondering this as I pulled the door open, Phone Lady's voice again suddenly audible over other conversations, music, and the beeping register.

". . . just one of those days," she was saying. "And did you hear about the shooting in California? Five kids, they are saying. Five. That's the most since—"

I shut the door so hard behind me it rattled the glass, not that anyone noticed. Everyone's always in their own world, when it's still an option.

CHAPTER

5

"SEE?" JILLY yelled. "Making memories! You and me! Just like the yearbook!"

At least, that was what I thought she said. It was hard to be sure, as we were in the center of a tightly packed crowd of people dancing and also screaming at each other over the thumping, bass-driven music. All this in the living room of an A-frame house that had apparently been the place to party for everyone at our school for the last year. Jilly had been saying hello to people all night. So far, I hadn't recognized a soul.

But I was here, in the early minutes of my first full day as a high school graduate, a warm beer in one hand. Our commencement, held in an amphitheater at the U, had been long and dull, a fact made even more difficult by the hot, humid night. Each time I looked up from my place in the rows of chairs—Steve Baroff beside me, red-eyed, giggling occasionally—all I could see were people fanning themselves with programs, the movement back and forth almost hypnotic. I felt awake only during the few minutes I was on my feet, walking to the stage and then across it to get my diploma. The crowd had been told repeatedly not to cheer for individual graduates—a directive totally ignored, so I still heard William's voice shouting "Bravo!" somewhere in the distance.

It wasn't just the heat hanging over us. There was also that day's school shooting, the details of which I'd done my best to avoid. This was not easy, as my classmates were discussing it as we lined up, and then the principal made mention of it not once but three times during his prepared remarks. I understood the reasons for this. It was the world we were living in, our reality, and as another public high school, we couldn't pretend otherwise. There had been a time, not that many months ago, when I, too, would have been glued to the news sites on my phone or the TV, sharing with anyone each new detail of breaking news. But then, another had happened. And one more. Now knowing was just too much.

I felt a bump at my back and turned as much as I could, considering the tight space, to see the boy Jilly had introduced me to earlier—Jeff? Jay?—was back beside me, a fresh beer for each of us in his hands. His friend was behind Jilly, his arms around her waist as she leaned back into him, smiling as he whispered something in her ear. This was as Out There as I'd ever been and I was trying to be a good sport about it. So when Jeff—I was pretty sure it was Jeff—held one of the cups out to me, I took it.

"It's punch!" he yelled in my ear. "Keg was out!"

I looked down at the drink, a bright blue concoction with specks of something floating in it. "Great," I yelled back. No way in hell was I drinking that. "Thanks."

He nodded, slipping his now free hand around my waist as he started bopping up and down to the beat. Tall and thin, with very large ears and visible tattoos under his shirt collar, he went to another school in the area, wore a chain wallet, and had already squashed my foot more times than I could count with the heavy boots he was wearing. But he seemed nice enough, and I knew Jilly was thrilled to see me with any guy other than William. Sure enough, as I thought this, she untangled herself long enough to lean forward toward me again.

"Isn't this the *best?*" she hollered, spilling some of her beer on me. "Bring on college. I am so ready!!"

I nodded, smiling at her while at the same time quite aware of Jeff's arm tightening around me to pull me back in his direction. I felt myself tense, by reflex, and tried to put a bit more space between us. No luck: he was latched on, and now leaning into my other ear.

"I've never seen you out here before," he said. "What's your story?"

How do you even answer such a question? Stories, as a rule, had to be told. Could you really do that while pushed together on a hot dance floor where you couldn't even hear yourself think?

Maybe I was overthinking this, I thought. I'd just give him the quickest answer I could. I turned toward him, formulating my response, but when I opened my mouth to begin, suddenly he was kissing me.

In no way did I see it coming. There was not a lean in,

the slow shrinkage of space between us. Just lips, big ones, suddenly engulfing mine. He tasted like beer, and all I could feel was his tongue.

Immediately, I wrenched my head away from his, although his hand was still tight on my hip, holding me in place. "Don't," I said, in the loudest voice I'd used all night.

"What?" He smiled at me, sleepily, then ran his other hand down my back. "We're just dancing, baby."

I turned, trying to catch Jilly's eye, but a group of girls in shiny plastic CLASS OF 16! tiaras, boas around their necks, had wound between us. The music seemed louder, suddenly, and my face was hot as I tried again to pull loose from Jeff's grip. I was starting to panic, feeling wholly trapped, as the last girl bumped past me, her feathers tickling my face. It was that same feeling I got sometimes of things being too much, too full, more than I could take. I had a flash of people running from a building, arms over their heads, and my stomach lurched.

Breathe, I told myself, closing my eyes for a second. *You're here, you're okay.* But the images kept coming, wide shots, narrow ones, helicopter view. And then, suddenly, something totally different: a boy on the beach in a white shirt, hand reaching out, an instant of comfort, safety, home. Even though it hadn't happened in months, I could feel what was about to happen, the panic rising like a liquid, filling me up. I pulled away from Jeff again, and as he yanked me back, my vision started to blur.

I closed my eyes, saying that familiar prayer. *Ethan*, I

thought. *Ethan*. Then I felt someone standing right in front of me. I blinked, and found I was face-to-face with Ambrose Little.

"Conga!" he yelled past me at Jeff, who just looked at him, confused. Then he reached for my hand and without thinking, I grabbed on tight and let him pull me away.

⚜

"Did you see the ears on that guy? You think the world sounds really loud to him, like, all the time?"

I was trying to catch my breath, which was made harder by the worry that I might not be able to do it. For once, I was glad for Ambrose's nattering, if not clinging to his stupid words with every inhale.

"I mean, I'm all about distinctive features," he continued, as I glanced over to see his own trademark curl, damp with sweat, tumble over into his eyes. "And it's not like he can help it. Cards you're dealt, and all that. But I bet he got called Jughead a lot as a kid. And if he didn't, someone was falling down on the job. Hey, are you going to drink that?"

I blinked, then looked down at the cup in my hand, which I'd forgotten I was holding. "It's blue," I managed to say.

"Pie in the Sky, i.e., Blueberry Yum Punch and vodka. Cheap, strong, and yes, blue. What, you don't like it?"

I handed him the cup, still focusing on inhaling as he took a big swig, winced, and then set it down between us. We were outside the A-frame, on the front deck, where we'd ended up after our conga exit from Jeff and the dance floor. Nearby, a keg stood, surrounded by crumpled cups; in a dim corner, a couple was making out. It wasn't cold outside at all, but I had chills. Still.

"Ambrose!" One of the boa girls, tall with red hair and freckles, stumbled through the door and over to us. "There you are. I lost you!"

"And now I'm found," he replied, smiling. "You're amazing, Grace."

She beamed, her face seeming to almost light up in the dark. I had a flash of that girl in the country club parking lot, looking at him in the same way. Attention from a cute boy— you could power the world with it.

"Dance with me," she said now, extending a hand to him. The lone outside light was behind her, catching the feathers of her boa as they trembled in the mild breeze. Too much, all at once, again. I looked away. "You promised, remember?"

"I am a man of my word," Ambrose replied, reaching out to her. Instead of taking her hand, though, he opened his palm flat, prompting her to do the same. "But Louna and I here are talking business. I'll come find you."

Grace dropped her hand, her mouth forming a pout. "I don't like waiting."

"Five minutes," he told her. He spread his fingers, and I watched the mechanics of her moving her hand into his, suddenly so intimate, so quickly. Then he let go. "Meet me at the punch bowl. I'll be the one about to sweep you off your feet."

There was that look again, like a surge of electricity moving over her face. "I'm counting on it," she said, and then turned, walking away slowly the way someone does when they want to be watched, and know that they will be.

Once she was back inside, Ambrose picked up my cup again, finishing off the contents. As he crumpled it in his hand, I said, "Are you serious, with all this?"

"What this?"

I nodded at the door, which Grace had left slightly open behind her. "The way you talked to her. Is it a joke, or not?"

"I never joke when it comes to pretty girls," he replied.

Of course he didn't.

"Don't feel bad about not understanding me, though," he said. "I'm kind of an enigma. Mysterious, hard to know."

"People that are hard to know don't often *announce* the fact they are hard to know," I pointed out.

"That's part of the enigma thing. Always staying unexpected. So what happened to you back there?"

I blinked, surprised by this sudden left turn in conversation. "It was hot," I said. "I got light-headed."

"So old Jughead groping you wasn't an issue."

I reached up, tucking a piece of hair behind my ear. "It was a grope, wasn't it?"

"More like a grip." He stretched his legs out in front of him, leaning back on his palms. "If you have to clutch a girl, you're doing something wrong. Definitely not a mysterious enigma."

"My friend set me up with him," I said.

"Might be time for a new friend."

I shook my head. "No. She means well. I haven't . . . I'm not that social lately. She's trying to change that."

"Not social? What's that like?"

As if on cue, the door slid open again. At first I thought it was Grace, as the figure that emerged also had a boa and tiara. As she got closer, however, I realized it was one of her friends, a shorter girl, curvier, with dark hair. "Ambrose! Are you hiding from me?"

"I thought you knew you were It," he told her with a smile.

She struck a pose, one hand on her hip. "You know that's true. I am all It *and* a bag of chips. Now come on back inside, you promised to take a shot with me."

"You had me at chips. Just give me five minutes."

Again, a pout. Was I the only girl who didn't have this move already down? "I don't wait for anyone."

"I'm not just anyone. I'm Ambrose." He winked—winked!—at her. "Five minutes. I'll be the one ready for some chips."

She shifted her weight to the other leg. "Hope you're hungry."

I was struggling not to make a disgusted face when I realized that I wasn't having trouble breathing anymore. For all the ridiculousness of these exchanges, the distraction had been helpful. "See you inside," Ambrose said now, and after a beat, the girl turned and walked away, fluffing her hair as she went.

"Wow," I said, as the door shut behind her.

"Agreed. I'm all for innuendo, but you can take it too far."

"How do you even know those girls?" I asked. "Didn't you just move to town?"

"They picked me up when I was walking here."

"You walked here?" The A-frame wasn't in the country, but neither was it in the town center. "Why?"

"I walk everywhere." He lifted one foot, then the other. "Just me, Pete, and Repeat."

"By choice?"

"By order of the state of California," he replied. "I'm currently between licenses."

I was pretty sure that wasn't even a thing. "Is this about wrecking your mom's car?"

"Partially. So are you not social by choice, or due to your personality?"

Again, I was struck by how he could turn the subject from himself to me as easily as flicking a wrist. "What do you mean, my personality?"

He shrugged. "You are a bit prickly."

"I am not prickly," I said, sounding exactly that way. I took a breath, resetting. "I just . . . it's been a hard year. Dating hasn't exactly been a priority."

He shuddered. "God, who wants to date?"

"Not you, apparently."

"I like the process, not the endgame. Courtship is my thing."

I just looked at him. "Did you really just say courtship was your *thing*?"

"Prickly and hard of hearing, are we?" I made a face, which he returned, before saying, "There's a reason they call it the thrill of the chase."

"So you don't do commitment."

"Why would I? That's what they do with crazy people," he said. I sighed. "Look, it's not like I'm tricking anyone. I am clear in the fact that my intention is to have, well, no intentions."

"Did you not just promise a dance, a shot, and a bag of chips?"

"That's not a relationship, it's a list. There's a difference."

The door slid open again. I was expecting yet another girl in a boa, but it was Jilly who stuck her head out, scanning the deck one way, then the other. When she saw me, she exhaled and hurried over.

"I have been so worried!" She'd taken off her shoes, which were actually a pair of mine, at some point. "What happened to you? One minute we were having fun dancing and then you were gone."

"I got light-headed," I said.

"And groped," Ambrose added. "Jughead and his big ears were all over her. You finally get a chance to make her social and *that's* the route you choose?"

It said something about how concerned Jilly was that up to this point, she hadn't paid much attention to Ambrose. Usually, she didn't miss anything, especially a male anything. Now she'd spotted him, and she was pissed. "Who the hell are you?"

"Ambrose Little," he said, sticking out his hand. "I work with Louna."

"No, you don't."

"How do you figure?"

"Because she's my best friend and I know everything about her, including whom she works with. I've never seen you in my life."

"Well. Don't *you* think a lot of yourself. You don't know someone, so they don't exist?"

She just looked at him, not used to being off her game in this way. Then, prioritizing, she waved him off, turning back to me. "I had no idea Eric was getting handsy. I'm sorry. It was crazy out there."

Man, I'd been way off on the name. Not that I felt bad about it, at this point. "It's okay. It's just been a long day, and . . ."

"I know." She looked at Ambrose. "Who is this guy?"

"Ambrose Little. I work with Louna."

"No," she said firmly. "You don't."

"Actually . . ." I began. Now she looked confused. "Since this afternoon, he kind of does. His sister is a client. He was dancing nearby when Eric was getting grabby and he . . ."

"Performed a conga extraction," Ambrose finished for me. "Just one of my many specialties."

Jilly gave him a level gaze, contemplating his face. Finally she said, "I don't think I like you."

"A common reaction," he replied. "I'll win you over. Eventually."

She looked at me, flabbergasted. All I could say was, "I know."

The door slid open again. This time, all I could see was an arm, a boa wrapped around it. Was it Grace? Bag of chips? Another girl? I hated that I was actually curious. "Am-*brose*! Where are you?"

"I guess that's my cue." He sat up, brushing his hands off. Then to me, he said, "You okay? All better now?"

If only, I thought. Was there even such a thing? I could feel Jilly watching me, aware of this moment, or whatever it was, between his question and my answer. "I'm fine," I said. "Thanks again."

"No problem." He stood up, running a hand through his hair, then did a little bow to Jilly. "Lovely making your acquaintance."

"You, too," she replied, obviously guarded.

"See? You're coming around." He grinned, then turned on one foot, slid his hands in his pockets, and started to the door, where all the boas were now gathered, a wall of girl, waiting for him. He raised his arms, giving a fanfare as they all hooted, then reached to pull him in.

Jilly looked pensive as she took a seat on my other side. "Is it weird that I am strangely attracted to him, even as I dislike him totally?"

"Yes," I said flatly.

"I figured. He's not really my type anyway," she decided. "Too good-looking, and he knows it. Not to mention he just screams of asshole."

"You think?" I asked.

"Don't you?"

If she'd posed this question earlier that day, or even at the wedding where we'd first met, my answer certainly would have been yes. Ambrose *was* cocky, entirely too confident in his own charm. He had little or no regard for other people's time or feelings and was about as shallow in his "intentions" as anyone I'd ever met. And now he was most likely working each one of those boa girls against the others, adding to his list.

And yet, I couldn't deny what had happened on the dance floor earlier. It wasn't how Ambrose appeared when, in my panic, everything had gone wavery, that whooshing about to begin in my ears that would take me down. Nor was it the way he'd sat with me afterward, peppering the night with his prattle as I tried to fill my lungs with air. Instead, it was a beat in between, something small: when he took my hand and began to pull me out of the crowd, and I felt myself—my prickly, antisocial self—squeeze his fingers once, tightly. He squeezed back. Like a question and then an answer or call and response, without either of us saying a word.

I stayed at the party for another hour or so, for Jilly more than myself. I had pledged to make memories; I wanted to at least try to have them be good ones. So we danced, just the two of us, and toasted our futures with beer from a fresh keg when it arrived. I didn't see Ambrose again, although I had to admit I did look for him every time I saw a flash of pink feathers in my peripheral vision.

At three thirty a.m., we piled into a rideshare with some guys Jilly knew and headed home with all the windows down, the night pouring in. I was dropped off second, and my house was dark. Once inside, I could see William asleep on the couch, where he often crashed when he and my mom stayed up talking late. His shoes were off, arms folded over his chest; he literally slept like a dead person. I picked the afghan off a nearby chair, shaking it out, then covered him. He didn't budge.

I knew I should be tired too, as I'd been up close to twenty-four hours straight. But even under the covers in my cool room with the fan on, I wasn't able to sleep. Finally, I picked up my phone from where it was charging on the nightstand and opened up one of my news apps. The story was right at the top, as I knew it would be, the featured picture that of a brick building, ambulances lined up beside it. I scrolled down past the bullet points of the story, then the introduction, looking for the only words that mattered to me.

ELIZABETH HAWKINS, 17.

DEMETRIOUS BARCLAY, 16.

SIERRA COPELAND, 17.

MARCUS SHEFFIELD, 15.

WILLA MARTIN, 16.

In the coming days, there would be pictures, remembrances, funerals. But tonight, there were just these names, no faces yet to match, the barest of bare facts. That was the way it was when it wasn't personal, when your own heart didn't lurch at the sight of that particular combination of letters. When they were just other people's children, brothers, sisters, loved ones.

ETHAN CARUSO, 17, seven months earlier, was different. He had been mine.

CHAPTER
6

THE SAND was chilly on my feet as I stepped onto it that August night. With the music still audible from the patio, I hooked the straps of my shoes onto my thumb, then slid my phone into the pocket of my dress. Ahead, the beach was flat and dark, dotted with the lights from hotels and, farther along, houses. Thinking I'd only go a little way before I turned around, I started walking.

If he hadn't been wearing that white shirt, bright almost to the point of glowing, I might not have even seen him. But he was. The boy who had asked me to dance, standing by the water's edge. I couldn't miss him. No, more than that. I can never picture him in anything else.

The real surprise, though, was that he saw *me*. When you come across someone on the beach at night, contemplating the ocean, you don't exactly interrupt. It's one of those unwritten rules. So I'd just walked behind him, keeping my head down, when I heard him say, "All done for the night?"

It's funny, the little details you remember from the things you cannot forget. The sand cool on my feet. The weight of my shoes, shifting as they swung in my hand. And again, that shirt bright in contrast to my own black dress, so dark I wondered later how he'd even seen me at all.

"Yeah," I answered. "I got off early, for once."

"Is it early?" He looked back behind him, over the dunes, where the party was still going on, shadows of figures distantly visible moving above. "Man. It feels late to me."

I wasn't sure what to say to this, and felt like maybe I should keep moving, give him the space he'd clearly come out here to claim. But he was the one who had started talking.

"Weddings take a lot out of you," I answered. "Or so I hear."

"You hear? You should know. You go to tons, right?"

"I *work* at tons," I corrected him. "It's different from being a guest. You're at a distance, an observer. Almost scientific."

"Huh," he said. He had a bit of a Northern accent, enough to notice. "I never thought about it that way. Then again, I mow yards for my job."

"That's not emotional?"

"Maybe for the grass."

I laughed. "I never thought about it *that* way."

"Oh, the world of landscaping is fascinating. Except that it's totally not."

We stood there for a second, both of us facing the crashing waves. Out on the horizon, I could see a fishing boat, its lights twinkling as the water shifted.

From behind us, there was a loud whoop, followed by cheering, and we both turned to look. In profile, I saw he had long lashes, a jut I hadn't noticed to his chin. "Your family's having fun," I said.

"My dad's family," he corrected me immediately. *O-kay,*

I thought. He gave me an apologetic smile. "Sorry. It's just . . .
complicated."

"Family usually is," I said.

"Is yours?"

I considered this for a moment. "Not really."

He laughed. "Oh, I get it. You *are* still on the clock.
Counseling morose guests gone AWOL from the ceremony,
just part of the job."

"No, no," I protested, holding up my hand. "I just mean . . .
my family is only me and my mom. Well, and William.
Not much to complicate."

"William?"

"Her best friend, my godfather-basically-my-father-
except-he's-not," I explained, using the term I'd come up
with back in elementary school during Meet My Family
week, when this issue first arose. "My real dad died when I
was three."

"Wow. Sorry."

I shrugged. "I didn't really know him, at least that I remember. So it's not like I miss him or anything."

He slid his hands in his pockets, leaning back on his heels.
"My dad and I used to be super close. I was his little buddy,
all that. Then, three years ago, he ditched my mom for his
secretary. Such a stereotype. He couldn't even be original
about *cheating.*"

His voice was tinged with disgust, saying this. Now I
said, "I'm sorry."

A shrug. "Not your fault. And yet *you* manage to apologize anyway. He never has. Weird how that works, huh?"

"Definitely," I said. "How's your mom doing?"

"She's fine," he replied. "Remarried, too, by this point. She's over it."

"And you?"

Silence. Then, "Not quite there yet. Even though I did agree to take this road trip with him, to this wedding, and be a groomsman. It was supposed to be this big re-bonding experience."

I dug a toe into the wet sand, wiggling it until it disappeared. "And how's that going?"

"I'm out here, alone, in the dark. Or at least I was until you came along," he replied. "You tell me."

"Ethan!"

The voice was behind us, coming from the steps that led up to the hotel. When I turned, I saw a heavyset woman in a green metallic dress, her hair done in an updo, peering down at us. The boy beside me said, "Yeah?"

"You're missing everything!" she called out. "Joe and Margy will be leaving soon!"

"Okay," he replied. "Just a sec."

Placated, she turned, adjusting her hair, then started back toward the party, her shadow stretching long down the stairs behind her. Ethan turned back to the water, a tired look on his face. "My aunt Didi. Who has kind of taken my estrangement from my dad personally."

"Family is complicated," I said.

"Exactly. Unless you're . . ." He raised his eyebrows at me. "What's your name?"

"Louna," I said.

"Like the moon?"

"Like Louis and Natalie, young vegans in love, circa 1999." Now I made a face.

"Wow," he said, looking impressed. "I think this is a story I have to hear."

I looked back at the steps, where Aunt Didi was now just a green blur in the distance. "Too bad you have to go back."

"Yeah." He glanced over as well. "Too bad."

We stood there for a second, facing each other. His shirttails, now untucked, were ruffling in the wind. I'd never had this feeling before, that something big was about to happen, and there was nothing I had to do but wait for it. A beat. Then another. Finally, Ethan stepped back from me, away from the thrown brightness of the hotel and into the dimness of the beach beyond. The wind blew my hair, the straps of my shoes twisting around each other as he smiled at me, then gestured for me to join him there.

I didn't even hesitate. So much of life is not being sure of anything. How I wished, later, I'd been able to savor them, those few steps and moments when for once, I just knew.

❧

We walked for what felt like a long time, just talking. First about my mom and dad and their marriage in the woods with the chickens, and then how his parents imploded in the midst of a huge home renovation that was never completed. ("She wanted an exercise and yoga room, and he wanted a wine cellar. They ended up with a divorce. Nice, right?") His cynicism, at least about this subject, was a comfort to me, and made it easy for me to tell him about my mother and William's views on love and marriage and how, unfortunately or not, they'd been passed on to me.

"I don't *not* believe in love," he told me, as we passed the last of the hotels and began to see houses up on the dunes. "I'm just not sure about marriage as an institution."

"Maybe you'll be the more barefoot, chicken-keeping, lifetime partner but no ring kind of person," I suggested.

"Because that's what happens to guys like me from New Jersey who play lacrosse and mow lawns."

"Maybe it is."

He laughed again, throwing his head back. You had to love—or okay, maybe just like—a person who could revel in the humor of something so fully. It made me want to laugh, too.

"I can get behind the idea of a good marriage," I said, as we stepped around some abandoned beach chairs. "Like my best friend Jilly, her parents. They run a food truck company, have five kids between two and seventeen, and their lives are total chaos. But they can't keep their hands off each other. I've never seen two people more in love."

Ethan looked up at the sky. "When it works, it works, I guess."

"That's entirely too vague for me. I need to know *how* it works," I said. "Preferably with diagrams and bullet points. I want a guarantee."

"Wow. That's a big ask," he said.

"It is," I told him. "But some people get it, right? That surety that something, someone, really is forever. My mom wouldn't have a business otherwise."

"I don't think anybody ever really knows what's going to happen," he said. "We're all just out here hoping for the best."

I thought of all the weddings I'd worked, from the small church ones with finger food to the huge, multi-venue kind where no expense was spared. How sure were any of them, really, even after checking every box: aisle walk, vows, rings, first dance, toasts, and cake? Like going through these motions, or variations of such, were the way of guaranteeing something would last. But I, of all people, knew this just wasn't true. We loved a third wedding, after all.

A few minutes later, I saw a bonfire burning ahead, a few dark figures standing around it. We went wide around them, but could still hear their voices, as well as music coming from a truck, doors open, parked in the sand by the dunes. Once past, I was surprised to see the beach ahead of us narrow to a thin strip, the tide running over a few sandbars there. In the dark, I'd just assumed it went on for miles. We kept going, all the way to the edge.

"Well, here we are," Ethan said. "The end of the world."

I smiled, turning slightly to take in the full view. "It's different than I expected."

"The big stuff always is," he said.

Behind us, I heard a swell of music, something easy and slow; it had to be deafening by the bonfire. Where we were, though, it was caught in the wind and carried, just distant enough to seem ghostlike. Or maybe that was the wrong word. Perhaps I wouldn't have used it at that moment, but only now.

Ethan walked out a little farther into the sand and water, the wind catching that white shirt, again sending the back billowing behind him. It was like he was glowing, more alive than anything I'd ever seen, when he turned back to me, holding out his hand. "Okay, I'll only ask once more, I promise. Want to dance?"

Could I hear the music, still? In my memory, the answer is yes. But in retrospect everything is perfect, as are all the other details of this night. At that moment, though, everything was brand-new, including the way I felt as I stepped forward, locking my fingers into his as he pulled me in closer. Me and Ethan, dancing in the dark at the end of the world. It was like I'd waited all my life to have something like this, and I knew even then, at the start, that it would be hard, so hard to lose. The big stuff always is.

CHAPTER
7

"I'M HERE! I'm here!"

He wasn't. In fact, he was barely through the door, racing toward the conference table, where the rest of us had been sitting for a good seven minutes. I turned to my mother, who valued promptness above all else, but she wouldn't look at me. Nobody likes an I Told You So.

"Sorry," Ambrose said as he basically threw himself, panting, into the seat beside me. A chair on wheels, it began rolling, putting him in motion as he added, "There was an accident on Main Street."

William, across the table, followed this movement with his eyes, intrigued. He always loved a shit show. I said, "Didn't you walk here, though?"

"Yes," Ambrose replied, putting out a hand, finally, to stop himself. Then he grabbed the side of the table and began trying to return the chair into position, one clumsy pull at a time. "But I had to stop and"—yank—"rubberneck. I'm only"—yank—"human."

I seriously thought my mom would just go ahead and fire him that second. He was late. Clearly inept. And still yanking. Instead she said, "Was everyone okay?"

"Looked like it. Airbag deployed, though, and there was an ambulance." Finally back where he'd begun at the table, he settled into his chair, then pulled a hand through his mussed-up hair. That one curl tumbled, and a piece of pink boa, stringy and wavering, rose up above him. No one else seemed to notice. "I could have garnered more detail, but it was important to me that I be on time."

I rolled my eyes. "You weren't, though."

"Well, we're all here now, so let's get started," my mother said. "Ambrose, first thing each morning we go over that day's schedule. You'll find it on that wall. Louna, give him a pad for notes, would you?"

After the tape dispenser incident, I had my reservations about trusting him with any office supplies. But I did as I was told, reaching across the table to pick up one of the yellow legal pads stacked there, along with a black pen from the nearby cup. When I pushed it over to Ambrose, he looked delighted, centering it in front of him, and uncapping the pen. I watched as he wrote his name at the top, like he was about to take a spelling test in third grade, followed by a number one with a dot.

"All of our upcoming events and tasks will be listed here," my mom said, gesturing to the whiteboard behind her, which was divided into two sections. On one side was a calendar of that month, with all of our events represented in William's block print. The other was the current week, with more detailed listings of every meeting, task, and errand that needed completing. I was grateful to see KIRBY'S listed right at the top of that day, Friday, which meant a two-hour car ride by myself nursing what I was pretty sure was my first hangover.

1. WHITEBOARD IS SCHEDULE, Ambrose wrote. The pen was squeaking.

"As you can see," my mom continued, "our next event is the Charlotte McDonald Wedding. We'll be overseeing the rehearsal dinner tonight at the Lakeview Armory. Tomorrow we'll have what we call a double hander, which means a church ceremony followed by a reception at another location."

2. TWO HANDS THIS WEEKEND, Ambrose added to his list.

"You'll see the locations are abbreviated next to the schedule," William said. "VB and BH: Village Baptist and Barn Hill."

3. CODES ARE INVOLVED.

Why was I reading this? I made a point of looking away.

"As you can see," my mom was saying, "William and I have three meetings today, and there is a lot to be done out of the office, most importantly the pickup of flowers. I'll expect you and Louna to get that done first, and follow up with the rest of the errands."

"Wait, what?" I said. "We don't both have to go to Kirby's. That's a one-person job."

"It's Ambrose's first day. He's shadowing you, learning the ropes."

The pen squeaked again. I couldn't help myself: I looked.

4. I'M A SHADOW!

"I don't need help." I pointed to the board. "Look, it says right there that programs need to be folded and place cards organized. That's all inside work you guys can oversee from your meetings."

"I think it's better if he goes along for the flowers," she said. "You can't be sure when you'll need an extra hand."

"Never," I said. "That's when. I never have. Ever."

William, fingers tented beneath his chin, looked amused. Ambrose said, "You guys, Louna's not my number one fan. Although I thought that might have changed, after last night."

William raised his eyebrows. I heard my mom's chair creak as she turned to look at me, saying, "Last night?"

"Well, *this* sounds interesting," William said.

"It's not," I assured him. "And it has nothing to do with work, which is what I thought we were supposed to be talking about."

"This girl, she's all business," Ambrose said. "That's what I love about her. Short version is I saved her from a jugheaded groper."

"A grouper?" William asked. "Like the fish?"

"Groper. As in, one who gropes. Was groping. Has groped." Ambrose clicked his pen open, then shut, punctuating this conjugation. "It was on the dance floor, at this party."

"You were dancing?" William asked. From his expression, you would have thought Ambrose had said I'd stripped naked as well. "At a party?"

"Why is that so shocking?" I demanded.

He looked at my mom, and they both burst out laughing. Ambrose clicked his pen open again.

5. *LOUNA DOESN'T GET OUT MUCH.*

"I'm going to Kirby's," I announced, pushing out my chair with a bit too much force; now I had to grab the table to keep from rolling away. "I'll call on my way back for the lunch order."

With this, I collected my purse and walked out of the conference room, making it clear decisions Had Been Made. And I really did feel that way, all the way to the front door of the office. Then my mother called my name.

I turned back to see her standing by the reception area. Her voice was low, confidential, as she came closer, then said, "I need you to take Ambrose with you."

"Why?"

"Because we have a very high-strung bride coming in here in five minutes, followed by a potential client whose wedding could make us a lot of money. We won't be able to supervise and can't risk another tape explosion."

"I don't understand why you hired him," I said.

"Because his mother asked me to and swore he could actually be a good worker if directed appropriately." I made a face, conveying my doubt about this. "Other than me and William, you're the best director I know."

"Don't kiss up to me. It's embarrassing."

She smiled. "You know, you might find you actually enjoy having company."

"I don't dislike people," I said. "I'm just not fond of *him*."

This was an important distinction, I felt. But she barely seemed to hear me, already turning to call his name as she gestured for him to join us. He brought the pen and pad with him. Of course.

"They're expecting you by ten sharp," she told me, handing over her copy of the invoice. "Make sure you get everything."

I took the paper from her, not answering, and turned back to the door. Before I could push it open, though, he reached around and did it for me. "After you."

My first thought was to just stop in my tracks, right where I was. The next was how petulant I was acting, like a child. Strange how you could barely know a person and they were still able to bring out the worst in you. I took a breath, nodded at him, then stepped through the door. Up close, I saw there was another tiny pink boa feather in his hair.

⌘

He would not. Stop. Touching. Everything.

It had started with the vents, which he spent the first five minutes of the drive—I was watching the dashboard clock—turning this way and that to achieve what he referred to as "maximum cooling velocity." Then he moved on to his side of the dual thermostat dial, turning it to basically Arctic, followed by loosening and tightening his seat belt. Now it was the radio.

"*Stop*," I said, as he changed the station yet again. When he'd asked if he could, I'd said yes, thinking he'd do it once or twice. This was our fourth round of my presets, and my headache was increasing with each push of a button. "Just leave it on one thing, would you please?"

"I can't listen to bad music," he explained. "It's like a thing with me."

"Fine." I hit the AM/FM button. "Talk radio it is."

I realized my mistake almost instantly. As it was the top of the hour, the national news was on.

"Authorities have released the names of the five victims of yesterday's shooting in California." The reporter's voice, seemingly like everyone on public radio, was level and calm. "All were students at Riverton High School, as was the gunman, a sixteen-year-old male who was a sophomore. Classmates and teachers have stated he was quiet, but showed no previous signs of violence."

I took a breath, focusing on my hands on the wheel. Ambrose was messing with his seat belt again.

"Fifteen-year-old Lacey Tornquist was a neighbor of the shooter," the voice continued. Then that of a girl, speaking quickly, breathless. "He wasn't a bad kid, but he did get picked on some. I never thought he'd do something like this, though. Never in a million years." The reporter again. "The shooter's name has not yet been released to the media. In Russia, government officials—"

I hit the button again, bringing us back to music. Ambrose looked over. "*Now* who's messing with the radio?"

I didn't answer, instead just focusing on breathing and driving. He reached out to turn the A/C down another notch. "Crazy about that shooting, huh? I watched some of the coverage with Milly's mom this morning, when she made us pancakes. Heavy stuff."

A truck switched lanes in front of me, and I hit the brakes, giving it space. "Who's Milly?"

"Oh, just this girl from last night. I crashed on her couch." He tugged at his belt again. "They were saying the kid had a fixation on other school shootings."

I realized I was gripping the steering wheel. Ten and two, I thought, moving my hands on the wheel.

"Like, he'd done a report on that one in Brownwood. Stood up in front of a current events class and talked all about it. How creepy is that?"

I swallowed, suddenly aware of the prickly feeling space between my ears. The truck switched back to the other lane. "I can't—"

"Seriously. Me neither. I mean, I didn't love high school either, but come on. No need to take it out on everyone else." A pause. "Hey, are you okay?"

I wasn't. But I was also behind the wheel, in heavy traffic, and knew to acknowledge this would be the worst thing I could do. "Why . . ." I began, then heard a crack in my voice. I swallowed. "Why didn't you like high school?"

He pushed the curl aside. "Well, it was really myriad reasons. First, I don't do well in standardized learning environments. Also, I have problems with conventional forms of authority and a compromised attention span, and can be super annoying." As if to underline this, he changed the radio station again. "Those are direct quotes, by the way."

"From counselors?"

"And teachers. Psychiatrists. Peer evaluations."

"Your peers said you were annoying, I assume?"

"Nope, that was one of my shrinks." I raised my eyebrows. "I know! I was like, wait, that's not a doctor term! Is annoying a diagnosis now? And if so, can I get meds for it?"

He laughed then, in a can-you-even-believe-it kind of way, shaking his head. Then he looked out the window, drumming his fingers on one knee.

I could see my exit now, the one that would take us onto the two-lane road that made up the rest of the trip. I put on my blinker, switching lanes so carefully you would have thought I was taking the driving test with a DMV worker beside me. Only when we reached the top of the ramp, the heavy traffic now a distant roar below, did I realize I'd been holding my breath. *Keep talking*, I told myself.

"Did you really go home with one of those girls last night?"

He stretched the seat belt away from him, then let it snap back. "Well, yes, in the technical sense. But nothing really happened. I crashed on her couch, and in the morning her mom came out in her bathrobe and offered me breakfast."

"Doesn't Bee worry when you don't come home?"

"Nah. I check in. And remember, I'm annoying. She needs a break every now and then."

"She seems like a really nice girl," I said.

"She is." He said this simply; it was clear it was fact. "It's not easy always having to be the good one, but she's a natural. You have any siblings?"

I shook my head. "Nope. Just me and my mom."

"Huh," he said.

Don't ask, I told myself. Then I asked. "What?"

"Nothing," he said. I waited, making it clear I expected more. "Just that, you know, it explains things. How you like to be alone."

"I don't like to be alone," I said.

"Right. You just don't want to be with *me.*"

I looked over at him. "That's not exactly true."

"Right. You basically did all you could to not have to be with me right now, including telling your mom you don't like me," he pointed out. I blinked, surprised. He'd been in another room, after all. He said, "My annoyingness does not affect my hearing. I'm like a dog, it's so good."

"I'll have to remember that." I cleared my throat. "Anyway, I'm sorry I said that. It's just . . . I'm used to working alone, and—"

"Look, you don't have to explain yourself," he said easily. "I'm not for everyone."

Again, this was said with such ease, a plain truth. What was it like to be so confident even in your failings that you weren't the least bit bothered when other people pointed them out? I was almost envious.

We were close to Kirby's now; I could see the greenhouses, as well as the bursts of color that were their outdoor plantings, in the distance. When it came to florists, my mom only recommended the best, usually choosing companies that catered to the exact needs of the client. If you wanted perfect, sculpted centerpieces of roses and lilies, picking Lakeview Florist or Occasions was easy. But if your taste was more natural, bohemian wildflowers-in-mason-jars—increasingly popular among younger brides—Kirby's was the place.

I pulled into the dusty lot, right up to the squat building that housed the office. This was a family business, another reason my mom preferred them. If you called with a problem, there was no corporate voicemail system, just a hand cupping the receiver while someone bellowed for Mr. or Mrs. Kirby, who were usually out in the fields tending the plants themselves. "Okay," I said, reaching back for my bag and pulling out the invoice. "We're here for Gerbera daisies, glads, lilies, and sunflowers. Ten buckets total. Mrs. Kirby will always try to add on an extra bucket or two she's trying to move, but we don't have room so we have to be firm."

"Ten buckets," he repeated. "Gerberas, glads, sunflowers, lilies. No extras."

Huh. Maybe he was right about that hearing. "Correct. It shouldn't take longer than a half hour total if we don't get caught up talking."

"Keep it short. All business. Thirty minutes max."

My phone rang then: Jilly, most likely wanting to catch up while en route from one KitKat activity to another. As I hit IGNORE, preferring to wait until I was alone, Ambrose said, "Wait, what was that? Your ringtone?"

"Nothing," I told him.

"It sounded like this awful pop song—"

"Nope. Let's go."

I pushed open my door, getting out as he did the same, then followed me through the propped-open screen door.

Inside, rows of plants sat on makeshift tables made of sawhorses and plywood, a row of walk-in coolers along one wall.

"Louna Barrett." A woman's voice came from behind a tall basket of ornamental greenery. "Right on time, as always."

"Hey, Mrs. Kirby," I replied. "How are you?"

She stepped out, wiping her hands on her apron. She was a tall and broad black woman with a melodic voice, and everything she said sounded important. "Very good, very good. Have some gorgeous peonies I want to show you, on special. Your mom's favorite."

"They are," I agreed. "But space is tight."

"You can always make room for a few extra blooms," she replied, then noticed Ambrose. "Who's this? A boyfriend?"

"No," I said, a bit too quickly. "This is Ambrose. He's working with us for the summer."

"Oh. Well. I'm sure you can forgive me for getting hopeful that you might have found another romantic prospect." She turned to him, shaking her head. "So heartbreaking what happened with that boy of hers."

This was so unexpected that for a moment, I couldn't even respond. Mrs. Kirby was a talker, always had been. The previous fall, I'd come out here to collect a client's rehearsal dinner flowers and, in an unusual move for me—everything when it came to Ethan was different—mentioned I had a boyfriend. It was almost embarrassing, thinking back to how happy I'd been, how I'd worked this fact, and him, into just about any conversation. When she asked after him the next time I saw her, I was so raw I told the truth. Both mistakes. Big ones.

Ambrose was looking at me. This he couldn't miss, even without the good hearing. I said, "We're really kind of pressed for time, and my mom wants pictures before we pack up the car. Can we go ahead and look at what you have?"

Mrs. Kirby, like any long-winded person, was used to being redirected. "Of course, sweetie, whatever you want," she said. "But you *have* to see these peonies. I can't let you leave without at least a glimpse."

She started toward the back, and I immediately fell in behind her, making a point of not looking Ambrose's way at all. Whatever was on his face as he worked this out, or guessed at it—surprise, pity, empathy—I knew I did not want to see it. I would take annoying, instead, all day long.

Forty-five minutes later, we were pulling back onto the two-lane highway, eleven buckets of flowers strapped with bungee cords into the back of my banged-up Suburban. I'd caved on the peonies, mostly just because I didn't have it in me to face down the hard sell. And they *were* beautiful, fragile and fragrant with lacy edges. They'd look gorgeous in the jars I'd be unpacking and cleaning later that day for Charlotte McDonald's wedding, and if she didn't agree, I'd eat the cost myself. They were my mom's favorite.

I kept waiting for Ambrose to ask me about Ethan. While we waited for Mrs. Kirby to confer with her husband, who came in from the fields in overalls and a straw hat, about prices. As we carted the buckets to the car, arranging them like a puzzle to make everything fit snugly. And now, when we were finally alone and back on the road, the car around us so fragrant that I had to crack my window.

But he didn't. Instead, he messed with the vents again, the seat belt, the radio. Also, he sneezed; it happened, especially when you weren't used to so many flowers in such a small space. Over the course of about three miles, I went from dreading him bringing it up to just wishing he would. At least then, it would be happening and not *about* to happen. After another mile, I figured I'd just go ahead and tell him, to get it over with.

"Can we stop?" he asked suddenly, nodding at a little store that was just ahead. "I'm parched."

Of course he couldn't just say thirsty, I thought, annoyed. "Sure," I said, glancing at the dashboard clock. "We have to be quick, though."

The store was small and dusty, an older man behind the counter. As soon as we walked in, a dog approached us, quickly wagging its tail. It was skinny and small, its fur scruffy, poking out in wiry tufts above its eyebrows and around the snout. Kind of like a canine Brillo pad. Panting.

Ambrose immediately dropped down to greet it, which made it even more excited, its entire body twisting and writhing as it got petted. "Your dog is awesome," he called out to the man, who was reading a newspaper, a pencil behind his ear. In return, he just grunted.

I walked over to the drink cooler, pulling out an iced tea. "What do you want?" I asked Ambrose, who was busy scratching the dog's neck, making one leg bang excitedly against the floor.

"Something fruity with lots of sugar," he replied. "I know, I know! You *are* a good boy!"

This time, the man looked over, irritated, and I was surprised to feel a wave of protectiveness. It was a fact Ambrose got on people's nerves. But this guy had only been around him a few seconds. I grabbed a tropical punch that was bright pink, then took both drinks over to the counter, putting them down. Just as I did, a car beeped outside and the dog started barking, the noise sudden and high-pitched.

"Shut *up*," the man growled as he punched a few buttons on the register. "Goddamn dog. Four seventy-two."

I gave him a five, highly aware as the noise continued, a mix of a yip and a screech. "Hey, buddy," Ambrose was saying, "it's okay."

"Barks every time he hears a beep," the man said, pushing my change across to me. "And it's like nails on a chalkboard."

I said nothing to this, just took the drinks and started for the door. "Let's go," I said to Ambrose, who was still trying to quiet the dog down. "There's bound to be traffic."

Another series of yaps, one right after the other. The man pushed himself to his feet, grumbling under his breath, then came around the counter, walking with a noticeable limp over to a back door. "Out," he said to the dog, as he pushed it open. "Go play in traffic."

The dog got quiet and sat down. "Good boy," Ambrose told him.

The man sighed. "*Out*," he said again, this time snapping his fingers. Slowly, the dog stood, then walked out the door, and the man dropped it shut behind him. As he shuffled back behind the counter, Ambrose tracked him with his eyes.

"Come on," I said quietly. A beat. Then another. Finally, he followed me outside.

We got in the car and I cranked the engine, then handed him his drink. I'd just shifted into reverse when he said, "Hey, I need a bathroom break. Long ride ahead and all."

"We're already back in the car," I said.

"I'll hurry. Promise."

I sat back. Quickly, he unbuckled his seat belt and hopped out, walking around the building toward the sign that said RESTROOMS.

I was just reaching forward to change the radio station (now an addiction for both of us, clearly) when the passenger door suddenly opened again and he tumbled inside. "Go," he said. He was holding something in his arms.

"What?"

"Go. Drive. Now!"

It was only after I shifted into reverse again, for some reason blindly following this directive, that I looked over and saw that what he was clutching was, in fact, the dog.

"Ambrose. You stole that man's dog?"

"I prefer to look at it as a rescue," he corrected me as it wriggled wildly in my side vision.

I looked over my shoulder. "Are you serious right now?"

"I couldn't just leave him there," he said, as if I was the

one acting irrationally. "Can you go a little faster? Just until we're clear of the parking lot."

I glanced in the rearview, but of course no one was following us. Still, I hit the gas hard as I pulled out, spraying gravel. The dog started barking again.

"See how happy he is?" Ambrose asked, as we picked up speed. He rolled down his window and the dog immediately stuck his head out, the wind ruffling the bursts of hair over his eyes. I looked over at both of them, then in the rearview, where now all I could see was flowers, bobbing in the breeze. Only then did I realize minutes had passed since I'd been thinking about Ethan and having to tell Ambrose that story. This should have made me happy, I knew, or at least relieved. But instead I felt sad. Sometimes forgetting was just as bad as remembering.

❧

"Is that a *dog*?"

I'd been worried about catching flack for the peonies. But as I lugged them in the office's back door, my mom didn't even notice.

"Yep," I said, brushing past her to put the bucket down. "Do you want these all here together?"

"Sure," she said, watching Ambrose as he tied an old scarf I'd found in my backseat around the dog's neck. The dog, who had not calmed down one bit during the hour drive, kept trying to lick him.

I walked back to the van, pulling open the other door and reaching for a bucket of tall gladiolas in bright pinks and purples. A moment later, Ambrose was beside me, removing the Gerbera daisies. "I think he's thirsty," he said to me. "You think I can grab him some water?"

"My mom's not exactly an animal person," I advised him. We both looked over at her: she was studying the dog as it gnawed on the scarf. "Whatever you do, I'd proceed with caution."

"Right. Thanks."

We went inside, putting the buckets down. Glancing into the conference room, I saw William at the table, unloading mason jars from a cardboard box. He called out, "Did you bring lunch? I'm starving."

"One sec," I told him. "We're just getting the flowers in."

He glanced around me, out at the car and Ambrose. "Is that—"

"Yes," my mother, still in the doorway, told him. "They brought a dog back, too. Which was not on the list."

I grabbed a bottled water from a nearby counter, along with a plastic thermos cup that had long ago lost its bottom half. When I went back outside, Ambrose was at the van, pulling out the sunflowers. "Here," I said, handing them both to him. "Just try to keep things low key."

"I always do," he said cheerfully. I couldn't tell if he was kidding.

I unloaded the lunch stuff, then left William and Mom at the table with their salads and went back outside, where the dog was now lapping water out of the thermos top. When he saw me, he stopped, lifting his dripping snout, and started wagging his tail.

"He likes you," Ambrose told me.

"I smell like lunch," I replied, not quite convinced. Still, I bent down, scratching the brittle hairs behind the dog's ears.

The truth was, I wasn't much of an animal person. I remembered a time, back in first grade, when I'd wanted a cat or dog more than anything. But my mom worked so much, and she claimed her former life on the farm had been quite enough animal caretaking, thank you, so eventually I stopped asking. It wasn't that I didn't like pets; I just figured they were for other people, like nose piercings and gluten-free diets.

Ambrose, however, felt differently. It was obvious by the way he was watching the dog drink, as if he was both adorable and genius. "I didn't hear him get called anything, did you? Guess that means we can name him whatever we want."

We? I thought. Out loud I said, "What's Bee going to say about this?"

"Oh, she'll be fine. She loves animals." The dog finished off the water, then sat back and shook its jowls, sending droplets flying. "And anyway, she won't have to deal with him. He'll go everywhere with me."

"On foot," I said, clarifying. He nodded. "What's going to happen when you crash at people's houses, like last night?"

"This is a small dog," he replied. "Compact. Won't be a problem."

"You'll have to feed it. And take it to the vet, make sure it's healthy. And what about in the fall, when you go back to school?"

He looked at me then. "You think way ahead, don't you?"

"No," I said, although I couldn't see why this was a bad thing. "I just *think*. I don't just take a dog and deal with the consequences later."

"Right now, there aren't consequences, though," he replied. "There's just a happy dog. What do you think about the name Jerry?"

The dog leaned down and began licking the empty bowl hard enough to make it scrape against the pavement.

"Why didn't you ask me about what Mrs. Kirby said?"

It was like I'd both planned to say this, and totally had not. My discomfort earlier, when this discussion had seemed inevitable, had passed with all the excitement of the abduction and ensuing ride home. Now I didn't feel like I just wanted to get it over with: instead, I was genuinely curious. Ambrose clearly had no problems traversing or outright bursting over any other boundaries in conversation or otherwise. So why not this one?

"You mean about your boyfriend?" he said.

"Yeah."

"Did you want me to ask?"

"No," I said. "I never do. I hate talking about it. But that's never stopped you before."

"Are we already at a point where our relationship is in nevers?" he asked. "That was fast."

"You know what I mean."

"I'm not sure I do." He stood, the dog watching him, tail still wagging. "Look, Louna. I might be a dog stealer, as far as you're concerned, but I am able to follow the basic rules of civility. If I was going to talk about a bad breakup, I'd want to be the one to bring it up. You did not."

A bad breakup? I thought. Then I said, "I don't always have the choice."

"Clearly. So why would I make it worse by then pushing for more details? People will tell you what they want you to know. I'm annoying, not an asshole."

I had to admit this was not what I was expecting. But as I went back over what Mrs. Kirby had said again, I realized it made sense he'd drawn this conclusion. Everyone had breakups they didn't want to talk about. Why would he assume it was anything else?

As if to punctuate the moment, the dog burped, spitting water. I opened my mouth to say something, to respond, but realized, again to my surprise, that I had a lump in my throat. I swallowed. "I don't think he's a Jerry."

"No?" He squatted down, giving the dog another scratch. "You might be right. No worries. He'll tell us his name when he wants us to know it."

"He'll tell us?"

"Well, in his way." He patted his head. "Stay here. I promise I'll come back. Okay?"

In response, the dog wagged its entire back end. As we walked away, it was still going full speed.

It was the shortest of walks back to the conference room, not nearly enough time to explain what I'd been thinking when I asked him about what Mrs. Kirby had said. The truth was, I felt I owed it to Ethan that he not be just a boy I once loved, much less one more face in a news story you dreaded having to hear. He was more than that, and yet talking about him to others felt, too often, like appropriating something. What did it take to claim a person, really? One perfect night? A few weeks of phone calls, hundreds of texts, all of them full of future plans and promises made? I'd spent less than a day with Ethan, but still felt he knew me better than just about anyone. You can't measure love by time put in, but the weight of those moments. Some in life are light, like a touch. Others, you can't help but stagger beneath.

This was on my mind all afternoon as Ambrose and I rinsed mason jars, packed them with flowers, then put them in lined boxes to be transported to the armory for table décor at the rehearsal dinner. Occasionally he went to check on the dog, bringing him snacks, more water, an old dishtowel I'd found under the sink to curl up on, but otherwise we worked in silence. *People will tell you what they want you to know,* he'd said. If that was true, I would have brought up Ethan right away, not just with him but everyone I met. That's what you do about the best thing that's ever happened to you. Unless, I guess, it is also the worst.

At six p.m., Mom and William left for the venue, releasing us to our respective evenings. I was expecting to be asked to transport Ambrose and the dog to wherever their next place might be, but then, as I was locking up, a black VW Jetta pulled up at the curb. A pretty redhead with seriously ripped shoulders, wearing yoga clothes, sunglasses perched on her head, was behind the wheel.

"Hey," she called out to me. "I'm looking for Ambrose?"

"He's around back," I replied. "Should be out in a sec."

"Thanks." She smiled, then pulled down her mirror, taking out a lip gloss and applying a coat. Was this Milly? Someone else? Of course I wouldn't ask. He hadn't told me.

A moment later Ambrose came around the corner holding the scarf, the dog lunging excitedly at the opposite end. "Annika," he said. "Namaste!"

She smiled. "I didn't know you had a dog."

"I am full of surprises." He climbed into the passenger seat, then patted his lap. As the dog leapt in, Annika burst out laughing, reaching over to rub his head with one hand. Ambrose waved at me, and I nodded, then started over to my own car. When I looked back a moment later, they were pulling out of the lot, the dog's head poking out the window. On the way home, I changed the radio station six times before I decided, finally, on silence.

CHAPTER

8

"OKAY, SO that's the Big Dipper," I said, pointing. "See how it looks like a ladle? And below it is the Little Dipper. And under that, the little one that looks like a crown? That's Cassiopeia."

Ethan turned his head to the side: I felt his hair brush my cheek. "And what about that one?"

"Which?"

He lifted his arm, moving a finger in a circle. "That clump there, at the bottom."

"I have no idea."

He shifted again, this time facing me. "I thought you said you knew this stuff."

"Some of it," I said, rolling toward him as well. "Okay, I know those three."

He laughed, that sudden burst that was even more startling close up. "And here I thought you could get us home strictly by celestial navigation."

"Nope. We'd be screwed," I told him. "Sorry."

"Hey, at least you can name a few. I've always just made up my own."

"Your own constellations?"

"Sure. It's like inkblots. You can tell a lot about a person by what they see in the sky." He moved onto his back again. "Take that weird square, over there. I'd call that Dented Laundry Hamper."

"It just doesn't have the same ring at Cassiopeia."

"But it's clear what it is." He pointed again. "Okay, and that one, over on the left? That's Dish Scrubber."

Now that I looked, I could sort of see the resemblance. "So what does it say about you that so far it's all household items that you see?"

"I'm glad you asked," he replied, and I smiled, already recognizing this as a classic Ethan expression. "I think it speaks to my domesticity. Also, lack of imagination."

"What about that one?" I asked, lifting my finger to point.

He didn't even hesitate. "Potholder."

"And that, the cluster by the Big Dipper?"

"EKG."

"That's not a household item."

"Well, maybe not at your house."

This time, I laughed, and as I did, he reached up, taking my pointing finger and pulling it toward him. I shifted my grip, interlocking my hand with his as he placed it on his chest, then curled up against him.

After the dance—sweet, awkward, perfect—we'd walked past the end of the world, through the shifting tides. It was then he'd taken my hand, wordless, easily. A stretch of dark, damp sand later, we found ourselves on the other side of the Colby peninsula. When the lights of the boardwalk appeared in the distance, we both stopped walking.

"Not yet," he said, and I knew exactly what he meant. We sat down and started looking at the stars.

I'd always been nervous about boys. I wasn't like Jilly, coming alive when faced with the opposite sex, the very presence of a guy causing the inherent glow in her to brighten. Instead, I was always jumpy, too aware of the particulars. The mechanics of a hand on mine, or an arm over my shoulder. The way my lips fit his in a kiss, specifics of saliva and tongue as if I was being graded on form. The kind of passion and attraction I saw in movies or read about in books seemed impossible to me, entirely too fraught with details and elbows.

From the start, Ethan was different. I felt so comfortable with him. Even just standing near him, there at the breaking waves, I'd wanted to lean in closer. It was the same way I felt now, as he reached his free hand to smooth back my hair. When he kissed me, I thought of nothing but how he tasted.

For the rest of that night, in my memory anyway, we were always in contact. My hand in his, his arm over my shoulder. The easy way he cupped my waist to pull me against him as we lay there in the sand, and later, crossed the length of the empty beach. We walked for an hour, maybe longer, talking the entire time, before we finally came up on the boardwalk.

Everything seemed bright and different after so long in the darkness, even though most of the businesses were closed. There was one neon sign lit, however, in the window of a narrow storefront. COFFEE AND PIE, it read. Two bikes were parked just outside.

I looked at Ethan. "We have to," he said, answering the question I hadn't even asked. I shook the sand out of my shoes, then dropped them onto the boards beneath my feet. My hair felt wild as I tried to smooth it, my lips raw from kissing. When I looked up at Ethan, I saw sand along his temple.

"Hold on," I said, reaching up. As I did, he lowered his head, leaning into my fingers. It was such a simple, fleeting moment, but later, when I'd think of it, I would sob until my chest ached. The big moments with Ethan weren't, well, big. Instead, it was these tiny increments and gestures that I clung to in order to hold on to him. It was why, now, I was never able to tell this story all at once. My memory fractured in certain places, wanting to just stop right there. On the boardwalk, in the thrown light of a neon sign. His head dipped down as I pulled my fingers through his hair. Sand falling onto my feet. That night still in progress, with daylight hours away.

CHAPTER

9

"NOW?"

"No."

A pause. "Now?"

I shook my head. Another pause. Then, finally, William gave me the nod.

"Okay," I said slowly. "*Now.*"

Ambrose leaned down over the ring bearer, a kindergartner named Ira, saying, "Okay, dude. It's go time." He rubbed his shoulders like a boxer's trainer, about to send him into the ring. "You got this! *Walk!*"

I sighed as Ira, in his tiny tux, carrying a white satin pillow with the two rings very loosely sewn on, started forward. In BRR, my mom reached into her pocket for some M&Ms.

One, two, three, four, five, I counted, then nodded at Ambrose. He said something to the two flower girls—both redheads and plentifully freckled—that made them giggle, then gave them the go-ahead. The older one began tossing rose petals carefully, as I'd demonstrated; the younger threw most of hers out in one big clump. Well, you couldn't have everything.

"Oh, my God, y'all, I'm so nervous!" Julie, the maid of honor, said loudly as the first bridesmaid and groomsman began their walk. My mother and William had christened her an SS—Spotlight Stealer—at the rehearsal dinner the night before, when her speech stretched to twenty minutes, only ending with her sobbing happy tears, reportedly much to the bride's obvious annoyance. Weddings were like truth serum, or so my mom always said. Whatever your personality, it would come out in spades. "Does anybody have a mint?" Julie said. "I'm *serious*. I need a mint!"

I was reaching into my pocket for one when Ambrose beat me to it, stepping back beside her as the next couple from the party began walking. "The flavor is cool waterfall," he told her, holding out a roll. "I find it both surprising and refreshing."

"Oh, bless you." Julie helped herself to one, popping it into her mouth, then smoothed back her hair. "Do I look okay? I'm a wreck!"

The groomsman she'd been paired with rolled his eyes. Short and stubby with a red face, he had a whiny wife, plus two small children who'd been running around like wild animals. I'd seen him taking multiple gulps from a flask during lineup, either thinking no one would notice or just not caring. There were lives you envied, I guess, and those you didn't.

"You're stunning," Ambrose told her as I walked back to where the bride, Charlotte, was standing with her father, blinking rapidly as she looked ahead at the packed church.

"Excited?" I said to her, the word we used instead of nervous. She nodded, blinking again. "You're going to do great. Remember, it's supposed to be fun!" I saw her face relax, slightly—I'd take what I could get—and then Julie's voice drifted back to us. "Oh, God, I'm next! I'm a total wreck! Does anyone have a tissue?"

Charlotte tensed right back up, a full body clench. Her dad glared. Ambrose, oblivious, gave Julie a tissue.

I looked ahead, into the church. In the back row, my mom was looking right at the bride. I had no doubt that even from a distance she was following this entire exchange solely by body cues and expressions. By the time she turned her attention to me, I was already sliding in closer to Charlotte, cupping a hand on her elbow.

"You look gorgeous," I told her. She and her dad were the only ones left now, Julie and her groomsman halfway down the aisle. "And remember, this is your day."

"I'm going to fucking kill her tomorrow," she declared through gritted teeth. Her lipstick was perfect.

"And not a soul would blame you," I replied smoothly. "Ready to get married?"

She sucked in a breath as I bent down, fluffing out the beaded train of her ivory, full-skirted dress one last time. When I stood, I saw Julie up at the front of the church, dramatically dabbing her eyes as the photographer, oblivious, moved in for the candid shot. As the organ began again, William, stealthy like a shark, moved in to say something to Julie. Then everyone stood, blocking my view.

"Wow," Ambrose said, a few minutes later, after we'd eased shut the back doors of the church, then taken our places by the side entrance where we'd wait to corral everyone post-ceremony. "That was intense. It's like coordinating an explosion."

"We might have had one, if Julie had kept talking," I told him. "In the future, remember we only use words like 'stunning' for the bride in the bride's earshot."

"Oh, sorry," he said. "She seemed like she needed some confidence."

"She's a desperate attention seeker who had no qualms about hijacking her so-called best friend's wedding," I replied. "The worst thing you can do is give someone like that attention."

"And a mint is attention?"

"If you don't offer them to the bride first."

"Do you realize you sound like a crazy person?"

Suddenly William appeared behind us, slightly out of breath from taking the outside route around the church. "Jesus, that maid of honor is a piece of work. Did you see those soap opera tears? I half expected her to swan into a faint and stop the whole ceremony."

I smiled. "What did you say to her?"

"I told her to shape up, remember who she was there for, and do her job." He shook his head, annoyed. "We're going to have to watch her at the reception. Five bucks says she inflicts bodily harm diving for the bouquet."

"I bet she's dying to get married," I mused as, up front, Charlotte and her groom took each other's hands. I couldn't see Julie at all.

"And nobody will have her because she's so obnoxious,"

William said. "Always a bridesmaid, until nobody even asks you to do *that* anymore."

I was so used to this kind of exchange, having it was like breathing. So I didn't notice until we paused that Ambrose was watching us, his expression aghast. "You guys are horrible," he said.

"Did I try to upstage a wedding just now?" I asked.

"Was I the one yelling loudly about a mint just seconds before my best friend walked down the aisle?" William said.

Ambrose just looked at us. I said, "He's got super hearing, too."

William pulled out his phone, glancing at the screen. "Your mom's reporting a loud talker. I'll be back."

I stepped back, giving him room to slip around us and down the side aisle to a row close to the front, where he slid in on the end. A beat. Then a very pointed expression to a woman in a flowered dress a few people down from him: I got quiet and I wasn't even saying anything.

"It's so weird to me," Ambrose said, as the vows began, "how you can be so cynical in this job. Aren't weddings all about hope?"

"Marriages are about hope," I said. "Weddings are pure logistics."

"Is he married?" he asked, nodding at William, who was now studying the younger flower girl as she fidgeted, tugging at the zipper of her dress.

"Nope," I said. "He's never even gotten close. The last boyfriend was the dad of one of my friends, and that was all the way back in middle school."

I had a flash of Mr. Bobkin, Elinor Bobkin's dad, newly divorced, who had met William at one of my choral performances in seventh grade. They'd dated for about three months, Mr. Bobkin had started talking about shopping for furniture together, and William fled. Since then, there'd been no one except the occasional fling, usually on vacations he took with his friends. But I only got sparse details on those, via eavesdropping, and sadly, William could always hear me coming.

"What about your mom?" Ambrose asked.

"Same way. Dateless for years, no faith in the power of love and romance." Realizing this sounded harsh even to me, I added, "Look, the wedding business jades a person. Clearly. This is only your first. By the end of the summer, you'll probably be just as bad as we are."

He was watching Charlotte as she said her vows, a smile on her face. "We? You feel that way, too?"

I shrugged. "I'm not totally cynical. But I don't believe in the fairy tale, if that's what you're asking."

"The fairy tale? What's that?"

A ripple across the crowd as the groom laughed, the priest joining in. "The idea that everything will be perfect, forever."

"Nobody really believes that, though."

"They *do*, though," I said. "These brides, they come in, with their new engagement rings all shiny on their fingers, and they want the ideal day. Flowers, food, venue, music, even napkins have to be perfect. And we do it, because that's our job and we're good at it. But the marriage: that's up to them. And it takes a lot more than putting peonies in mason jars."

Ambrose considered this as the priest spoke at the front of the church. "You know, if you really think about it, *I* should be the one who doesn't believe in all this," he said after a moment. "I've only been to three weddings, all my mother's. I was in every one of them. Each ended in divorce."

"This is the first wedding you've attended that you weren't in?"

"Yep," he replied. "It's like seeing the man behind the curtain. And that man is scary."

"Sorry," I said.

"But that's the thing," he replied. "It's okay. Because when I *do* get asked to another wedding, I won't go into it thinking about everything that can go wrong. I'll just enjoy the party and the moment."

"Good for you. I wish I could," I said.

"You can, though."

"Nope. Too late." I cleared my throat. "That ship has sailed. Once you see how things can go, you can't unknow it."

I felt him look at me, and realized this sounded harsh. But it was the truth. It took a lot to have hope in this world where so little evidence of it existed. We may all start in the same place, at a church, watching a couple begin a whole new life together. But what we glimpse beyond that is different for each of us, a funhouse mirror reflection of our own experience. Maybe if nothing bad had ever happened, you didn't even consider those clouds and storms ahead. But for the rest of us, even the brightest sunshine carried a chance of rain. It was only a matter of time.

༺ ༻

"Interloper at ten o'clock," I said to Ambrose. "Want to take this one?"

"Sure," he replied, moving over to intercept an older man making a beeline for the buffet despite our repeated reminders that we'd be going by tables. My mother hated a long, snaky line of hungry guests, but there were always the few who tried to circumvent the system. I watched, somewhat proud, as he politely redirected the man to his seat. When he flashed me a thumbs-up, though, I only nodded.

Two hours into the event, I had to admit my mom had, again, been right. He was a fast learner, with the charm that initially bugged me actually being an asset at times like this. If you're going to come between someone bold enough to jump the line and the prime rib, you have to do it with a light touch, and Ambrose had that in spades. So I'd let him do the heavy lifting while I kept the lines of people who were actually supposed to be eating moving smoothly. Half the room down, half to go. This was me being optimistic, I realized, taking note of it for once. And just like that, the universe noticed as well.

"Excuse me." I turned to see a woman in a red dress approaching, a toddler with pigtails on her hip. She was thin and angular, with black-framed glasses you just knew cost a fortune. "Have you seen my son? He's the ring bearer?"

"Ira?" I asked. She nodded, switching her daughter to her other side. "I haven't seen him since the wedding party came in."

She turned. "I thought he was with his cousins, over there at the kids' table, but they haven't seen him either. Where is he?"

I scanned the room: no sign of a kid in a tight-fitting tux. "Let me check the lobby. Maybe he went to the bathroom?"

"Not by himself," she replied, gesturing to what I assumed was her husband, a heavyset guy at the nearby bar. *Now*, she mouthed, and he started over.

"People are hungry," Ambrose said as he walked back up to me. "I just almost came to fisticuffs with a woman. She was clutching a plate and prepared to use it."

Normally I would have questioned the use of "fisticuffs"—sometimes I wondered what era Ambrose actually came from—but there was no time. "Have you seen Ira?"

"Little dude?" I nodded. "No. Why?"

"He may be missing." I said this in a low voice: the last thing we needed was unnecessary panic. "I'm going to check the lobby. You take outside."

"Ira!" the mother yelled. So much for staying calm. "Has anyone seen my son?"

I walked quickly to the lobby, Ambrose right behind me. As I turned down a nearby hallway, he headed for the outside doors. Older couple, clump of teenagers probably up to no good, staff member pushing a laundry cart. No Ira. Outside the men's bathroom, I knocked, hard, then pushed open the door. "Ira? Are you in there?"

"Who?" someone yelled back.

"A kid in a tux. Do you see him?"

A pause. "Nope. Just me, as far as I can tell."

I let the door drop, regrouping, then pulled out my phone. RING BEARER MISSING, I texted my mom and William. IN LOBBY LOOKING. Then I headed back toward the ballroom, scanning around me as I went. Outside, I could see Ambrose in the parking lot, his hands cupped to his mouth.

"Ira!" I recognized William's voice before I took a corner, almost crashing into him. He said, "Definitely not in the ballroom. Mom's starting to freak."

"Bathroom's clear. I'll go help Ambrose look outside."

"Your mom's sweeping the kitchen. I'll ask at the desk and do another pass through here."

We broke, neither of us running. Yet. As I pushed open the heavy glass doors to the parking lot, I could hear Ambrose. "Ira! Buddy! You out here?" Somewhere, a dog barked.

I heard my phone beep and grabbed it: my mom, to all of us. NO SIGN YET. ANYONE?

Shit, I thought, just as a big truck rumbled by on the street outside. Hearing a voice behind me, I swung around, but it was only a couple in formal wear, obviously late, hurrying toward the front entrance. "Ira!" I called. The dog barked again.

"He's not in this lot," Ambrose reported, jogging toward me. "I've cased the whole place. Twice."

"Mom says he's not anywhere they've checked either," I said. "This could be bad. Ira!"

Another dog bark. Ambrose turned toward the sound. "Ira!"

Bark.

"Ira!" I called. Bark.

"This way," he said, starting to walk again. I followed him, checking between cars—God forbid—as I went. My phone beeped again. MOM WANTS POLICE, William reported. Uh-oh.

"Ira!" I called again, hearing a subsequent woof as I followed Ambrose's blue shirt around some hedges to a loading bay bright with floodlights. Now I *was* running, my flats slapping the pavement. We passed a Dumpster and some smelly garbage cans before I spotted Ambrose's dog, tied to a drainpipe. Beside him was Ira, patting his back.

"Oh, my God," I said, slowing to a walk as I pulled out my phone. FOUND HIM, I texted. "Ira! What are you doing all the way out here?"

He turned, looking at us. The dog, seeing Ambrose, immediately got to his feet and began wiggling. "I saw a dog," Ira explained. "I love dogs."

"Of course you do," I replied, walking over to a nearby door and pulling it open, startling a table of people talking just on his other side. I scanned the ballroom until I found my mom, then gave her the high sign. As she started hurrying over, Ira's mom in tow, I said, "You hungry? There's mac and cheese."

Score: his eyes widened. I stuck out my hand, he took it, and I led him inside.

"Ira! Where have you been? You scared Mommy to

death!" his mom shrieked when she saw him. "Come here!"

He dropped my hand. "I want mac and cheese," he announced as he started over to her.

My mom, smiling calmly at the onlooking table as she passed them, said to me, "What happened? If we'd had to call the police I never would have lived it down. Can you imagine?"

"He just wandered out this door," I said, pulling it shut behind me so she wouldn't see the dog. "Next time we'll know to keep an eye on it if there are kids here."

"Next time I'll keep the ring bearer on a leash," she grumbled, then looked at her phone. "William is reporting everyone's going rogue at the buffet. He needs muscle."

"I'm on it," I said.

"No, you found the lost child." She squared her shoulders, readjusting the diamond pendant she always wore to the center of her neck. "Take five minutes. Then go find the caterer to talk cake cutting."

"Okay."

She squeezed my arm, then started over to the buffet line, which had indeed become snaky and fidgeting in our absence. I opened the door again, slipping out into the loading bay. Ambrose was crouched down in front of the dog, scratching his ears. "Who's a hero? That's right, *you* are! Good boy!"

I could see a cloud of wiry hair coming off the dog, rising into the light behind him. "I thought you and I just saved the day."

He glanced back at me. "Because Ira here told us where to look. You heard that bark! It was like breadcrumbs through the forest."

Of course it was. "You're calling him Ira now?"

"It's his name." He was still scratching, the cloud of hair growing wider. How could a dog shed so much and not be bald? "That was his way of telling us."

"The barking," I said, clarifying.

"Yep."

"Ira!" I called out. The dog didn't even look at me, much less bark. I looked at Ambrose.

"Do you always answer to *your* name?" he asked.

I sighed. Even without the drama of a lost child, this wedding felt longer than others. "I have to go deal with the cake. Are you coming?"

I started back around the building, having decided to take the long way for some extra fresh air. A moment later, he fell into step beside me, brushing his hands against each other. "I have to hand it to you. This job is harder than it looks."

"What did it look like?"

"Standing around while being bossy," he replied. I raised my eyebrows. "Louna. You literally *dragged* me into my mother's ceremony by one arm."

"You were holding up the schedule," I replied, hating how prim I sounded.

"My point is, there's a lot behind the scenes the layman or guest would never know about. Like a secret world."

I rolled my eyes. "You make it sound magical."

"You don't think it is?"

"I think it's work," I replied.

"*Magical* work." He laughed at the face I made, hearing this, then added, "You know, you can act the part all you want. But my take on you is you're not as cynical as you make yourself out to be."

"You have a take on me now?"

"I have a take on everyone. I'm an observer, a witness."

"Usually those people listen more than they talk," I pointed out.

"Maybe." He slipped his hands into his pockets, shaking that curl out of his eyes. "My point is, I've been around you a lot the last few days and I've seen things."

"Well," I said. "That doesn't sound ominous at all."

"A cynic," he continued, ignoring this, "would not have looked as relieved as you did when we found Ira. Also, a cynic would have made sure the boss knew whose dog caused the lost child to wander off in the first place. You, instead, covered for me and Ira, the dog."

"I think you're confusing a cynic with an asshole," I told him.

"Maybe. But I saw how you reacted, both times. You're not that hardened yet, even if you prefer to think otherwise."

A car drove around us, the bass thumping. I said, "The key word is *yet*."

"It is," he agreed. "Because you still have a choice in the matter."

"Or it's only a matter of time," I countered.

"Okay, *now* you sound like a cynic." He tipped his head back, looking up at the stars overhead. "But you're not fooling me. I know what I saw."

To this I said nothing. What was the point? It wasn't like I was proud of my hard little rock of a heart. Everyone's life shapes them in their own unique way. No one could really understand how the events of the last year, highs and lows, had honed me into what I now was, sharper in places, more calloused in others. And of course I'd been worried about a lost child. I wasn't a monster. Yet.

We were back at the front doors to the club now, where a large party was exiting the reception, cigars in hand. As we approached, two men, suits rumpled and cheeks rosy, opened a door for us at the same time. In reply, Ambrose spread his arms, clearly loving an entrance. Before he stepped in, though, he turned his head, cupping a hand to his mouth.

"Ira!" he called out. Of course, the dog barked.

❦

"Call me crazy," my mom said, loosening the strap of one of her shoes. "But I'm thinking they might go the distance."

"Natalie Barrett." William gave her a warning look. "Don't you dare tell me you've become an optimist. I don't think I can take it."

"Never," she replied, as he topped off both their glasses, then dropped the bottle with a clank back into the ice bucket. "I just got that sense. They don't seem like the divorce type."

"Which is the same as being married happily, yes?"

My mom considered this as she took a sip of her drink.

"I don't think it's that simple. There's a whole spectrum between those two, at least in my experience. Like all the variations of gray."

William didn't seem to buy it, even before he said, "Gray is gray, as far as I'm concerned."

"I disagree." She eased the other strap, wincing as she did so. "I remember being so unhappy at times in my own marriage, for various reasons. And yet the thought of it ending, of choosing to do that . . . I never would have even thought of it. And if I had, I'm sure I would have considered it the much worse option."

"Worse than being unhappy?"

"Well, yes," she replied. "Like, in a marriage, it's not just whether you see the glass as half-full or half-empty. It's whether you see it those two ways, or any of the other endless fractions that are possible."

William winced. "This conversation is making my head hurt. I give them six years. And she leaves, for someone else. Three kids."

My mom leaned her head to the side, considering this. "I don't know. What do you think, Louna?"

I blinked, not having expected to be asked to weigh in. This was their game, not mine, even though I had seen Charlotte and her groom laughing happily as they climbed into the car to leave together. For them, and her in particular . . . I wished they'd always put each other first. Out loud, though, I said, "I have no idea."

"Smart girl." William raised his glass at me. "She who doesn't gamble can never lose."

"Or win," my mom pointed out.

"Details," he replied, and they both laughed, then clinked glasses.

I felt a yawn coming on and reached up, covering my mouth, wishing we could just go ahead and do our final sweep so we, too, could head home. Before that would happen, though, I had to collect all the vases we'd rented from the tables, and I wasn't about to do it alone. Ambrose, however, was nowhere in sight.

Just as I thought this, I heard voices from over by the back door where Ira had escaped. When I turned, there Ambrose was with, of all people, Julie the annoying maid of honor. She was holding her shoes in one hand, the thrown bouquet—which, as William predicted, she'd dived for with vigor—in the other. As Ambrose said something to her, she tipped her head back and laughed again, putting a hand on his arm.

There's something messy about people at the end of weddings. Clothes, once pressed, are rumpled and creased. Hair escapes from chignons and gets wild from dancing. Makeup runs, as do stockings and tights, and women almost always shed their shoes, men their jackets. There's nothing neat about that feeling when the finiteness of the event hits and you're suddenly more aware than ever that tomorrow is just another regular day. Maybe this was what made people drag out the night, stretching the time left a little longer. I understood it: I'd done it. But we were working here, not attending. Ambrose could get messy off the clock. I wanted to go home.

"Hey," I called out, and they both looked over at me. "Let's grab these vases so we can start getting out of here."

"Sure thing, boss," he replied. "Be there in five seconds."

The boss thing was new, since an incident earlier when I'd told him that no, he *couldn't* accept when one of the bridesmaids asked him to dance. I assumed he'd known this already, having extended the same offer to me at his own mother's wedding. My assumptions were always wrong when it came to Ambrose.

"No *dancing?*" he said, once I'd told him to decline. Still, I could feel the bridesmaid, ever hopeful, hovering behind me. "Aren't we here to make sure the party is perfect?"

"You really think that much of your conga skills?"

"Well, no," he replied, although clearly, he did. "But a good wedding is at least ninety-five percent based on a great dance floor experience. I can help with that."

In the business less than a week and he was quoting statistics. Made-up ones, but statistics. "We're not here to enjoy the party. We're here to make sure everyone else does."

"What if their enjoyment could be enhanced by us contributing our own?"

"It doesn't work that way," I said, as a girl in her late twenties, wearing a pink dress, began crossing the floor in his direction, that telltale look on her face. What was he, a dancing magnet? "Just politely say no, tell them you're working, and move off the dance floor. If you're not here, you can't be asked."

He pointed at me. "That's my motto in general when it comes to dancing. You have to put yourself out there!" I looked at his finger. He lowered it, slowly. "I mean, unless you're working. Sorry, boss."

"I'm not your boss," I grumbled, starting toward the buffet line. When I looked back, he was shaking his head, smiling, as the girl in pink tried to lead him farther into the shifting crowd. When he backed away, she made a sad face, then mimed wiping a tear. Jesus.

Just recalling this was making me even crankier, so I got to my feet, collecting the vase from the table where I'd been sitting, then the one next to it. I was all set to snap at Ambrose as he finally did come over, but then I saw he was carrying three others, one in each hand and another pressed to his chest. "Where should I pour these out?" he asked.

"Just put them in the crate for now and we'll do it outside," I said. I always hated a wedding when we had to collect equipment after the fact, preferring the ones my mom called Zero Footprint, where we just left it all for the venue to deal with. As I picked up another vase, I saw Julie crossing the room, shoes now on, the bouquet dangling down beside her. "What was she saying to you?"

"Who?" I nodded at her. "Jules? Nothing much. Just wondering where an out of towner could grab a martini at this late hour. I told her I knew just the place."

"You're going out with her tonight?"

"It's just a drink. And a ride for me and Ira, which is a good thing. Our dogs are tired."

Ha-ha, I thought as I walked over to the wooden rack we'd stored under the cake table and slid the vases into them. The flowers, white roses mixed with those peonies

I'd caved on, had held up well, still perky as they bobbed in their water.

"So what happens to these now?" Ambrose asked, as he added his vases to the rack.

"The flowers?" I asked. "Usually we toss them."

"Really? Seems wasteful."

"Maybe," I said. "But after picking them up, arranging them, putting them out on tables, and then collecting them back up, I feel like our relationship has run its full course."

I could feel him watching me as I slid another vase in, a few petals falling off one rose as I did so. "Do you look at everything in terms of coupling and uncoupling?"

I shrugged, getting to my feet again. "Unavoidable effect of the business, I guess. Grab those across the room, will you? I'll get this side."

"You got it, boss." This time, I didn't have the energy to correct him.

"I need to hit the bathroom, so I'll take final sweep," William called out as he and my mom, ritual completed, got up from their chairs. "What's left besides that and vases?"

"Cake top from the fridge," my mom told him. "Charlotte's mom is supposed to come by the office for it first thing Monday."

"And then we're done," he replied, holding up a hand. She slapped him five—the champagne was showing—and they headed in their separate directions as Ambrose and I finished filling the rack and carried it outside to the van. There, in the glare of a parking lot light, we dumped the water out of the vases one by one, putting the flowers on the curb beside. By the time we were done, all I could smell were roses.

"So long, fellas," Ambrose told the blooms, a solemn look on his face. "It's not you, it's us."

I rolled my eyes but didn't say anything, instead focusing on getting the rack secured for the trip back to the office. By the time William and my mom came out, I'd slipped my feet out of the backs of my own shoes, feeling ever closer to the night's end and my own barefoot drive home.

"Good job, team," my mom said as she pulled her keys out of her purse. "Kudos to Ambrose and Louna in particular for finding a wayward child."

"Thank you, ma'am," he replied, giving her a salute. "It was the least I could do for the company."

William laughed. "I like this kid. So dedicated!"

The child wouldn't have been lost if it wasn't for his dog, I wanted to say. I didn't.

"Monday," my mom continued, "we turn our full attention to the Elinor Lin Wedding. It's a double hander, with a very detail-oriented bride. So rest up."

With that, William climbed into the van, taking off his suit jacket, while my mom headed to her car. I reached back, taking down the bun I always wore when working, then ran a hand through my hair as I dug for my own keys. When I looked up, Ambrose was getting to his feet, a bunch of the discarded blooms in his arms. He'd wrapped them with a crumpled program, fashioning a huge, trailing bouquet, which he held out to me.

"Oh," I said, suddenly feeling bad about how short I'd been with him all night. Not that it was exactly proper to give a co-worker flowers, but still, a nice gesture. "You shouldn't—"

"No?" He looked down at them. "You said you were throwing them out, so I thought it was okay if I took them."

I heard footsteps, and then Julie stepped out from behind the next row of cars. "Ambrose? You ready to go get that drink?"

He was still looking at me. "Of course," I told him. "It's fine."

"See you Monday, Louna," he said, then started over to her, holding the flowers out in greeting. Taking them, she ducked her head down to breathe in the scent, and I thought of her waiting for the bride to throw the bouquet earlier, how she'd gone into a crouch, eyes sharp, determined to be the lucky one. It was so calculated, so different from this, unexpected in that way only weddings could be.

"See you," I replied, not that either of them heard me as they started toward the loading bay, I assumed to collect Ira. I waited until they were out of sight before I walked back to the curb, where all the blossoms still lay, petals around them. I picked up one peony and a rose, then thought better and left them where they were. There's a difference between things given and those you simply find. Julie knew it, and I did, too. I never expected anything from anyone. Which was not the same thing as not wanting, ever, to be surprised.

"WHICH IS which?" I asked, squinting into the dark pan.

"Does it matter? Just dig in."

I looked at Ethan as he poked his own fork into what I thought was the slice of blueberry crumble, scooping out a huge bite. "You can't just jam them all together and make some hybrid. We got six flavors. Each needs to be tasted individually."

"Lulu," he said. "It's one thirty in the morning and we're sitting in the dark. Just eat."

I had a nickname now, something else I'd never experienced before. The numbers in that category just kept growing. And yet, I was clearly the same Louna, compelled to add, "That man clearly takes his pies seriously. The way he advised us you would have thought we were buying a car. Or life insurance."

"But we weren't. Here." The next thing I knew, his fork was up against my lips, and I smelled custard. "This one's some kind of fruity mush. It's good."

I took the bite, messily. "That's the lemon-orange crumb."

This I remembered specifically, because it had sounded

so good. Once inside the coffee shop, we discovered the
owner, a guy in an EAT SLEEP FISH baseball hat, was closing up. At the register, a dark-haired boy and his girlfriend,
clearly regulars, were getting one last hit of caffeine to go.

"Anywhere else close by to eat at this hour?" Ethan asked
them as they paid up.

The girl, wearing shorts and a T-shirt that said CLEM-
ENTINE'S, looked at the boy. "World of Waffles, but it's not
exactly walking distance. Or there's the Wheelhouse."

"No," the guy said flatly. "The coffee there tastes like
burnt towels."

"There's a twenty-four-hour café at the Big Club," she
suggested. "Lousy coffee, but great people-watching."

"Auden," the guy said. "Are you *trying* to give terrible
suggestions?"

"At least *I'm* suggesting," she replied. To us she said,
"Look, this place is as good as it gets even in daylight hours.
Your best bet is to take some pie and drinks to go."

"Please do," said the guy behind the counter. "I'll even
give you a deal. Pie is never as good the second day."

Choosing had taken time with so many selections, all
looking delicious, and the owner walking us through the
particulars of each. In the end, we'd left with two large coffees, a pie pan filled with one of just about everything, and
two forks. The slices looked gorgeous in the case. In the dark,
though, it was all about the taste.

"Oh, man." Ethan sat back, whistling between his teeth,
then pointed at the pan. "This one, on the right, is IT. Chocolate and crunchy. And maybe orange?"

I reached across him with my own utensil, taking some. "Pot de crème and mandarin. He said that one was his favorite."

Ethan helped himself to another huge forkful. As he moved it toward his mouth, a mandarin slipped off, landing on my arm with a splat. "Whoops. Sorry."

"Look at you," I said, as he picked it up, still chewing. There was a spot of chocolate on his nose. "You're a mess."

"Try to catch this," he said, rearing back with the segment. I opened my mouth. He threw it, going wide, and hit my ear. "Bad throw. Sorry."

"Give me that," I said, taking the pie plate. I dug out another mandarin, pinching it between my fingers, and he set down his fork, readying himself, mouth open. I started laughing even before I launched it, sending it sailing over his head.

He turned, watching it hit the sand. "Well, if you were aiming for the water, I'd call that close."

"I was," I said, and then he smiled at me and reached out, pulling me in for a kiss. He tasted like chocolate, and as a breeze blew over us, swirling up sand, I closed my eyes tightly, thinking no, now I wanted to stay in *this* moment, forever.

This was weird, I knew, as I'd only met him a few hours ago. But with our walk, the dance, all the talking, and now pie, Ethan was already familiar in his quirks and tells. The way he squinted, tightly, before saying something he felt strongly. The slow lope of his big, tall guy walk. The feeling of his class ring, cold and smooth, against my fingers when he took my hand. The trill of his ringtone, a pop song so unexpected that the first time I'd heard it, I'd had to laugh.

We'd been sitting in the sand, sharing pictures on our phones. I showed him Jilly, my mom and William, and the one picture of myself I actually liked, which had been taken under a gazebo at a wedding the previous spring. In turn, I got to see him with the guys he'd been friends with since preschool, posing shirtless, all of their hair wet and cow-licked, by a backyard swimming pool. I'd just been leaning in closer to examine a shot of him on the soccer field when the phone rang, the tone a clip of a girl singing over a bouncy, fizzy beat.

"What is that?" I said, laughing as he scrambled to si-lence it.

"Don't do it," he said, holding up a hand. "Do *not* mock. You don't know the whole story."

I waited.

"If you must know," he said, looking down at the phone, "it's Lexi Navigator."

"Seriously?" All I knew about Lexi Navigator, a teenage singer with a statuesque build and a huge amount of dark hair, were the skimpy outfits and plentiful feathers and body glitter that were her trademark. She was the kind of enter-tainer defined by the fact that I could name at least three of her outlandish getups off the top of my head, but not *one* of her songs. "I would not have guessed that."

"I said don't mock," he reminded me.

"Then tell me the story."

A sigh. Then he squinted. "Okay. So, it's the beginning of

junior year and my buddy Sam's dad, who's an entertainment lawyer, gets this block of tickets to a Lexi Navigator show. We're not doing anything, and it's the whole VIP thing: limo, backstage passes, all that. So we go."

"No girls? Just you?"

"What, six guys can't hit up a Lexi Navigator show in the name of male bonding? You gotta live, right?" I bit my lip, trying not to laugh. "So the seats are, like, third row. We're all just laughing, making fun of the opening act, having fun. Then she comes out, and there's fireworks and confetti and she's in this dress that shoots lasers, wearing a wire basket on her head . . ."

"Wait, a wire basket?"

He shrugged. "That's what it looked like. And the show is crazy, right? All these greased-up dancers, balloons falling, little girls screaming all around us. Then, about halfway through, she goes into this more mellow part, brings down the lights, puts a stool on the stage, takes a seat."

"Still wearing the basket?"

"No, by then she'd changed, like, ten times. She had on, like, a crown of snakes and a bikini tuxedo."

"Of course she did."

"So she starts talking about the next song," he continued, "and how it was inspired by her grandmother dying the year before. And then she starts singing, and about a verse in, she's crying."

"Really."

"Yup." He squinted. "And we're all sitting there, only a

few feet away, and I can see the tears and they're real, and suddenly I start thinking about my grandmother."

"Your grandmother's passed, too?"

"No, she's fine. Healthy as a horse. Which is what makes this all so stupid." He sighed. "So I'm watching, and she's crying, and I'm thinking about Nana, and you know, maybe I get a little emotional myself."

I waited a second. Then I said, "Maybe?"

"I did." He coughed. "And, unfortunately, it was seen. And documented by my buddies."

I reached over, taking his hand again. "Oh, dear."

"Exactly." He folded his fingers through mine. "And of course they won't let it go, even when she changes into a mermaid costume with a real flipper. They're threatening to post it everywhere, immediately, and I just want to die. And kill them. Or kill them, and then die."

I laughed. "That seems kind of extreme."

"You don't know my guys," he said. "We've been mocking each other since we were in diapers. It's like an art form. I'm never going to live this down."

"So what did you do?"

"We have this thing called striking a deal," he said, rubbing his free hand over his face. "Like an exchange program for embarrassment. You pick one to trump another. I was willing to do just about anything."

"Obviously."

"So," he continued, "I agreed to have a Lexi Navigator song as my ringtone until graduation. And if anyone asks about it—and of course, they do—I have to tell them I'm her number one fan and show this picture."

With that, he turned on his phone again, typing in a passcode. A few swipes and there it was: Ethan, in a BROWN-WOOD LACROSSE T-shirt, next to Lexi Navigator, who was wearing a red leather bodysuit and devil horns, her face covered in glitter. You gotta live, indeed.

"And this is better than the world knowing you cried at her song?" I said, clarifying.

"Of course it is!" he said. "This way I just look quirky. With the tears, possibly mentally unstable."

"You sure about that?" I asked, looking at the picture again.

He made a face. "Anyway, the deal is this: if I ever *don't* answer by saying I'm a big fan and showing the picture and they hear about it, they'll post the video and kill me with shame. We shook on it."

I raised my eyebrows. "And these are your friends?"

He flipped to the next picture, of all of them around Lexi Navigator. "My best friends. Believe it or not."

"I believe it," I said, leaning against him as he moved to another picture of their group, this time in the limo. All cute, athletic boys, clean-cut and grinning. Jilly would have been in heaven. "But I have a question."

"She smelled great," he said. "Everyone asks that."

"Not my question," I replied.

"Oh. Sorry."

"The deal is you have to say you heart Lexi and show the picture when people ask about the ringtone, correct?"

"Yup. Until graduation."

"But when I asked," I continued, "you told me the real story. Why?"

He put the pie pan aside and turned to face me, now wrapping both of his hands around mine. "Lulu. I'm pretty much having the best night of my life. Why would I tell you anything but the truth?"

I felt my face get warm, hearing this. It wasn't the nickname, or the assurance that I wasn't the only one who felt this night was special, although I'd turn over these things again and again later, remembering. Instead, it was this last question, the inverse of how I knew I, myself, felt concerning just about everyone else in the world. For safety's sake, we learn to be less honest at the beginnings of things, not more. But Ethan was different. With him and me, it was always about the truth. Why would I tell you anything but? It was the closest thing to "I love you" a boy had ever said to me. Maybe it meant even more.

CHAPTER

11

IF YOU'D asked me, it was only a matter of time before something like this happened. But of course, nobody had asked me.

"Is Ambrose here?"

I looked up from my laptop, where I'd been studying the seating arrangements for that weekend's wedding. A pretty girl in shorts and a button-down shirt, her red hair pulled back in a headband, was standing just inside the main door of the office, a picnic basket over one arm.

"Um," I said, looking toward the back room. He wasn't there; he'd left a few minutes earlier with another girl, whom he'd introduced to me as Hajar. "He's actually at lunch."

"Oh." Her disappointment was immediate and obvious. "Do you know where he went?"

I shook my head. "Sorry."

She twisted her mouth, either pouting or thinking or both. Then she set the basket down, pulling out her phone, and quickly typed in a message. A moment later, I heard a ping. "Oh," she said. "He says he's in a meeting?"

The fact this was phrased as a question suggested I was

supposed to dispute it, or at least give an answer. Instead, I just shrugged, smiling, and went back to my tables.

I heard her type something else. Then she said, "Well, I guess you can do sandwiches for dinner, too, right?"

I was not sure why I was still involved in this exchange. Glancing up, I saw she was watching me, again expecting a response. "Guess so."

At this, she smiled, like I'd said much more than these two words. "Okay if I leave a quick note?" she asked, picking up a Natalie Barrett Weddings pad from the table between us. This time she didn't wait for an answer. She just started writing.

Too many tables at this wedding, I thought to myself as I went back to my work. At least it was a sit-down dinner, so we wouldn't be directing traffic at a buffet.

"If you could give this to him," the girl said, forcing me to look up *again*, "that would be great." She was holding out a piece of paper, folded into a neat square.

I put it on the table, above my own papers. "Sure thing."

"Thanks so much!" A clink, then a creak, as she hoisted the basket again and started for the door. Once outside, she slid on a pair of sunglasses before walking away.

I filled in another table with names, all the while aware of the folded note nearby, AMBROSE written on the top in a curling, girlish hand. I had the oddest urge to open and read it, although I had no idea why. His love life was none of my business or concern. But it was annoying to have to run interference for him while he was off having lunch and I was still working.

That said, I had to admit (but would not have aloud, not to anyone) that having Ambrose as a co-worker wasn't actually all that bad. Sure, there was his tendency to break things—a stapler and tape measure had suffered the same fate as the tape dispenser in his short employ—as well as the constant chatter that now filled the time I used to spend organizing place cards in silence. But in truth, he *was* funny, and I often had to bite back my own laughs as he prattled on about his various misadventures while we sat working side by side. Like, perhaps, scheduling two lunches at once. I couldn't wait to hear about that one.

About twenty minutes later, stomach grumbling, I took my own break, walking over to the coffee shop for an egg salad bagel. The line was long, and I ended up back by Phone Lady, who was set up at the window counter.

". . . so I said, you don't have to tell *me* about health concerns," she was saying, her voice carrying as always. "I'm a cancer survivor! Four squamous cells in two years scraped off my shoulders and back. And I still managed to pay my rent and bills."

A pause, but a short one. Whoever Phone Lady was always talking to, they never seemed to get much of a word in.

"I never wanted a tenant anyway. We renovated that garage apartment for Martin, so he'd have a place for his pinball machines and model trains. That's how good I was to him! And you know how that turned out."

Ahead of me, a woman in a black business suit, an ID badge of some sort clipped to her jacket, exhaled loudly. I wanted to tell her to save her breath. I'd heard people outright tell Phone Lady to hush and she barely batted an eye.

"I know my rights as a landlord," she continued now. "And I'm not afraid to evict, no sir. But it's just so unfortunate. I thought having someone in that apartment would be a good thing. Just my luck. I don't get good things, I guess."

Hearing this, I craned my neck to see how many people were still ahead of me. I could handle Phone Lady's complaining, her detailed stories of the slights of co-workers and relatives, even the long-winded stories about her cats' health issues. But the sad stuff and self-pity just wasn't worth an egg salad sandwich to me. I had enough of that in my own head.

Luckily, the businesswoman and guy behind her had simple orders, so soon enough I was on my way. As I pushed out the door, holding it for a man carrying a baby, Phone Lady was saying something about having joined a dating website. *Better him than me*, I thought. The stories just went on and on, whether or not anyone was there to listen.

I'd planned to bring my food back to the office to eat. On my way, though, I saw Ira, tied up by a bench in a shady spot right next to the stationery store, a blue bandana around his neck. Clearly, Ambrose had discovered that the couple that owned the store, Emily and Florence, were huge animal lovers. I was actually surprised he wasn't already just hanging out inside. When Ira saw me, he sat up, wagging his tail.

"Hey, bud," I said. He responded by wiggling harder, his front end now joining in, going the opposite direction. "You thirsty?"

He wasn't. His water bowl, a custom job with his name on

it—something I just *knew* a girl had purchased for Ambrose—
was full. Still, when I took a seat and untwisted my own bottle, I poured a bit in, topping him off. Obligingly, he drank.
Then, after sniffing at my sandwich from a distance, his long
whiskers twitching, he turned in a circle and lay at my feet,
his head on my shoe. Again, I was not a dog person. Or an
animal person. But it seemed rude to move, so I didn't.

A moment later, my phone rang. Even without the caller
ID I would have known it was Jilly, based only on the noise
in the background—children's voices, engaged in some sort
of argument, a baby wailing. "Hello?" I said.

"Hang on," she replied. Then: "Everyone HUSH I am on
the PHONE or NO ICE CREAM for ANYONE."

The noise volume dropped noticeably, although I could
still hear Bean, sputtering.

"Hey," Jilly said to me. "What are you doing?"

When I heard from Jilly while she was in the throes
of sibling caregiver duty and I was doing something alone,
peacefully, I was always self-conscious about it. "Working," I
said. "And eating lunch. What's up?"

The phone was pierced by a bloodcurdling shriek, which
she ignored, saying, "Oh, the regular. Shuttling between food
trucks and lessons, play dates and diaper changes."

"You just passed the ice cream place," I heard Crawford
say in his flat monotone.

"Shit," she said. The girls howled in protest, saying something about bad words. "Oh, like you haven't heard it before.
And there are other ice cream places."

"Not like that one." Crawford again.

you please shut up for one second and let me talk to
she snapped. Silence. Temporarily. "Okay, quickly: I
left it with Devon that we'd meet him and his buddy tonight
at À la Carte for dinner at seven thirty."

"Devon?" I asked. "Who's that?"

"The mock UN guy I met at the student government convention. I told you." She hadn't. But Jilly was always talking to different guys, so I wasn't exactly shocked that one
had slipped her mind. "Remember? They're civilized dinner
people. He had on a sport jacket!"

Which was the equivalent of her kryptonite. But not
mine, and I hadn't agreed to anything even resembling this.
"Jilly. I don't want to have dinner with strangers."

"And you don't want to go dancing with strangers. Or
go to a party with strangers. You don't want to do anything
with anyone."

"How did we go from strangers to anyone?"

"Everyone will be a stranger as long as you insist on never
meeting people! What happened to making memories?"

I sighed, looking down at Ira, who was drooling on the
pavement beside my foot. "Why do all our memories have to
involve people I don't know?"

"Because," she said, as Bean hollered again, "this is the
summer for you to get used to meeting guys again. You have
to get these first few bumpy awful dates out of the way.
Swine before pearls, and all that."

"And when, exactly, will the pearls arrive?"

"In the fall at college, probably. But if you've already done this, the awkward hard part, meeting them will be easier."

"So you're saying I should head into dinner tonight expecting disaster."

"Well, that's a bit strong. More likely a lack of chemistry, or just boredom. But just consider the numbers. With Ethan, you hit the lottery your first shot. It takes a few tries, just based on odds, before you can expect to win again."

This was just the kind of twisted Jilly logic that always sucked me in, the type that sounded outright crazy . . . until it didn't. "Fine," I said. "Have you seen the guy I'm supposed to be paired up with, or is he purely a theoretical?"

"I have actually laid eyes on him. His name is Tyler. He had on a sport coat, too, for what it's worth."

Which was nothing, as I saw enough formal wear. In my mind, though, I pictured rolling dice, slowly warming to the idea of aiming to gather losses rather than worrying about winning. If I really was cynical girl, then this was *my* kryptonite. "Okay. I'll see you at seven thirty."

"All *right!*" she crowed, and I heard her beep the horn as punctuation. "That's my girl. I gotta go. Love ya!"

"Love ya back," I replied, although I was pretty sure she didn't hear me. As I put down my phone, I had a flash of the jughead guy at the party: in her thinking, strike one. How many more before I'd earned a decent hit? I guessed I would find out.

Just as I thought this, I saw the girl with the picnic basket coming back across the courtyard. At the exact same time— how was this possible?—Ambrose and Hajar were approaching via the opposite entrance. They were holding hands, each of them carrying a cup from Lotus Sushi. Ira and I were in the middle, the dead center point where these two parties would collide. I felt my stomach clench. Ira started barking.

"Ira!" Ambrose called out, seeing only the dog. Ira barked again, excited, while I made a point of looking directly at the girl with the basket, willing Ambrose to follow my gaze. Finally he did, suddenly slowing his pace, as if he could put off this confrontation with space alone. Nope.

"Ambrose?" I heard basket girl say, from my left-hand side.

"Jenna!" he replied, from my right. Beside him, Hajar, in a red maxi dress and sandals, gave a tentative smile. "You're here!"

"I brought you lunch," she said, not smiling at all. "Like we discussed last night?"

Now Hajar's face changed. She looked at Ambrose. "I thought you stayed in last night."

"I did," he said quickly. Jenna put a hand on her hip, physically contesting this. "With Jenna. Actually."

Now everyone looked tense. Except for Ira, who was wagging away, trying to get to Ambrose.

"I'm going back to work," I said delicately, moving to step around the dog.

"I should, too," Ambrose said immediately. "The boss is a real bear about lunch breaks."

He wasn't getting away that easily, though. "Were you really with this girl last night?" asked Hajar as I slipped past her. Ira, having no luck with Ambrose, tried to follow, his nose bumping my leg. "You lied to me?"

"I didn't lie," he said. "The plan was to hang at her house and watch a movie. And—"

"He stayed until three a.m.," Jenna finished. "Him *and* his dog."

Hajar looked at Jenna. "Well, did he tell *you* we were together this weekend? He went out to eat with my entire family."

Clearly, this was news to Jenna, who responded with, "So you'd already done that when we met on Monday at the movie theater?"

I was clear of this threesome now, free to go. I felt bad for Ira, though, his stretched-out leash still tangled around one of Jenna's ankles, looking from the girls back to Ambrose like a confused child.

"Monday?" Hajar demanded. "You said you had to stay home with your sister."

"Who then decided she wanted to go to a movie," Ambrose said quickly. Glares at him from both directions. "Ladies, I *did* go to the movies Monday and I stayed in last night. I haven't been untruthful to anyone here."

"Oh, so you don't lie," Jenna said. "You just don't tell the whole truth."

"Is there a difference?" Hajar asked.

"Well, if we're splitting hairs," Ambrose said, "then yes. It's vast, actually."

"Vast?" Jenna repeated, whether because she didn't get the sentiment or the word itself, I wasn't sure. Hajar, over the semantics, just loosened the top of her drink and threw the contents at Ambrose, then walked away.

Whoa, I thought as Ira dove for the ice cubes. Jenna unwound his leash from her foot, then shifted the basket to the other arm.

"Well," Ambrose said, rather magnanimously, smiling at her, "and then there were two."

"You're an asshole," she replied. Then she walked away as well.

In the silence that followed, I wished more than ever that I'd abandoned this scene when I had the chance. I was embarrassed enough; I couldn't imagine how Ambrose felt. But as he crouched down in front of Ira, shirt stained wet with cola, and scratched his ears, he appeared largely unaffected, as if this kind of thing happened all the time.

"She left you a note," I told him, just to say something. "Jenna. Before, when she came by."

"Oh, thanks." He stood again, then checked Ira's bowl. "But I'm pretty sure whatever it says no longer pertains."

I nodded, then started toward the office. A moment later, he fell into step behind me. I said, "Can I ask you something?"

"Sure." So agreeable. I was beginning to think this *was* a regular occurrence.

"Why do you do that?"

"Do what?"

I stopped and faced him, shielding my eyes with one hand. "Juggle two girls at once. It clearly won't work, at least not for long. And you can't *enjoy* getting busted."

"Well," he replied, "I don't consider it busted. I didn't lie to anyone, nor did I make any promises about exclusivity."

"But it was clearly assumed."

"That's on them, not me." I cocked my head to the side, making it clear I doubted this logic. "Look, I like hanging out with girls, plural. Commitment doesn't really work for me."

"Maybe because you're always hanging out with girls, plural?" I suggested.

"No," he countered, "because it's too serious. Everything gets, like, heavy, immediately. And all the questions: Where are you going? Who with? When will you be back? Why haven't you called? What's that glitter in your hair?"

"Glitter?"

He sighed. "Let me put it this way. You know that feeling, when you very first meet someone and there's a spark, that undeniable attraction, and everything about them seems new and interesting and perfect?"

A boy on a beach, his hand outstretched. White shirt billowing in the dark. "Yeah," I said. "Sure."

"It's the best, right? Like magic, that awesome." I nodded. "So why, if you could, wouldn't you want that *all* the time, every time?"

"Because," I said, then realized immediately this was not an answer. I swallowed, taking a breath. "Then you only have beginnings, over and over again. Nothing substantial."

"But substantial is complicated. *Substantial*," he said, pointing at me, "is questions about glitter in your hair, or why you won't tag along shopping, or whether you find her friends annoying."

"So you don't want anything that lasts," I said, clarifying. "Only a bunch of magical first nights and days, strung along one right after the other."

He smiled. "Doesn't sound bad, does it? All the upsides of dating, none of the down."

"Except when you get a drink thrown at you," I pointed out.

He shrugged. "Shirts can be washed."

We started walking again: it had been over an hour for each of us, and while my mom wasn't exactly a bear, she would notice.

"Let me guess," he said. "You think I'm terrible."

"Not necessarily. It's just . . . not my way, I guess." I thought for a second. "What's funny is that Jilly was just saying, basically, that I need to be more *like* you."

"Really?" I nodded. "How so?"

I paused, wondering how exactly to say this, what I wanted to reveal. "My last relationship—my boyfriend—it was basically all one perfect early beginning. We met at the beach, clicked immediately, spent a whole night talking. Then we were long distance, so there was never a chance of anything getting old."

He was quiet, listening to this. "Sounds nice."

"It was." I swallowed again. "Anyway, I haven't dated since. I haven't wanted to. And she maintains it's because my expectations were set so high, right off the bat. Like no one will ever compete."

"Do you think that?"

"I don't know," I said. This was the truth. "But maybe going into things hoping they will is the wrong approach. Like, if I date someone expecting nothing, I'd be better off."

"I don't expect nothing of the person," he corrected me. "Just the relationship."

"You're just having fun, though," I said. "No ties. No forever."

"Ugh, no." He winced. "And who wants to be tied?"

"I didn't mind it with my boyfriend," I said. "Which is exactly why your way wouldn't work for me."

He considered this. "Sure it would. You just have to do it."

"Oh, right," I said. "Because it would be that easy for *you* to change your ways, totally."

"I could," he said, confident.

"Ambrose. You're seriously saying that it would be no problem at all for you to decide to date only one person, with an eye toward the long term, starting right now."

"Yeah, if I wanted to. Easily."

We were at the office door now. Through the glass, I could see my mom and William at the conference table, that week's bride, Elinor Lin, between them. She was smart and gorgeous and had already had a dramatic, vocal meltdown about napkin holders. It was mid-June of my last summer doing this job. If I couldn't sell cucumbers or sling coffee, maybe there was another way to endure.

"Want to bet on it?" I asked Ambrose.

He raised an eyebrow. "I'm listening."

"What about this," I said. "For a set period, I agree to date the way you do, multiple people, no commitment. At the same time, you find one girl and see her exclusively. We see who bows out first."

"Oh, it'll be you," he said confidently.

"We haven't even set the stakes," I said, offended.

"I'm very competitive," he explained. "Okay, specifics. What's the time period?"

"Three weeks?" I wasn't totally sure, but I thought I saw him waver. "What, too long?"

"I was thinking maybe not long enough," he replied. "If I'm going to commit, I need to really go for it."

"Four," I said.

"Seven. That will get us to Bee's wedding."

I had to admit, I was surprised. "Agreed. Other fine print?"

"You can't just go on a couple of dates and call it multiple because that's what it would be for you. If you're going to be me, you have to be all me. Lots of dates. Like, every night."

"Ambrose," I said. "I have to work."

"I work!" I just looked at him. "Let's say you have to do at least three a week."

"Three?" I said. "One."

"Please," he replied, looking offended. "Two or no deal."

I sighed. "Fine. Two it is. And what does the winner get?"

"Hmmm." He leaned against the door, rubbing his chin like it actually helped him think. "If I win, I get to decide who you go out with next. And it can be anybody, you can't dispute or refuse, no takesies backsies."

"Takesies backsies? What are you, twelve?" I said. "And what about if I win?"

"You won't," he said, again so confidently. "But if we're talking hypothetical, that would mean I couldn't be a one-woman man, so you also get to pick *my* next prospect."

I stuck out my hand. "I have to admit," I said, "I'm not totally sure why you're agreeing to this."

"Because you think I can't do it," he replied. "And it's only for seven weeks."

"After which," I said, "you'll go back to dating the entire town and getting drinks thrown at you."

"While you," he added, "will be stuck with the person of my choosing, demanding the origin of the glitter in your hair."

We shook. It was a rare thing for me, lately or otherwise, to feel going into something that I already had an edge. But this time, I did. It was just dating, all beginnings, no endings. He was right—it did sound nice. And anyway, how hard could it be?

CHAPTER
12

"OKAY," DEVON said, holding up his hand. "LEGIONNAIRES."

As Tyler thought for a second, then jotted on his napkin, I tried to catch Jilly's eye. But she was studying her water glass, or pretending to. "Got one!" he announced.

"No way," Devon said.

"Yep." Tyler cleared his throat, loudly. "REASONING LIE."

"Nice!" Devon said, reaching across the table for a high five. The tenth, since I'd started counting soon after we sat down. Each one sounded a louder slap than the rest, but again, that might have just been me.

"My turn." Tyler looked at me. "You want to get in on this yet? Run with the big dogs?"

When we'd first arrived at the table and found them deep in an anagram competition, I'd actually thought it was kind of cute. After it became clear they played this game with intense focus and pride riding on every exchange, I started to see it differently. Never before had I seen such smack talk over wordplay. And that wasn't even mentioning the fact they'd basically entirely ignored us.

"I'm good," I said, taking another sip of the coffee drink I'd ordered to help me stay awake.

"Suit yourself. Are *you* ready?" he asked Devon, who was hunched over his own napkin, pen in hand. "To get your clock cleaned? Your ass handed to you? Your—"

"Just spit it out, Stevenson."

"Okay." Tyler grinned at me. "REVOLUTIONARY. Go!"

As Devon began scribbling, Tyler cackled, draining the last of the soda from his own glass with a slurp. When our waiter, a bodybuilding type, walked by, I watched Jilly's eyes follow him. This time, she saw me watching her and mouthed an apology.

I just shrugged. Sure, the guys were kind of duds, but it wasn't like anyone was groping me. And I'd gotten a decent dinner out of it, plus got to hang out with Jilly, something I was realizing I needed to do as much as I could before we both headed off to school in August. Not focusing on the dating aspect of, well, dating was actually a good approach. Who knew?

"Got it!" Devon yelled, hitting the table and making my fork jump. "UNTO REAL IVORY."

"Nice," Tyler said. Another five. "You girls have to join in! Unless you're *scared*. . . ."

"You don't scare me," Jilly said flatly in response. She pushed out her chair. "We're going to the bathroom."

"All right," said Tyler, then signaled to Devon to pick up his pen again. We were almost to the restroom when I heard one of them yell, "A THIGHBONE GROOM TOT!"

"Keep going," she said from behind me, as palms slapped again. "Do *not* turn around."

Once inside the restroom, I went into a stall, while she leaned against the sinks, contemplating her reflection. After a moment she said, "I can't believe I picked these guys. Normally my judgment in these things is aces."

"It was the sport coats," I told her. "They blinded you."

"Probably." I heard the water running. "I'm just sorry for you. I finally convince you to go on a real date with me and this happens. Now you'll never agree to anything again."

I flushed, then came out to join her, pumping soap into my hands. "No, I will. My pride is at stake now, remember? Or at least for the next seven weeks."

"Oh, right." She fluffed her bangs. "I guess I have Ambrose to thank for that, huh? I finally got my wingman. Or woman. Or whatever."

"And it only took our entire lives so far," I told her.

"True. Watch, though: while you specifically *aren't* looking for someone great, you'll find them. I'm out here digging for years and you will just stumble over a gold nugget by accident."

"Is that what you think is happening tonight?" I asked. "Because Tyler is no gold nugget."

"I'm just saying there are *types*," she replied. "Those of us who are always seeking, like me, and those who get found, like you. That's why I think, no offense, that Ambrose might win this bet. He's a seeker, too."

"Who has to commit to someone," I reminded her.

"For seven weeks," she said, flipping her hand. "My point

is that to win, all he has to do is be himself with one person. You have to be someone else with many. The math doesn't work for me."

"If he's himself, he won't last with the same person for seven weeks," I reminded her. "In his default setting, he'd flirt with a parking meter."

"This is true." She opened her bag, taking out a lipstick. "But I just worry about you suddenly plunging into the dating pool. I don't think I've taught you enough."

I looked at her through the mirror. "Then why have you been encouraging me to do just that for all these months? Are you forgetting that you said I should do this earlier today? What happened to swine before pearls and rolling the dice?"

"It's not the same thing, though," she said. "What I was suggesting was just getting back out there and seeing what happens, with the knowledge that it might not be Ethan all over again. This is *aiming* for that. It's totally different."

"But it's something," I pointed out. "Which is more than I have been doing."

She sighed. "Look, you know I'll support you no matter what. But is it so bad that I do want another big, perfect love for you? I feel like it's the least the universe can do, after what you lost."

"I'm only seventeen, Jilly. This is seven weeks. The universe has plenty of time."

With this, she bit her lip, a rare emotional response, then put out a hand, squeezing my arm. "Well, if you need a lot of dates that will probably not be great, you came to the right person. I have sort of a knack in that department. And I would like to see Ambrose go down, if only for the sport of it."

"I'll let you help pick whom he has to date when I win," I promised her. "I'm thinking maybe a Tyler or Devon type girl. Lots of high fives."

"Too bad for now that's what *we're* stuck with." She dropped her lipstick back in her bag. "You know, that waiter's kind of cute and he's been super friendly with me. Wonder what he's up to later?"

"You're going to ditch the sport coats right here at dinner?"

"Oh, please. I doubt they'd even notice if we didn't go back to the table."

I pushed open the door, glancing back into the restaurant. Tyler and Devon were now building structures with the silverware and leftover plates, both of them clearly focused. "We can't just leave," I said.

"Spoken like a true person who gets found," she told me. "Us seekers have no patience for lost causes."

Maybe this was true. But in the end, she would give them another thirty minutes—during which time we as a group exchanged about six words—before pleading a headache and early morning the next day and getting us out of there. When Tyler asked me for my number, I was surprised to say the least, and almost told him I didn't see the point. We had zero chemistry and the last thing I wanted was a repeat of this dinner or some variation of it. But Jilly was more right than I'd known: when you've only been found, you can't become a ruthless seeker just like that. So in the end, I gave it to him anyway.

———

"Seriously? Anagrams?"

I looked around me, wondering if I'd misjudged how loudly Ambrose had asked this question. Nope. Even Phone Lady, at a table a few feet away, had given us her attention, briefly pausing her own high-volume conversation.

"Yes," I said in almost a whisper, like this would compensate. "Aggressive ones. It was cutthroat."

"Whoa." The line inched forward, slowly. Lately, the coffee order had become Ambrose's job, but with Elinor Lin and her mother back for yet another meeting, it was that much more important, so I'd come along for backup. "So I'm guessing the night did not end with a hot make-out session."

"No," I said flatly. "He barely spoke to me the whole dinner, actually. But then he asked for my number, which was weird."

"Why?"

"Why did he ask for my number?"

"No," he said, "I know that. You're a hot girl and he loves word games. What I'm wondering is why you think it was weird."

I barely had time to process being referred to as "hot," which was a first, before answering. "Why would he want to see me again if he had no interest in me when I was right in front of him?"

"Well, I wasn't there," he replied as the line moved up a bit more, "but if I was a betting man, I'd say he had no idea you didn't have a good time."

"I think it was pretty obvious."

"Maybe to *you*. But some people—guys in particular—are oblivious. It's what makes dating so easy when you aren't that way. It's like having a secret power."

From behind me, I now heard Phone Lady talking, saying something about steep vet bills and highway robbery. "And that's you," I surmised. "Superman."

"No," he said, tossing that curl out of his face. "But the bottom line is, all anyone really wants from another person is their attention. It's so easy to give and counts for so much. It's stupid *not* to do it."

Hearing this, I thought of all the times I'd seen Ambrose leaning into a girl while she talked, his interest rapt and evident. Starting with that very first night in the parking lot of the club when he was AWOL for his mom's wedding, all the way up to . . . well, moments earlier, when he'd made Emily, one of the stationery store owners, blush when he complimented her dress. Would I have felt differently the night before if between word games Tyler had focused entirely on me? I couldn't say. But it wouldn't have hurt.

"I think I'm going to win this bet," I announced as we moved up in line. "If you give attention to every female you meet, there's no way you'll be able to keep a girlfriend."

"There's nothing wrong with attention," he said easily. "I just can't openly flirt. Luckily, I know the difference."

I turned, facing him. "Does this mean you've already

met someone with possible life-partner potential?"

I was pretty sure he winced at this last part, but he recovered quickly. "First of all, my life is not seven weeks. Or at least I hope it isn't. Second, finding one person to be with for that time isn't as easy as a dinner date. It takes time and focus."

"Or," I countered, "you could just take the first girl you would have that one perfect first night with and see if she can go the distance."

"True," he replied. "But the only girl I met last night was a total train wreck. I basically had to dodge out the back door of a club and take off on foot. Long story."

"Was this before or after you gave her your full attention?"

He ignored this, instead moving up to the register, where we'd finally arrived. The Lumberjack was behind the counter, in red-and-white plaid this time. "Long time, no see," he said, giving me a nod. "Where've you been?"

"She's dating everyone," Ambrose told him. "It keeps a girl busy."

I blushed instantly, then cleared my throat. "I have someone else to do the coffee run now," I said, nodding at Ambrose. "Except on special occasions."

"Special," he repeated, giving me a grin. "Sounds complicated. Hit me."

"Okay," I said, then read it out to him: my mom and William's regulars—I was getting her the extra shot she requested, as she was clearly tired—plus two very complicated whip-free and sugar-substitute drinks for the Lins. "Plus four waters, no ice, extra lemon."

618

"Child's play," he told me as he turned to the espresso machine, banging cups and pouring milk. "I thought you said this was hard."

"Oh," I said. "Well, next time I'll be sure to be more challenging."

He looked back at me, smiling again. "You do that."

I laughed, then reached into my pocket for the petty cash I'd grabbed for the order. Once I pulled it out, I realized Ambrose was looking at me, one eyebrow raised. "What?" I said.

"Who's giving full attention now?" he asked, just as the steam starting hissing.

"I'm placing an order," I told him.

"If that's what we're calling it," he replied.

"I believe we were talking about you," I said. "As in, you need to get cracking. Seven weeks is ticking past and you don't want to get disqualified. You better find a lifer, stat."

"It's been one day," he said in a flat voice. "You just worry about yourself."

"I'm not worried. I have Jilly. She's been wanting me to date for *months*. She can't wait to set me up."

"Oh, right. And her taste is impeccable. Jughead and Anagram. Sounds like a cop show."

Lumberjack came back to the counter, sliding four waters across to me. As I grabbed a drink carrier and started loading it, he said, "Sorry to eavesdrop, but it's an occupational hazard. Did I hear you guys betting on dates?"

"It was her idea," Ambrose told him. "And I'm very competitive."

"Shut up." I felt myself blush again. To Lumberjack I said,

"It's just a stupid thing. I need to date more and him less. We're seeing if we can do it."

"I can totally do it," Ambrose added. "Her, I'm not so sure."

"Date more?" the Lumberjack said to me, ignoring this. "I can't imagine you'd have a lack of offers."

Now I was definitely blushing. Why had I come for coffees? Even an idiot could read off a list. I said, "Well . . . it's complicated. I guess."

He looked me for a second, half-smiling, then turned back to the machine. Again, I could feel Ambrose staring at me.

"She likes a man in plaid," he said eventually, under his breath. "Noted."

"Please shut up," I whispered back. Then I concentrated on listening to Phone Lady, now going on about her first husband, until our drinks were done and Lumberjack brought them to the counter and rang us up.

"Twenty-two eleven," he said. I slid the cash in my hand across to him, then filled another drink carrier, handing it to Ambrose. After I collected my change, he grabbed a napkin and scribbled something on the back, then handed it over as well. "Well, if you need any help with the bet, let me know. I'm competitive, too."

I looked down at the napkin: LEO, it said, with a number underneath. "Um . . . okay."

"I protest," Ambrose said. "The rule about the dating bet is you don't talk to dates about the bet."

"We never made that rule," I told him.

"I'm making it now."

Someone cleared their throat behind us. "Let's go," I said, then looked at Leo. "Thanks."

"No problem," he said, then smiled at the next customer who stepped up, already giving their order. As we wound past the remaining line, I felt clumsy, so thrown off by what had just happened that I had to steady the drink carrier with my other hand. When I was with Jughead, Anagram, and any of the other boys Jilly had dragged me out with, I'd just felt like I was going through the motions, holding up my end of a bargain I didn't really even remember agreeing to. But this, an unexpected boy taking me by surprise, was both different and familiar at the same time.

"Attention," Ambrose announced, as he pushed the door open for me. Stepping through, I heard Phone Lady still talking, and wondered if she ever got tired of her own voice. "Like I said, it means everything."

Everything was a lot to deal with, though, when you had gotten used to nothing. I needed increments: a few somethings, maybe an anything first. I looked down at the napkin, which I realized I was clutching in my hand, the neat block print, the number in blue ink. If I texted, how would he respond? If we spoke, what would his voice sound like on the other end of the line? Again, too familiar. I slid it into my back pocket, and tried to do what I did best, and forget.

CHAPTER
13

"WHAT TIME is it?"

"You're not supposed to ask that. Remember?"

We'd made this rule around four a.m., when it was dark and we still had a while until daybreak. Now, though, two hours and change later, the sky was turning lighter and pink, the stars fading even as I tried to keep track of them. Morning was here.

And we were where we'd started, just below the hotel, on the sand. After finishing our pie and coffee, we'd walked back along the boardwalk, then the narrow main road of Colby, passing a couple of blinking streetlights and only a handful of cars. When the hotel sign had appeared in front of us, bright in floodlights, I'd wanted to keep walking, going as far in the other direction as we could. But Ethan's dad was leaving at eight a.m. sharp for the long drive back to New Jersey. So instead, we went to the beach, where we found a row of folded chaise lounges, took one, and curled up together.

I'd never felt so close with anyone, ever. Maybe this was because of what had happened earlier, beneath the pier. My

lips had been sticky with fruit and chocolate, Ethan's breath
sugar-sweet coffee as he eased me back into the damp, cool
sand. I'd expected to be nervous my first time, and never
would have thought it would have happened like this. But
as he slipped my dress off my shoulders, then eased up
the skirt, I'd found myself arching up to meet him as if I'd
known every move ahead of time and had only to do them.
He'd asked if I was sure so many times after sliding on the
condom that I finally covered his mouth with my own to
silence him. It hurt a bit, which I'd expected, and I'd cried
after, which I had not. We stayed there for a long time, the
wind blowing sand across us now and then, my knees pulled
to my chest, my head on his shoulder. For the first time in
hours, we didn't talk, and in that silence I heard everything
else I needed to.

Now, in his arms, facing the water, I could smell salt on
his shirt and beneath it the slight tinge of his cologne, as well
as sweat. It would only be a matter of time before someone
came along, walking with their dog or kid, making it clear
that the beach, and the night, were no longer ours alone.
Thinking this, I squeezed my eyes shut tightly, again willing
time to stop. Like the game Ethan played with his friends,
striking a deal—I would have given anything for a few more
hours.

A gull called overhead, swooping. Somewhere a car horn
beeped.

"Ten hours," Ethan said, right above my ear. I turned,
looking up at him. In daylight I was noticing new things: the
freckle on his chin, a scar above one eyebrow, the little bit

of stubble already coming in. "That's how long a drive it is to Brownwood from here."

"Half a day," I said. "That's not so bad."

"When you come," he told me, shifting, "I'll take you to Spinnaker's, where they have the best pretzels and limeade. And to the town bell, the largest in the state, which is pretty much the only other exciting thing around."

"More exciting than limeade?"

"I know, it's hard to believe," he agreed.

"And when you come to Lakeview," I replied, running a finger down the buttons of his shirt, "I'll take you to Luna Blu for fried pickles and to see the Angel."

"Angel?"

"It's a sculpture, a metal one, right outside of this office downtown. The woman's a realtor or something? It's huge, with these crazy wings made of bottle caps. When the wind blows, it spins."

"Wow. That is better than our big bell for sure."

"I can't wait," I said.

"Me neither."

With every silence now, I was more aware of the passing of time.

"I'm so glad I left the wedding and came down here last night," he said. I couldn't decide if I wanted to close my eyes and just listen to him, or keep them open so I could have him in my gaze as long as possible.

"Not as glad as I am," I replied, as he kissed my hair. "For once, I really did do something epic."

He laughed: I'd told him about Jilly's directive, of course.

I felt like I'd told him everything. "I think that's the first time I've been referred to in those terms."

"But not the last. At least as long as I'm around."

"Oh, you'll be around." He slid his arm to encircle my waist. "Don't worry about that."

I heard it, then: the opening, bouncy notes of that same Lexi Navigator song. It seemed like days ago he'd shared that story with me, not hours, and I wished I'd enjoyed having so much still ahead while I had the chance. The ring of a phone was yet more proof of the intrusion of the world, even if it did have a nice beat.

"My dad," Ethan said, answering it. "Hello? Yeah, I'm up. Nah, couldn't sleep so I came down to the beach."

I loved that I was a secret. I'd remember that later.

"Let's just grab something on the way. I'll meet you in the lot at eight." A pause. "Because that's what we said last night."

Reflexively, I closed my eyes, curling more tightly against him.

"I'm not ready to go yet," he said, the words reverberating in me. "Seven thirty, then."

A pause. Another gull swooped over us, crying.

"Fine. Okay. Yeah. See you."

He hung up. I didn't want to ask, but anyone could tell when you bargained and lost. "How soon?" I said quietly.

He was quiet a moment. "Thirty-five minutes."

I opened my eyes, lifting my head, and moved so I was over him, looking down into his face. "I don't want you to go."

"I don't want to go." He reached up, tucking a piece of my hair, windblown, sand-tinged, behind my ear. "But it's a long drive, and he's ready."

I swallowed, then tried to smile. "I'm going to hate that Lexi Navigator song even more now. It's like she took you away from me."

"Hey, don't hate on Lexi," he said. "It's a good song!"

"But not the one that made you cry," I pointed out.

He reached up, taking the finger I'd extended to his chin and grabbing it. "That's between you and me, Lulu. I trust you."

I smiled. "I won't let you down."

"You never could," he said, so easily that it was this, finally, that made the tears well up in my eyes. "Hey. Don't cry. You know I'm easily emotional."

"I'm sorry," I said, wiping my free hand over my face. "This has been so great. I don't want to end it on a bad note."

"End?" He sat up. "Nothing's ending here, at least for me. This is just a pause, until we're together again."

"To see big bells and have limeade," I managed to get out.

"And eat pickles with angels," he added.

With that, I was sure I would lose it, and probably would have if he hadn't leaned in closer to me, kissing me long and hard, his fingers pressed against my back. I'd never felt so happy and sad at once, the absolute convergence of two opposing emotions, and together they made my heart full enough to feel like it might break. When we finally pulled back from each other, I was sobbing.

"Don't," he said, then swallowed himself, looking past me. "We'll talk all the time. And text, and make plans right away to see each other again. Like, today."

"Okay," I said, barely managing to get the word out.

"We *will*," he said, thinking I was doubting this, but I wasn't. I never doubted him. There just wasn't enough time.

I reached over to his other wrist, tilting his watch to see the face. It was 6:46. "You should probably go."

He pulled a hand through his hair, then cleared his throat but didn't say anything. A woman with two kids, one in a bathing suit, was coming down the beach toward us now, a cup of coffee in her hand.

"Walk me up?" he said.

I got to my feet, picking up my shoes from the sand beside the chair as Ethan stood as well and found his own. Then we started toward the steps that led to the hotel. He was holding my hand, our fingers tightly entwined. Even in motion, I wanted to be as close to him as possible.

I didn't put on my shoes after climbing the last step, or even when we circled the pool to the hotel entrance. Instead, I waited until the last possible moment, standing in front of the doors there, before sliding my feet into the straps and buckling them. The night had been barefoot, and the night was over. As Ethan shook out his socks, then put on his own shoes, a housekeeper carrying a load of towels came out the door, glancing at us with eyebrows raised. Some stories tell themselves.

We were halfway to the lobby elevators when I realized

we might really be about to say good-bye. When I slowed my steps, he said, "I'm just going to get my stuff. I'll come back down and we'll go out together. Okay?"

The relief I felt hearing this was immense; a reprieve, if only a short one. I nodded as he leaned in, kissing my forehead. Then the elevator came and he stepped in, smiling at me just before the doors closed.

I walked over to the lobby bathroom, pushing the heavy door open and going inside. When I saw myself in the mirror, I laughed out loud: my hair was wild, windblown and tangled, my lips swollen from kissing, the straps of my dress tied crookedly, one higher than the other. As I reached up, trying to smooth my hair, a small piece of dune grass dislodged itself from somewhere, falling into the sink in front of me. I reached down, picking it up, then turned it in my fingers slowly one way, then another. *This is what it will feel like when he's gone*, I told myself, but the thought was too big. Not yet.

Back out in the lobby, Ethan was standing by the front doors, a duffel bag at his feet. He'd tucked in his shirt and splashed some cold water on his face: his skin was cool as he kissed me, a cheek brushing my own. "Found your phone," he said, reaching into his jacket pocket and handing it to me. "You're going to need it."

"Are you saying you're going to call?"

"Probably before we even leave the lot."

I smiled. "Then you'll need my number."

He pulled out his phone, swiping to the contacts, and

handed it over. I could feel him watching me, so close, as I typed in my name and the digits, then hit SAVE. "There. Done."

He took it back, then sighed. "I don't want to be done."

"Me neither."

A car pulled up outside, just past the overhang of the hotel. I could tell by Ethan's face that it was his dad. The car did look new, and expensive, low to the ground and cherry red.

"Just stay," I said quietly, before I could stop myself.

"I wish I could," he replied, then pulled me closer, burying his face in my hair. *Is this the end?* I thought. Or would there be another kiss, another moment, more time, just like I wanted? But then he was pulling back from me, still holding my hand. "I gotta go, though. I'm so sorry."

"It's okay," I managed to get out. "I'll be there for limeade before you know it."

"I'm holding you to that." Then he did kiss me again, one hand touching my face, lingering there even as he finally pulled away. "This isn't over, Lulu. It's only the beginning. Right?"

"The beginning," I repeated. "Okay."

I saw him draw in a big breath, then let it out before he turned, starting toward the revolving doors. When he was almost there, he turned, dropping the bag and jogging back over to me. As soon as he was close enough, I had my arms around him.

"I love you," he said, close to my ear.

"I love you, too," I replied. Then I kissed him, trying to put everything I felt and had into this last bit of contact. When he pulled away, it was all I could do not to sob.

And then he was walking over to the doors, pushing through them and outside. I got only the briefest glance of his dad, also tall, stocky, and dark-haired, watching him approach from over the roof of the car. He popped the trunk, and Ethan dropped his bag in, then walked back to the passenger door to climb inside. I knew I'd already gotten my good-bye, several of them, but I still couldn't make myself move as his dad got behind the wheel, starting the car. Just as they drove off, two women approached from outside, pushing the doors into motion. My last glimpse of Ethan was this combination of the doors turning and the car moving, in a prism of motion and spinning that left me dizzy and yearning. As if the whole world itself tilted, not just my own.

CHAPTER

14

"WAIT, THEY'RE not coming?" my mom said, as William waved his free hand, trying to quiet her. "But the photographer will be here in ten minutes!"

". . . of course I understand," William said into the phone at his ear, using his firm voice. Just hearing it, I sat up straighter in my own chair. "But we'd agreed you'd participate in this photo shoot. There's no way we'll find someone else on such short notice."

"Remind her this was part of our deal," my mom said. He flapped at her again. "If they stand us up for this, no discount on the rehearsal dinner fee. I might even mark it up."

Yikes, I thought, raising my eyebrows. When I snuck a look at my mom, she looked so incensed I quickly went back to folding programs.

"Well, that's unfortunate," William said into the phone, sitting back in his chair. "And of course we'll discuss how it affects our fee. . . . Fine. Okay. Right."

"No," my mom said flatly, as he hung up the phone. "No way she just canceled on us for this. I won't accept it."

"You know I usually am a big fan of denial," he replied with a sigh, "but we probably need to call the photographer and reschedule. We can't shoot wedding images without a bride."

Just then, as if on cue, the front door chimed. When I looked over, a petite woman with close-cut black curls was entering, pulling a case behind her. A light setup was over her shoulder. "Morning," she called out, totally oblivious to the mood of the room. "Where do you want me?"

My mom groaned, putting her head in her hands. This was dramatic for her, but I understood the frustration. Ever since Natalie Barrett Weddings had been chosen as a finalist for Local Business of the Year by *Lakeview Monthly* she'd been on edge, doing everything she could to better our chances of winning. This included, but was not limited to, eschewing the staff photographer the magazine had sent to get some quick candids in favor of a professional taking pictures of a real-life couple in our office. One of our upcoming brides, Marlo Wagner, had been all set up to come in with her fiancé that morning until the phone call a few minutes earlier. We'd had a lot of problems in the office, but lacking a bride and groom at the same time had never been one of them.

"I'll call the magazine," William said now, picking up the phone again. "Tell them we need another day."

"Don't bother," my mom told him through her hands. "They already made it clear that if they don't have these images by business close today they're going with stock ones. *Stock*, William. Can you even imagine?"

"There has to be a solution to this," he said, as the photographer started unpacking cameras and lenses from her case. "We don't need a real bride and groom. Just two people to play the part."

"No one wants to see us cutting a cake," my mom said. "We're too old and grizzled."

"Speak for yourself. I got carded buying prosecco the other day," he replied, somewhat haughtily. "And I wasn't thinking about us."

I was moving on to the next stack of programs when I became acutely aware of the fact that I was being watched. Sure enough, when I paused and glanced up, they were both looking right at me.

"No," I said firmly. "No way."

"She has a point," my mom said, although she kept her eyes on me. "We're not in the *child* bride business. However, if we just did body part shots—"

"What?" I asked, horrified.

"—it would easily work," William finished, as if I hadn't said anything. "Hands cutting a cake, hands holding a bouquet, shots from the back. Yes. I think it's doable."

"Do neither of you hear me saying *no* over here?" I said.

"I guess we don't *necessarily* need a groom," my mom told William, answering this question for me. "Although I did like the symmetry aspect of some of your ideas."

"I'm not speaking to either of you," I announced, going back to what I was doing. The door chimed again, cheerful, and I made a point of not looking up. The silence that followed, however, was familiar. As in a recent way.

"What?" I heard Ambrose say. He'd been out getting the first coffee order of the morning. "What is it?"

Now I had to speak up. "*No*," I said loudly.

"Okay, okay," Ambrose, assuming this was directed at him, said quickly. "Fine. I did eat one of these doughnuts I just got us without offering them around first."

My mom and William were still studying him, much like hungry cats in cartoons eye plump birds whistling on a swing.

"Fine, it was two," Ambrose added. "I'm sorry! I was hungry. Also—"

"This isn't about doughnuts," my mother told him. She looked at me again. "It's about helping out when the company is in a serious bind."

"Oh." Ambrose exhaled. "Well, sure. What do you need?"

"See?" she said, pointing at him. "Now that's loyalty."

"I am not going to pretend to be engaged to Ambrose!" I said.

"Engaged?" He grinned at me. "Oh, this should be fun."

This was not the word in my head when, half an hour later, I left the conference room with my nails still wet from a rush manicure from Liza, a nail tech from the nearby salon whom my mother coaxed over with a crisp fifty-dollar bill. Because this was supposed to be shots of a casual client meeting, I'd kept on the sundress I'd worn to work that day. As I walked toward Ambrose and the photographer, now set up in the reception area, I saw he had on a new, crisp shirt. Also, he was smiling at me in a way that made it clear he still thought this was hilarious.

"Now, I think first we'll just do some shots of you flipping through the books of other weddings," the photographer said, gesturing for me to sit down on one of the chaises. "Because we're not doing faces, I'll blur your profiles in editing, focusing more on your hands, together, on the pages."

Ambrose patted the seat beside him. "Come on, honey. Time for our close-up."

I looked at my mother, who held up ten fingers, symbolizing the hundred bucks I'd been promised for going through with this. It was not enough. Still, I sat down.

"Okay," the photographer said, squatting down and lifting the camera. "Now, let's have the groom open the book and hold it in his lap. Louna, lean into him and point to something on the page."

"Should we talk motivation?" Ambrose said to me. "Want to develop our backstory? How long we've been together, all that?"

"No," I said flatly, jabbing a finger at a picture of a cake, flowers trailing off it.

"I think," he continued, ignoring me, "that we met cute. Like, you dropped a kitten, and I picked it up for you."

"Why would I drop a kitten?"

"Well, clearly, it was an accident," he replied, sliding his other arm around me. I told myself not to stiffen, then glared at William, who had the nerve to laugh out loud. "Your hair smells good, by the way. Is that vanilla?"

I didn't respond to this. The photographer, now shooting, said, "Louna, can you relax your mouth? You look kind of angry."

"Imagine that," I said under my breath.

From the albums, we moved on to posing with the cake

William had bought just for the shoot, a grocery store variety he'd carefully decorated with fresh flowers. The photographer put us beside it, then arranged our hands—Ambrose's above, mine below—on a silver cake cutter.

"Now, just put it on the edge," she called out, checking her light meter. "And, Ambrose, shift your hand so we can see the ring on Louna's finger a bit better. It's just so pretty!"

"Three months' salary," he told her, insisting, still, on being in character. "But my baby deserved a rock!"

My mom, who was the actual owner of this ring, snorted. William said, "You guys actually look really cute together, if you don't mind me saying."

I was about to tell him that, in fact, I did, when Ambrose moved in closer behind me, his mouth right at my ear. "FYI, your tag is sticking out. Let me get it. It's what a fiancé would do."

A second later, I felt his fingers on the small of my back, smoothing down the fabric of my dress there. And the weirdest, craziest thing happened: I felt something. That unmistakable, sudden rush of feeling when your body responds to a touch in that certain, specific way. As I blinked, trying to process this, I realized that despite my reluctance, I hadn't stiffened even once in all the times he'd touched me so far. So weird.

"Great," the photographer called out, clicking away. "Now, Louna, turn your head and look up at Ambrose. Again, I'll blur your features. But I love this staging."

I swallowed—calm down, Barrett—then did as I was told, turning toward him. With one of his hands over mine, the other beside me against the table, it was almost like easing into an embrace, and I was surprised, again, by how natural it felt. No elbows or awkwardness; I just fit there.

"What?" Ambrose said, looking down at me.

"Nothing," I replied, as the photographer moved in closer, getting even more of us together. It seemed like she shot forever, us frozen in that spot. Even so, when we broke apart, the space between us felt huge, much bigger than it was. As if somehow *it* was the odd thing now.

❧

"Okay," Jilly said, extracting a lock of her hair from Bean's sticky grip. "Tell me again *exactly* what you said to the Lumberjack."

"His name is Leo."

"Whatever. Just read."

I looked down at my phone, between us on the bed. At my desk, Crawford was now reading my dictionary the way anyone else might a newspaper, flipping through for the big stories. "'Hey, it's Louna. Going to a party tonight, want to come?'"

She considered this, wrinkling her nose. "It's a bit conversational for my taste."

"It's eleven words," I pointed out.

"Yes, but it's how they *sound*." Bean let out a wail, and Jilly put her on the floor, where she promptly made a beeline for my closet, her hands slapping the hardwood. "I would have been like, 'Party Tuesday you in'. No punctuation, because you're a busy girl, and let him ask who it is, don't tell him."

"Why not?"

"Because it adds mystery!" she said. "And mystery is everything, especially at the beginning."

"Well, it's done now," I told her. "He already responded."

"And said what?"

I hit the screen, scrolling down. "'Sure. Off at 7.'"

From her serious face, studying the screen, you could have thought this was an ancient scroll that needed to be translated. "Yeah. He's got the upper hand now. It's obvious."

"How?" I asked.

"He responded with 'Sure.' It's like you're twisting his arm, begging him. He's agreeing, not accepting."

"You get all that from 'sure'?"

"It's syntax. Context. You have to read between the lines."

"There aren't lines, it's, like, one sentence."

"Two," Crawford corrected me from the desk. "That was two sentences."

"Are you supposed to be listening?" Jilly asked him. "Read your book."

"It's the dictionary."

"Even better." She got to her feet, walking over to the closet, where Bean was now trying to chew on one of my shoes. Picking her up, she said, "Let's just work with what we have. He's off at seven. Now, you absolutely can't go to his work and meet him there—"

"Why not?" I asked. "Isn't that why he told me that?"

"Because that looks even more desperate! You never meet anyone halfway, you make them come to *you*. He's already had 'sure.' You need to call the rest of the shots."

"This is insane," I said. "I refuse to believe everyone strategizes at this level when it comes to a simple date."

"Don't call it a date," she corrected me. "Too formal. You're hanging out at a party. With a group."

There was a bang outside my door as KitKat entered, each carrying a bag of pretzels. "What are you guys doing?" Jilly demanded. "Did you let yourselves in?"

"No, William did," Kat told her. "And he offered snacks."

"No fair," Crawford said. "I'm hungry."

"Mom says you need to drive us to the truck so Dad can take us to gymnastics," Kit told Jilly, popping a pretzel in her mouth.

"I thought she was doing that. I have a party to get to."

"She's tired. She said she needs to lie down."

Jilly and I exchanged a look. Her mom went nonstop. When she got tired, it usually meant something. As in, another Baker something. "I am going to East U in August," she said to me, under her breath. "Baby or no baby."

"Who's having a baby?" Crawford asked.

"Nobody," we said in unison. Jilly shifted Bean to her other hip, then looked at KitKat, now sitting on the bed together, crunching. "Fine. I'll drive you guys, then circle back and get ready. Louna, let's meet at six forty-five at my house. In the meantime, text the Lumberjack again but *only* give the party address I gave you. Nothing else. You have to have *hand*. It's important."

"Louna knows a real lumberjack?" Crawford asked.

"No," I told him,

"I want more pretzels," Kit announced, crumpling up the bag. "Can I go ask William?"

"No," Jilly replied. "We're leaving. All of us. Now! Let's go."

Crawford put the dictionary back, the twins got to their feet, and Jilly followed, Bean squirming for me as she passed. I patted her chubby hand, giving it a kiss, and she laughed.

"Why would anyone want to add to this?" Jilly said, once everyone else had thumped down the stairs. "It's madness already."

"Love makes people do crazy things, I guess."

At this, she harrumphed, then waved over her shoulder as she left. As usual after a Baker departure, the room felt bigger and quieter. I sat down on my bed, looking over the text exchanges with Leo. To me, they were just words, all the nuances and meanings Jilly saw invisible. Was this really how it worked, when you were seeking? It seemed so complicated. Regardless, I did as she'd said and sent the address of the party, nothing else. A moment later, he texted back with just a K. From sentences to words to just letters. It was hard to see this as progress and not the other way around.

CHAPTER
15

BY THE time I'd gotten ready—changing my shirt twice, redoing makeup once—I still had nearly an hour before I was set to meet Jilly. So I went downstairs to look for William.

He was in the kitchen. William loved to cook, had even toyed with going to culinary school at one point after college. But he hated the small kitchen at his otherwise perfect-for-him high-rise, modern apartment, preferring to keep it pristine at all times and not smelling of garlic. So when he felt like cooking, he always came over to our house, where he could spread out across the island and counters and know whatever he made would be enthusiastically welcomed. (My mom and I were Lean Cuisine and takeout types: about all she could make was toast, and my strength was chocolate chip cookies. These were great staples, don't get me wrong. But you couldn't exactly eat them every night.) There was no set schedule when William would cook, though, which added a surprise element.

"What's the occasion?" I asked him as I came in.

He glanced over his shoulder, chopping at something. "Your mother read another article about clean eating and getting in shape. She's inspired and requested a home-cooked, healthy meal."

"Again?"

"We could both do with a lifestyle change," he replied, the knife banging as he made more cuts. "We're going to start cooking more, and walking every night, as well."

Sure you are, I thought. They made these diet and exercise pledges every few months, proclaiming it the Start of a New Era. It was usually only a week at best before I found them once again on the couch after work splitting a bucket of chicken and watching *Big New York* or *Big Chicago,* their favorite reality shows. I knew better than to point this out, though. "Sounds great. What are you making?"

"Chicken paillard with asparagus and shaved parmesan and a pear salad," he replied. "I'm just hoping you guys have lemons. It's the one thing I forgot."

"William. You know we don't have lemons. We don't even have bread right now."

"What?" He looked aghast. Wiping his hands on his apron—a plain linen one he always brought from home—he went over to the fridge, pulling it open. "Dear God, there is *nothing* in these produce drawers. Not even a bag of spinach!"

"I'd be less surprised to find a live animal," I told him.

He shut the door, shaking his head. "I always wonder how you managed to get to eighteen without scurvy."

"Hey, we order salads from Tossed almost every night," I said, defending myself. "Just because it's not here doesn't mean I don't eat it."

"Well, thank God for that." He sighed, looking at the

onion and chicken breasts out on the island. "I need lemons, though. They're key to the dish."

"I can run and get you some," I said. "Farmer Fred's is, like, two seconds away."

"Farmer Fred's?" he repeated. "No. I don't cook enough to lower myself to that kind of standard. I'm going to Spice and Thyme. While I'm there, I'll grab some prosciutto and melon, as we do need an appetizer. And maybe some of those Belgian macaroons for dessert."

"What happened to healthy eating?"

"They're *Belgian* and organic, Louna. Are you coming or what?"

Fifteen minutes later, we were at Spice and Thyme, the gourmet market, where the fragrant notes of expensive coffee hit you the second you stepped through the sliding doors. It was practically required that you pause just to inhale. We both did.

"I want heaven to smell just like this," William said.

"And movie popcorn," I added.

"Well, of course."

He grabbed a basket and we started over to the produce, which was so beautiful and arranged so meticulously it felt like a shame to remove any of it. As William took two lemons, I examined a nearby artichoke that was so big and perfect it looked fake.

"I make a great sauce for those with Greek yogurt and dill," he told me, adding it to the basket. "For another night. Now that we're eating healthy."

"Right," I said, already picturing it rotting in our fridge.

"Excuse me, but can you point me toward the kumquats? They're on special right now, correct?" a woman pushing a cart asked William. She had a list in her hand, glasses perched on the tip of her nose.

"Um," he said. "I don't work here."

She flushed instantly. "Oh, sorry!"

"But I do know they are over there, by the persimmons," he said gallantly, pointing. "On sale, I'm not sure."

"Thank you," she said quickly, clearly embarrassed, as she turned her cart and headed that way.

"Five minutes," I said to him once she was out of earshot. "That's how long it took."

"Better than three, I guess," he replied, picking up a melon and knocking it. "And I was even holding a *basket*. Honestly."

For as long as I could remember, no matter where we went in the world of retail, it was a given William would be mistaken for an employee and asked for directions, fitting room access, or, in my favorite situations, advice on purchases. Somehow, he just exuded authority and knowledge, even when he was off the clock. He got annoyed, but personally, I found it hilarious.

We moved on to the meat section, stopping at each of the free sample stations along the way. (Another one of our rituals.) We were standing by the case, him studying the prosciutto, when the guy working came up from the other side. He was dark haired, very muscled, and had tattoos up both arms, as well as a thick gauge in one ear.

"William!" he said, his voice friendly. "Where you been?

You never came to report back on that Parma."

I was looking at a piece of tongue—ugh—and so didn't see, at first, that William was blushing. It was only when he answered with a stammer that I noticed. "I, um, have been busy. But it was good. A little salty for my taste."

The guy leaned on top of the case, his massive arms flexing. "Agreed. I cut it with a bit of this new blue we got, a cow's milk, very silky and tart. The Meridien, have you tried it?"

"No," William said. "I'm not, um, so I need some prosciutto?"

The guy looked at him, then me, and smiled. "Sure. Quarter pound or half?"

"Half."

"Great. And I'll throw in a bit of this new Black Forest I want you to try. You have the Wasilla goat at home still, yes? You've got to pair them on a baguette. It's incredible. Just a sec."

As the guy opened the case and drew out a huge slab of meat, then walked over to the slicer, I looked pointedly at William. He ignored me, focused instead on the ground sausage display. Finally, I poked him.

"What?"

"Who is that guy?" I asked, my voice low. He blushed again. "He's cute, William."

"I barely know him," he replied, going darker red. "We talked meat and cheese at closing once."

"I think he likes you."

"Louna. Stop it."

"William," the guy called out over the clanging of the slicer. "You want this thin? Are you making that melon dish we had at dinner that time?"

I gaped at him. "Y-yes," he stammered. I could literally feel heat coming off his face. "That would, um, be great."

"Excuse me," a man carrying a baguette said, coming up to us. "Where is the bulk nut section?"

"Over by the flowers," William told him, clearly grateful for once for this distraction. "Straight ahead, then left."

"You had him over for *dinner*?" I demanded, as the man walked away, taking a wrong turn immediately. "When was this?"

"Hush," he said, fiddling with the lemons in his basket.

"Here you go," the meat guy said, dropping two plastic bags on the counter. "The prosciutto you like, with a sample of the Black Forest. You want me to walk over to cheeses with you so you can sample that Meridien?"

"Sure," I said, smiling at him.

"No," William told him, at the same time. "I, um . . . we have to go. I'm cooking and the chicken is . . . Next time."

"Sure thing." The guy smiled at me and then, wider, at William. "I'll look forward to it."

William grabbed the meat, tossing it in his basket, then hustled away, vanishing around a display of flavored popcorn. I turned back to the guy, sticking out my hand. "I'm Louna. And you are?"

"Matt," he replied. We shook. "You're William's . . ."

"Goddaughter," I said, which was the easy explanation.

"He's a great guy," he told me, looking at the popcorn. "And, um . . . still single? Yes?"

"Yes," I replied.

"Good to know," he said, then knocked the counter between us, smiled, and walked away.

I found William dabbing his brow by the macaroons. "You didn't tell me you'd had anyone over for a date."

"It was one time," he said. I waited. "Look, he's nice. I'm just . . . not ready for anything."

"William. You haven't dated since I was in middle school."

"Exactly. I wouldn't even know where to start."

"With prosciutto and melon, apparently," I said. He blushed again. "Look, if I can get back out there dating, so can you."

He looked at me. "You're dating again?"

"Kind of. Ambrose and I made a bet. I'm actually meeting the Lumberjack at a party tonight."

He looked surprised. "Really?"

I nodded. "It's nothing serious. That's the whole point. I just have to date, but Ambrose has to commit for seven weeks. Whoever caves first has to get set up by the other with their person of choice."

"Ambrose gets to set you up?" he asked.

"If he wins," I said. "Which he won't."

"You should hope not. Because he'd pick himself for sure."

Now my eyes widened. "What? No. That's not how it works."

"You said he could pick anyone, correct?" He crossed the

aisle, scanning the boxes. "So he says it's him, and then you have no choice but to go out with him. Pretty genius. I take it that part was his idea?"

Come to think of it, it had been. But that meant nothing, either. "Ambrose does *not* want to go out with me, William. We barely even like each other."

"So you say," he said, picking up a box and putting it in the basket. "I hear a lot of laughing when you two are in the office. And you looked pretty cozy at that photoshoot."

"Sir, can you help me with the curry sauces?" a woman in a sundress called out from one aisle down. "I need one that's mild but fragrant."

"I have to get out of here," William hissed to me, starting toward the register. Still, he couldn't help himself, saying to the woman as he passed her, "Tamil's, in mild. Don't use too much."

"Thank you!"

At the registers, I was determined to bring up the Ambrose thing again, demanding why on earth he thought that, of all things, would be the outcome of our bet. Because we looked good pretending to slice a cake? But just as I started to say this, his phone rang: it was my mother, calling about some issue with the photographer of the Elinor Lin Wedding that weekend, serious enough that they kept talking the entire ride back home. As we pulled up in the driveway, I could see Jilly in her backyard, alone for once, waiting for me. No time to ask more questions, which was maybe a good thing after all. But as I said good-bye to him, then crossed the grass to Jilly's, I couldn't help but consider the fact that William's intuition was usually dead on. Then again, everyone can be wrong sometimes.

⁂

"There he is," Jilly said, her voice low. "Act cool."

This had to be the worst thing to say to a nervous person. I thought about telling her so, but I was too on edge watching Leo make his way across the crowded living room. Instead I asked, "Whose party is this, anyway?"

"Jack from Turbo Taco," she said, sipping her beer. "His parents have that truck with the racing flames on it? They sell the hottest hot sauce in town. People have been hospitalized."

"Wow," I said, as Leo stopped to talk to two girls who had their backs to us. He had on yet another plaid shirt, short sleeved this time, and no apron. Not that he would wear an apron to a party. Okay, I was nervous *and* crazy. I took another gulp of my beer, which was warm even though I'd only just gotten it. "God, I feel so out of place. Why did I agree to do this again?"

"Because the Lumberjack is cute and you want to beat Ambrose," she replied cheerfully, adjusting the neckline of her dress. "Speaking of which, there he is. I guess he found it after all."

I glanced over to where she was looking. Sure enough, there was Ambrose in the kitchen, popping a beer open on the countertop. When he saw us, he waved, pushing that curl from his forehead. Ira was on the deck outside, being petted by a group of girls holding red cups. This time, he had on a polka-dot bandana. Apparently, this was his signature look now. "Found it?" I asked.

"Ambrose hadn't heard of the neighborhood when I told him about this party."

Now I turned, giving her my full attention. "You invited him?"

"Yeah, when I gave him that ride the other night." She was scanning the crowd, not looking at me. When she realized I was staring at her, she blinked. "What?"

"I thought you couldn't stand him."

She flipped her hand. "Oh, that was just a first impression. He's okay."

Between this and William's melon-prosciutto date, I suddenly felt like no one was telling me anything. "You gave Ambrose a ride? When?"

"Last week," she said easily. "I was doing register for my dad downtown, after the bars closed, and I saw him and his dog walking. I couldn't just drive past them, especially at two a.m."

"I'm surprised he was alone," I remarked, as Leo looked up and saw me, waving a hand. I waved back, and the girls he was talking to both turned to look at me. I sucked down more of my beer.

"He said he'd just dodged some girl at a club," she replied. "Crazy story. Had to run out the back door."

"I think I heard about that."

"I'm sure you did." She took another sip. "Anyway, I just drove him back to his sister's. He invited me in for a snack, but I said no. Being around food all night in close quarters and all. Plus I felt super greasy."

"He asked you in?"

"Yeah." She was looking around again, and took a second to meet my eyes. "Why? Is that weird? You guys are just friends, right?"

"Not even that," I said quickly. "We just work together."

"And make bets together."

"That's strictly for bragging rights," I told her, thinking about what William had said.

"That's what I thought." She tucked a piece of hair behind one ear. "I don't think he's my type anyway. Too loosey-goosey. Not a sport coat in sight."

"Remember how that worked out last time, though," I reminded her. "Maybe it's not the best indicator."

"True," she agreed. "I guess you never know."

Leo had wrapped up his conversation and was now making his way toward us, winding through the growing crowd. My date, even though I wasn't supposed to call him that, and yet now all I could think about was Jilly and Ambrose, together. It would never happen. Would it?

"Hey there," Leo said, sliding in beside me. "Where'd you get the beers?"

"Outside," I told him. "Follow me."

We cut through the kitchen, which boasted an impressive display of hot sauces stacked on the wide windowsill, and out onto the side deck, where the keg was set up under a tangle of Christmas lights. Ira, tied nearby, saw me immediately and began wagging his tail.

"Hey there, bud," I said, bending down to scratch his ears. He'd had a haircut and smelled like powder, clearly freshly bathed. "Ten to one Ambrose met a pretty dog groomer," I said out loud. "Am I right?"

"What?" Leo asked from the keg.

"Nothing," I said, standing back up and facing him. "Do you want to go back inside? Or—"

"Let's stay here for a bit," he replied. "Less chance of bumping into more people from high school."

We walked over to a bench that ran along the deck, where I took a seat. Ira, now on a diagonal from me, let out a whine and then lay down, his head on his paws. "You're from here, too?" I said, as Leo leaned on the nearby railing. "I didn't realize."

"Born and bred," he replied. "Class of 2015, Kiffney-Brown."

I raised my eyebrows. "So you're smart."

"By the numbers. I was a big-time math nerd before I started writing."

More new information. "You write?"

A nod. "I'm in the program at the U. Workshops, independent study, all that stuff. I was doing both tracks, but now I'm strictly fiction."

"What kind of stuff?"

"The novel I'm working on right now is kind of a streamof-consciousness take on the dwindling of human contact in society," he replied, as easily as anyone else might rattle off their birthdate and astrological sign. Clearly, he'd said this before. "It's futuristic, but also set in present day. I'm playing with time a lot. It's challenging."

"Huh," I said, before realizing this was about the stupidest response I could have offered. I added, "I love to read. But I've never been very good at writing if it wasn't, like, papers for school."

"Oh, it's totally different," he said, taking a sip of his beer as two girls in thick sandals clomped over to the keg. "Anyone can be taught to present a basic argument or summarize information. Fiction is a skill. You either have it, or you don't."

"And you do."

"Well, yeah." He must have known this sounded arrogant, because he smiled at me, diluting it somewhat. "But I'm still learning. I have this awesome professor, McCallum McClatchy. You ever read his books?"

I shook my head, not exactly wanting to share that the current novel on *my* bedside table was a fantasy novel about girls put under a spell that made them into tigers. They then had to fight a series of other tigers, also former humans, in order to turn back. I'd once been a big fan of contemporary fiction. Since I lost Ethan, though, real life had been bad enough all around me on a daily basis. Between the covers of a book, I wanted anything else.

"Oh, he's great," Leo continued. "Irish born, really sparse in terms of his prose, but with thick language. His whole first book takes place in a potato field over the course of one day, and it's told from the point of view of the *plow*."

"Wow," I said.

"It's incredible." I'd never seen him this excited about coffee. "I'll loan you one of my copies. If you don't mind highlights and margin notes."

"I don't," I said.

"Great. I'll bring it to work tomorrow." He smiled at me again. "It can be kind of a tough read, with all the footnotes and flashbacks. McCallum is my inspiration when it comes to time shifting on the page. But I can walk you through it."

I'd said I wasn't good at writing fiction, not reading it, I thought, but then told myself to stop being so judgmental. When you loved something, you wanted everyone else to love it in the same way. Right? Right.

Just then, my phone rang. With it buried in my bag, which was over my shoulder, it took a second to grab it, during which Leo raised his eyebrows at my ringtone. Who was being judgmental now?

"Hello?"

"Wave at me," a voice said.

I glanced at the screen: Ambrose. "What?"

"I'm inside, in the living room. Facing you right now. Wave at me. Make it look urgent."

"You need an urgent wave?"

"Just do it. Please?" Then he hung up.

I turned, peering over a group of girls huddled in the open sliding-glass door. Ambrose was indeed all the way across the room from me, a red cup now in his hands. A girl with broad shoulders and a high ponytail was facing him, her hands on her hips. He looked like he might be sweating.

"What's going on?" Leo asked.

"Not sure," I said, then waved at Ambrose. He looked surprised, then glanced both ways, as if wondering if it was too late to avoid being spotted. I waved again, this time with a bit more arm. The girl in front of him turned around, narrowing her eyes at me.

"What was that, your ringtone?" Leo asked me. "It sounded like . . ."

"It's nothing," I told him, as the girl with the ponytail turned back to Ambrose, sticking her finger in his face. I watched as he slid out from in front of her, talking the entire time, then made a beeline across the room, dodging in and out of people, before popping out the door a minute or two later. Ira, spotting him, began wiggling, his tail going crazy.

"Thanks," he said to me as he slid in beside me, bumping my leg with his. Not only did I not feel awkward, I didn't even move over. "Melissa was getting a *bit* clingy."

I looked back at the living room, where Melissa, with her big shoulders, was now glaring at me. "What did you tell her?"

"That you are my ex-girlfriend and we've gotten back together since she and I hung out, and you are very jealous," he replied smoothly, now scratching a grateful Ira behind his ears.

"Excuse me?" I said.

"It's fine, our road trip to the mountains was weeks ago."

"You went to the mountains with that girl?"

"I needed some clear air," he explained. "Don't you, sometimes?"

I just looked at him. Across from me, Leo snorted into his beer.

"Anyway, don't let me interrupt *your* night," he said, bending down to untie Ira from the deck rail. "We'll just make our exit and hope for better results at the next party."

"There's always another party, isn't there?" I asked.

"Hope so," he said cheerfully. "Because this one is too small for me and Melissa. You might want to avoid her, you know, just to be on the safe side."

"Won't she wonder why Louna's talking to another guy if she's with you?" Leo asked.

"No, I told her she has a wandering eye and is super promiscuous," Ambrose told him. "That's why we broke up."

"You did *what?*" I said.

"I'm going now!" he said, wrapping the leash around his wrist. "You two kids have fun."

"Leo! What are you doing here?"

Once again, Ambrose was saved by the blonde—this time, a very pretty girl with long straight hair wearing denim shorts and a peasant blouse, gladiator sandals wrapped around her tan legs. Everything about her screamed beach and flowy, and I instantly was aware of my own drab ensemble.

"Lauren," said Leo, breaking into a smile. "Hey."

They embraced, her kissing his cheek, then both turned to face us. "Hi," she said, sticking her hand out. "I'm Lauren."

"Louna," I said.

"She's the girl I met at work, the one I told you about," Leo explained. "And this is . . ."

"Ambrose," Ambrose said, offering his own hand. He was looking right at her, of course; full attention, focused. "And this is Ira."

"Hello, Ira," Lauren said, crouching down to pet him. "Aren't you a handsome boy?"

"He takes after me," Ambrose told her. I rolled my eyes.

Lauren got back to her feet, then gave Leo a friendly punch to the arm. "You jerk. You didn't tell me you'd be here when I said how I was dreading it earlier."

"I didn't know it was the same party," he told her.

"I'm newly single," Lauren explained to me. Ambrose, hearing this, visibly increased his attention level. "And Leo's been on me to try to get back out there and date. But it's hard."

"I know it," I told her. "I'm in the same boat. My best friend basically had to drag me here."

"Then you get it!" She sighed, tucking a piece of hair behind her ear, which was studded with a row of gold and diamond hoops. I'd never seen anyone so, well . . . shimmery. "Once you get dumped, the last thing you want is to offer up your heart again, right?"

"Someone dumped *you*?" Ambrose asked, aghast. "What are they, crazy?"

In response, Lauren smiled gratefully. "You're sweet. And, well, yes. We were together for four years."

"And had known each other since kindergarten, where

we met," Leo added. "We were the Fearsome Threesome on the playground."

"Never date one of your best friends," Lauren said to me. "When it ends, you lose so much more than a boyfriend. It sucks."

On this last word, her voice broke a bit, and she smiled, embarrassed. Leo put his arm around her, and she put her head on his shoulder. "Patrick's a doofus. You'll find someone else. Someone better."

"Which I guess is why I'm here," she said with a sigh. "I'll stay for one beer. Then I'm going home to get into bed and eat ice cream."

"That sounds like a plan," Ambrose said. He reached over, grabbing a red cup and filling it, then presented it with a flourish. "Personally, I like Rocky Road after a bad breakup. It's like a metaphor, fitting."

"Thanks," she said. "Lately I've been mainlining rainbow sherbet. I was hoping it had antidepressant powers."

"Just avoid the chocolate peanut butter or pralines and cream. Too couply for the newly single."

"That's good advice," she said.

"Ambrose was just leaving," I told her.

"Only because I had no reason to stay," he said. "Now we're talking ice cream, so I do."

Lauren blushed slightly, then looked down into her beer. "I'm warning you, I might be terrible company. If I get buzzed I'll probably start telling you my entire sad story."

"I love sad stories. So does Ira," Ambrose told her. The

dog, for his part, started tugging toward the stairs that led down to the yard, clearly sending a message. "Oh, looks like someone needs a walk. I'll be back in a sec."

"I'll come with you, if you want," Lauren offered.

"Yeah?" he said, pushing that curl out of his face.

"It's not like I really want to stay here," she said.

"Lead the way, then."

Ambrose waved his hand, motioning for her to go first. She glanced at Leo, shrugged with a smile, and then started down the steps, Ambrose and Ira following along behind her. I could hear their voices, already chatting, as they disappeared into the dark of the yard below.

"He'd better behave himself," Leo said, as we watched them cut across the grass, their shadows thrown in the moonlight. "That girl's a real prize."

I believed this, even though I'd just met her, and was pretty sure Ambrose got it, too. And watching this particular departure, I knew something was happening. Even from a distance, you could tell when two people simply clicked. Starting with a nighttime walk, well—that just sealed the deal.

CHAPTER

16

ETHAN DID phone me from the parking lot, just as he'd promised. I missed the call.

In my defense, I was packed in the elevator with a group of people who'd just arrived, all talking over each other. If I heard a ringtone of soaring soprano, backed by moaning violins, I probably just assumed it belonged to one of them. It wasn't until I got off on my floor and it rang again in the quiet of the hallway that I realized the noise was coming from my pocket. I pulled it out.

"You might be annoyed now," he said, in lieu of hello, "but that song will grow on you. Someday, it might even make you cry."

When I remembered this later, it broke whatever pieces were left of my heart. But that was later.

"You put a Lexi Navigator song as my ringtone?" I asked.

"While I was getting my bag," he told me. "And before you get mad about me jacking your password for Tunage," he said, "you really should make it harder to figure out."

"How did you know it was William?" I asked.

"You did say he was the alarm code at the house," he told

me. I had, while telling a story about how this was the way I learned to spell his name as a kid. William was our password for everything. "I took a guess."

"Well," I said, still working through all this. I'd had to stop walking just to catch up, so to speak. "Now you know all my secrets."

"Don't worry. They're safe with me."

I turned, looking out over the balcony to the street below. Somewhere, a red car was driving steadily away from me, putting a mile, then another mile between us.

"What am I supposed to tell people when they ask me why I have a Lexi Navigator ringtone?" I asked him now.

"That you are her biggest fan because your boyfriend loves her," he replied. Boyfriend. I liked the sound of that. "And then you show them your screensaver."

"My—" I pulled my phone down, flipping to that setting. Sure enough, there was Ethan grinning next to Lexi Navigator in her stage outfit. I put it back to my ear. "Okay. That's pretty cute."

"I'm glad you think so. As we were driving off I started to worry that maybe you would hate it. Hold on a sec." I heard a voice in the background, then Ethan saying something. "Look, we're stopping for gas and snacks. I'll call back in a bit, okay? You'll know me by 'Pay Attention, the Words Are Changing.'"

"What?"

"The name of the song about her grandmother, Lulu. Come on! How are you going to date Lexi Navigator's number one fan if you don't know her biggest hits?"

I smiled, turning back to my room. "I'll get right on that."

"You can start with your Tunage library, under Recently Purchased. Talk to you in a few!"

With that he was gone, leaving me to just stare, open mouthed, as I went to my music app to find, yes, five new songs, all by Lexi Navigator. I'd listen to them all, over and over again, in between the dozens of short conversations we'd have in the following hours as we each headed back to our respective homes. With Ethan in my ear, the drive back to Lakeview felt, and looked, entirely different. *I* felt like a different girl. I would never again be who I was when I walked down those beach stairs, took off my shoes, and stepped into the sand. And I was so, so glad.

Once home, we talked constantly, and when we weren't talking, we were texting or chatting face-to-face on HiThere! He'd linked the S.O. (significant other) part of his Ume.com page to my profile right after our first phone conversation, at the same time I was adding his to my own. Despite my having dated a few guys already, it wasn't until Ethan that I understood what all the love songs and sappy movie endings really were all about. I finally understood Jilly's buoyant romanticism, the hopefulness that seeps into every part of your life when you know someone loves you in that way. I ate, slept, and dreamed Ethan. When he wasn't in my ear or on my screen in one way or another, I was running over our night together in my mind, hour by hour, so I'd be sure not to forget a single detail.

As we'd promised, we immediately began to make plans to get together again. His dad, still eager to get on Ethan's good side post-divorce, said he'd buy him a ticket down for his fall break, which was in mid-October, overlapping by a few days with mine. I circled the days on my desk calendar and began a countdown on my phone, getting teased regularly by my mom, William, and Jilly about my visible impatience with how slowly time was passing.

"I have never seen you like this," Jilly said to me, staring as I hummed along to Lexi Navigator on the car radio as we drove to school the first day of senior year. "It's like you've been body swapped or something."

"What?" I said. "You've been in love tons of times."

"Not like that. This, what's going on here?" She swirled her finger at me. "It's some serious first love stuff. Sometimes I look over at you and you're just sitting there, smiling at nothing."

"I am not."

"You are. And I'm jealous." She sighed, checking her reflection in the visor mirror. "I want an Ethan, too."

I couldn't blame her. To me, he was perfect: this gorgeous, funny, smart boy who thought I, Lulu, hung the moon as well. It was like my life had been silent in a way before, and now there was a soundtrack, the very best music playing along in the background at every moment. You didn't miss it when it wasn't there. You didn't know to. But once it was, nothing ever sounded the same again.

"Tell me where you are now," I'd say to Ethan when we talked before school, and then at lunch, and after last period, and several more times up until bed, when he was the last voice I heard before going to sleep.

"Walking across the quad to practice, stuffing my face with a bag of Cheese-pops," he said. "Where are you?"

"Heading to the coffee shop for afternoon caffeine for Mom and William."

"Double shot for her, or no?"

"Just the one. She already sounded like she was buzzing."

He just knew me so well, already. Mostly because we talked so much, but there was something else, as well. The time we'd been together had been so short and yet so intense that everything was sped up, like the difference between dog and people years. I already felt like I'd known him forever. This was what love was. I knew it now. And it changed everything.

"When this boy does come," William said to me in early September, as I sat texting with Ethan after school as he rode the bus to a lacrosse game, "I'm going to have to sit him down and have a talk."

"You?" my mom asked from her desk, where she was busy checking a spreadsheet of attendees to the next wedding. "Isn't that my job?"

"I'm the father figure. If anyone gets to sit cleaning a gun while making the boy squirm talking about honor and chivalry, it's me."

"A gun?" I said.

"You maced yourself the last time you tried to carry pepper spray," my mom told him.

"Well, I obviously wouldn't do that while giving this talk," he replied snippily.

"No one is lecturing Ethan about anything," I told them

both, using my own stern voice. "We're all just going to make him feel welcome and show him the best of Lakeview."

"Which is what?" William asked.

"Louna, of course," my mom said. "That's what he's coming for after all, right?"

At this, I blushed, even as my phone beeped, Ethan responding to my last message. NOW WHAT ARE YOU DOING?

PUTTING UP WITH MY MOM AND WILLIAM TEASING ME ABOUT YOU.

HA! CAN'T WAIT TO MEET THEM.

"Look at our girl," William said then. "She's crazy in love. We didn't ruin her with our bad attitudes after all."

"Not yet," my mom said. "Remember, they've only spent one night together."

William gave her a look. "Natalie, for God's sake. Let the girl have her fun. It's not her fault we're all dried up and unlovable."

"Speak for yourself. I am very lovable."

William snorted. My mom caught my eye, then mouthed an *I'm sorry*, looking genuinely apologetic. I knew in truth she was happy for me, but just worried, as her own love story hadn't ended well. But this was different. I was different. And Ethan, well, was Ethan. He would never do anything to hurt me. It never occurred to me that, in fact, it might be someone else.

CHAPTER

17

SURELY AMBROSE had always been a person who hummed.
I probably just hadn't noticed.

"Isn't it time for morning coffee run?" I asked him, as he
launched into the second go-round of a currently popular
dance song, wordlessly. "You know how my mom gets without her caffeine."

He paused the instrumentals. "I thought you'd want to
do it. To see Leo. Don't you?"

I shifted in my seat, then realized I was literally squirming at this question and made myself still. "I'm kind of deep
in these place cards right now."

He looked over from his own stack, equal in size to mine.
"You are?"

"Well, yeah."

I tried to sound breezy, offhand, two things I never was.
It didn't work, a fact made clear when he gave me his full
focus of attention. "Hold on. I thought you guys had a good
time the other night."

"We did," I said, folding another card. The paper was
thick and embossed, each name done by a professional cal-

ligrapher. Wreck it, you pay for it, had been my mom's directive. Never before had paper made me nervous. "I'm just,
you know. . . ."

Usually, when you trail off, people just finish the sentence for you in their own heads. Ambrose's was clearly still
full of beats and choruses, because he said, "You're what?"

"I'm *busy*," I told him. "And it's your job."

He drew back. "Gosh. Okay. Sorry. I'll go right now."

With that, he pushed out his chair and got to his feet,
then headed to the back office, where my mom and William
were conferring with the valet parking company about Elinor Lin's rehearsal dinner, whistling as he went. I was *sure*
he'd never done that before.

So he was happy. No crime in that. And just because he'd
had a great time with Lauren the night before—he hadn't
said so exactly, but the music-making spoke volumes—didn't
mean he was going to win our bet and me lose. I only had
to keep going on dates, just like I'd done with Leo. I wasn't
humming, mind you. But I'd done it.

I winced to myself even as I thought this. After Lauren
and Ambrose had left the night before, Leo and I had talked
for another hour or so, mostly about his writing, the conversation interrupted occasionally by Jilly, coming to complain
that the party sucked and she wanted to go home. Finally,
around eleven, she bumped into some guy she knew from yet
another food truck—the community was wide reaching—and
decided she wanted to stay indefinitely just as I was ready
to leave. In the end, I got a ride with Leo on the back of his

fixed-gear bike, where I felt every bump and rattle of the handful of miles back to my house.

Once there, I could tell he expected to be invited in by the way he kept glancing at the door. But William's car was still there and I didn't feel like making introductions. In the end, we sat on the curb, the bike lying beside us like a literal third and fourth wheel. I was tired of talking, tired in general, and trying to come up with a good exit strategy, but Leo was still going full speed about his writing.

"Really, it's all process," he explained to me. "You have to *dig*, you know? Fiction is blood, sweat, tears, shit, all mixed together. Like the lotus from the mud. If you nurture it, something beautiful comes."

I could admit this all sounded exotic and dramatic at one point. But that had been a few hours earlier, and I still didn't understand exactly what his book in progress was about. "That's cool," I said, a response I'd taken to alternating with a few others like "Wow," "Interesting," and, just for variety, "I never saw it like that." For someone so interested in words, he didn't seem to notice this repetition.

Now he smiled, like I was cute, before reaching out and rubbing his thumb along the side of my mouth, then down my chin. I was thinking maybe I had something on my face, and wondering for how long, when he suddenly moved in to kiss me. It was swift and abrupt and took me by total surprise, even before he leaned me back into the grass with one smooth movement. I had a flash of a vampire whipping a cape over his head, which was not exactly romantic, and then his mouth was on mine, tongue wriggling.

Ugh. I let it go on for a long enough period so as not to seem totally rude, then sat back up. "Well," I said, as he pulled back, his eyes sort of dazed, "I should go. It's late."

"Now?" He looked at the house again. "Really?"

"Yeah." I made an effort to look apologetic, like this was not actually my choice. "I have an early day, and all. . . ."

"Yeah, okay, cool," he said, cutting me off. "I get it."

I stood up, aware of the dampness from the grass on my back. "I'll see you around work, I guess?"

"Sure."

I started up the walk, relieved to finally be wrapping things up. I'd only taken a few steps, though, when he said, "It's the bet, right? Just dates, nothing more. FYI, I didn't really want that either."

Pausing, I said, "Okay."

"It is," he replied, pulling a cigarette out of his pocket. Ugh. At least he'd waited. "Okay, I mean."

Right, I thought. He was still there on the curb when I went inside.

So that was my night. Not totally terrible, just weird. It did not, however, leave me humming, whistling, and walking with a literal bounce in my step, something I noticed as Ambrose passed me, heading out for the coffees.

"You want anything?" he asked. "Maybe a nice melty doughnut?"

"No," I told him. Then, realizing I sounded surly, I added, "Thanks, though."

He gave me a thumbs-up, then pushed out the door. Ira, tied up to the nearby bench and wearing a green bandana, got right to his feet, wagging happily. As Ambrose bent over him, petting his head, I saw he was whistling again.

Just then, my phone rang. Enough time had passed that, sometimes, I didn't even notice my Lexi Navigator ringtone anymore. Today, though, for whatever reason, the opening chords made my heart hurt in a way it had not in a while.

"Hey," Jilly said, sounding especially cheerful herself, considering it was morning and I knew she had all four kids with her for a full day. "Happy Wednesday!"

"Is it?" I asked, doing another card with a bit of extra force on the fold.

"Sure!" she replied. "It's hump day, sunny and gorgeous, and we are on the way to get one of the best biscuits in town. It's perfect!"

I blinked. In the background, Crawford spoke for me, saying, "You're being weird today."

"Oh, hush. Can't a person be happy once in a while?" she asked. To me she said, "The GRAVY Truck is actually right over near you. Can you take a break? I want you to meet Michael Salem."

"Does he always go by his first and last names?"

"Salem is his *middle* name," she corrected me, "and I think it's cute."

"This the guy from the party last night?" I asked.

"I met him there, yes," she replied. "But he's not just a guy from a party, if you know what I mean."

"What *do* you mean?" I asked.

"Just that, you know . . ." She lowered her voice. "I like him. A lot. Like, very much a lot."

I was about to tell her she'd only just met him, that it couldn't possibly be that serious. But I knew the tone of her voice, that buoyant giggle, the sudden glint the world got on a morning after like this. Clearly, epic was going around. Too bad I'd already had my turn.

"That's great, Jilly," I said. "I'm so happy for you."

"Well, I mean, it's early," she replied, sounding anything but under-confident. "But he's just . . . he's so *nice*, Louna. And totally not my type! He had on a hoodie and carried a skateboard the entire time we were together. And he's a redhead. With freckles!"

I smiled. "I can't wait to meet him."

"Then come to the truck. Their chicken biscuits are to die for."

"I wanted a muffin," Crawford said.

"Me, too," said KitKat. "We hate biscuits."

"Hush up," Jilly sang out, hardly bothered. "Louna?"

I looked back at the office, where my mom was still on the phone. "I can't. We've got this huge rehearsal dinner and wedding this weekend. There's tons to do."

"Oh. Okay." She sounded disappointed. For about two seconds. "But you will meet him, and soon, okay? We'll double date, you and the Lumberjack. Hey, how did that go, anyway? You looked like you were having fun."

"It was fine," I told her, as Ambrose came back in with the

coffees, then hummed his way past me, giving me a jaunty salute with his free hand. I tried not to grimace, probably failed. "I'll fill you in later."

"Do that. Or call if you do get a break. I'm in the car or the truck until at least five. Have a great day!"

"Okay," I said, not even trying to match her enthusiasm. I put down my phone, then picked up another card, folding it and adding it to the stack. As I reached for another one, a book suddenly dropped onto the table beside me. A slim paperback, the cover featured a line drawing of a field, one crow flying overhead. HARVEST, it said on the cover. I looked at Ambrose, who was taking his seat beside me. "What's this?"

"A loan from Leo," he replied, starting in on his own stack of cards. "He said to take your time with it."

I pulled the book over, flipping it open. A NOVEL BY MC-CALLUM MCCLATCHY, said the title page. I turned another page, which had passages highlighted, notes scribbled in the margins, and read the first line.

In a world, in a field, a plow sits. Harvest has come.

"Oh, for God's sake," I said out loud, pushing it aside.

Ambrose glanced at me. "Are you okay?"

"I'm fine," I said, a bit too forcefully. "I just want . . . to work."

"Sure." He folded another card. "Let's work."

A moment later, he started humming again.

⸎

"Candles," William said, handing me the long plastic lighter. "Don't forget the ones by the gazebo."

I nodded, then walked over to the nearest table, set with thick linens and gold-rimmed china, a huge collection of white lilies at its center. As I bent over the three pillar candles arranged just so around the place settings, I breathed in their fragrant smell, hoping it might improve my mood. It couldn't hurt.

So the week hadn't been great. At least it was busy, with the details for this weekend's Elinor Lin rehearsal dinner and wedding distracting me from Ambrose's cheerful mood and Jilly's own epic night, which I'd heard all about in the days since. Michael Salem (he was indeed always referred to by this double moniker) had just graduated from the Fountain School, skateboarded in competitions, had four siblings, too, just like her! She'd showed me a picture, of him leaning out of the GRAVY Truck, smiling, a dour-looking Crawford reflected in his big, white-framed sunglasses. He was cute, and, yes, not her type at all. You just never knew, I guess.

I moved on to the next table, lighting the candles there. Behind me, distantly, I could hear my mom talking with Elinor Lin's mother, who had proven to be the biggest wrinkle in the fabric of this weekend's events. Mothers of the bride were always a factor: they had Emotions and Opinions and were often enlisted to convey certain messages or directives the bride was too timid to deliver herself. Elinor Lin didn't need anyone to speak for her, though: she was smart, assertive, and knew exactly what she wanted. I'd thought she was tough until I met Mrs. Lin, who was all of these things but louder, bossier, and ready to spar at any second about whatever didn't suit her. In another world, she and my mom might have been friends, purely out of their similarities. In this one, though, they were anything but.

"People will need direction as they come in," Mrs. Lin was saying as she dabbed her face with a Kleenex, of which she kept an impressive supply in the bodice of whatever she was wearing. The first time I'd noticed her yanking out a tissue from this area, it had startled me, but now it was all I could do not to reach over and do the same when the pollen count got high. You got to know people in weird ways at weddings. "And it's rude to not have someone there to greet them."

"Elinor felt," my mom replied, using the two word prefix she always utilized with Mrs. Lin in these conversations, "that having the table assignments in the gazebo as guests entered would be enough."

"Well, I don't. So put someone there."

With that, she walked away. I risked a glance at my mom, who was watching her go, face calm but eyes narrowed. There really was no counterargument to a person telling you that you are wrong and then what to do, even if you were Natalie Barrett, and I felt a rush of protectiveness toward her. When she glanced at me, though, I quickly went back to the candles.

Just as I lit the wick of a round candle in a glass votive, someone leaned over me and blew it out. Annoyed, I glanced up. Ambrose.

"Sorry," he said quickly. "I just can't light a candle without making a wish and blowing it out. It's some kind of birth-day neurosis."

I looked at the plastic lighter in his hand. "Then you defi-nitely should not be doing this particular job."

"It's okay," he assured me. "I'm just lighting them, wish-ing and blowing, then lighting them again."

Granted, it had been a long day. Just about anything had the potential to cross the line of Just Too Damn Much. But there was something about this that shot me over it. "Are you serious?" I demanded.

"What?"

"That is the stupidest, most waste-of-time thing I've ever heard."

"Ouch." He raised his eyebrows. "Are you mad at me about something?"

"It's not professional! Making wishes, lighting candles twice. You're here representing our company. You need to act like it."

I watched him as he took an exaggeratedly slow look around the backyard of the historic mansion that was our venue. Besides us, there was only the string quartet, tuning up, and a couple of caterers. "Okay. I'll stop. Sorry."

With that, he went on to another table, and I went back to my own work. I found myself pausing, though, with the next candle I lit, thinking of what he'd said. But I didn't make a wish. What was the point?

By six fifty-five, when all the candles were done and the first guests were pulling up at the valet stand, my mom came over to me. "I'm going to need you to stand by the gazebo and direct the guests to their tables."

Her face was sour as she said this, clearly not happy. That made two of us. "Sure," I told her. "But I don't think we need it. People can figure it out for themselves."

She gave me a smile, squeezing my arm, and walked away. Over in the gazebo, I double-checked that all the tea lights were lit, the seat assignments lined up neatly on the table in front of them. When an older couple came through, I smiled, ready to guide them, but they just took their cards and walked on, not even looking at me. One point to Natalie Barrett.

As another group of guests approached, I looked across the tables to the small pond on the backyard's edge, where Ambrose was standing with William, talking about something. His face was animated as he gestured, smiling frequently, as William nodded politely, seeming kind of charmed. I thought of Jilly earlier, and all day really, the unique quality to a person's voice when you know they are just as happy to hear themselves say something as they are to tell it to you. Of course I couldn't say Ambrose was definitely talking about Lauren: it could have been Ira, or anything. And yet.

"Louna?"

I turned to see Ben Reed standing by the place card table, wearing a shirt and tie and smiling at me. He'd sat beside me for an entire semester of the most boring World Civ class ever, during which we'd taken turns keeping each other awake and always partnered for projects. He was a nice guy, funny and sweet, with a longtime girlfriend, Amy Tellman, who he'd dated since middle school. "Hey," I said, then gave him a hug. "What are you doing here?"

"Tennis," he explained. Ben had played for the varsity team; until that moment, I'd never seen him without a racket poking out of his backpack. "Albert Lin and I grew up doing the camps and tournaments together. Our moms are tight. What about you? How do you know Elinor and Mark?"

"My mom's the wedding planner. I'm working," I explained, then turned to the table, scanning the cards until I found his name. I picked it up, holding it out to him. "And you are at table six."

"Thank you," he said, taking it from me. He glanced out into the yard. "Looks fancy. Now I wish I'd brought a date."

"How is Amy?"

He winced, hearing this, basically answering the question. "I wouldn't know. We broke up a couple of weeks ago."

"What?" I said, shocked. He winced again. Whoops. "I'm . . . God, I'm sorry. You guys were so . . . wow. I'm sorry."

He nodded. "Thanks. It was her decision. Last summer before college, wanting to make a fresh start at UC Berkeley, blah blah. I should have seen it coming."

"Well, I didn't."

"Me neither. I'm basically gutted." He sighed, looking down at his card. "Anyway. It's great to see you. Especially without having old Partone droning on about global implications in front of us."

"He did love the big consequences," I agreed, as two women entered the gazebo. "Have fun tonight."

At this, he made a face, then smiled as he started across the lawn to his table. Halfway there, he turned back and glanced at me, looking away quickly when he saw I was still watching him.

"Wait, what is this? The tables? How do we know which number we are?"

I sighed inwardly, then turned around to help the two women. One point to Mrs. Lin. No matter the issue, there was always an ongoing tally, somehow.

⚜

The end of a rehearsal dinner is different from that of a wedding. Even if it's late, there's still that sense of anticipation and excitement, the big event still ahead. That is, if you're a guest. When you're working, it's one down, one to go.

"You're sure? You won't get upset?"

I gave Ambrose an apologetic look, knowing I deserved this. "No. And I shouldn't have earlier. I'm just super grumpy, for some reason. I'm sorry."

"It's okay," he said. Then, as I watched, he briefly closed his eyes, blowing out the pillar between us. I wondered what he wished for. I'd never ask, though. "I didn't realize Leo was such a bust as a date."

"He wasn't," I told him, blowing out the next candle. "It's me."

"Lauren seems to think otherwise."

"You talked to Lauren about this?"

"Well, yeah," he said. He glanced at me. "You weren't yourself, and Leo is her best friend. I figured she'd have insight."

I suppose I deserved this, too, but it was harder to take somehow. "Did she?"

"She said," he replied, moving to the next table, "that he is great if you've known him forever, like she has, but that in college he's become a bit . . ."

I waited, curious about exactly what adjective would follow. This was not a case when you filled it in.

". . . insufferable," he finished. He blew out another candle. "She blames his writing professor and hopes it's just a phase. But she understood he probably isn't the best boyfriend material right now."

"Good thing I'm not the one who has to stick in the long-term relationship," I commented.

"Oh, I've got you beat, no question," he replied. "Lauren will make it easy."

After all the whistling, humming, bouncy steps, and general good cheer, the fact he felt this way shouldn't have been any kind of surprise to me. But hearing it, for whatever reason, was still difficult. I had a flash of him standing behind me, cutting that cake, then quickly pushed it away. "She seems great," I said.

"She's awesome." He moved over to the next table. "Don't feel bad, it was just a super stroke of luck she showed up when she did that night."

"I'm still in this," I reminded him. "All I have to do is date a bunch of people once, and I'm doing that."

"True, true," he agreed. Out on the street, someone zoomed past, tires squealing. I could only hope it wasn't one of the valets. "So you're saying you have another prospect already lined up?"

"I'm working on it," I said, which wasn't exactly a lie, if thinking counted as working. What I'd actually been mulling, a bit worriedly, was that if Jilly was so into Michael Salem, I'd be losing the one person who was happy to set me up repeatedly. Unless he had a friend. Or, um, lots of friends.

"Well, good," Ambrose said. "It's no fun if we can't keep it interesting."

"Don't worry about that. You just focus on you," I said, walking over to another table and bending over the row of small votives there to blow them out. Once done, I looked up to see him staring at me. "What?"

"You really don't make a wish? Like, ever?"

"It's not my birthday, and this isn't a cake," I pointed out.

"Yeah, but it doesn't have to be. Why wouldn't you ask for something, given the chance?"

"Birthdays are special. These are just candles."

"Still counts," he said firmly.

"Ambrose, come on."

"What? You don't need anything? Your life is perfect?"

"It's just a wish," I said. "I don't want to burst your bubble, but just because you make them doesn't increase the chances of them working."

"You're still putting it out there, though," he countered. "Into the universe. Has to count."

I looked down at the row of four flames in front of me,

still lit. "Let's just agree to disagree, okay? It's your thing, like stealing dogs and doing the conga. Doesn't mean it has to be mine, right?"

"That's how you sum me up?" he asked, and I smiled. "Dog stealer and conga dancer?"

"And wish maker," I added. "I'm just not. That's okay, right?"

He held my gaze for a second, and I had the fleeting thought, out of nowhere, that he might say it wasn't. Instead, though, he came over and bent down, then closed his eyes, blowing out the row from one end to another. When he was done, he gave me a smile, then walked off to the next table. It wasn't until later, driving home, that I realized he'd never answered my question. But I knew the real reply to his. My last birthday, I'd closed my eyes and thought of nothing when I leaned over my cake. You stop believing in wishes when the only one you want to make can never come true.

CHAPTER
18

THAT MORNING, I texted Ethan as soon as I woke up, like I did every day. I never got out of bed until I saw his return message pop up on my screen.

MORNING, LULU. HAVE A GOOD ONE.

With that, I pushed back the covers, getting to my feet, and went to take a shower, dropping my phone onto the speaker just outside the bathroom on my way. I didn't listen to Lexi Navigator that particular day, even though it was my go-to rise and shine music. Instead, it was news, just headlines, none of which I remembered after toweling myself off.

Once dressed, I grabbed my backpack and headed downstairs, where my mother was still in her bathrobe watching *Daybreak USA*, her favorite morning show. For the two hours it was on each day, she'd keep up a running commentary on the four hosts, weighing in on their hair and makeup, their reactions as they interviewed guests, and their interplay with each other. Everyone had something, I guess, and my mom's was a morning news program.

"Melissa is just too thin these days," she said to me, as I popped a bagel in the toaster, checking the clock. "I know she's going through that divorce, but she needs to take care of herself."

I glanced at the screen, where Melissa Scott, in a teal dress, was reporting on the stock market. She looked fine to me. "What do you and William have going on today?"

"Just prep for Rachel Quaker's rehearsal dinner, and the wedding tomorrow," she replied. During the school year, I only worked on weekends, so I was less up to date on the various events we had planned. This one, though, I remembered, if only for the unique last name.

"This is the one with the bucking bronco, right?" I asked.

She sighed, closing her eyes. On the TV, Drew Tate, the meteorologist, was now pointing at a weather map. "It's a mechanical bull, and I can't believe you're bringing it up when it's not absolutely necessary."

"Sorry," I said, stifling a laugh. It wasn't easy to throw something at my mom she wasn't experienced with, but Rachel Quaker, a native Texan, had done just that when she requested a rodeo-themed rehearsal dinner. Besides the bull, there would be special-ordered barbecue and ribs trucked in from her home state, complimentary cowboy hats for all guests, and beribboned baskets full of wet naps. My mother had been complaining about it for weeks. The only upside was that the wedding itself was as traditional as the dinner was not: big church, big guest list, really big money. If my mom had a price for dealing with electronic animals, they'd clearly met it.

"Mark my words, someone will break their neck. We can only pray it is not the bride or groom," she replied, which had been her mantra since the planning had gotten underway months earlier. She took a sip of her coffee, nodding at the TV. "Look at Patrick Williams. He's had so much Botox he can't even look concerned for those poor people on that wrecked ferry."

My bagel popped up and I grabbed it, taking another look at the screen. This time, I could see her point. Patrick Williams had never met a cosmetic procedure he didn't like, and HD kept no secrets. "I gotta go. I told Jilly I'd meet her early to study for that Spanish quiz."

"Be sure to eat that whole bagel," she called after me as I started for the door. "I've got enough worries with Melissa."

In the car, I ate half as I headed out of our neighborhood, then turned onto the main road to school. At the first stoplight, my phone beeped. It was Jilly, driving KitKat and Crawford to school, like she did every day.

LUNCHBOX FAIL. BE THERE ASAP. COURTYARD?

I glanced at the light, still red, then quickly replied with a thumbs-up. As traffic starting moving again, I heard my ringtone.

"*Hola, niña bonita,*" Ethan said when I picked up. "*¿Estás lista para la prueba?*"

"I think the fact that I have no idea what you are saying does not bode well for this quiz today," I replied.

"I asked if you were ready for the test," he said, laughing. "Also I called you a pretty girl."

"Well, that's nice." I smiled. "And the answer is clearly no."

I heard someone's voice in the background; he drove to his own school every day with three of his buddies, and the collective volume was always high. "Will you guys shut up? I'm trying to talk to my girlfriend."

I felt my face flush. That never got old.

"You're *always* talking to your girlfriend," someone said. "And aren't we stopping for doughnuts? It's Friday."

"No can do, I said I'd meet Coach in his office before the late bell," Ethan said. To me he added, "Still not sure what this is about. Got me kind of in knots."

"It's got to be good," I told him, as I had the night before, and the day before that. Getting called in for a special meeting with his lacrosse coach could only mean something really good or bad, according to Ethan. My money was on the former, but I understood his worry. "Be sure to text me, though. I'm curious."

"You and me both." Another chorus of laughter from the background. "I'd better go, we're almost there. Talk at lunch?"

"Yep," I said, as school came up in the distance. Usually I got to mine first, as he and his buddies were always stopping for food en route. "I can tell you how badly I bombed that quiz."

"*Vas a hacer bien,*" he replied.

"I don't know what that means!"

"You'll do fine," he told me, laughing. "Love you, Lulu."

"Love you, too," I told him. "Talk soon."

I pulled into the lot, then wound around, looking for a parking space. By the time I found one, in the lower part dotted with dusty potholes, my console clock said 7:55. I had twenty minutes to find Jilly, cram like crazy, and then hope for the best for the quiz.

When I got to the bench in the courtyard where we always met, she wasn't there, so I sat down and pulled out my book to go over verb tenses. I thought about Ethan, going to his coach's office at probably right that same moment, and closed my eyes, thinking a good thought for him.

By the time the bell rang, Jilly still hadn't shown up. *So much for studying,* I thought, although I wasn't exactly surprised. Everything at the Baker house was nuts, but the mornings were especially so, which was why Jilly had such a low grade in Spanish: she was always late. I was just bad at it. Apparently.

When I got to class, Señor Richards was already giving out the quizzes. I slid into a seat and opened my bag, taking out a pen and checking the door again for Jilly as he handed me mine. I scanned the first question: no idea. Great.

The late bell rang, and after the normal amount of backpack zipping and general settling-in noises, the room fell silent around me. As I worked down the page I realized I wasn't entirely clueless, which was encouraging. Up at the front of the room, Señor Richards was on his laptop, brow furrowed as he scanned the screen.

By the time I'd finished the quiz as best I could, it was eight forty-five and I was one of the last ones to hand in my paper. As I did, I glanced outside for Jilly. A half hour was late, even for her. A few moments later, Señor Richards got to his feet, coming around to lean against the desk, and told us in Spanish to open our books to page 176. THE SUBJUNC-TIVE, the title heading said in English. The upshot seemed to be that you used it when you weren't certain. Well, I thought, that would come in handy for me.

Just then, outside the half-open door, I heard someone running down the hallway. For a minute I thought it was Jilly, but then they passed by, a blur in my side vision as Señor Richards directed our attention to the board, where he was busy writing something in his boxy print.

At 9:05, when the bell rang signaling the end of the period, I immediately pulled out my phone, expecting to see a string of increasingly panicked texts from her over the last fifty minutes. But there was nothing except a bunch of news alerts, which I didn't bother to read. I had a long way to go in the five minutes we were given between classes if I wasn't going to be late myself, to Art History.

As usual, everyone seemed to be moving super slowly when I was in a rush. The hallway was packed with people on their phones or talking loudly to each other as I wound through bodies and backpacks, trying to get to the one staircase that was usually less crowded than the others. By the time I got downstairs, I only had two and a half minutes until the bell. I did notice a lot of people standing around the TV in the main office, looking at something, but it didn't occur to me to see what it was.

Once outside, I passed a couple making out and two guys walking super slowly with instrument cases as I headed for the steps that led to the Art and Theatre building. I pulled my backpack closer and started up them, taking the last couple two at a time, then popped out right by my classroom's back door, which Ms. DiMarcello, bless her, kept propped open because she knew it was a valued shortcut.

"Louna!"

When I heard Jilly's voice, some aspect of it—tone, volume, a trembling—made me stop where I was. I turned around to see her coming toward me across the grass, where you weren't allowed to walk, her footsteps leaving prints in the dew. She had one hand to her mouth, and her eyes were wide. Without even knowing why, I suddenly felt cold.

"Oh, my God," I said, rushing over to meet her. "What happened? Are you okay? Is it one of the kids?"

The bell rang then, loud and piercing. She reached out, her fingers clamping my upper left arm. "No, it's not . . . Louna, there's been a shooting."

"A what?" I said. Just behind me, I could hear my teacher rapping her hand on the wooden desk to quiet everyone down, just like she always did. "I don't understand."

In response, she pulled out her phone. BREAKING, it said in yellow block letters on the screen, above an image of a flat, cinderblock building with a flagpole out front, a tiger painted on its side. SHOOTER CONFIRMED AT HIGH SCHOOL, BROWN-WOOD, NEW JERSEY.

I just looked at the words, trying to make sense of them.

"Oh, my God," I said, immediately pulling out my own phone, fingers shaking as I selected Ethan's number. It went straight to voicemail, but that wasn't unusual: he wasn't allowed to have his phone out in class. Still, I fired off a text— YOU OK???—for when he would see it. Because Ethan was fine. He had to be. What were the chances?

"I was late, with Crawford's stupid lunchbox thing, and I heard them break in on the radio," she said. She was still holding my arm. "It was in the gym, at least that's what they were saying."

Ethan's first class was English: I knew this as well as, if not better than, the fact that Spanish was my own. "He wouldn't have been in the gym," I said. "He starts in the main building."

"Oh, good," she said. She eased her grip, finally, letting her hand drop. "I just, when I heard Brownwood, and they said there were fatalities—"

I looked back at my screen and the two words I'd sent, willing the dots to appear beneath them that would signal he was typing a response. Nothing.

"Louna?" I heard Ms. DiMarcello call from the door behind me. "Time to come in. We're starting."

"One second," I called over my shoulder. I looked at Jilly. "He's fine, right? It's a huge school, he always says so."

"I'm sure he is," she said. "And it sounds like he wasn't even near there."

"Yeah." I swallowed, looking at my phone again. "I should . . . I guess I'll go in to class?"

"Okay," she said. Neither of us moved. "I'm sure he'll text you any minute."

I heard footsteps and looked behind her to see a school resource officer coming toward us. There were two: one was wide and muscular, built like a fireplug, the other skinny and tall. This was the skinny one. "Ladies, it's past late bell. Move along to your second periods."

"I'm going," Jilly told him, then looked at me again. "Text me. The minute you hear."

"I will," I said. He was still standing there, watching us. I slipped my phone in my pocket and went inside.

For the next fifty minutes, Ms. DiMarcello stood in front of the board, lecturing about the Surrealists. Not that I could have told you then, or now, what she said: I wrote not one word on the empty white page of the notebook in front of me, my eyes instead on my phone's screen, which I had hidden under my coat in my lap. Our school, like Ethan's and most others, had a strict in-class no-screen policy that I usually followed. But that day, I would have fought someone to keep it close and on. By the time the bell rang, there was still no word.

The minute I got back outside, I dialed him again. This time, it went straight to voicemail without even ringing. Clearly, I was not the only one calling. I pulled up my texts.

PLEASE LET ME KNOW YOU ARE OKAY.

No dots. I felt suddenly sick, and lurched over to a nearby trash can, pulling my hair back. But nothing happened. Just people pushing past, talking, on their way to class, like any other day.

Then, a beep. *Thank God*, I thought, tears springing to my eyes.

ANY WORD?

Jilly. I typed her back NO, then started walking down to the main building, still gripping my phone in my hand. My next class was Western Civ, all the way down by the bus parking lot. It wasn't until I was about halfway there that I remembered something about my conversation with Ethan that morning.

Said I'd meet Coach in his office before the late bell.

I stopped walking right where I was, causing someone to bump me from behind. They exhaled, then cut around me as I opened my news app. The latest wasn't hard to find: it was right at the top. BREAKING STORY: SHOOTING AT NJ HIGH SCHOOL. I clicked the link, which took me to a picture of that same school building and flagpole, this time with cop cars parked all around the front of it. Three bullet points, designed for scanning quickly, were below.

SHOTS FIRED JUST BEFORE FIRST PERIOD, AROUND 8:20 A.M.
MULTIPLE VICTIMS REPORTEDLY IN GYM AREA
SHOOTER BELIEVED TO BE CURRENT STUDENT, ACTING ALONE

8:20, I thought. I'd just gotten my Spanish quiz. Ethan should have been in English, trying not to look at the hair of the girl in front of him, which he maintained was so greasy it literally dripped onto his desk. I knew this. I knew everything about him. So how did I not know if he was all right?

The hallway was emptying as everyone went into classrooms and down the nearby staircase. Moments earlier, it had been packed, elbow to elbow, with me just one of a sea of people. Now I stood there, staring at my screen, until all the doors around me shut and I was the only one left, standing alone. I told myself I wasn't moving until I knew something, that I'd stop time in this interim. Later, it would seem silly that I thought I could do this, have some control over events already unfolded. But I believed in a lot of things, before. I never heard from Ethan again.

CHAPTER
19

"DO YOU want a tissue?" William said to my mother, in an attempt at humor. He nodded at Mrs. Lin's ample bosom, where a Kleenex was indeed poking out, at the ready. "Because I know where to find one."

In response, my mother just blinked, trying to hold back the tears of frustration that were brimming in her eyes. Just moments earlier, she'd found out via text that the next week's wedding, for which we'd done tons of legwork and put down multiple deposits, had been called off. Then, as she was absorbing that news, Mrs. Lin approached and unloaded a loud, shrieking tirade about her sudden, strong dislike of the tulle bows tied on the backs of the chairs, which had been her idea in the first place. It was the latest in a long day of similar takedowns over tiny details; anyone else would have cracked hours earlier. It took my mom until now, almost eight p.m. and three hours past the ceremony, but finally, she'd gotten there.

As William patted her shoulder, moving his hand in that familiar soothing circle, I forced myself to take a deep breath. I hated to see my mother upset. Mostly because it never happened, so it was kind of scary, like the world—or my world—was tilting the wrong way on its axis.

"Louna, I'm fine," she said to me now, clearly aware of this. "I'm pissed off, not sad. And it's mostly about the Marlo Wagner cancellation. At least now we know why she bailed on the photo shoot."

"Being yelled at about the chair bows did not help matters, though," William said, moving his hand now in the other direction. "Considering we were clear we were against it from the start. Who wants their chair gift wrapped? And then she takes her bad decision out on you? Unacceptable."

"I hate this wedding," my mother grumbled, wiping her eyes with a tissue not snatched from someone's chest.

"And I hate that woman," William told her. "But let's look at the upside, shall we? No Wagner wedding next weekend means we can actually go on that freebie trip to check out St. Samara for the Kerr wedding."

"Oh, God," my mother groaned. "Are you still even thinking about that? We don't do out of town weddings. And now you want to try one on an *island*?"

"Correction. I want to take a free *trip* to an island under the guise of considering a wedding there," he told her. "Just think about it. Beach, clear blue water, cocktails with umbrellas, all expenses paid. If you didn't already deserve it, you definitely do after tonight."

As if to punctuate this, Mrs. Lin began at that moment to lay into a member of the catering staff. The woman, startled, cowered back, a tray of empty glasses trembling above her. I looked over to the head table, where Elinor Lin was huddled close with her new husband, their heads ducked together, both of them smiling. While part of me wished she'd take responsibility for the tornado that was her mother, I had to admit she looked awfully happy. And God knew she probably deserved it. We'd only dealt with Mrs. Lin for a few weeks. I couldn't imagine an entire life.

As I thought this, Ambrose walked up to our little confab. "All clear on the fainting junior bridesmaid," he reported. "I just checked on her again and she's fine."

Hearing this, I glanced over at the head table, where, sure enough, the tween who'd passed out during the vows earlier was now giggling with one of the flower girls. We were used to people getting woozy, if not blacking out altogether. It was why my mom always gave her "don't lock your knees and standing will be a breeze" speech at rehearsals, especially when it was hot outside. Inevitably, though, we had a few people go down, and this girl had done it in spectacular fashion, crashing into a flower arrangement and taking it with her. When she came to and realized what happened, she was so embarrassed she burst into tears.

I'd led her into a side room, water in hand, prepared to stay with her there until the ceremony ended. But it was Ambrose who proved to be crucial in the moment.

"You think that was bad?" he asked her, sliding into the folding chair adjacent to her own. "I'll tell you about embarrassing. This one time? I was trying to walk backward while talking to a girl and didn't see the curb. Fell over it, landed right on my tailbone, screamed like a baby. It was horrifying."

The junior bridesmaid, face red, just looked at him. "Really?"

"Oh, yeah," he said, waving his hand easily. "And that was nothing. Another time, at school, I was giving this presentation on toxic waste and my pants fell down. I was into baggy clothes then, but man, not *that* baggy."

At this, I laughed: I couldn't help myself. He grinned at me, then at the girl, who now had the barest semblance of a smile. "And another time," he continued, lowering his voice slightly, "I was messing with this tape dispenser and it exploded in front of my boss and this seriously pretty girl who worked with me. There was *smoke*, and I had to get down on the floor and clean it all up, in front of everyone."

I blinked, remembering. He sure hadn't seemed embarrassed. And I was pretty now, in this retelling? Just as I thought this, he looked up at me, the tween now tittering beside him, and I felt myself smile. I'd realized a lot of things about Ambrose that day and since, but this one always surprised me. He was kind. So kind. Who knew?

Now I watched as he adjusted his tie, then said to us, "DJ says they'll do the bouquet and garter toss in fifteen. Next, another half hour of dancing, followed by the grand exit. Then we can start kicking people out."

"Starting with Mrs. Lin," I said, as my mother gave me a smile.

"Good luck with that," he replied. "She just read me the riot act about the dessert forks. I don't even know what those are."

My mother, hearing this, turned to look at the near-est table, taking in the place settings there. Even when she thought someone was crazy, she still wanted things to be just right. It was either a professional strength or weakness: I had not yet figured out which.

"Oh, and Louna," Ambrose added, as she picked up a fork, conferring with William, "that guy at table ten asked if I knew where you were. Just a hunch, but I'm betting he doesn't know your strict policy about dancing."

"I don't have a policy about dancing," I told him. "Just dancing at weddings at which I am *working*."

"Well, you better tell him. Because here he comes."

Sure enough, when I turned, Ben Reed was approaching from behind me, that same familiar easygoing smile on his face. My mom and William moved aside, giving me space, and I expected Ambrose to follow suit. But of course, he stayed right where he was.

"Hey," Ben said. "You disappeared."

"This is the kind of wedding that keeps you running," I explained. "Having a good time?"

"Yeah." He glanced at Ambrose. "Um, actually, I wanted to ask you something."

Now, surely, Ambrose would leave us alone. He didn't. I turned my body, to at least block him out. "Sure," I said.

Ben glanced across the country club lawn, where the dance floor, set up under a white tent, was packed with people. "I wondered if you might want to d—"

Just then, there was a burst of loud laughter from the

table behind us, followed by the clinking of glasses. But I'd gotten the idea.

"I can't," I said. "I'm not allowed to when I'm working."

Ben looked confused. "Like, at all?"

"Well, no." I looked at my mom and William, now discussing the forks. "Because we're part of the staff, it's frowned upon."

"So you can't go out, even after it's over?"

Now I was perplexed. Ambrose, however, had not missed anything. "He asked you if you wanted to *do* something," he said, leaning into my ear. "I think you misheard?"

I felt my face get red, along with a sudden surge of fury that he was even part of this exchange. "I'm so sorry," I said to Ben, shaking my head. "I thought . . . I thought you asked me to dance."

"Oh," he said. For some reason he looked at Ambrose. Maybe he thought he might have to interpret this, as well? "No. But I can. I mean, I will. I just thought because you were working—"

"That's what I meant," I said, stepping over his words. "I mean, when I said that. Clients can't totally forbid me to be social. Yet, anyway."

At this, he smiled, and it occurred to me, distantly, that this would be the kind of meet-cute story someone in another situation might tell, years later, part of a beginning. "Good. Because I was beginning to wonder if this was a slave labor sort of situation."

"It can be. But not like that."

We both stood there a second, recalibrating. Then I felt Ambrose lean into my ear again. "You still haven't answered his actual question, FYI."

"Will you *butt out?*" I said to him through clenched teeth, adding a swat for good measure. This time, he backed away. A bit. With Ben watching, like we were both crazy. I took a breath, composing myself. "I'd love to do something once this is all over. If, you know, you're still asking."

He smiled. "I am. How about this week? A movie, dinner . . ."

"Great," I said. "Just text me. Let me give you my number."

As he pulled out his phone, opening up the contacts and handing it to me, I wondered why Ambrose was so interested in this, especially since he had his own perfect, awesome girl and, in his mind, our bet pretty much sealed up. I was going to ask him after I'd typed in my number and Ben walked away. By then, though, he was gone.

❧

Two and a half hours later, I was busy untangling yet another tulle bow from a chair. It was ten thirty, long past the originally projected end of the Lin wedding, and we'd just seen the last of the guests out the doors to their cars. This was a full hour after the departure of the bride and groom, which, despite the happy cuddling I'd seen at the head table earlier, did not—as far as my system went, anyway—bode well for their union. While the guests threw birdseed and glitter (great for pictures, awful if you didn't want it on you and your clothes for eternity), Elinor and her groom came out to the limo to make their grand exit. They smiled for the camera and their friends and family. But in the final view I had from my vantage point near the country club gates, she was tugging her bias-cut, fluted dress as if he'd sat on it, her face annoyed, while he sat back against the seat, rolling his eyes. For them, I wished for forgiveness.

Maybe, I realized, I believed in wishes after all. At least for other people. Thinking this, I glanced over at Ambrose, who was collecting the large flower arrangements from the tables and toting them to Mrs. Lin's car. What she planned to do in her hotel room with twenty towering vases of lilies, roses, and greenery was anyone's guess. She'd made it very clear, however, that she would be taking anything the family paid for with her when she (finally) (blessedly) left. For the time being, however, she was still walking around barking orders. Ambrose and I were the only ones left to hear them, however; my mom and William had taken their ritualistic toast and commentary elsewhere.

"And these programs," I heard her saying now, grabbing up the stack I'd brought from the church after the ceremony and put on the cake table. "Are the serving pieces ours?"

"No, they belong to the caterer," Ambrose told her from behind a wobbling iris.

"Oh." Mrs. Lin glanced around. "Well, the cocktail napkins, then."

She picked them up, then headed my way, toward the exit. I made a point of bending down deeply over the chair in front of me, as if untying the bow there was on the level of splitting an atom. Even so, she said, "I'll want all this fabric from these bows, as well. Tulle isn't cheap."

"Will do," Ambrose said cheerfully. I shot him a look, which he didn't see, too busy trying to keep up with her as she marched across the grass. Not for the first time, I wondered how he managed always to be so good natured, especially when my own patience had long ago worn thin.

By eleven fifteen, all that was left were the tents, tables, and chairs, which the venue would deal with (although I did see Mrs. Lin, on one of her final passes, studying them as if considering whether they, too, would fit in her rental car). It wasn't until she drove off, the sedan packed to the ceiling, that my mother and William reappeared. They were in a much better mood, red-cheeked and giggly. What Mrs. Lin gives, champagne takes away.

"Ding-dong, the witch is gone," William said, as her taillights turned out of the gates. "That was one for the record books."

"Mark my words," my mother said, "I will not deal with that woman again. If she forgot something, one of you has to get it to her."

"I doubt that's going to happen," Ambrose told her. "She took just about anything not nailed down."

"But the question," William said, pointing at him, "is did *you* take anything?"

My mom and I looked at each other, not understanding. Then Ambrose, smiling, reached into his pocket, pulling out a handful of tissues. "Yep."

"Damn!" William cackled. "I owe you twenty bucks."

"Am I drunk? I don't think I'm drunk," my mom said to me. "But I don't understand."

William was still tittering, pulling out his wallet, while Ambrose carefully folded the tissues. Then, suddenly, I got it. "You took those from her *bosom*?"

Hearing me say this, William busted out laughing again. My mom, trying to look stern, said, "Okay, despite her behavior, that is not appropriate."

"Oh, I think it's *very* appropriate," William told her, handing over a twenty to Ambrose, who took it with a grin. "She basically had them there in full view, like a human tissue dispenser. Don't tell me you weren't tempted."

"I was tempted to punch her in the face," my mom said. "But I guess this is the next best thing."

"And the *next* best," William said, "is us finally being done with this event for good. Next weekend, St. Samara."

"I have not agreed to that, William," my mom said.

"I already called Dr. Kerr, who contacted his travel agent. We leave Friday morning."

"What?"

"Natalie." He put his hands on her shoulders. "When was the last time we got to go anywhere in mid-summer, much less a tropical island? I need this. *We* need this. We're going."

My mom, exasperated, looked at me. I said, "I think it sounds great. You totally should do it."

"See? Even Louna thinks so." He dropped his hands. "Oh, I can't wait. I am going to buy a straw hat just for the occasion. I'll get you one, too."

"I don't want a straw hat."

"You'll change your mind," he said easily. "Now come on. Let's go finish that bottle at your place. Then we can go online and order resort wear."

My mom still didn't look convinced, but she followed him to the van, climbing into the passenger seat. To be honest, I couldn't remember the last time she'd taken a vacation, and never during wedding season. Everything was different this summer.

As they drove off, my phone beeped. It was Ben. Already. Interesting.

KNOW YOU MIGHT STILL BE WORKING BUT
I WAS THINKING LATE NIGHT BREAKFAST.
WORLD OF WAFFLES?

"Well, that's romantic," Ambrose, who was somehow looking over my shoulder *again*, said. "Pancakes and thee? That's a seriously awesome first date. You have to do it."

I just looked at him until, slowly, he took a step back. "Why are you so invested in this? You were on us like a chaperone earlier."

"I'm a curious person," he said, like this was an excuse. "Also I have a lot invested in winning this bet."

"I thought you said you had it in the bag. That Lauren makes it easy."

"I do, and she does. But now you're bringing in pancakes. I have to stay vigilant."

I looked back at my phone. It was late evening, the whole

night ahead of us. Pancakes would be a great start. And yet I knew I wouldn't. I'd had the most epic of nights once. Things like that didn't happen again.

WISH I COULD. WIPED. TEXT ME TOMORROW?

The little dots appeared: he'd been waiting. SURE. SLEEP GOOD.

"What?" Ambrose said. I looked at him. "You just made a face."

"Did I?"

"Yeah." He read the screen—of course he did—then clicked his tongue. "And I don't get it, either. That is good play he's giving. Pancakes? Telling you how to sleep? How can you not be into that?"

I put my phone back in my pocket. "It's not him."

"Then what is it?"

I looked up at him, trying to figure out how to answer this. In the weeks since we'd gone to Kirby's together, I'd been waiting for the subject of Ethan to come up some other way between us. A passing mention from my mom, or William, or even Jilly. But it hadn't. As far as he knew, I'd just had a bad breakup.

"Just too much like a first date I had with someone else," I said. "Nobody wants to be a pale imitation."

He studied me a second. Then he said, "That boyfriend of yours must have really been something. If the split ruined pancakes for you and everything."

"Yeah," I said. "Plus, I'm tired. But don't worry. Ben and I *will* have a great date this week. Don't count me out yet. I'm still on track to win."

I expected him to laugh at this, or respond in kind with his typical bravado. Instead, he said nothing, just stood there until I was acutely aware of his silence. "Okay," he said finally. "We'll see."

I smiled, shifting my bag to my other arm. It seemed a weird way to leave things, heavy in a sense I couldn't explain. Without thinking, I reached forward to his jacket pocket, pulling out one of those folded Kleenexes. "Sorry," I said. "Couldn't resist."

"Must be going around," he replied.

A car pulled into the lot then, curving around to stop in front of us. It was Lauren, in a black tank dress and silver bracelets, her hair in loose waves. Ira was in the front seat, panting, his signature bandana—yellow this time—tied jauntily around his neck. "Hey," she said. "All done here?"

I slipped the tissue into my pocket as Ambrose said, "Yep. Let's go."

She waved at me as he climbed into the front seat, Ira jumping into the back and just as quickly poking his head up through the space between them. *Just one big happy family*, I thought, as they drove off. On my own way home, I passed the World of Waffles, lit up and busy as it seemed to be all times of the night, and wondered if I'd made a mistake. Just as quickly, though, I'd passed by, and it was behind me.

CHAPTER
20

BY THE beginning of the following week, my mom was finally coming around to the idea of a couple of days away. She was predicting the trip would be a disaster, mind you, and saying she'd never agree to an actual wedding that far offsite in a million years. But for her, this was progress.

"See that?" she said to me on Tuesday morning, as she sat in front of *Daybreak USA* with her coffee. Melissa Scott was narrating a segment entitled "Tourist Traps!" that detailed various scams crooks used on people while on vacation. Or, as it might as well have been called, Exhibit A. "They ask you for help, then they steal your passport, then you can never get home. It's evil genius."

"You can get another passport," I pointed out, sticking a straw in the smoothie I'd just made. "You don't have to, like, live there forever."

Mom grumbled as Melissa held up the travel wallet the current expert recommended, which basically made it possible to attach your currency and documents to your body in a series of what looked like double knots. "I mean, really.

I can't wear something like that! I just shouldn't go. This is ridiculous."

I slid into the seat beside her, facing our kitchen TV. "Mom," I said. "What's your real issue, here? This can't just be about an offsite wedding. It's too crazy even for you."

She gave me a look. "Oh, *that's* nice. Thank you."

"You know what I mean. Seriously, what gives?"

In response, she looked down at her coffee cup, running her finger around the rim. "I've just never been much of the vacation type. That's it."

"Because you didn't have the opportunity," I said. "Also, you were stuck with me."

"I have never been *stuck* with you," she replied. Then she reached over, brushing my hair back with her free hand. "You are the best thing that ever happened to me."

"Okay," I said, "but you're still not answering my question."

Exasperated, she dropped her hand. "Look. I know it's not a popular or common thing, but I *like* working. I prefer it, actually. If I'm not doing my job then I feel at loose ends. Which is bad enough here at home. But we're going to be on an island. With no escape."

I raised my eyebrows. "Are you *serious*? But you always talk about how much you hate your job."

"I do *not*," she replied immediately, clearly dismayed. "No, no. I say that certain aspects get on my nerves, and specific brides or circumstances. But the job itself? Never."

I sat back, trying to process this. It did actually fit, now that I thought about it. "So what you're saying is that all those times I wanted to go the beach, or the mountains, or the amusement park, we *could* have and you just didn't *want* to?"

She bit her lip. "Well, maybe not every time."

I shook my head. "Wow."

"I'm sorry," she told me. She squeezed my hand. "Look. There was a point in my life, when I was still married to your dad, when I was free to do whatever I wanted. I felt like I should have been so happy. And I wasn't. Then everything fell apart, and I ended up at Linens, Etc. as a single parent, and didn't *expect* to be happy ever again. But when I met William, and we started doing this business, it was like suddenly things just clicked for me. I'd found my *thing*, you know, my It. When you come to something like that late, you're always afraid you'll lose it again. It makes everything about it feel precious."

"Mom, you were, like, twenty-two when you started this business," I pointed out.

"Twenty-two, divorced from a trust-fund poet, and I'd spent the last few years raising chickens and making bracelets for a living." She sighed. "Finding my calling felt like a blessing. And you don't take blessings for granted."

"You're allowed a day off, though. Even God took one."

"And like Him, I get my Sundays," she said. "That's enough."

She got up then, crossing the kitchen to refill her coffee cup. On the TV, Dan Jersey, the news anchor, was somberly reporting on the stock market while a graphic of highs and lows hovered over one shoulder. I studied it, thinking about what she'd said. The calling part I couldn't relate to, not yet anyway, and I loved vacations. But this idea of coming across something so right for you after feeling like you never would, and then being terrified of scaring it away—well, that wasn't so hard to understand.

"We have four weddings left before Bee's," I said to her now, as she took her seat again, folding one leg up underneath her. "They won't be affected by you relaxing a bit. I'll make sure they're waiting for you the minute you return. Promise."

"Well, it looks like I don't have a choice," she said, sighing. "William already bought us matching hats and caftans. I'm going, like it or not."

The way she said this, you still would have thought she was being packed off to work camp in Siberia. But you never know what you can do until you try, and if you're lucky, what you love will always be waiting for you. That's just how it is in most cases. Not all. But most.

⌘

"The thing is," Julian said, leaning over the table, closer to me, "what most people don't realize is that discounting alien life isn't just foolish. It's arrogant."

I picked up my iced tea, taking a sip. In the first fifteen minutes at the Thai restaurant, we'd covered the basics—school, family, music—just like every other date I'd gone on so far. Then, suddenly, we were talking extraterrestrials. It hadn't even been a natural segue, either. Julian, the nephew of one of the ladies who owned the stationery store beside our office, just plunged right in.

"I'm sorry?" I said, as our waitress paused by my elbow, refilling the tiny bit I'd already consumed.

"It takes a lot of balls to just assume you are the only form of life in the universe," he explained, taking off his baseball cap and smoothing back the dreadlocks beneath it. "That's what my talk is about this weekend. The full title is 'The Hubris of Earthlings: How Narrow-Mindedness Endangers Our Understanding of the Universe.'"

His aunt, Florence, had mentioned he was in town for a conference at the U. That's what I got for being so worried about the bet that I didn't ask questions. When she said he was my age, a nice guy, and looking for someone to hang out with, I'd just jumped right in.

"So you're, like, an expert," I said now, as he checked his phone—prominently between us and lighting up with messages regularly—on the table. "You must be, if you're speaking."

"Well, anyone can give a talk if you sign up early enough," he said, typing some response while not looking at me. "But, yes, I consider myself a scholar when it comes to outer galaxies. We should all be students of the greater world, though. It's our duty. To do otherwise is, frankly . . ."

He looked down at his phone again as a new message came in.

"Arrogant," I finished for him. He didn't hear me.

After the entrees arrived, I excused myself to the restroom, where I took as long as possible washing my hands and reapplying lipstick. If I had to kiss a few frogs to find another prince, I was definitely working my way through the amphibian world. Why was it so hard to find someone I actually liked to talk to? Although really, at this point, I would have taken just some continuous eye contact. Or, well, attention.

Just as I thought this, my own phone beeped. When I pulled it out, I saw a text from Ambrose. CHECKING IN, he wrote. We'd agreed on this, for safety's sake, as it was a date not at a party or with another couple. YOU GOOD?

HE LIKES ALIENS, I responded.

WHO DOESN'T?

I sighed, ignoring this, then put my phone in my pocket and headed back to the table. I knew the drill now. All I had to do was get through dinner, politely decline dessert, and then offer a firm handshake before heading home. I had to admit, though, that even week and three dates into the bet, I was already kind of over it. But I couldn't quit, after all my big talk. Even if August seemed ages, even galaxies, away.

❦

"How'd the airport go?" Ambrose asked.

I sank into one of the leather chaises of the office, letting out a big breath. "Excruciating. But they are on the plane. I went into the terminal and watched the screen until it said DEPARTED, just to be sure."

"I'm glad," he said. "When she unpacked her entire carry-on searching for her passport and it was in her *hand*, I thought for sure she was going to just bag the whole trip."

"Oh, we had, like, two more incidents like that while en route," I told him, rubbing my eyes. "I'm starting to think it's a good thing she never goes away. I don't think I could take it."

"But she's gone," he said, wrapping a rubber band around the stack of place cards he'd been counting and dropping them into the bin at his feet. "And we have the weekend off. Just as soon as we finish all this."

I looked at the arrangement of vases, guestbook, cake toppers, napkins, and other nuptial-related items piled on the table in front of me. It had all been purchased for the Margo Wagner Wedding, which had been booked for the next day. A moderately expensive, mid-size double hander with a shabby chic theme, it was to have been the kind of event my mom and William could do with their eyes closed. And it would have been lovely, I was sure of it, if Margo's fiancé hadn't called it off with a little over a week to go.

It was too late to get back any deposits or return stuff, even if she wanted to, which she did not. In fact, the specific orders, delivered by her grim-faced mother, were that she "never hear about this unpleasantness again." We could always use extra supplies for emergencies, but there was still something sad about boxing up all this stuff that had been bought, I knew, with such great plans and hopes. I reached over, picking up the cake topper: it was a groom holding a bride in his arms, both of them grinning.

"I'll wrap up the candles and candleholders," I said to Ambrose now, getting to my feet. I ripped open a box of tissue paper, pulling out a piece, and picked up a small blue votive. The colors for the wedding were to have been yellow and blue, the bride and groom's favorites, respectively. "But to be honest, I never liked the whole green idea."

Ambrose glanced over at me. "Green idea?"

"The tablecloths," I said, nodding at the stack of them on a nearby chair. "My mom hates anything but white. But Margo was all about the symbolism, you know, of merging yellow and blue together. So for the reception, she wanted a lot of green."

He laughed. "Man, in this business people can find meaning in everything. Even the color wheel."

"Weddings make people do weird things," I told him, wrapping another votive. "That's the one truth that never changes."

"I'm starting to understand that," he replied.

As we worked quietly for a few minutes, I thought of Margo Wagner, a girl fond of heavy makeup and statement necklaces whom I had met a couple of times at the office. All brides tend to be obsessed with their events, but I remembered her being mostly focused on her huge engagement ring, which she was constantly turning to catch the light. Perhaps, I thought now, it was like a crystal ball, and looking into it she saw everything turning out perfectly, with yellow and blue and then all that green. Or she just liked the way it shined. Maybe both.

"So," Ambrose said now, as I wrapped a larger pillar candle, "what's the latest on the dating front? You've been awfully quiet since Alien Lover. Hope you haven't had trouble keeping up your end of the bet."

"Nope," I said. "Last night I doubled with Jilly and Michael Salem with one of his friends, also a food truck kid."

"Wow, that's a big community, huh? It's like homeschooling."

"It is," I agreed. "This guy, Martin, his parents do dumplings. I hear they are delicious."

"And what about Martin?"

I sighed, picking up another votive. "Very nice, super cute, and totally hung up on his ex."

He made a face. "Yikes."

"Yeah. Her name is Eloise. To me she *kind* of sounds like a nightmare, but he is hopeful it's just a matter of time before she comes to her senses." I tucked a piece of hair behind my ear. "It wasn't awful, though. At least I got to see Jilly."

"She's been busy?"

"She's always busy. But now she's in love, which means any of her spare time is all about Michael Salem," I said.

"That always sucks. When your friends go totally MIA."

"Nah, I'm happy for her. She deserves it." I bent down, arranging the candles in the box at my feet. "Jilly has always been a hopeless romantic, but she's never really had a serious boyfriend. It's a first for her, all this walking into the sunset. So it's huge."

I could feel him looking at me as I stood back up, bunching up some more paper. "What about you, though?"

"I just told you. Alien guy on Monday, Martin last night, and Ben and I are trying to work out something this weekend, since I'll be free. So not only I am totally still in this,

I'm actually ahead of what we agreed on. Which is why I'm already thinking about good prospects for you when you can't go the distance with Lauren. Maybe Eloise will still be available."

"Maybe," he said, and I laughed. "But I wasn't talking about the bet."

I looked at him. "Oh. Then what did you mean?"

"The whole in love, hopeless romantic, huge thing. When do you get that?"

"Have to win the bet first," I said, and laughed again.

He didn't. "I'm serious, Louna. The bet aside, you want that, right? The sunset walk?"

Immediately, I felt myself tense, my guard going up. "I mean, sure," I said, trying to sound light, easy. "Who doesn't? But it only happens so often."

"You think there's a limit on sunset walks?"

"I think," I said, "that we're all entitled to great loves, but not an endless amount. If you've had one, it takes a while for another to come around."

"A great love is just that, though. Great."

"Yeah?" I asked.

"So it doesn't usually involve a bad breakup, like yours did. Which is the opposite of great."

Now I was kind of stuck. I cleared my throat, recalibrating. "Things end," I told him. "Even with the best—or greatest—of beginnings. And yellow and blue make green. Such is life, right?"

I wrapped another large pillar in tissue, then put it in the box. After a few moments of silence, Ambrose said, "I can't decide if you're really this cynical or just guarded."

"Maybe both," I said.

I was trying to be funny, or at least lighten the mood. It was bad enough to be surrounded by the evidence of a romance that had crashed and burned; did we really have to share our own war stories, as well? The moment I thought this, though, I felt a pang in my heart. Ethan wasn't a battle for me. Loving him had been the easiest thing I'd ever done. Maybe that was why I was so sure if anything else ever came even close, it would be nothing but hard.

Just then the door opened, the beep sounding overhead. I looked over to see Lauren coming in, wearing flip-flops and a sundress, another girl following along behind her. "Hope it's okay we dropped in," she said to Ambrose, waving at me. I waved back. "I just really wanted Maya to meet you."

"It's fine," Ambrose said, putting down the guestbook he'd been about to pack up and walking over to them. "The famous Maya. It's great to finally make your acquaintance."

"And you are the infamous Ambrose," the girl, who was taller than Lauren, with dark hair and a nose ring and wearing jeans and a tank top, replied. "Who has my cousin in the best mood I've seen her in for months."

At this, Lauren blushed, but still reached out to take Ambrose's hand, wrapping her fingers around it. "Maya got the brunt of my breakup darkness," she explained to us. "I went a bit goth for a while there."

"If you can even imagine that," Maya said.

"I can't. Lauren is all sunshine," Ambrose replied, and of course at this she beamed, glittering even more. I went back to my candles. "So. Big day's tomorrow, huh?"

"Yep," Maya said, glancing at the cake topper. "And I hear you can actually attend?"

"I can," he replied, and Lauren smiled even wider. "We had a last-minute cancellation. Hence all this stuff and no use for it."

Maya picked up a bottle of bubbles tied with a ribbon from a nearby basket. "Wow. Looks like it was going to be a big deal."

"All weddings seem big once you work a job like this," he replied. "No matter the size, it's the small details that kill you."

He sounded just like my mother. I bit back a smile, bending over my box.

"Well, I guess it's good we decided to forgo all that for the most part, then," Maya replied.

"Maya's getting married tomorrow," Lauren explained to me.

"You are? Congratulations," I said. "Where's the ceremony?"

She and Lauren looked at each other, then laughed. "Good question. Right now, it looks like it might be at that Jump Java a few doors down, in that little patio part out back. Unless we can find someplace better."

I raised my eyebrows. "The patio? Aren't there just smoking tables out there?"

"We're hoping to relocate the ashtrays," Lauren said easily, as Maya moved her hand over the votives left on the table. "Maya and Roger want it low key, and Leo's boss okayed it, as long as we don't linger during the evening rush. It's all about the party after, anyway."

"And where's that?" I asked.

"Probably we'll all just go up to the Incubator for drinks," Maya said. "That's our favorite bar. We actually met there."

I looked at Ambrose, who had gone back to piling blue-and-yellow-edged napkins into the box. "Wow. After all we see around here, it sounds so easy."

This word just came to me, and I was grateful for it. Better than the next one, which was sad. But maybe the whole Margo thing was getting to me. Maya said, "Well, Roger just hated the idea of a big, expensive thing, you know? And we're doing a party in a couple of months in Michigan for his whole family, so none of them are coming. It's just us and my mom, the friend who got ordained on the Internet to marry us, and a few others."

"It's going to be perfect," Lauren said.

"Oh, totally," Maya added. To me she said, "What are these?"

I glanced over to see her holding a box of small cards, tied with a bow. "Oh, those are for the wish wall. Or, were."

"Wish wall?" she said. "What's that?"

I looked at Ambrose, wanting to offer him the chance to explain. But he looked clueless. So much for already being an expert. "At the ceremony, we were going to set up this bulletin board on an easel," I told her, pointing to where it was leaning against a nearby chair. "Then during the reception, everyone writes out a wish for the bride and groom on one of these cards and tacks it up. At the end of the night, we take them down and arrange them back in the box. The idea is that every night from the first one you are married, you open one, together."

"Oh." She looked at the box. "That's kind of cute."

"It's big right now," I told her.

"Louna, however, doesn't believe in wishes," Ambrose added.

"I don't believe in making one every time you blow out a *candle*," I corrected him. "But this is kind of nice, for the couple. People seem to like it."

Maya put the box down, then picked up the cake topper again. "I can see the appeal. I mean, Roger didn't want to do any of this, but. . . ."

I looked at Ambrose, who raised his eyebrows. Lauren said, "But you didn't either, right? I mean, you're good with the simple plan?"

"Oh, sure," Maya replied quickly. "I mean, it's just about us being together with the people we love. It doesn't matter where we are. And that patio seems nice. You said we could put some flowers out, and then bring them up to the Incubator and put them on the picnic tables outside there. That sounds good."

"It'll be great," Lauren said.

"Perfect," Ambrose added. Maya just stood there, holding the cake topper. "Um . . . are you okay?"

"I'm fine, just fine." Her voice cracked, clearly, on this last word. She looked at me. "Do you have a restroom I can use?"

"Down the hall to the right," I told her, pointing. She nodded, releasing the topper, and then went that way. A moment later, we heard the door shut, then lock, behind her.

Lauren looked at Ambrose. "Oh, my God. I had no idea she wanted any of this . . . I would have helped her."

"She didn't tell you she did." He put an arm around her, and as I watched how effortlessly, easily, she leaned into him, I thought of myself doing the same thing. Then, quickly, of something, anything else. Ambrose said to her, "Weddings are emotional, even the small ones. I'm sure that's all this is about."

"I mean, I asked her if she was sure about the patio, if she didn't want to do it somewhere nicer, but they're both students and don't have much to spare. Leo offering Jump Java seemed like the perfect solution. And the Incubator . . . well. . . ."

"It's a very thematic name," Ambrose assured her. "First comes love, then comes marriage, then comes Maya . . ."

"With a baby in an incubator?" She looked stricken. "Now *I* want to cry."

"What's wrong with incubators? They save lives!"

"Ambrose," I said quietly.

"I should go check on her," Lauren said. "She seemed really upset."

"Here, take a water." I reached over to grab one off a nearby table. "It always helps."

She did, then started down the hallway, her flip-flops thwacking against the carpet. When she was gone, he looked at me.

"Okay," he said. "You have to do something."

"Me?" I asked.

"A bride is in distress! That's your specialty."

"A bride," I corrected him. "Not *our* bride. She said herself all this"—I gestured at the stuff still piled around us—"wasn't what she wanted."

"Come on. I've only worked here a few weeks and even I can recognize a CG when I see one."

I blinked, surprised he'd learned this abbreviation. "A Controlling Groom is only our problem if it's our event. And this isn't."

He looked at the tables again, then at me. "Okay. But what if it was?"

"But it's not."

"But it *could* be," he said. "If we decided to help, maybe find a better place, donate some of this stuff. It could totally be."

"You want to get my mother involved in this?" I asked. "Are you insane?"

"No, no. I'm not talking about her. I mean us." He moved his hand, fingers wiggling, back and forth between us. It reminded me, instantly, of that first night we'd met at his mother's wedding, when he wanted me to heal. It seemed like ages ago now. "You and me. We could do this."

"But I don't want to," I said.

"Did you not just see that?" he demanded, pointing at

the bathroom door. Lauren must have joined her cousin inside, as I couldn't see anyone. "This is the only wedding that girl will ever have. Do you want to be responsible for it taking place among ashtrays and the sound of coffee grinding?"

"Or," I said, lowering my voice to a whisper, "it is a first marriage, soon regretted, and she does everything exactly to her heart's desire the next time."

He just looked at me. "I can't believe you just said that. And by the way, whispering didn't make it any less heartless."

I sighed. "Ambrose. I know you like to save things. Dogs, children, the day. But not everybody wants it. Or needs it."

"But some people do," he shot back. "And those cases, if you can help, you should. Why wouldn't you?"

"Because it's not your problem? Or responsibility?"

"I don't see it that way."

"Then you plan the wedding," I told him. "You know enough by now. Take this stuff and go nuts, if that's what you want. It's fine with me."

Hearing this, he studied my face, saying nothing, for long enough that I started to get self-conscious. "It must have really been awful," he said. "What happened to you."

I swallowed. "I don't know what you're talking about."

"You do, though. A boy, a great love lost, the only sunset walk you're allowed." He shook his head. "You can't even see the hope in anything."

"I see plenty of hope," I retorted, feeling defensive. "But this is a business."

"Which is built on the whole idea of people wanting to

mark publicly the very moment they agree to be together forever, once and for all."

"And it's lovely when it works out that way," I said. "Once and for all, and all. But sometimes, it doesn't. I'm part of this kind of thing enough. I don't need to do it on my free time, as well. Don't you get that?"

He didn't answer this question. In fact, he said nothing, and then, distantly, I heard the bathroom door open. By the time the girls returned, I was back at work wrapping a candle like it was my job, which, in fact, it was.

"Sorry about that," Maya said to us. "Pre-wedding jitters, I guess."

"We're going to do a wish wall," Lauren told Ambrose. "It won't be hard to pull together, right?"

"You can use this one," he said, nodding at the box of cards on the table. "Louna said so."

At this, both Lauren and Maya turned to me. "Oh, wow, really?" Maya asked, her face flushed. "That's so nice! Thank you."

I nodded, this time staying silent myself.

"And I was thinking," Ambrose said, "that while the patio idea is nice, I think you can do better. Why don't you guys come back to my house and take a look at the backyard? Bee's garden is awesome and we have plenty of space for tables."

The girls looked at each other. Maya said, "Really?"

"Why not? At least there won't be ashtrays."

"Or incubators," Lauren said. "Oh, and we could put flowers in mason jars! Those are cheap, right?"

"I think so," Maya replied. "And you know what else isn't expensive? Those little white lights, like Christmas ones, that we could string up. I wonder if they sell them in summer."

"Even if they don't," Ambrose said, "someone has to have some in their attic. We'll ask around."

"Oh, I love this!" Maya said, clapping her hands, a smile on her face. "I mean, I know we wanted to keep things simple, but . . ."

". . . this will be simply beautiful," Lauren finished for her.

Maya looked like she might tear up again, or already was. "Thank you," she said to Ambrose, clearly meaning it. Then she looked at me. "Seriously."

"Oh," I said, holding up a hand. "This is all him."

And it was. I was acutely aware of this for the next forty-five minutes, as I finished the work day with them so close by, excitedly planning away. I focused on my packing, getting the tissue wrapped just right, clearly labeling each bin with its contents. Everything in its place, just as it should be, even as this crazy, last-minute event came together only steps away. But as they left at five, still chattering excitedly, and I locked up alone, I couldn't help feeling like I'd lost. What, though, at least this time, I couldn't say.

CHAPTER

21

WHAT DO you say when there's nothing left to tell? Just the final details, the flimsy bits, or maybe not so flimsy at all, that round out the end of the story. This is the part no one ever wants to share. But here it is anyway.

I ditched school after first period the day of the shooting. I just couldn't stay there, looking at my phone's screen, empty of messages and calls from Ethan. The guard wasn't at the school parking lot gatehouse when I left, but if he had been, I don't even know what I would have said, what magic words I could have summoned to win my release. I was speechless, silent, and all I could do was cry. And I didn't even know anything for sure yet.

That would come later, hours after I showed up tear-stained and shaky at the office, giving William what he would later call, when he told his part of this story, "the scare of his life." He was not a news person, and my mother never paid attention to anything on TV or radio other than *Daybreak USA*, which she'd cut off early that morning. So they'd had no idea what was going on, instead immersed in the details of their bucking bronco wedding. We'd had to go next door to the stationery store, where they had a TV in the back, all of us crammed into their tiny office watching live coverage. I remember my mother kept looking at me, her face more worried than I had ever seen it, while William held my hand, his other arm over my shoulder. So close, and yet nothing, and no one, could get to me.

I tried calling Ethan every few minutes, and checked his Ume.com page, where other people were also begging him to update. He'd last logged in the night before, posting a picture of his cleats after a particularly muddy practice. I'd look at them a million times.

Later, at home, after a pizza arrived that no one ate, my mom and William kept leaving the room for huddled conversations of which I caught only a word here and there: "contact," "question," "interfering," "necessary." They asked if I had a number for Ethan's parents, an address, anything. I didn't. But even if I had, I wasn't sure I could have called at that point. Ethan would never have made me worry. He would have gotten in touch, somehow, as soon as possible. So I knew, by then. But I didn't want to know.

It sounds so weird now. All of this, in retrospect, seems tear-streaked and damp. How I could sit so silently in front of a TV for hour upon hour, fingers gripping my own fingers, until that moment early the next morning when the names of the victims were released. There were four before him, and, I knew by the math, two after. I didn't hear those, though. When I saw his name on the screen, everything went black.

It would be days later that I'd finally piece together the whole story. Partly from a friend of the family who answered

the phone at the Carusos' when William finally got through
and explained who he was. Some from the news stories that
put together timelines, marking the exact spot in the gym
where Ethan had come running after hearing the shots that
killed two female volleyball players. He'd tried to talk the
guy into putting down the gun, witnesses who looked to
be in shock themselves told Patrick Williams, who went to
Brownwood to report live on location. I'd sat with my mother
watching *Daybreak USA* so many mornings, and now, suddenly, they were talking about someone I knew. Someone I
loved. The picture of Ethan all the news outlets showed, pro-
vided by the family, was one I hadn't seen, a candid from junior prom the year before. Every time it went up on-screen,
I wanted to believe, somehow, it wasn't him after all. Like if
I didn't know that Ethan, it couldn't be mine who was gone.

I watched everything I could, even after the major net-
works moved on. Nothing about the shooter, though. His
name and details were of no interest to me, not deserving of
a single breath I was still struggling to take. But the special
reports on the victims, details true or not ("Ethan Caruso
loved soccer, lacrosse, and, his friends say, Lexi Navigator")
I soaked in like water. And when they weren't on, and I was
alone, I ran over our own story, that one night, again and
again in my mind. Every bit, from the minute I stepped into
the damp sand until he drove away, a flash of red through
those whirling revolving doors. Like if I repeated it enough, I
could conjure him up, bring him back, and this would all be
the bad dream I wished it was.

I wanted to go to the service. When it was announced

on the memorial page his friends had put up, I immediately made plans to make the trip, William and my mother offering to come with me. The night before we were to leave for the airport, though, I started throwing up, the sickest I had ever been. It was like my grief was toxic, turning my very body against me. After I passed out walking from the bathroom back to my bed, my mom put her foot down and told me I had to stay home. I didn't speak to her for three days.

They had a group memorial that was televised, a "healing event" for the community. Students held candles, teachers linked arms, everyone cried. The lacrosse coach, between his own sobs, talked about how, on that morning, he'd asked Ethan to his gym office to tell him about some interest from a college recruiter. When Lexi Navigator, in a plain black dress and minimal glitter, was introduced to sing her song about loss, a favorite of one of the victims, I held my pillow to my mouth and screamed.

There were more details. Like how I missed a full week of school, staying in my bed and sobbing. The way Jilly came by every afternoon and crawled in beside me, her arms around my waist, holding me as I tried to sleep. The brightness of the sky outside, the filtered sunlight through the tree just past my window, the most beautiful fall, everyone agreed. It probably was. But even though I was there, and lived it, I couldn't have said so. The dead aren't the only ones who vanish: you, too, can disappear in plain sight if enough is taken from you. I was still missing, in many ways. And I wasn't sure I wanted to be found.

CHAPTER

22

I KNOW YOU WANT NO PART OF THIS, BUT I
NEED A PUNCHBOWL.

This was the third text I had gotten from Ambrose, and it
was only nine a.m. So much for my bonus, unexpected non-
working Saturday. I picked up my coffee, taking a sip, and
reminded myself that Jilly and I had an entire day planned at
the pool together. It wouldn't be relaxing—nothing was with
Crawford, KitKat, and Bean in tow, as they would be—but
at least I'd be off the clock. If I turned off my phone.

NOBODY LIKES PUNCH, I texted back. DO PITCHERS
OF SOMETHING INSTEAD. LESS MESSY/GERMY.

In response, he sent me a thumbs-up, the same response
I'd gotten when called earlier to advise on one of those plastic aisles you roll out for everyone to proceed down (they
never stay put and look awful) and the merits of mushroom
appetizers versus meatballs (as one of our favorite caterers, Delia, always said: vegetarians aside, everyone loves
meatballs). It was clear that in the last fourteen hours or so
this impromptu, easy backyard wedding had morphed into

something more complicated. And who needed that?

Not me, I thought as I found my bathing suit and pulled it on, then tied my hair up in a ponytail. I was searching the hall closet for some sunscreen when my phone rang. I sighed, not in the mood for more questions, but then I saw it was my mother.

"Hey," I answered, "how's life in the tropics?"

"Wonderful," she replied. I blinked, surprised, then looked at the screen again, confirming it was in fact her I was talking to. "It's just so relaxing and gorgeous. I should have done this years ago."

This time, I looked at the clock. With the time difference, it was just after ten, which meant either she was still loopy from a late night before or she was already hitting the mimosas. *When in Rome*, I thought. "Wow," I said. "I have to say I'm surprised, with how much you resisted."

"Oh, that," she said, batting away days of complaints and stress as easily as a circling gnat. "Classic workholeic behavior. I'm textbook, according to John."

Okay, she was clearly drunk. "Do you mean workaholic? And who's John?"

"Oh, sorry." She laughed, the sound surprisingly . . . tinkly. Which was a word I had never associated with my mother, well, ever. "John Sheldon. He's a former CEO and author we met on the plane. Wrote an entire book about the overworked business, corporate, obnoxious mentality all too prevalent these days. Workholes. Like assholes, but worse."

"Right," I said. "So you know this guy now?"

Another light laugh. "Well, we ended up chatting the

entire flight, and then he invited us to dinner at his place. He keeps a second home here, to recharge and get away from the Nothing Olympics."

"What?"

"It's another one of his terms in his book. The competition we're all in daily, so fiercely, to climb ahead of each other. And what's the final prize? Nothing."

Now I was getting concerned. "Is William around?"

"Sure. He's right here. Hold on."

Something rubbing the phone, followed by a muffled voice, sounded in my ear. Then William came on, sounding perfectly normal. Thank goodness. "Hey, Lou. Everything okay back home?"

"Yeah," I said slowly. "How's it going there?"

"Oh, great," he replied. "I mean, everyone thinks I'm a concierge. But at least the tips are good."

They both laughed at this. Normally, I would have, too. But I was distracted. "Mom sounds kind of crazy."

He laughed. "I know, right? She's a smitten kitten. You should see her when she's actually with this guy. It's like the cartoons, hearts in her eyes."

"Are you serious?"

"Totally." I heard my mother say something, to which he replied, "Oh, please, it's totally true and you know it. If I didn't love you so much I'd be jealous to the point of depression. Also, all the drinks are included."

More laughter. Meanwhile, I still couldn't find the sunscreen.

"Hold on," I said to William. "Mom actually *likes* this guy?"

"I know, it's insane. They only just met! But he's taking her out on his boat today for lunch."

"But she hates the water."

"Apparently it's different here? Or she is." He snorted. "Anyway, don't worry. We spent half of last night researching him on the Internet and he's legit. Not my type, of course. But we can't all get so lucky in first class."

"We're just friends," I heard my mom call out, which was reassuring. Until she added, "For now, anyway."

My phone beeped again: it was Jilly. "I need to go," I said. "Call me later?"

"Will do," William said cheerfully. "Miss you!"

"Love you!" my mom chimed in.

Everyone is insane, I thought as I clicked over to Jilly. "Hey," I said. "Are we still on for ten?"

She sighed, answering this question. "I'm so sorry. Kitty has an earache and I have to take her to urgent care. Even if it's not an infection, and it totally is, she can't swim."

"Oh," I said. "Well, I can come along, help with the kids."

"That's so nice of you!" she replied, as some kind of shrieking—in Baker family style, of indeterminate source—erupted behind her. "But to be honest, Michael Salem already offered to take them to the park with his little brothers for me. We're all going for lunch at the truck later. You could meet us there, if you want."

"Oh, that's okay. I'll just hang out here, I guess."

"I'm sorry," she said again. "But what are you doing tonight? Did you finally make plans with Ben?"

"We're supposed to talk this afternoon, when he's off work."

Ever since the previous weekend and his invite to World of Waffles, we'd been trying to make something else happen. But Thursday, the guy who worked at Jumbo Smoothie the shift after him didn't show up and he had to close. Then the night before, when he was free after nine, I'd just come from dinner over at the Bakers', where they were testing out a new sandwich, the Good Gouda-lee Goo, and was too stuffed to do anything. We would work it out, though, if only because I had a bet to win.

"Well, let me know if you guys end up going out," she said. "I'll be kid free by seven if all goes as it should. And you know how often that happens."

I did. But I told her I'd see her later anyway, then hung up, sitting back against the wall. It was now mid-morning, and the whole day stretched out in front of me. I was sure I'd spend it answering wedding questions for Ambrose, and expected more texts as I changed, then went downstairs and made breakfast. But my phone stayed silent. In my heart, I'd been alone for a long while. But this was the first time in ages that I'd felt like it.

This is good, I told myself, climbing the stairs back to my room with a big cup of coffee in hand. I had a closet to clean out before I left for school, a task I'd been putting off for ages. I grabbed a garbage bag for thrift shop donations and another for trash, then pulled open the door and got to work. An hour later, I was sweaty and sneezing from dust, and both bags were full. There was a third pile as well, marked JILLY, of the clothes of hers she'd abandoned among my own. All that was still left to deal with was the one outfit off to the side.

I'd brought that black dress to Colby that August week-end in a garment bag, the shoes still new in their box. Coming home that Sunday morning, sleepless and giddy, I'd tossed them both into a plastic hotel laundry bag which, when I dumped it out later, also poured forth a fair amount of sand. I got the dress dry cleaned, something I'd later regret so much. Even so, more than once, I'd press my face to it, wishing to find just the slightest bit of Ethan's smell, the ocean, and that night still on it somewhere. Otherwise I just left it, hanging on its single hook, the shoes lined up beneath it. Like the shroud for the body of the girl I once was and would never be again. Now it had been almost nine months. Maybe it was time.

I pushed my hair off my damp forehead, then picked up Jilly's pile, turning to toss it outside the door before I walked over to the dress. I reached out, touching the bodice, then felt the tiny row of sequins, almost invisible, along the hem. In my mind, time blurred, moving sideways: Ethan sliding a strap off my shoulder, the skirt blowing across my bare legs, down at the end of the world. I bit my lip, imagining myself sliding it from the hanger, folding it carefully, and putting it in the donate bag. It wouldn't carry my memory: that would always stay with me. I knew that now. And yet, I remained unable to take those few steps to do this last task. Yet.

My phone beeped from where it was on my bed. I ran out

and grabbed it so quickly I would have been embarrassed had anyone been watching. Which, of course, no one was.

KIND OF A TABLE EMERGENCY. SUGGESTIONS?

WE HAVE A FEW, I typed back. HOW MANY YOU NEED?

AS MANY AS YOU GOT. I'LL HAVE SOMEONE PICK THEM UP.

I looked back into the closet at the dress, those shoes, and wished yet another time I could slide back into them, like Cinderella under the fairy godmother's spell, take a spin and begin all over. But it was just an outfit, and Ethan was gone. Things would change, but never that. No matter how many times I told anyone, it would always be the end of this story. But maybe not, I was beginning to see, of mine.

NO, I'LL BRING THEM, I wrote Ambrose back. JUST TELL ME WHERE.

⁂

Bee's house was a pretty bungalow at the end of a cul-de-sac with sunflowers blooming up the front walk. Much better than a smoking patio. As I climbed out of my car and started for the front door, I realized I was actually curious to see what Ambrose had come up with. After knocking a few times with no response, I heard voices from the backyard and headed that way.

"They're supposed to be in the *trees*," someone wailed just as I came up to the gate. "You don't put lights on bushes!"

"Says who?" another voice, sounding equally frustrated, replied.

"Everyone! God, Roger, just stop. That looks awful. Give them to me."

I leaned over the gate carefully, looking into the yard. Across the bright green grass, Maya and her groom were standing by a holly bush with a few lights flung across it, the rest in a tangle at their feet. Even though they were facing away from me, the tension was clear: her arms were crossed, his, on his hips.

"Hello?" I called out. "I was told to bring tables?"

Maya turned, seeing me. "Oh, Louna, hi! Honey, go help her. I'll get some backup."

As she ran, barefoot, across the grass and up the back porch steps to the house, Roger made his way over to me. He was about my height, skinny, with black curly hair, wearing a T-shirt that said I DIG FOSSILS. Pit stains were visible beneath both his arms.

"Do we need tables?" he said to me, in lieu of a hello. "I was thinking everyone could just sit on blankets."

"Just doing as I was asked," I said cheerfully, starting back to my car.

His response to this was an audible grumbling. Maybe Ambrose had called this right and he was a CG after all. "Up until last night, we were getting married at a coffee shop."

"I heard that," I said, surprised and yet not at how swiftly I'd shifted into my ever-pleasant-I'm-staying-out-of-this work mode. "I brought six. That's all we had."

"*Six?*" he said. "How many people are they inviting now?"

Instead of replying, I popped the back of my Suburban, sliding the top table out so he could grab one end of it. He didn't, instead now focused on his phone. I looked back into the car, realizing I was probably going to have to ask him to help me, when suddenly I felt hands grab the other end.

"Got it," Ambrose said, sliding it farther out. "Yo, Roger! You and Maya take this. We'll get the next one."

"Sure thing," I heard Maya say cheerfully. Nothing from Roger. A moment later they were walking awkwardly, the table between them, up the path to the side gate.

I pulled the next table out, Ambrose took the end, and we put it between us, following them. "So how's it going?" I asked. "I sensed some light tension."

"Oh, no, there's heavy tension," he replied, shaking that curl out of his face. The door of the house opened and Bee and Lauren came out, making their way down the walk. "In the truck there, ladies! We've got four more to carry around!"

"I meant tension about the *lights*," I corrected him, dodging a rosebush as it came up on my left.

"Oh, there's that, too." He glanced behind him, adjusting his trajectory toward the gate. "Turns out you really kind of need a ladder if you want them in the trees."

"You don't have a ladder?"

"My plan was to hurl them," he explained.

A word I had never, in all my years, used while discussing wedding prep. "Somebody on this block has to have one. You just need to go and ask."

"How can I do that, though," he replied, shifting his grip

on the table, "when every time we add any tiny wrinkle Roger sighs loudly and Maya starts crying?"

"Why are they even here?" I asked. "You know my mom never allows the bride or groom at the event pre-ceremony, even if they want to be. It's asking for trouble."

"I don't have that many people!" he shot back. I raised my eyebrows. "Sorry. It's just . . . this isn't as easy as I thought it would be. Like, it's not easy. At all. Shoot, I just banged my leg on this fence. Watch it as you come through, okay?"

"Ambrose!" Maya yelled from behind him. "Where do we want these?"

"Arranged in an orderly and yet not rigid fashion!" he replied.

"What?"

In return, he grimaced. I'd honestly never seen him so stressed, and had to fight the urge to laugh, which was absolutely the wrong response, I knew. "Just put it down," he said, his voice tight. "I'll figure it out."

"I don't understand why we need tables," Roger was saying as we put ours next to the one they'd dropped unceremoniously by a large tree. "What happened to my blanket idea?"

"You can't expect people to sit on the ground and balance a plate in their lap at a wedding," Ambrose told him.

"Why not? Not everyone needs a chair."

I was facing Ambrose, so I saw his expression—one of sudden realization, then dread—as he heard this last word. I said carefully, "You do have chairs, right?"

He just looked at me as Lauren yelped. "Ouch, I just

totally whacked my leg. You guys, hazard over here by the gate!"

"Ambrose, where do you want this table?" Bee asked.

"He said in an orderly but not rigid fashion," Maya told her.

"What the hell does that mean?"

Before Ambrose could respond, a huge clump of lights fell from the tree above us, landing with a clank on the grass. So the hurling had worked. Sort of.

"Jesus," Roger said. "That could have killed someone!"

Maya sniffled, putting her hand to her mouth, as Bee and Lauren exchanged looks. But I was focused only on Ambrose, looking around the backyard with obvious, rising panic on his face.

"Go find a ladder," I told him. "I've got this."

CHAPTER
23

MY MOTHER always said that a good wedding is eighty percent organization, fifteen percent guest behavior, and five percent luck. But really, no matter the size or type, you took all the luck you could get.

So far, we'd had some. Like the fact that Bee's neighbor two doors down was a contractor who had several ladders, one of which he happily climbed, lights in hand, then draped them across the branches as I directed him. He also had six folding chairs in his garage, which we were able to add to the five that Bee found wrapped in spiderwebs behind her water heater, where they'd been left by the previous owner of the house. We still needed more, though, which was why it was especially fortunate the Bakers kept an ample supply in their own garage to set up, along with small tables, for impromptu food truck seating. One call to Jilly—sure enough, Kitty had an ear infection—and she'd offered to bring as many as we needed of each. When I told Ambrose, he exhaled such a big breath I thought he might collapse outright.

"Thank God," he said. "If I had to hear Roger talking about blankets one more time I would have lost my mind."

"She and Michael Salem are going to try to bring them by five at the latest. Ceremony is at six, right?"

"That's the plan," he said, unpacking another mason jar from the box at his feet. "It should be super-fast. Then we'll immediately start receptioning."

"Not exactly a word," I pointed out, lending a hand with the jars. "What about food? Are you doing it right away, or waiting?"

"It's all finger stuff that has to be heated," he said. "So I figured we'd do it in waves. That's why I put that one table down at the bottom of the stairs. We can run out the trays, plop them down, and let everyone have at them."

Plop, like hurl, was a word I hadn't heard much before in terms of planning. "You may get a mob scene, though, especially if people are hungry. Might be better to pass some, so they can't all rush one spot."

"Oh." He stopped unpacking. "I didn't think about that. We don't have servers, though."

"I can help with that," I told him, picking out another jar. "And I'm sure we can enlist a couple of others. There's a certain kind of wedding guest that likes a job. You just have to ID them."

This, of course, was different from someone trying to wrest control of the event. There were types who just thrived on managing a guestbook or collecting bouquets from bridesmaids for the cake table, and William was great at spotting them within minutes of arrival. Without him there, I'd just have to trust my own instincts.

"Oh, I don't want you to have to stick around," Ambrose

said now, as we finally emptied the box. A dozen jars for six tables: eighteen would be better, but it would do. "I'm sure you have plans tonight."

Instantly, I felt embarrassed. Here I was inviting myself to the very wedding I'd been adamant only the day before I wanted no part of. *Stupid*, I thought, and wished for a second I'd ignored his text and just stayed home, maybe tried again to deal with that dress. Then, though, I looked in the wide window in front of us and saw Maya at the kitchen island, bent over the crowns she and Lauren were weaving from flowers picked in Bee's garden. She was smiling as she said something, then covered her mouth and laughed.

"Not until later tonight," I told him. "I mean, I don't want to force myself on you. But if you need my help, you have it."

Ambrose looked up at me. "I think it's obvious that need is not even strong enough a word. Please stay."

Now I smiled. "Okay. Now let's talk tablecloths."

It was a short conversation, as this detail, like many others, had been overlooked. "Oh, shit," Lauren said, when we went inside to report this. "With the whole blanket debate those totally slipped my mind."

"You don't absolutely need them," I pointed out. "It's just the tables are kind of banged up."

"So we need six tablecloths," Ambrose said, looking around the kitchen as if they might suddenly materialize. *That* would be luck. "And probably some plates."

"Probably?" I asked.

"We have lots of napkins!" he told me. "It's finger food."

"People will get a new napkin for every item they eat?"

asked Roger, who unlike the tablecloths, had suddenly appeared. "That's so bad for the earth."

"Roger, it's a napkin, not fracking," Lauren told him, sounding more peeved than I thought was possible for her.

"It's still wasteful. What we should do is give everyone one plate and one cup when they arrive, and they keep it until the end."

"What?" Maya said.

"Oh, shit." Ambrose sighed. "Cups."

"We don't have cups?" Lauren asked.

"I am not asking people to carry around their plate for three hours!" Maya said, her voice more adamant than I'd heard it all day.

"Three hours?" Roger said. "How long are we planning to do this?"

"I can't believe you forgot cups," Lauren said to Ambrose.

"I'm in charge of *everything*," he shot back. "You can't keep up with paper goods?"

"I was dealing with flowers!" she said.

Uh-oh, I thought. Nothing could fray nerves like this kind of detail, and my instinct told me words might be about to be spoken that would not be able to be taken back. "You ordered a keg, yes?" I asked Ambrose. He nodded. "Then they'll bring cups with it. As far as plates, there's a dollar store two blocks away where they also have paper tablecloths. They're cheap and will rip eventually, but at least they'll look nice when people arrive."

"Dollar store," Ambrose repeated. "Right. Let's go."

"Go?" Lauren said. "You're supposed to be helping with

the bouquets. You promised, like, an hour ago."

"Did you not hear me say I'm kind of busy dealing with all the other details?" he said. In return, she glared at him. *That got ugly fast,* I thought.

A knock sounded on the glass door in front of us. When I looked up, Leo was standing there, in black pants and white shirt, carrying a guitar case and an amp. "Where do I plug in?" he called out, his voice muffled.

"Plug in?" Roger said. "We're going electric with this?"

"I thought he was just doing his DJ thing on his computer," Lauren whispered to Maya. "I didn't even know he played."

"You're his best friend," Ambrose pointed out.

"Oh, shut up," she said. Then, turning on her heel, she stomped off. Maya looked at me, like I was supposed to do something, before following her.

"Ambrose!" Bee called from down the hallway. "Steve and Emily just got here with the food. Did you mean to have them buy forty pizzas?"

"Forty?" Roger said. "I didn't even know we were having pizza. Now we definitely need to do my assigned plate idea."

"They're going to be bite-sized!" Ambrose shouted, sounding slightly hysterical. Everyone got quiet, quickly. Until Leo, still outside, knocked again, harder this time.

"I'll just go to the dollar store," I said quietly to Ambrose, happy for any reason to put distance between me and Leo. "See you in a bit."

Everyone started talking again as I slipped out, pulling my keys from my pocket. I exhaled, relieved, when the front screen door swung shut behind me.

I'd just cranked the engine and put my car into gear when I heard a knocking on the back window. As I turned to look, the passenger door rattled open and Ambrose jumped in. "Drive. Fast. Get us out of here," he said, yanking it shut behind him.

"But—"

"Louna. I'm begging you. Just go."

I remembered the last time he'd leapt into that seat unexpectedly and told me to floor it. Then, we'd stolen a dog. This time, who knew? Whatever happened, though, it was better than that lonely dusty closet I'd been in earlier, or maybe forever. *You gotta live*, I heard Ethan say, something I'd almost forgotten. So I drove.

⚜

"Man," Ambrose said, as we stood in the paper goods aisle at $1Dollar. "This place is *amazing*."

I looked at the display of napkins before me, then at him. "It's a dollar store. Surely you've seen one before."

"Nope," he said, crouching down in front of the tablecloths and riffling through them. "My mom's not much for discounts."

After her wedding, and the ongoing prep for Bee's upcoming one, I actually believed this. Just then, I heard a familiar buzz—his phone. He pulled it out, glancing at it, then put it back in his pocket.

"Hopefully not another crisis," I said, checking out a stack of hand towels bound with a crooked ribbon.

"No. Just Lauren." His voice was flat. Of course I noticed.

"So," I said slowly, "everything okay with you guys? Seemed pretty tense back there."

He sighed, sitting back on his heels. "She's just wound tightly with all this. Wanting Maya to be happy and all that."

"What about you guys, though?" I asked. *"You're* still happy, right?"

"I guess," he replied. Not exactly a ringing endorsement. "It's harder, you know, going long term. Or maybe it's just hard with her."

"Relationships take work," I pointed out.

"Yeah, but the question is, how much. And how soon." He glanced at me. "I think you might win this bet after all, is what I'm saying."

I had to admit, this was a surprise. Suddenly, things looked different. I had to think before I answered. "I'd rather you be happy," I told him

"Yeah?" he asked. I nodded. Then he said, slowly, "Well, that's good to know."

We just stood there, looking at each other, and suddenly, I felt it. It wasn't a beach at night, the perfect moment, or an ideal beginning. Far from it. But something was happening, just like that moment I leaned into him, our hands cutting the cake. I just didn't know what it was.

Or maybe I did.

"So," I said quickly, "tablecloths, plates, forks. You said you have napkins?"

"Napkins," he repeated. "Right. Only about forty."

"Big ones?"

"Very small. Like cocktail size." I sighed, then reached

out, collecting seven packs of twenty large ones and tossing . them in the basket I was holding. "Do we need that many, really? Only thirty people are coming."

"People are messy and like multiple napkins and they're a buck each, Roger," I said.

"Hey," he said, holding up his hand. "I would never ask you to carry the same plate around for three hours."

"Thank goodness," I replied. "If you did, we'd no longer be friends for sure."

I moved down the aisle, checking out some white crepe paper rolls that were on special for a quarter each. A year or so ago, we'd done some table décor with tulle that could probably be recreated, and it was better than just plain cloths.

"So you're saying we're friends."

I turned back to him. "Aren't we?"

"Well, I was in from the start," he replied. "But you . . . you're a harder nut to crack."

"Now I'm a nut?"

"I'm just saying . . . I'm glad to hear it. That's all." He smiled. "You know, you're not the easiest person to win over."

"I didn't realize you were trying to," I replied, trying to make a joke.

"From the start," he repeated, not kidding at all.

And just like that, it was back between us, whatever it was, rising up again. I could see it in the seriousness of his face, hear it in the quiet of his voice, the inhale he'd just taken as if he was about to speak. I realized I was scared of what might happen next, that whatever words he chose to say next would be too much for me, but at the same time I was desperate to hear them. What a weird push and pull in this world, at that moment. And yet, I would have stayed there, on the edge, forever.

But then his phone rang, loud between us, and he didn't say anything. At least to me.

"Hello?" he answered, then listened a second. "Non-alcoholic beer? No. That is not what I ordered. I'm saying tell them that!" A pause. "Fine. I'll be home in a minute."

He hung up, looking stressed, then glanced at me again. "We should go," he said. "The crises keep multiplying."

"Yeah, let's do it," I told him.

Moment passed. I was safe, I told myself. But why was I also sad?

He started down the aisle then, toward the register, and I followed, dropping a few rolls of the crepe paper in the basket as I went. Even as we paid and left, though, heading back to the chaos, I kept thinking back to that moment on the edge of what had been and what could be. When the world had opened up, unfolding a potential that both dazzled and terrified me.

<hr/>

"Wow," Jilly whispered to me, as we stood together at the back of the crowd. "Those tablecloths look great with the crepe paper. Did you do that?"

I glanced over at the nearest table, lined with two mason jars of sunflowers and a blue glass votive, the candle flickering warmly inside. "I helped. But this was really Ambrose's thing."

"Impressive," she said. "The student becomes the master."

"What?"

"It's a martial arts movie thing," she explained, smiling at Michael Salem, who was standing beside her in a button down and shorts, holding her hand. "His favorite."

To this, I only nodded, as the groom and Andrew, his friend who was officiating, took their places under the big tree at the end of our makeshift aisle. Roger was in a suit that looked like it was hot and uncomfortable—I hadn't made it to the wish wall yet, but if I had, I would have considered, for him, breathable fabric—Andrew in khaki pants, sandals, and a flowing white shirt. Off to the side, in William's typical spot, was Ambrose, who then signaled to Leo to start the music. When he caught my eye, I looked away.

I was still processing what had happened—or not—at the dollar store. We hadn't talked again, as the entire ride home Ambrose had been putting out fires involving both the beer snafu and a blown breaker due to Leo's guitar amp. Then, as soon as we'd arrived, Lauren was waiting in the driveway, arms crossed, clearly unhappy and ready for A Discussion. I'd slipped inside to help with the keg and everything else, but had to assume whatever had followed had not gone well, as I'd gotten a text from him soon after that said only: CONGRATS. YOU WIN.

Now, as the song on Leo's phone, attached to a speaker, began, everyone turned to the porch, where Maya stood with her mom. She was a gorgeous bride, in a plain white sheath and her grandmother's gold cross on a thin necklace, her something old and borrowed. The new was her flower

crown, made herself. The blue, the beads on her white sandals, was visible with each step she took as she started down
the stairs.

She smiled at me as she passed, and I nodded, then bent
down to adjust a bit of her hem that was doubled over, catching on the grass. A tiny detail, but one people would notice.
And if you could fix something, why wouldn't you?

"I still feel weird we're here," Jilly said in my ear as Maya
and Roger turned to face each other. "We don't even know
these people."

"You saved everyone from eating nothing but pizza," I
told her again. "You've earned an invite."

That had been another wrinkle. Ambrose's list for the
friends who'd gone grocery shopping had requested pizzas
on the front, with frozen egg rolls and meatballs and other
finger food continued on the back. When they didn't turn it
over and then did their own strange math about how many
they'd need, we ended up with forty frozen pies and nothing else. Luckily, Jilly and Michael Salem hadn't left her
house yet, and between their two trucks were able to produce enough grilled cheese and ham and chicken biscuits
on the fly to nicely round out the menu. It had taken only
a quick canvas of the early arriving guests to find a couple
of people happy to preheat the oven and arrange things on
cookie sheets, all of which were now warming up as Maya
and Roger said their vows. Then all we had to do was plop
them on trays and we'd be good.

Now I watched as the bride and groom took each other's
hands, their very short ceremony already speeding toward

its pinnacle and conclusion. When they began their vows, I looked up at the twinkling lights in the trees as a breeze blew across the yard and all of us assembled. Then I looked up at Ambrose again, his face in profile, watching as Maya slid a ring on Roger's finger. What had he meant, that it was good to know I wanted him to be happy? I wanted to think about it, and yet didn't, at the same time.

Moments later, the bride and groom came back down the aisle, Roger flushed and actually smiling, Maya waving her bouquet over her head. As everyone cheered, throwing the flower petals we'd collected from pruning Bee's older roses, my phone buzzed. I pulled it out: Ben.

OFF AT 8. DINNER?

I glanced up at Ambrose, who was talking to Andrew, shaking his hand. Leo was starting the playlist that was his gift to the bride and groom. I'd looked at it earlier when he'd been taking a smoke break. It was mostly slow, folky music mixed with the occasional rap song, not exactly ideal for dancing. Not that I was going to say anything. At that point, I'd planned to be long gone by the time the party really got going, yet somehow I was still here. And now, I realized, I wanted to stay.

KIND OF GOT CAUGHT UP, I wrote back. TOMORROW? Then I slid it back in my pocket, not waiting for a response.

A half hour later, three of the six tablecloths were ripped, we were out of grilled cheese squares, and Leo had been overthrown as DJ by a group of people demanding danceable music. Michael Salem had started up the GRAVY Truck to produce some more biscuits, while Jilly and I took our turn at the wish wall, which had been set up just by the backyard gate. As I straightened the box of cards and replaced the pens in their holder, I wondered if I'd ever attend any wedding without lapsing into organizer mode. Probably not.

"So what's the idea here again?" Jilly asked.

"You write a wish for the bride and groom," I told her.

"What if you don't know them at all?"

"Then you write what you would want someone to wish for you at *your* wedding," I said. "Peace, friendship, never fighting over who washes the dishes. That kind of thing."

"I love washing dishes, though," she said, considering her card. "Maybe I'll just wish for lots of good food. That's what my parents say is key to their marriage."

"You can go a long way on grilled cheese sandwiches, I guess."

"Or they can." She bent over the table and began to write. "What are you going to say?"

I wasn't actually sure, at that moment. As I thought, I glanced around the yard again, taking in the crowd of people dancing by that big tree, the white tables lined with candles, one guest's baby toddling over to Ira, who had a white, bejeweled bandana tied around his neck for the occasion. I didn't realize I'd been actually looking for something—or someone—specific until I spotted Ambrose, standing at the back of the GRAVY Truck talking to Michael

Salem. He was in the middle of saying something, using his hands to make a point, and I watched him for a minute, surprising myself again with how much I wanted him to see me, as well. When he did, and broke into a grin, I felt my face flush.

"I don't think you can wish that for the bride and groom," Jilly said. "Maybe for you, though."

I looked at her. "What are you talking about?"

She rolled her eyes. "Oh, please, Louna. You and Ambrose have so much chemistry you're basically flammable."

"Jilly," I said, my voice low, "he could not *be* more on the rebound."

"Which means you won the bet, and so can pick yourself for him to go out with next," she replied, folding her card and sticking it on the wall. "It's perfect. You can act like you can't stand him all you want. But that blush doesn't lie."

"It's not like that," I said, although if asked, I wasn't sure I could say what it *was* like, actually. I opened my card. "And I never planned to pick me."

"Plans change," she said. "You know that better than anyone."

She was right. But so was I. Even driving back with the tables earlier, I'd had no idea I might be where I was now, on the edge of something with the last person I'd ever expect. You would think I'd have learned that the world is full of surprises, though, and maybe not just the kind that break your heart.

I put my pen to the paper and began to write. I'd made so

many wishes for so many couples quietly in my head as they drove away, but writing the words out made it seem more real, possible. For them, and maybe for me.

FOR YOU, I WISH FOR SECOND CHANCES.

I folded it shut, then put it on the wall before I could change my mind, right above Jilly's. As Michael Salem called out to her and she started his way, I crossed the backyard, moving toward the music. When I looked back at the wish wall from a distance, it was a sea of squares: I couldn't even find mine among them. So many things we ask for, hope for, prayers put out into a world so wide: there was no way they could all be answered. But you had to keep asking. If you didn't, nothing even had a chance of coming true.

On the dance floor, Roger and Maya were in the center, holding hands, him even sweatier, her flower crown lopsided. Andrew, his white shirt also damp, bopped beside them, along with Maya's mom and some other friends, all in a circle. Behind them, Bee was twirling in the arms of the contractor neighbor, while Lauren boogied with Kevin Yu, Bee's med student groom-to-be. Yet again, I found myself on the outside of all this, a line only I could see dividing us. This time, though, there was no rule: I could cross over it. Isn't that the way everything begins? A night, a love, a once and for all.

When I saw Ambrose coming toward me from the other side of the floor, the moment seemed even more fated, like my wish *had* come true. All this time I'd been waiting for my second chance. Maybe he'd been here all along.

"Hey," I said to him, holding out my hand. "Dancing is healing. Want to heal?"

"Yeah. Sure. Of course," he said quickly, but didn't move. "It's about time, right?"

I cocked my head to the side. "What's wrong?"

"Nothing," he said, equally fast, too fast. He flashed me a smile, compensating, then dropped it when he saw my own serious expression. Behind me, I could hear someone whooping: a girl in a black dress twirled past, her hem brushing my leg. "I was just . . . at the truck, talking with Jilly."

"Oh," I said, confused. "Okay."

He looked over at Bee, doing a shimmy as Kevin clapped his hands. "I told her . . . how I feel about you. How I've felt."

This was big, I knew. Huge. But it didn't match—what he was saying and how he was saying it. Like a rhythm slightly off, the beat you somehow can't clap to. "And?"

His face softened, and he stepped closer. Around us, the music was picking up, faster, people whooping it up. "Why didn't you tell me? About the shooting? About Ethan?"

Ethan. It was the last name I wanted to hear. It didn't belong in this place, at this moment. All around me people were happy, flushed and in motion, the way the world had been on that crisp fall morning not even a year ago. How stupid I was to think Ambrose and I could somehow be happy, too, after such a bumpy, uneven beginning. To really be happy, you needed epic, like Ethan, and we weren't that. Not even close.

"Jilly told you?" I said, my voice sounding light, like it was rising away from me.

"She was looking out for you," he said. "She's protective. I get it. What you went through . . ."

"Don't pity me," I said quickly, stepping back. "Don't do that. I don't need it."

"I'm not," he replied, moving closer to close the gap between us. "I just feel like an idiot, all that stuff I said about breakups and you being cynical. You must have felt—"

"I don't feel anything," I said, cutting him off. "It's fine."

"Hey." He reached out for my arm, but I shook him off, the response reflexive, immediate. "Look. I just wanted to say I'm sorry. I didn't know. And if I said stupid things. I'm just . . . sorry."

The music was changing now, the current song winding down, another, slower one coming in behind it. A perfect transition, and how common is that? I hated that I noticed.

"I'm sorry, too," I said, stepping back farther. "And I should go, actually. I told Ben I'd meet him."

He blinked at me. "You did?"

"Yeah," I said. "I mean, I didn't know I'd won the bet, yet. And I kind of like this dating thing. I can see why you're so into it."

"I don't want to do it anymore, though," he said immediately. "And I don't care about the bet. You're more than that. You always have been. That was just a way to win you."

I wished the music would stop. I wished everything would stop. But wishes don't mean anything. I'd been right about that all along.

"You don't want me," I told him. "Nothing will ever be as good as what I had. I'll never be what I was."

"Louna." He tried to reach for my hand; again, I pulled away. "Don't say that."

"I have to go," I said, my voice breaking. "I have somewhere to be."

He looked at me for a second, and I wondered about all the other ways this might have gone, possibilities spinning out into the future. Not that it mattered.

"Fine. Go," he said. "But know this. I meant what I said to Jilly. How I feel about you. Nothing's changed for me."

That must be nice, I thought. Me, I could never count on anything without it shifting shape right before my eyes.

Somehow, I was moving off the edge of the dance floor, across that line. Then I went farther, over the grass, through the gate, and out to my car. I'd always wondered about the people who leave weddings early, the impetus for not seeing the whole thing through to the end. Everyone has their reasons, as unique and varied as faces and thumbprints. You could speculate all you want and still never get close. But I felt sure that as I departed, alone, no one was watching me.

CHAPTER 24

THIS WAS better. Of course it was.

"Are you going to finish that?" Ben asked, nodding at the last of the doughnut on my plate. This was a running joke, testament both to his bottomless appetite and the fact we always ended up eating together. Almost three weeks of dating, and these things happen. It was all normal, exactly how it was supposed to go.

"Go ahead," I said, pushing it over to him.

He grinned, then picked it up, taking a bite. "The day you deny me your leftovers, I'll know we're finished."

"*That's* how you'll know?" I asked. "You'll miss every other sign?"

"Food is my language," he explained, sipping his iced coffee. "That's the way it works with us stubborn types. We miss other, normal cues."

Another inside thing between us: how we referred to his tenaciousness in asking me, and actually getting me, to go out with him. Already, we had A Story, our own folklore: that semester of Western Civ, just friends, followed by the Lin wedding and then multiple attempts to get together, all thwarted by his schedule or mine. Finally, he saw me driving home one night, pulled a U-turn, and followed me to the next intersection, where he texted me an invite for a slice of pizza. I went, we ate, then kissed, and the rest was . . . well, this.

It was nice, the kind of story you wanted to tell, but I couldn't help but recognize the tiny cracks in our origin tale's foundation that only I could see. Like how on That Night I'd been coming from Maya and Roger's wedding, still reeling from everything Ambrose had said to me. The fact that when I got Ben's text at that light, I was typing back no before I realized he was right behind me. Small details, I knew, not really part of the outcome. And that was what mattered, anyway, the fact that we'd ended up together, over two slices, everything unfolding in a normal way. No instant dislike, dragging across parking lots, stealing of dogs and other annoying behavior, not a single weird bet or secret left unrevealed too long. If our relationship was a wedding, it would have been proceeding Just Fine, with no surprises or real problems. Unlike me and Ambrose and whatever we might have been, most assuredly a Disaster.

So, yes. This was good. And I didn't have to worry about dating other people, because I'd won the bet. Though it didn't feel like much of a victory. It didn't feel like anything.

"You have foam on your nose," Ben said now, pulling his phone out of his pocket. "It's super cute. Let's snap a pic."

I made myself smile as I settled in against him, focusing my gaze on the tiny circle on his phone that was the camera. Ben was big into documentation of us on his Ume.com page and other social media sites. The first few times I'd scrolled through his feed and seen so much of my own face it had been alarming, although now I thought it was cute. Most of the time, anyway.

"Man," he said, sliding his phone back in his pocket as I checked my watch out of habit, even though I wasn't expected at work. "That woman sure can talk. Does she really think we need to hear about her lab results?"

I followed his gaze over my shoulder, where Phone Lady, at the next table, was indeed deep in conversation with someone about a recent "scan and blood draw, ordered by the doctor, and you know *that's* never good." I hadn't even heard her until now, which said something about my level of attention. "She's always does that," I told him. "I think it's like therapy for her, or something."

"Sharing her most personal details with the coffee-buying public?"

"I didn't say I understood it," I said. "I'm just reporting the facts."

He smiled at me: three for three inside jokes in one meal. This one he'd first said to me that night at the pizza place. That he knew we were both going off to school soon, and it was probably not a good time to get involved, but that he'd been thinking about me nonstop and had to take a shot anyway. "I'm not pressuring you," was his exact phrasing, "but these are the facts." Another tiny imperfection, how I had rephrased his words, but close enough.

Which, really, would be the name I'd give our relationship, not that I could ever say it aloud. We weren't madly in love yet, but I liked him a lot. It wasn't exactly epic, but we had a story. Not totally perfect, but, well, close enough. And I hadn't expected that anyway, from him or any other guy, really. You only get so many sunset walks.

As I thought this, Ben leaned forward, surprising me with a quick kiss. I jumped, startled: I was still adjusting to this aspect of him, a kind of dive-bomb affection that was cute, really. At the moment, I was quite aware of Leo, behind the nearby counter, who'd been shooting me looks ever since we'd arrived for breakfast a half hour earlier. Ben had ordered for us, sparing me direct contact, for which I had been grateful. As he headed for the bathroom, though, Leo made a beeline right for me.

"I have to admit," he said, in a dramatic way that made me suspect he'd planned what he was going to say ahead of time, "I'm surprised."

I looked around the busy shop: other customers, pastry display, Phone Lady now talking about her difficulties with her mother. "About what?"

He nodded toward the men's room. "You're here with someone who isn't Ambrose. Kind of weird, considering he dumped my best friend for you."

"What?" I said. "No, he didn't."

"'No, he didn't,'" he repeated in a high voice, mocking me. *What a jerk,* I thought. "Funny, because that's exactly what he told Lauren. Here she was, busy planning a wedding for her cousin and best friend, and you guys run off and hook up at the dollar store behind her back. Nice."

"I didn't hook up with anyone at the dollar store," I said,

as a man at the next table glanced over at me. When I glared at him, he quickly turned back around. "And if Ambrose brought me into their breakup, that's all him. I had nothing to do with it."

This was true. Sure, I'd thought for a *second* I had some feelings for Ambrose, but I'd been caught up in the moment, the wedding, not to mention spending basically all my time with him for the entire summer. Just as quickly, though, on the dance floor, I'd realized my mistake, come to my senses, and gotten out of there. If Ben and I had our origin story, this was the opposite, but it served the same purpose. The more I told it, the more I believed it. No cracks.

"Everything okay?" Ben asked, returning to the table and putting his hands on the back of my chair.

"Yeah," I said, glancing at Leo. "We were just catching up."

"I gotta get back to work," he announced, as if I'd been the one tearing him away from his job. "See you around, Louna."

I nodded, and then, thankfully, he was leaving, going back behind the counter. "Nice guy," Ben observed. "I like the beard."

I smiled, turning around to look up at him. "Don't get any ideas."

In response, he leaned down, kissing the top of my head. Another sneak attack, but this time I didn't react. *Progress,* I thought, and had a flash of how we must look from the outside, a happy couple having breakfast and some mild PDA at the beginning of a late summer day. I wasn't sure what it meant that I did this often when it came to Ben and me, stepping outside of myself to consider us from a distance, like an observer rather than participant in the relationship. *Because you know you're going through the motions,* a dark, quiet voice replied, the one I heard sometimes late at night when I couldn't sleep. To be honest, this was the same time I found myself missing Ambrose—his breaking of office supplies, melty croissants, and, maybe, kindness—in a way I couldn't explain. In broad daylight, though, it was easy to silence: I pushed out my chair, getting to my feet, and it was gone.

"So you're off at six?" I asked Ben as we headed for the door, passing Phone Lady, who was still talking loudly, a bite of scone now in her mouth.

He pushed the door open, holding it for me. "Yeah. Then I've got some top-secret birthday stuff to do. But I'll see you around eight."

"Ben," I said, as he joined me outside, then took my hand. "You don't have to do anything for my birthday."

"Oh, right," he replied. "Because that's exactly how you hold on to a wonderful girlfriend, ignoring her big day. I'm *not* that thick-headed, Barrett."

"You're coming to the dinner," I told him. "Seriously. That's all I want."

"Too bad. You're getting more," he replied. I sighed. "Don't get mad. Just reporting the facts."

Ha-ha. The truth was, with everything that had been going on lately—this new relationship, plus getting ready to leave for school in a matter of weeks—my birthday, a little over a week away on July 22, kept slipping my mind. Normally I could have also blamed event fatigue, as this was thick in the marriage season. But after Maya and Roger's event, not to mention the ones every summer of my life so far, I'd decided to take a break from work to try to enjoy the time I had left at home wedding-free.

"Well, I think it's a wonderful idea," my mother had said when I proposed this a couple of hours after her return from St. Samara, as we sat drinking iced tea on the back porch. "God knows you've earned some time off. After this vacation, I'm even more aware of how important things other than work are to your quality of life."

"She's basically memorized John's book," William told me. "It's like she's in a cult now."

"Oh, stop it," my mom said. Then she blushed, slightly, the same way I'd noticed she did every time John was mentioned in conversation, which was, well, constantly, usually by her. "Enjoy your summer, Louna. We'll be fine."

"See, now I *know* you're in love," William told her. "Because the old Natalie would immediately be freaking out that we have four weddings ahead and will be down our best employee."

"That's nice," I said to him, touched. "Thanks."

"Don't get too excited. There's only Ambrose to compare you to," he replied, taking a swig of his tea. He was still wearing the straw hat he'd bought for the trip, which he now tipped back on his head and said, "What?"

I blinked. "Sorry?"

"You just made a weird face."

"Did I?" I picked up my own glass. "Didn't mean to. Maybe I'm not used to compliments?"

"Maybe," he said slowly, as I took a sip. My mother, across the patio table, was looking at her phone, another new habit since the vacation. John had already texted three times since I'd picked them up, by my count. "Well, I for one will miss you terribly and am selfish enough to hope you get bored out of your mind and decide to rejoin us on the front lines. But I'm not in love."

"Yet," my mother said, eyes still on her screen.

"Yet?" I asked. "Can you arrange a timeline for something like that?"

"No," she replied, putting the phone aside. "But you *can* set up a date with potential for it. Which is what William agreed to do while we were away, with his cheese friend."

"He's not my cheese friend," William said immediately. Now he was blushing. "And I made that promise after a night of champagne on an exotic island. I can't be held responsible."

"Nonsense," my mother said, waving her hand. "It counts. And you'll reach out to him this week, because John and I both saw you swear to it."

"John again," William said to me. "Get ready to hear that name a lot. I know I have. Next thing you know he'll be moving in."

"Doesn't he live in St. Samara?" I asked.

"He has a house there, for the necessary and all-too-rare act of recharging," my mother explained, as William rolled his eyes again. "But he's based in Lakeview and spends most of his time traveling, giving lectures. It's a fluid lifestyle, allowing for adjustments as needed."

"This is what I meant when I said she memorized the book," William told me. "She speaks in bullet points and catchphrases now."

"It's very good!" my mother said. "In fact, John is having additional copies sent for both of you, along with the accompanying workbook. I think you'll really benefit from it."

"Louna is seventeen, Natalie," William said. "She doesn't need to worry about being a workaholic yet."

"The term is a work*hole*, and it's not just about that," she replied, as her phone lit up again. Immediately, she grabbed it. Eyes on the screen, she was nonetheless able to say, "It's about the courage to go for what you *want*, not just what you think you need. Sometimes, we don't even know what that is."

"Well, I need to get home," William replied, standing up, his hand on his hat. "We've got that meeting at the office first thing tomorrow with Amber Dashwood about her three-ring circus of a wedding."

"Circus?" I asked. "How did I miss this?"

"It's a recent development," my mother said. "Apparently she decided a couple of weeks ago she wants a theme after all. So we're calling the tent a Big Top and hiring acrobats."

"Wow," I said, regretting for a second I'd decided to sit it out. "Sounds insane."

"She wanted exotic animals, too, but that's harder to pull together permit-wise," William said, collecting his bag. "Also, liability. Maybe Ambrose can bring that dog of his and we'll pretend?"

"He's not exactly ferocious," my mom said. "But what is she expecting on such short notice?"

I had a flash of Ira, his wiry snout and eyebrows, the way his tail thumped hard against whatever was nearby whenever Ambrose appeared. True love, that was, instant in the second he was rescued and we carried him away. As I thought this, I felt William looking at me again, and wondered if my face had yet again changed. But this time, he said nothing.

It wasn't until later that night, when he was gone and my mother had retired to her room with her already dog-eared and highlighted copy of *Workholes: How to Be the Person You Want to Be and Do the Job You Love* that I realized in the hours we'd spent together I'd never even mentioned the news about my own love life, and Ben. This didn't really mean anything; we'd talked mostly about their trip, with me leaning over their respective phones to look at pictures (William: scenery, food, and sunsets; my mother: herself in front of sunsets and scenery, with John). And anyway, the next morning during *Daybreak USA*, when she brought up my birthday, I said right away I was seeing someone that I wanted invited to the dinner she was hosting. In the weeks following, after William worked up the nerve to invite Matt, his cheese friend, out for drinks (twice) and dinner (three times) he'd decided to bring him along as well. Now here we were, all of us paired off, planning to come together to celebrate, well, me. Things were surely different. But not totally: we were still doing it a day early, as a wedding rehearsal was booked for the actual date.

As for me, with free days for the first time in recent

memory, I'd been getting stuff for school, hanging out with Jilly and the kids, and trying to get used to *not* being at work, which was harder than I'd expected. The first couple of days felt totally decadent, sleeping in, eating bowls of cereal in front of marathons of *Big New York* and *Chicago* in my pajamas, then reading until dinner. Then I'd finally drag myself into the shower so I could meet Ben, either alone or with his friends, for dinner or to hit the various farewell parties that were already starting. After a week or so, though, I was finding it harder to keep busy. Maybe I was more of a workhole than I realized.

When it came to Ben, though, everything was easy. We already knew each other enough that there were no real surprises. Word had gotten around school after the Brownwood shooting about my relationship with Ethan. He'd never mentioned it then, but the subject had come up a couple of times since we'd gotten together—that was part of our story, too, the events that came before—and just as easily been discussed before moving on. That was the difference, with a person you knew and one you didn't: I couldn't have kept that secret from Ben even if I wanted to.

But these were thoughts that only came in the middle of the night, when I allowed myself to retrace that Saturday of Maya and Roger's wedding, going over each moment for clues of how, in some way, I could have done things differently. It wasn't like the way I'd savored my night with Ethan, everything perfect from start to finish. With this, I could see nothing but the places where I could or should have done something else, all the way up to that moment on the dance floor, when everything had gotten to be too much and I'd chosen to run. What *had* I been thinking, in that moment? Even now as I replayed it, I wasn't sure. It was like Ethan suddenly being conjured was what it took to make it finally clear Ambrose and I were already too messy and strange to ever be anything else.

What I had with Ben, instead, was neat and tidy, easy. I saw it now, as we started across the parking lot, away from Jump Java, toward his car so he could go to work. It was the way we were reflected in the glass of the stationery store, his hand holding mine, how we walked in rhythm, not rushing or dragging, just right. Because of all those pictures, I knew just how we appeared. A good-looking boy, tall with broad shoulders, in jeans and a Jumbo Smoothie polo shirt; a girl wearing a sundress and flip-flops, dark hair in a messy bun, sunglasses parked on her head. When the reflection stopped, it seemed odd to me that we didn't, as well.

❦❧

"Of course I do," Jilly said, popping open another tube of sunscreen. "And we still have plenty of time."

I watched her, skeptical, as she squeezed a dollop into her open palm. "It's already July fifteenth. You leave in a little over a month."

"Exactly," she replied, pulling Bean, clothed in a swim diaper and a sunhat, closer to her. As she began to slather on the cream with one hand while keeping her in place with another, she added, "From the way you're talking, you'd think it was tomorrow."

To this I said nothing, watching as Bean squirmed in her grip. Ahead of us, some kid leaping into the pool did a cannonball, splashing water everywhere. "You are coming to my birthday dinner, though, right?"

"Louna." She looked at me. "Of course. Why are you being so weird about this?"

"I'm not the one being weird," I told her, meaning it. "I've been with Ben for three weeks and you haven't even hung out with us once. I met Michael Salem, like, immediately."

"I know Ben," she said, finally unleashing Bean, who immediately started across the beach chair between us. "Remember? We went to school together?"

"You don't know him as my boyfriend."

"Is he really that different?" she asked. "And besides, with all those pictures he's tagging you in on Ume I basically feel like I'm hanging out with you guys anyway."

Hearing this, I felt stung enough to sit back in my chair, busying myself with another coat of sunblock. I was just starting on my legs when Crawford, sitting fully clothed on Jilly's other side reading a thick novel, said, "She's right, you know. You are avoiding her."

Jilly sighed, adjusting her bathing suit straps as she sat back on her chair. "Crawford, shut up. How can I be avoiding her? She's right here."

"Avoiding her with her *boyfriend*," he said in his flat, nasal tone, not looking up from the page in front of him. "You told her you guys had plans last night and couldn't do dinner. But you sat on the couch and watched TV all night."

Silence. If shame was audible, however, Jilly's face would

have been at high volume. "Is that true?" I said finally. "You *lied* to me?"

"Yes," Crawford answered for her.

"No," she said at the same time, then sighed out loud, turning to face me. "Okay, fine. Maybe I've been reluctant to embrace you with Ben. But it's only because I feel so awful about everything that happened."

"She wasn't working at the truck a couple of nights ago when you wanted to go bowling, either," Crawford added from her other side. "She was just sitting around."

Jilly whipped her head around to face him. "Will you *stop*?"

"Sure," he said agreeably, turning a page as Bean, another bottle of sunscreen now in her grip, started over to his chair.

I swallowed, still taken aback by what I'd just heard. Finally I said, "I don't get it. What do you feel so awful about that you don't even want to hang out with me?"

"I don't want to hang out with you and *Ben*," she corrected me.

"Is that different?"

"Yes," she said emphatically, her entire body heaving with the word. She sat back again, putting her hands to her face, then dropped them. "Look, Louna. If I hadn't opened my big mouth about Ethan, you'd be with Ambrose. I screwed everything up for you. If I go out with you and Ben, it's like I think that's okay."

"I'm *saying* it's okay," I replied. "Also, you didn't screw anything up for me. Ambrose and I were never meant to be anything other than friends."

"See, I don't believe that though," she said.

"Well, I do." I sat up, pulling my legs to my chest. "I've told you a million times, you didn't do anything wrong by telling him about Ethan. You were just looking out for me."

"And I did it by giving him information he then threw back at you, scaring you off, and now you're with some other guy you barely even know."

"You were with Michael Salem after one night at a party!"

"Because he's my true love! You barely even talk about Ben except when you're pressuring me to make it so you don't have to be alone with him!"

"You guys are yelling," Crawford said.

He was right. Jilly sat back, smoothing her suit. I cleared my throat. Another kid did a cannonball. Splash.

"Not every relationship," I said slowly after a moment, "is the hot, heavy love story. Some of them are just, you know, more mellow."

"Mellow," she repeated. "That's what all those Valentines and love songs are about, for sure."

"Why do you care so much?" I demanded. "All you wanted was for me to be back out there. I'm out. I have a boyfriend."

"You'll notice," she said, "that you did not include happy in that list."

"Ben is a great guy."

"Not the same thing."

I exhaled, frustrated. "You understand that most of the time I was with Ambrose, he was driving me nuts, right? That we are total opposites?"

"What I understand," she said quietly, "is what I saw with my own eyes. He might have made you crazy. But when you were with him, there was a spark. It wasn't ever just mellow."

"Also we were completely wrong for each other," I said. "That's why it never would have worked out."

"Maybe," she said. "Or maybe not. And it's that maybe that is killing me. Maybe I denied you what I have with Michael Salem. And sitting and watching you pretend you have it now with someone else . . . I just can't do it. I'm sorry."

"Come on," I said now. "There was and is no chance for me and Ambrose. I haven't even seen him since that night, and I'm with Ben now. I'm sure he's moved on. You can, too. I promise."

"Okay, fine. I'll try," she said. Then she sighed, loudly, as Bean crawled back over to her, pulling up on the side of her chair. "And I'll go out with you and Ben, if that's what you want."

"It is," I replied, thinking how simple and easy this sounded. Just as quickly, I thought of Ambrose that first day we met, his own honest response: *I hate not getting what I want.* I wasn't what he wanted, though, not really. Just a fleeting thought for a moment, I was sure, despite what Jilly said. And I wanted mellow. Or, at least, I'd take it.

CHAPTER

25

MY MOTHER was not one to apologize unless the situation truly warranted it. In the last three minutes, by my count, she'd told me she was sorry at least five times.

"It's just," she continued, as I moved quickly around my room, finding my shoes and keys, "once you've promised clowns, you can't really walk back from it."

"It's fine," I told her again. "Just tell me where they are."

"On the I-15 off ramp, apparently. They say you can't miss them, as they're—"

"—clowns," I finished for her. "Got it. I'm on my way."

"I'm so sorry!" she said again. "If you can just get them here, that's all we need. Give Ben my apologies."

"I'm not even meeting him until seven thirty," I said, checking the clock just to be safe. It was six fifteen. "I'll see you soon. I'll be the one with the carful of clowns."

"Bless you."

Ten minutes later, I was pulling up behind a broken-down blue polka-dotted microbus where six men in jumpsuits and wigs, sporting various versions of red noses and carrying water bottles, were milling around. I unlocked my doors, they jumped in, and we headed to the Amber Dashwood reception, which was slated to begin in mere minutes at the Derby Estate across town. When we pulled up in front, William was waiting.

"Oh, thank God," he said, as they all exited, grabbing their bags of gear. "All right, everyone, follow this path here around to the patio area and await further instructions. We'll need you to greet arriving guests momentarily."

The clowns took off, adjusting rainbow wigs, big shoes slapping the pavement. As we watched them go I said, "I know it's crazy, but I kind of miss this job."

"That's crazy," he said, pulling out his phone and quickly typing a text. "But if you really mean it, feel free to stick around. I've got a whole group of performing dogs that need to behave during the passed appetizers."

"Dogs? I thought you guys were joking about Ira."

"Oh, it's not Ira," he said. "This is a professional dog *circus* your mother had come in from Virginia. You should see the dancing schnauzers."

"Wow," I said. A couple of cars turned into the Derby Estate lot, driving slowly, obviously looking for spaces. "Looks like you have some early birds."

"They probably didn't even wait until the vows were done," he grumbled, as one sedan parked, a couple in dress clothes climbing out. "I'll never understand people who are that desperate to get to a reception. Do they not get out much?"

I smiled, having heard this many times before, as another car drove past us, finding a spot. Despite my time away, I could still feel it, that slow simmer of excitement/dread in my stomach that always hit in the moments an event began. You just never knew how the night would go.

William's phone beeped. "Your mother is reporting surly bartenders," he reported, after looking at the screen. "I guess it's time for my patented attitude adjustment."

"I'll pray for them," I told him, as he straightened his tie.

"You just get out of here," he replied, giving me a quick kiss on the cheek. "Save yourself."

"Will do."

As he disappeared down the path, though, I stayed where I was, watching as a few more guests arrived. Around the house, I could see tables set up with white cloths and flower arrangements that even from a distance I could tell had come from Kirby's. I wondered if Ambrose had gone to fetch them, maybe with Ira, and if Mrs. Kirby had asked about me. They'd get used to my absence soon enough, though, and probably Ambrose's as well. Summer was almost over. After Bee's wedding, he had his own life to get back to. Wherever that would be.

"Excuse me," I heard someone say from behind me, "but is this the way to the Dashwood event?"

I turned, facing an older man in a dark suit and red tie. "Yes. It's around back."

He peered down the path, as if not sure he believed me, then looked back at the lot, as if reconsidering attending at all. Now that I noticed, there really wasn't clear signage. "Why don't you follow me," I told him. "This way."

Around back, I found my mother standing by the table

assignments, lighting a candle. When she saw me, her eyes widened. "This gentleman is a guest," I said, nodding at the man behind me. "The route isn't totally clear. You might want to have someone out front, just FYI."

"Oh, right," she said, smiling at the man as he approached her table. "Ambrose? Can you go around front and direct traffic?"

Up until that second, I hadn't even seen him. Suddenly, though, there he was, in a blue dress shirt and navy tie, standing right in front of me. He looked as uncomfortable as I suddenly felt.

"Hi," I said, feeling like it was my job to start whatever conversation, hopefully minimal, that was necessary.

"Hey," he replied, then immediately looked at my mom. "You need me out front?"

"Just wave people in this general direction," my mom told him, lighting another candle. "And make sure Louna leaves; she's got a hot date."

At this, I felt my face flush. I hadn't told my mom or William anything about what had almost happened between me and Ambrose on the dance floor. What was the point? You don't start stories that have no middle or end, and this one barely had a beginning either. Just a couple of sentences, messy ones, trailing off into nothingness. Period.

"Right," Ambrose said, turning and starting up the path. "Come on, Louna. You don't want to keep your man waiting."

"That's the spirit," my mom called out, totally oblivious. "Have fun, honey!"

Now even more uncomfortable, I kept my gaze focused on the back of Ambrose's shirt as I followed him up the path to the parking lot where, sure enough, a clump of guests were gathered, trying to decide if they were supposed to go through the main house, around, or some other route.

"Reception is this way, everyone," Ambrose called out, and, like lemmings in formal wear, they all headed toward us. "You'll find your table assignments just around back. Enjoy!"

I stepped aside on the grass as one woman in a purple dress and squeaking shoes, clearly intent on hitting the appetizers first, barreled past me, her obviously embarrassed date following along behind. Soon, everyone had followed, and it was just me and Ambrose again on the sidewalk, as more cars pulled into the lot.

"I can stay awhile, if you need help," I said, feeling like I should offer, well, something.

"I think I can handle pointing people in a certain direction," he replied, his voice cool. "But thanks."

Just go, I told myself, as a couple with two little girls in stiff pink dresses began to head our way, their voices carrying above us. *He doesn't want you here any more than you want to be.* But then I thought again about the short time remaining before I departed for school, and how everything already felt like it was wrapping up. Who knew when I'd have another chance to do the same with this?

"Look, Ambrose," I began, after he'd waved the family to the path. "I know this is awkward."

"Awkward?" he replied, shaking that curl out of his face.

"Why, because I basically declared my undying love for you and you walked away, never to be seen again until, well, now? How is that awkward?"

This was a lot to hear at once, so it took me a second to unpack it. Finally I said, "You didn't declare your undying love. You asked me about Ethan."

"I was working *up* to it," he replied. "I had to apologize first. I was processing the information I'd just heard."

"Ambrose—"

"It was a two-pronged approach," he continued. "I didn't think you'd take off before I had a chance to finish."

"Two-pronged?" I said. "You make it sound like a utensil."

"Why didn't you tell me it wasn't a bad breakup you were reeling from?" he demanded. "I didn't know what I was up against. I had no idea what you needed."

"It's not your job to give me what I need," I said. "And—"

"Excuse me, is the reception in this building?" a man in a seersucker suit asked from behind us.

"Around back," Ambrose said immediately, jabbing a finger. The man, looking apologetic, scurried off.

"Don't take this out on the guests," I said. "It's me you're mad at, remember?"

"But that's the thing, Louna. I'm not." He sighed, shaking his head. "Look. I know this isn't the time or place for this, but I'm going to say it anyway. I liked you from the start. Okay? That first day, my mom's wedding, when you grabbed me and dragged me inside, that was the beginning for me. It's why I asked you to dance. It's why I went out on the floor at that stupid party when Jughead was mauling you. It's why I did everything: the job, the bet, all of it. If I won, I was going to pick me for your next date, even if I was supposed to still be with someone else. I figured if there was no other way, then you'd have to give me a chance."

I blinked, trying to process this. "But you were so into Lauren."

"She was—is—great," he said. "And we had a couple of great, epic nights together. But it was you I looked forward to seeing every day, you I wanted to hang out with even when this job was boring and stressful. I just didn't know how to tell you, until that night at the dollar store when you said we were friends and you wanted me to be happy."

"You knew we were friends," I said softly.

"I hoped we were," he replied. More cars were coming into the lot now, the bulk of the guests arriving. "When you said it, though, I saw a chance. Like an opening, big enough to wriggle through. That's what I told Jilly, at the truck, that I'd been crazy about you all summer, but I knew you'd been hurt and wanted to be careful, to do things right. And she said it would be hard to compete with Ethan, for all kinds of reasons, so I should just be myself. I didn't get what she meant. So I asked her to explain."

Again, Ethan was there with us. It was like I could feel it. "I loved him so much," I said. "No one can ever understand what losing him was like."

"That's the thing, though." He exhaled, looking down. "I wasn't trying to get what it was about him. I just felt that finally, maybe, I was starting to understand you."

Oh, God, I thought, and just as suddenly felt a pang of

pure fear, a reaction to this idea of opening myself up again to all the things that could then hurt me. Lightning didn't strike twice, except when it did. How could I allow myself back into that place of sunset walks and once and for all without expecting what had already followed? It was scarier than anything. Except maybe not doing it, at all.

"Excuse me—"

"Around back!" Ambrose hollered, turning to face the crowd making its way from the lot. "The reception is in the backyard!"

"You're yelling at the guests," I said quietly.

"Sorry!" he shouted. Then he looked at me again, his face serious. "I wish you had stayed there, in front of me, that night. That you hadn't taken off."

I wish for a lot of things, I wanted to say, and yet I'd told him otherwise, and now it seemed wrong to change my mind. "But I did. And now . . ."

I didn't finish this sentence, and he didn't either. We just stood there, guests streaming past, following the crowd ahead of them in, finally, the proper direction. In the night there would be dancing dogs, clowns, giddy toasts, and teary good-byes. All of this ahead, yet to unfold. Beginnings were always the best.

"I'm sorry," I said to him. "About not telling you. And leaving. And everything else."

"I'm sorry, too," he replied. He swallowed, looking across the lot. "Next time I'll know to say how I feel first. Not bury the lead."

"And I," I added, "will be upfront about the things that really matter. No surprises."

We looked at each other again. A man in a bow tie behind Ambrose paused, looking around him, then started to follow the path, going the right way.

"Well," he said after a moment. "The good news is we will be really good to whomever we date next. You're welcome."

"Right back at you," I said, then smiled. "Take care, Ambrose."

"You, too," he replied. "Bye, Louna."

Then I walked away, across the lot to my car, and that was that. A proper good-bye. No one dashing away or leaving angry. No yelling or sudden, shattering disappearances, with everything left unfinished. It was new for me, as so much had been with Ambrose from the start, and it felt like this should make me feel better, more at peace. But as I climbed behind the wheel, I began to cry.

After all that, I needed something before seeing Ben. I decided it was coffee.

Jump Java was quieter in the evening, and luckily Leo wasn't working. There wasn't even a line. But Phone Lady was still there, at a table for one, talking away.

"Tall latte with extra foam," I told the barista, an Asian girl with a cute pixie haircut. As she nodded, turning to start making it, I decided I'd have a doughnut, too. You want what you want, and sometimes, it's sugar.

"That's just the thing," I could hear Phone Lady saying, her voice louder than ever in the less crowded space. "I never thought I would be dealing with all this. I had everything worked out, down to the minute. Yeah. Best laid plans . . ."

I looked at the clock by the espresso machine: it was just after seven. I was supposed to go by Jumbo Smoothie, pick up Ben, and then we'd head to dinner with some of his friends before hitting yet another party. Normally I liked the idea of a whole night still ahead of me. But right at that moment, I felt tired. And Phone Lady was still talking.

"No, I'm thinking I need to focus on me. You know, self-care. Everything's been so hard lately, and I just can't devote time to another person. Right?"

The pixie barista turned back to me, sliding my cup across the counter. I was just about to ask for that doughnut when the door banged open. A group of women in workout wear carrying yoga mats came in, all talking at once.

"Anything else?" she asked me.

"Um, no," I said, glancing behind me. Too many people in too small a space—the doughnut could wait. "Just this."

As she rang me up, the door opened again and more women in spandex and NAMASTE T-shirts entered, clearly from the same class. Distantly, I could still hear Phone Lady, which meant she had to be practically shouting.

I paid for my drink, grabbed a lid, and started to wind my way to the door through the ladies now lined up behind me, dodging flip-flopped feet and yoga bags. Despite my efforts, someone bumped me from behind just as I was passing Phone Lady's table, sending me stumbling into the back of her chair. When I hit it, she jerked forward, her phone falling from her grip and clattering across the floor.

"Oh, God, sorry," I said, putting down my drink on an adjacent table and going to fetch it. "That was all my fault."

"It's okay, I'll get it," she said quickly, right on my heels.

"No, let me," I said. "It's the least I can do."

She was still behind me, though, as I reached the phone, bending down to pick it up. "Don't . . ." she said.

I knew the second I held it in my hand something was weird. It wasn't just the screen, cracked, black and dead, or the way it felt cold in my hand. You can just tell when something doesn't work, or never did. All that talking, all those days. But no one was ever there on the other end.

She was still standing right behind me, close enough that I could feel her breath on my back before I slowly turned around. "Here," I said quietly, holding it out to her. "Sorry again."

"It's fine," she said, grabbing it from me. "Don't worry about it."

And then she was walking away, back to her table, her dead phone in her hand. Maybe she put it back to her ear right away, or waited until I was gone. I wouldn't know. I was too sad to look.

CHAPTER

26

"WHAT DO you think?" my mom asked, moving the daisies a bit more to the center. "Perfect, right?"

It was. All of it, from the table set out on the back deck with our best wedding linens, votives, and vases, to the spread of stuffed olives, spanakopita, and pimiento cheese, my favorites and William's specialties. For dinner, there would be thick steaks topped with onion rings and mashed potatoes that were mostly butter and cream, just like I'd requested.

"It's great," I said, even as she continued to putter, moving a fork a millimeter to one side, then back again. Through the kitchen window, I could see William, his apron on, standing with Matt at the kitchen island. As it was for Ben and John, this dinner would be Matt's first formal introduction to our little family, such as it was, and it felt both strange and nice to see our numbers double after all this time.

"You're nervous," I observed, as my mom moved the fork again.

"Nonsense," she replied, not looking at me. "I just want everything to be perfect for my only daughter's birthday party."

"Sure you do," I said, as she again glanced around the house to the driveway, where John was due any moment. "You know I'm going to like him, right?"

"Oh, I know," she said, although she didn't exactly sound fully confident. "It's just my first boyfriend in eighteen years. Kind of a big deal."

"Huge," I agreed. She shot me a look. "I mean in a good way! I'm going to be gone soon. You can't only hang out with William. Especially if he's part of a couple now, too."

With this, we both looked into the kitchen again, where William was pouring glasses of wine, one for him, one for Matt. He must have sensed our attention, because he turned, blushing slightly, then looked flustered. Matt, however, waved cheerily. I waved back.

"To be honest, I never thought something like this would happen for me," my mom said now, coming around to stand beside me. "You just get to the point where you think, well, that's over, you know? That part of my life. I was okay with it. I had what I thought I needed: you, and William, my work. It all made sense."

"But maybe," I said, reciting what I now knew to be one of her favorite lines from *Workholes,* "we don't always know what we need."

She beamed at me, proud. "Exactly."

William slid open the glass door, sticking his head out. "We're on target for everything to come together by six, just so you know. You both ready for the guests?"

"You make it sound so formal," I said.

"It's a celebration!" His phone beeped; he pulled it out,

glancing at it. "And as such, I think you might need shoes. I don't cook for barefoot people."

"I have flip-flops in the kitchen," I said.

"This is a party," he insisted. "Throw me a bone. Please?"

I looked at my mom, who shrugged so innocently it was obvious she was in on whatever he was up to. "What's going on?" I asked.

"Nothing," he said, as his phone beeped again. "Just want everything to be perfect."

My mom looked at me. "You might as well humor him. When he gets like this, there's really no other option."

"Fine," I said. "I'll go get some real shoes."

As I started inside, passing Matt, who was arranging cheeses on a platter, I heard William say something to my mom, his voice low. She replied, also quietly. Thick as thieves. Some things never change.

I climbed the stairs two at a time, glancing at the clock as I went. In my closet, I scanned the various options lined up against the wall, trying to decide which ones went best with what I had on. Then I saw the black sandals under that same colored dress, their beaded straps folded neatly around them. If I really was moving on, I thought, it was time to do it in all ways, not just some. I stepped closer, picking them up, and slid my bare foot into one. It still fit perfectly, the worn spot at the toe from all the walking that night instantly familiar, even as I'd long forgotten it.

I'd just finished buckling them when I heard voices outside my open window. Walking over, I expected to see Ben, or maybe Jilly and Michael Salem, who were also joining us. But the yard was empty, whoever had arrived already out of sight under the front porch overhang. When I headed back downstairs to greet them, though, there was only William, shutting the front door. When he saw me, he jumped, startled.

"You're supposed to be upstairs," he said, shifting what I now saw was a box in his arms, on the top the name of a bakery just down from the office.

"It only takes so long to pick out shoes," I said. "What's that?"

He looked down at the box as if he'd never seen it before. "This? Oh. Nothing."

"Looks like a cake," I pointed out.

"It *might* be a cake," he said. "It could also be any number of other things that come in boxes."

I cocked my head to the side. "Looks like a cake," I said again.

"Fine." He sighed, shaking his head and looking at the ceiling. "If you must know—"

"I must," I said. I always got such a kick out of seeing William squirm. It was like the best birthday present ever.

"—I made you a chocolate chip cheesecake last night for your birthday. It was perfect, until I tried to put it into the car to bring here and dropped it all over the console."

"I *love* your chocolate chip cheesecake," I said.

He gave me a pained look. "Are you trying to make me feel awful?"

"William." I smiled. "It's fine. I love any kind of cake, you know that. I'm just glad we're all together."

"Well, this is from Sweet Tooth, so it's going to be good," he pointed out, nodding at the box. "Thank goodness Ambrose was just leaving the office and could run out and get one. He's a lifesaver. I just hope he has good taste in desserts. I left it all up to him."

"Ambrose?" I said. "That's who was just here?"

"Well, you weren't supposed to know," he said, "but clearly my shoe subterfuge was as lame as I suspected."

I turned, looking out the glass panel by the door. The street was quiet, no one in sight. What did I want to see, anyway? We'd wrapped things up as neatly as could be expected after all our messy threads. End of story. Once and for all.

"William?" Matt called out from the kitchen. "I'm wondering about crackers or baguette with this artisanal blue. Can you weigh in?"

"Coming," he replied, setting the box down on the hallway table just as the doorbell rang. Immediately, my mom came inside from the back deck, smoothing her hair. I took a look through the glass: standing there was a dark-haired man in a sport jacket, holding a huge bouquet of flowers.

Behind me, William and Matt were huddled over the cheese plate, their voices low. I heard William laugh, the sound a comfort as always, then looked at my mom again, the smile that broke across John's face as she opened the door to face him. So much happiness at once; it was almost too much, like a bright light that made me squint.

This was how it was supposed to be, I thought, as I walked over to the Sweet Tooth box, looking down at it. Carefully, I eased it open, immediately smelling sugar: the cake was round and chocolate frosted, dotted with white icing roses. HAPPY BIRTHDAY, LOUNA, it said in an arc of perfect lettering on the top. And below, smaller: MAKE A WISH.

I blinked, immediately feeling a lump rise in my throat. *I left it all up to him*, William had told me. I thought of that night with the candles, how frustrated I'd been by Ambrose's insistence on blowing them out his way, and then of the wish wall at Maya and Roger's wedding, the second chances I'd asked for. I'd made so many wishes, though, that hadn't come true.

My mom was coming down the hallway now, John in tow: I saw she was holding his hand, her cheeks pink, happier than I'd ever seen her. "This is Louna," she said, taking my arm. "Louna, this is John Sheldon."

"It's lovely to meet you," I said, as the doorbell rang again.

"Happy birthday." Up close, I saw what I'd thought was one big bouquet was actually two smaller ones. He handed me a bunch of daisies, then gave my mother the other, gorgeous, frilly peonies. Her favorite. Nice. "Thanks for inviting me."

"Of course," I said, as the doorbell rang again. "One second, let me just get this. I think it's my boyfriend."

As I left them, I realized this was the first time I'd referred to him this way out loud. It felt strange in my mouth, in a way I hadn't expected, something I tried to swallow as I went down the hallway to the door. When I opened it, Ben was standing there with a bunch of balloons, more flowers, and what was clearly a tennis racket, wrapped in pink paper decorated with hearts. He had his phone in his hand and snapped a picture of my face before I could even manage to smile.

"Hey," I said, blinking. "Is this the surprise?"

"One of them," he replied, stepping forward and kissing me on the cheek. No dive bomb: I saw it coming, and didn't flinch a bit. "Sorry I'm late. There was all this traffic. A dog darted out in the road and some guy followed and got hit trying to grab it. Total gridlock."

Instantly, I felt cold. "A dog? Was . . . is everyone okay?"

"I don't know," he said, holding out the flowers to me. Roses this time, dark red. "It had just happened when I drove by. All I saw was a bandana in the road."

He stepped past me then, inside, but I just stood there in the open door, frozen to the spot. Behind me, I could hear my mother, William, and their dates talking, the happy sounds of people meeting who have something important in common. The world always goes on, even when your own part of it stops. I knew this better than anyone. I was aware, too, how quickly you could lose the things you thought would be around forever, or at least long enough for you to change your mind.

"Louna?" Ben asked from behind me. "You coming?"

MAKE A WISH, the cake had read, and right then I knew what mine was. *Please, God*, I thought, as I stepped over the threshold, hurrying down the stairs. When I got to the sidewalk, I reached down, unbuckling my shoes. Then I left them behind as I ran, barefoot, toward the growing sound of sirens.

At first, all I could see were red and blue lights, flashing.

Traffic had slowed to a crawl in both directions, a single officer trying to wave people through one lane at a time. On both sides of the street, people had gathered, either alone or in clumps, eerily silent as they watched the paramedics working on someone by the curb.

My heart was in my mouth, the beat filling my ears, as I rounded the corner, dodging around two women with strollers. One had a hand to her mouth, the other her baby in her arms, its chubby cheek pressed against her own. "Careful," she called out to me, her voice sharp; part admonishment, part warning. But I'd been that way all this time, and it hadn't changed a thing. Maybe it was better to barrel through life, breaking fragile things and catching on every jagged edge. Neat or messy, calm or crazy, I still ended up in this same place.

Finally, I reached the intersection, stumbling to a stop. I was vaguely aware of my feet hurting, skin split in places as I stood on the curb, scanning the stopped traffic all around me. Emergencies shouldn't feel the same, with similar colors and noises, when each one is so unique, all its own. I thought of myself all those months ago, standing in the emptying hallway at school, gradually more and more alone as I stood on the edge of knowing and not, a place I'd later tell myself I would have returned to a million times over if I could. But now, I realized it was really no better, that uncertainty. Even when there's still hope, it's hard to see, especially with tears in your eyes.

"Miss!" I heard as I stepped off the curb, in between two cars. I could feel the heat coming off them, the warmth of the pavement under my feet, one of which was definitely bleeding now. A policeman blurred in my side vision, still yelling at me. "You can't go there. Turn back!"

I didn't, pushing through past idling engines, the distant sound of radios, the hushed whispers of another set of bystanders, now watching me.

"Miss!" the cop yelled again. He was coming toward me now. I squeezed around a final bumper, feeling hot chrome on my leg, then looked to my right, where the EMTs were huddled over something bulky in the road, a blanket draped across it.

Everything got slower, suddenly: the banging approach of the cop's footsteps, the slow roll of a nearby car creeping forward, my own breath, now audible and jagged in my lungs. One of the paramedics was on his radio now, another racing along the opposite sidewalk with a gurney, wheels rattling. Every sound so specific and unique I already knew I'd remember it later, and forever. A sob escaped my lips, primal and terrifying, as I felt the cop grab my upper arm.

"Miss!" he barked, pulling me back. "You cannot be here. Go back to the sidewalk."

"*No*," I said. His broad shoulders and dark uniform were blocking my vision: all I could see was myself, thrashing, in the mirrored lenses of his sunglasses. The outside view, again, but this time I was fully within it as well. Why was it that you felt most alive at the moments so close to death? "You don't understand."

I was out of control, I knew this. He had to seize my other shoulder as I continued to try to dodge past. "Can I get some help here?" he barked over my head. Finally, I craned my neck enough to see around him. The paramedic was replacing his radio slowly, exchanging a look with his partner, who wasn't rushing anymore.

No, I thought, a million memories spilling over in my brain all at once. That damp sand on the dark beach, a boy in a white shirt, billowing, the bouncy notes of a pop song ringtone. All familiar, like a slideshow I'd watched so many times. But then, as the cop gripped my arms, pushing me back, something else: a room full of flowers. A scruffy dog in my side view, his head out the window. Candles lit and then re-lit, a group of people moving on a makeshift dance floor. All those weddings, and kisses, and leave-takings, the faces of so many brides and grooms blurring in my head. *Love is what it's all about*, William had said to me all those months ago, although at the time, these were just words. I wondered if he'd feel differently now. I knew I did. Because standing there, tears streaking my face, I would have given anything for another shot at what I'd passed up, uneven and imperfect as it was. Life didn't begin cleanly, and it surely never ended that way. We were blessed with whatever we had in the middle. It made sense that it be messy, too.

"Get *back*," the cop shouted, pushing me off him with both hands, and then I did lose my grip, stumbling over my own feet and bumping against a parked car behind me. I could feel people looking at me, the sudden glare of attention as I came back into my own body and awareness, this here, this now. I put my hands to my face, sinking to my knees in the grass by the sidewalk, my feet throbbing beneath me. I was still there, huddled into myself, when I felt something scratchy and alive brush my cheek, then nose. I opened my eyes.

Ira.

"Hey," I whispered, not quite sure he was real, even as I reached out, touching the wiry scruff at his neck. His tail, now waving, thumped the car behind him. "What are you—"

A shadow fell over me then, and I looked up, past his wriggling body, to see Ambrose standing above me. I thought I might be dreaming until I saw the pink soda in his hand, along with the end of the dog's leash, his wrinkled shirt, that one curl loose over his forehead in the heat. Not the idealized details of dreams or fantasies, but those of real life, this life. As he crouched down, his face worried, to get closer to me, he was about to say something, but I didn't give him the chance. Already, I was reaching up, my arms tight around his neck, and I pulled him to me and pressed my lips against his. At first I could feel his surprise, but then he was responding, his hand moving through my hair, fingers against my neck. It was primal and epic, nothing like mellow, and as it went on for what felt like forever, I could hear traffic beginning to resume, Ira circling us, barking, the world moving on. This time, though, I was okay to be left behind a few minutes for a kiss, a beginning, my own walk, sunset or not. Whatever I was allowed.

CHAPTER

27

"BEE? IT'S Louna. Can I come in?"

No answer. I looked down at the water in my hand, then my watch, which told me we had ten minutes before the ceremony was supposed to begin. Reaching down, I tried the knob. When it turned, I gently pushed it open.

"Bee?" I said again, peering inside. The room where she'd been getting ready was just above where the ceremony would take place, by the hotel's infinity pool: I could see the chairs we'd lined up earlier, now filled with guests, through the window. "Are you in here?" Still, nothing.

I pulled out my phone, ready to send a BRIDE AWOL text if necessary, then walked past the small sitting area, closer to the window. Down below, I could see William up by the flower-covered arch, checking his own watch. I saw him shoot a look down the aisle. A second later, my phone beeped. My mom.

WHERE IS SHE?

I walked over to the bathroom door, which was closed, and stood listening for a second. Nothing. Then, distantly, a sniffle. Shit.

BATHROOM, I texted back. Then I knocked. "Bee?"

A pause. "Yes?"

"It's Louna," I said. "We, um, need to get downstairs."

"One sec." I heard her blow her nose, which did not bode well, and looked at my watch again. When the door opened, though, she was smiling, even with a tissue in one hand.

"I'm allergic to something, can you believe it?" she asked, turning back to the bathroom counter, where I saw an array of over-the-counter allergy medicines lined up. "My big day and I can't stop sneezing."

"You still look beautiful," I said. It was true: even with a bit of a red nose, her hair was perfect, pearly pink lipstick in place, clearly happy. Whew.

She smiled at me. Then sneezed again. "Shoot," she moaned, grabbing two more tissues out of the nearby dispenser. "This is not how I wanted this to go!"

"It will be fine," I said, handing her the water. "I bet once you get outside it will stop."

"That's where most allergies originate, though," she said, blowing her nose. "You forget I'm marrying a med student. Who probably did not expect, after all this planning and money, to be wed to someone whose nose is redder than a clown's."

"I'm sure that is not what Kevin cares about," I told her, bending down to fluff the bottom of her form-fitting, lace-covered dress around her shoes. "Weddings are about love, and love tolerates everything. Even red noses."

"Nicely put." She cocked an eyebrow at me. "You're good at your job."

"I was trained by the best," I replied. "And I've got an extra pack of tissues. Slide one of these by your bouquet, and let's go. You don't want to keep everyone waiting."

Another sneeze, and she was following me out of the bathroom and then the room, as I texted ON OUR WAY to my mom. As I pushed the button for the elevator, she said, "I bet you have a lot of these kind of stories to tell, huh? Allergic brides. Cold feet. Missing grooms."

"Missing sons of brides," I reminded her. "It was your brother I had to drag in from the parking lot, remember?"

She sighed, making a face as the elevator doors slid open. "As if I could forget. You're a saint for putting up with him, much less dating him."

"Well, it's never dull," I agreed.

"What do you remember most, though?" she asked me, as we stepped inside. "Your best wedding story, ever. Humor me."

I had to think about it. There was the time the groom, nervous, stumbled backward into a pool during the vows. The mother-in-law who got drunk at the rehearsal dinner and made an hour-long toast, working her way around the room detailing every beef she had with guests in attendance. The missing ring bearer. The Disaster. Distinct as they happened, now they all seemed like one big wedding, ongoing, leading all the way up to this one, my last for the near future. I left for school in six days.

"There was this one girl," I said, as the elevator creaked into motion. "Back in the spring. She was in tears, so scared. Asked me if I believed in true love lasting forever. It felt like a test."

"What did you tell her?"

I thought back to Deborah, sitting on the floor of the anteroom, her expensive dress puffed out all around her. "Nothing," I said. "I didn't know what to say."

She looked at me, then down at the flowers she was holding, pink roses with white lilies, so fragrant I could smell nothing else. "Sounds intense. And maybe like a sign?"

"Maybe," I said. "But I'm hopeful it all worked out."

Just then, the doors slid open, and there was my mother with the bridesmaids and flower girl, all lined up with their backs to us, ready for the procession. But I was looking at the end of the line, to the boy in a black tux with a rogue curl on his forehead who now turned to face us, a smile breaking across his face. Seeing him, I knew what I'd say now if Debbie was again before me, posing this same question. I wouldn't even hesitate.

Yes. Definitely.

As I passed by, Ambrose looped an arm around my waist, pulling me into him. "I'm thinking about falling backward into the pool," he said, kissing my forehead. "Just to liven things up."

"We don't need any more life. Just focus on your job," I said, although I lingered in that spot, against him, that I'd come to love.

"Says the person who is supposed to be off the clock," he replied, although he did straighten up and get into formation. "You just can't do it, can you?"

"I can and I am," I told him. Or at least I was trying.

"Okay, let's do this," my mom called out, gesturing for Bee to get into her place next to Ambrose, who offered his arm, giving me a wink as he did so. I smiled as she took it, then moved around them to make my way to the doors that led to the patio. When I pushed them open, William gave the signal, and the string quartet by the pool began to play.

I love this part, I thought as I moved up the side aisle to my seat in the third row. Technically I *was* a guest today, although old habits clearly did die hard. And that was just fine, I thought, turning with the rest of the crowd to face the aisle as the mother of the bride began her walk. It was rare for things to be perfect and organized anyway, even with your best efforts. Embrace the messy and when things do come together just right, you'll always be pleasantly surprised.

This was a lesson I'd been learning a lot in the last couple of weeks, as one thing after another did just that. First, there was Ambrose. We'd been together ever since that night of my party, although bringing him back to the house and telling Ben everything that had happened was, well, awkward to say the least. He'd been angry, and rightfully so, leaving with his roses and racket and a few choice words about my character. By that night, every picture of us was deleted from his profile, not that I'd expected differently. I could only hope he would forgive me someday, as well as find a girl with whom to make his own epic, real story.

My mom and William were also still both coupled, bringing the number of our little band of cynics down to zero. We continued to let loose, though, when it came to brides, weddings, CGs, overbearing mothers-in-law, and people who charged the cupcakes before dinner was even served. As for Jilly, she was already crying about being separated from Michael Salem when she left for school at East U, even as I pointed out he would be less than an hour away, attending the U itself. Also, he drove a food truck, so was therefore mobile. On the upside for her, despite the naps, Mrs. Baker was *not* pregnant again. At least, not yet.

As for me, I'd leave for school, too, while Ambrose stayed in Lakeview, enrolling in part-time classes at the U as well and, surprisingly, continuing to work for Natalie Barrett Weddings. He'd promised me he was going to get his driver's license back, when the State of California allowed it, so he and Ira could make the short trip to see me when I couldn't come back home. I knew long-distance relationships often didn't work, especially new ones, but I wasn't giving a lot of thought to endings. I'd had enough of those.

And now here we were, with another wedding ceremony, so full of potential. Followed by the middle, with dancing and the toast, two hands holding a cake cutter, maybe even making a wish. And then the big finish. Well, you couldn't beat that: cans tied to a shiny bumper, a bouquet lofted high in the air, that final wave as the car pulled away. Everything in weddings and life had its phases, and if you were smart, you learned to appreciate them all.

What really mattered, though, were the people in those moments with you. Memories are what we have and what we keep, and I held mine close. The ones I knew well, like a night on the beach with a boy who would always live in my heart, and the ones yet to come with another. For now, though, I was choosing to believe we had time, plenty of it. But really, all I knew for sure was that somewhere soon in that long, messy middle stretching ahead, Ambrose would again reach out a hand, asking me to dance. And this time, I'd say yes.